I0766925

Jacob

War of the End Times

EAMON BLAKE

ISBN: 978-1-7385182-7-2

Acknowledgements

Book 3

This book, **Jacob - War of the End Times**, is the third in a series of books. It tells the epic story about a battle between the Gods and the forces of evil. For me, writing the books was a labour of love that began in 2016. Little did I know that over time, it was to grow into a story to be told in a series of five books.

Book 1 - Jacob - Journey of a God

Book 2 - Jacob - Walk of the Messengers

Book 3 - Jacob - War of the End Times

Book 4 - Jacob - Children of the Gods

Book 5 - Jacob - Battle for Olympus

These books would never have been written if it wasn't for the support and encouragement of my amazing family and friends who listened to my relentless telling of the stories and the ideas I had. A special 'Thank You' to you all, you know who you are.

I would like to take this opportunity to thank those who took the time to read and proof-read this book in a genre that, in a lot of cases, is alien to them. They were the ones who particularly encouraged and cajoled me into taking this epic story to its conclusion. Thank you, a million times, to Teresa Carroll, Rita Foley, Sean Blake, Tom Lillis, Vincent Reynolds, Eamonn Maguire, Raymond King, Vanessa Keogh and Thérése McGarry.

To my friend Damien Carroll: What can I say. Your regular emails and phone calls were a great help in getting some of my Dublin 'isms' out of the story making it a far better read. I am filled with gratitude.

I am eternally grateful to a very special group of people, the Poets and Authors in the 'All About Writing Group', for assisting me in getting my book to print ready; this would not have been possible without their valuable critique and editorial assistance, especially with grammar, layouts and storylines.

To my amazing niece, Niamh Blake, thank you so much for your wonderful cover designs.

I would also like to acknowledge PerpetuityPublications.com for their assistance in formatting my books and getting them ready for release. Thanks again Perpetuity Publications.

And finally, in memory of James, Sadie and Sean Blake - forever in our hearts, R.I.P.

Author's Profile

Eamon Blake is from Crumlin, a Southside suburb of Dublin, Ireland, a place he still has a great love for. It was there, between 1970 and 1975, where he attended the local secondary school, Meanscoil Naomh Colm. During fifth and sixth year, he had the pleasure of being taught English by the late Michael Condon, an inspirational teacher who had an amazing teaching technique commanding the greatest of respect from his pupils. Eamon believes that as a result of that teacher's style and perseverance he developed an interest in writing. It was in that same school where he developed his passion for real and classical history. *The history and mythology learned during that time lingered in Eamon's mind and those early influences only resurfaced in recent years, inspiring him to pen a series of five fantasy novels recounting the tale of a Dublin schoolboy discovering his extraordinary powers, and who he actually was.*

A widower with one son, Eamon, over the years, has successfully navigated various employment roles involving procurement, sales and marketing. His professional journey included delivering marketing presentations to major wholesale and retail chains, as well as participating in monthly sales and planning meetings. He believes the wealth of experience garnered during those years helped him develop his own writing style, ultimately leading to the Jacob series.

Eamon's first foray into writing began with him researching and publishing a book detailing the history and genealogy of his own family in central Dublin, dating back to the 1780s. Motivated by a desire to share this heritage, he produced and published enough copies exclusively for his extended family.

The idea for the Jacob series came to Eamon in the late summer of 2016 after he witnessed a charming yet humorous incident in Temple Bar, Dublin. This event led to the realisation that a fantastical story could be crafted by intertwining major historical events from Africa, America, Europe, the Far East as well as the Near East, linking them, and drawing inspiration from worldwide mythological realms featuring Centaurs, Dragons, Elves, The Gods, The Little People, Mer-Peoples, The Yeti and Wizards.

Contact author:

Email: thejacobsaga@gmail.com

Table of Contents

Prologue

For the Messengers, wherever they travelled, the forces of Hell seemed to be waiting, ready to wreak havoc. The guardians, with each conflict grew in confidence to become stronger and wiser, nevertheless they were very aware of how Hell was also evolving, and this at times was very challenging. There were many adventures both natural and supernatural but no matter how bad things got the sleeping gods were always ready to awaken and assist. This happened many times, especially for Magni of Asgard, who spent much of his time providing extra protection for Panya, who was pregnant with his brother Odi's babies. Jacob also slept lightly, always on alert, ready to impart words of wisdom, or go to the aid of his guardians, which he did on many occasions.

During their journeys, the messengers and their guardians travelled to quite a few iconic sites around the world, and in those places they certainly left their mark. They experienced exciting, even dangerous adventures, but it was their bonds that would, in the end, define them. Some formed relationships, became lovers, leading to them becoming parents; others met their partners from among those they encountered on their journey. Baldor remained alone but his happiness was only delayed, he would eventually find love and it's destined to come from an unexpected source.

Over the centuries they used their time to pass on the message but they also influenced, cajoled, and encouraged those they met to change their ways especially the ones who were moving towards The Darkness.

For the messengers and their guardians, the strange thing was, they never really aged. They started as nervous sixteen year old youths and as the years passed they entered their long sleep as very wise and mature deities that looked just like twenty year olds.

On that fateful day when, in groups of three, they left the temple, it was Panya, Thanases and Baldor who were the first to leave and they began a journey that was to span nearly eighteen hundred years. Almost immediately they encountered the power of Hell, they bore witness to the crucifixion and then the sack of Jerusalem, before suffering the wrath of a turned Sun God in Palmyra. In Armenia they watched the dedication of its beating heart. In Georgia they witnessed the depravity of the servants of evil. In the Midlands and Eastern Europe they assisted the various royal families in defending themselves against the onslaught of the Golden Hoard. In Ukraine they re-vealed themselves by rescuing the city of Kiev. During their time in Russia, 'passion' showed itself when Thanases met the love of his life and became a father to a son who was destined to become very powerful. It was there where Baldor became the 'Beacon of Light' that was to lead the slaves of St. Petersburg back to their homeland.

The second group to leave the temple was Oba, Jahiri and Jomo and they made their way south into Africa where they were to spend just over seventeen hundred years. Their adventures started almost immediately when they found themselves in a vicious battle involving the Serpents of Hell on the slopes of Mount Sinai. Even with the assistance of one of the most pow-erful wizards they suffered greatly before becoming stronger. On crossing into Egypt they met with the gods of North Africa and through them learned what was before them, but most of all they became staunch allies to the natural world. Their journey took them through the Atlas Mountains and into the Western Sahara Desert before taking them back towards the Great Rift Valley and then to the lands that were to become the birth place of the Zulu nation and they identified the one who would become ancestor to that same nation. They too had many adventures and bore witness to most of the great events in the history of the African pantheon. They rescued the Yoruba peoples with the assistance of the God Shango as well as thousands of warriors from the ancient tribes. They were there for the end of the Kingdom of Kush, but the one thing that made them different was they learned to communicate with the animal kingdom. They successfully passed the message to all those whom they were tasked allowing Jomo and Oba to finally show their love for each other. At around this time Jahiri was to realise the power of Olympus when he discovered that Jamilah, a girl whom he hadn't seen for nine hundred years, was still alive and placed into a deep sleep by Jacob.

Mulan and her guardians were next to leave the temple and, of all the messengers; it was them who suffered the most violent encounters. Their journey east took them to Uluru in Australia, where they were to find themselves protecting the tribes against an onslaught of serpents. It was also there, where the guardians fulfilled one of Jacob's prophesies, one was to become 'Lord of the Mountains' and the other 'Emperor of the Birds'. On arrival in South America, they became victims of a rogue god who succeeded in sending them to rest among the tombs of Elysium only to be resurrected after the arrival of powerful gods from the Mesoamerican pantheon. In Japan, China and Burma the attacks by the forces of Hell were relentless, causing the peoples of those lands to suffer greatly. It was on arrival into the domain of Lord Shiva when the greatest tragedy struck. Mulan fell, causing Jacob and Odi to awaken and come to the rescue. It was also the time when true love again showed itself. Girish met Manasa and she became pregnant. Garuda declared his love for Mulan and they both learned how the power of love could take them to the dream-world where they could spend as much time together as they needed.

The last group to leave the temple was Eala, Faer and Fafner, and they too were destined to have a tumultuous time. Their journey began with the birth of Jacob and Eala's children. Fafner departed to become Emperor of the Dragons leaving Faer to be the sole protector of Eala. For Faer it was an even more stressful time, he was tasked with rescuing a Celtic goddess from the bowels of Hell, a goddess who was to become the love of his life and the mother of his children. They were there for the fall of the Roman Empire. They witnessed the rise of the first King of the Franks and they assisted in making Charlemagne the Holy Roman Emperor, helping him to become known as the Father of Europe. They were there for the arrival of the Black Death and were the ones to call on the Goddess of the Snows to assist in defeating it. After many centuries had passed, Fafner returned to continue the journey. They suffered real tragedy when Fafner's wife was murdered by a Dark Angel who was eventually revealed to be one of the seven princes of Hell. On reaching London they were present during the reign of Henry V111 and a century later they bore witness to the plague and great fire. London was also the site of one of their biggest battles. After London they spent many peaceful years in the Dragon realm before reaching the Fair Lands where Faer had to assist in reviving the one he loved. It was there where they slept for two hundred years.

Before the four journeys ended there were seven children born and they were all destined to one day become powerful gods in their own right. Jacob and Eala had a girl and two boys whom they named Helena, Obelius and Demetrius. Manasa and Girish had a son to whom they gave the name

Hemish, Oba and Jomo named their son, Zane. Jahiri and Jamilah had a daughter they called Sagal and finally, Thanases and Irina named their son, Viktor. Panya was heavily pregnant but her twin girls were not due to be born for another two hundred years.

All four groups completed their tasks and went into their deep sleep. While sleeping, they were well protected by the power of the Light, ensuring they'd never be found. They rested knowing that their work was done and those who had received the 'Message' would continue to pass it down through the generations by keeping a low profile.

Even so this didn't deter the efforts by the forces of Hell, who continuously probed and never gave up searching. They brought famine, pestilence and war to any location they believed was visited by the messengers and soon genocide became a familiar word. They were responsible for the rise of the most ruthless tyrants and despots earth had ever seen, the very ones who would go on to usher millions of souls into the bowels of Hell to form the core of Lucifer's army.

It was now coming to the end of the second decade of the twenty-first century and among the Astrals many were prepared and others were beginning to stir. The waterfalls were slowing to a trickle and the volcanoes were quietening down. An eerie silence was becoming more sinister and fear was spreading all over the world. Rumblings beneath the temple alerted the stewards to the impending arrival of the gods and they knew the first to awaken would be Jacob.

So approaches the
War of the End Times

Jacob - War of the End Times

Chapter 1

In the bowels of hell he walked. His temper rising and his patience wearing thin. He believed he was being ignored and side lined. Although aware Lucifer's plans were about to come to fruition, his fury grew when he realised those plans didn't include him. With this in mind he used his strength to break through the toughened walls of Mount Vesuvius, where on exiting, he stood as Lord of the Titans. He bellowed in a loud and thunderous voice, "I am Cronus, bring me my crown."

His height, stature and build terrified all who saw him. His body looked to be made from charred granite. Every step he took pounded, sending tremors in all directions. He looked for familiar landmarks in the hope one of them would guide him back to reclaim his throne, nothing was familiar. He stomped his way towards the ruined city of Pompeii but still nothing showed to help him find his way. His loud ranting sent shivers down the spines of the scattering guides and tourists alike. He'd look at the people scurrying and hiding and found no pity. Compassion or feeling was something he lost way back in the mists of time.

Slightly to the North West he saw what looked like a large city. It was Naples, where on arrival; he demanded the whereabouts of Olympus and the location of Zeus, his usurper. The people of Naples got no warning of his arrival, or his plans, and those he captured only ever knew of him as a mythical Titan from the myths and legends of the ancient Greeks. The terrified citizens tried to tell him that up to now no one believed he ever existed, and this ignorance just fuelled his rage. He was not impressed with the lack of knowledge or with the lack of assistance. His loss of respect for mankind, gained after their expulsion from Paradise, ensured he didn't give them a chance to work out what he was after. Those he captured suffered and then died in a most horrific way. His penchant for squeezing the life from his captives had not abated and his lust for destruction was still deeply embedded within him. He then proceeded with the systematic destruction of the city, walking from south to north, east to west, through street after street with his arms outstretched bringing down buildings both old and new. He caused numerous deaths as he passed, allowing no one to escape. Those who tried suffered the most.

In response the Italian government unleashed an air onslaught using the most up to date planes and helicopter gunships. Their combined military was given permission for a full and sustained attack, an attack that achieved nothing other than cause Cronus's anger to grow. As is usual for military planners and advisers, they placed all their faith in modern weaponry and refused to listen to professors and experts in 'The Classics'. They refused to accept the existence of the ancient gods, or worse still, the more dangerous Titans. They didn't even seek the knowledge and experience gained by the Irish security forces during the battle of Dublin.

They had no knowledge or awareness that Cronus, as a Titan, was protected by a long forgotten magic causing each approaching missile to explode before impact. He seemed invincible and the more he was attacked the more the rage took him. He used fireballs, that seemed to be created from thin air, to take down the planes and helicopters, and it wasn't long before he eliminated the Italian air force as well as the assortment of ground forces that were sent against him. When his decimation of the military was complete he turned his attention back to his demolition of the city. His levelling of Naples was relentless and it seemed as though he was practising for a far more formidable challenge. He didn't tire, just moved on to his next target.

He turned his gaze towards the south east and decided to cross the mountains where on his way he spread fear everywhere he passed. He relished in his trail of destruction especially as he travelled through the small villages and towns that dotted this section of his journey.

After several hours he arrived on the shores of the Adriatic Sea, near the port city of Brindisi. He sneered as he looked out at the thousands of ships and smaller craft floating out at sea. These were the boats that had earlier been used to evacuate citizens from most of the immediate east coast of Italy and it was assumed they would be safe. They weren't, they were horrified while watching him move towards a sandy beach, and then walk into the shallow waters. They panicked when he used a left to right motion of his hand to cause what were initially small waves, to rise to great heights. When the waves spread out, they swamped the ships and boats, capsizing them and bringing on the demise of many evacuees.

He endured another military attack, this time by an alliance of NATO and the Russian Federation, who threw everything they had at him but again he was able to repel their efforts. The generals soon realised they were fighting an unknown force that seemed unbeatable and the troubling thing was, Cronus now knew he was unstoppable.

He paused for a moment and looked back at the devastation he had caused and on seeing a few survivors; to them he let his plans be known. "I am Cronus, Lord of the Titans. I will find my sons and bring havoc to their lives and loved ones. I plan to tear down their palaces and their temples, and by the time I'm finished I will have erased all memory of their existence." He then paused and faced east. "Olympus is near and I can smell their fear."

News helicopters kept their distance while using the most powerful cameras and sound equipment to broadcast these tragic yet momentous events. They broadcasted as he raised his arms and watched as he commanded the waters to part allowing him to cross from Italy to Albania. What he did defied physics and reminded the world of the power that once existed and was controlled by the Titans. The cameras picked up the once soft sand of the seabed and watched it harden; it was as though all of nature was in terror of him. Even the deep ravines he met were no obstacle, one leap and he was on the other side.

The helicopters following him flew in disbelief as he eventually entered Albania through the small coastal village of Golem. There was little time to plan an evacuation and the Albanians were overwhelmed. After destroying Golem he turned north and soon arrived at the outskirts of the city of Tirana, where on arrival, and in his loud and thunderous voice he yelled, "Look back at the destruction of your villages, towns and cities. You will suffer the same fate if you continue to hide from me what I seek. Do not stand in the way of my revenge." The people were bewildered; they were innocents and knew nothing of Olympus.

He showed no mercy towards Tirana and levelled the city in less than two hours. The death toll between his slaughter in Italy and his savaging of Tirana was approaching six million that day ensuring his wrath was continuously being broadcast throughout the world. Populations now in his path were in total fear as they realised their governments seemed incapable of protecting them.

All over the world shops sold out of books covering ancient Greek mythology. TV stations continuously broadcasted documentaries on Greek history, and professors of 'The Classics' were in high demand for interview.

The people of Greece were well aware of Cronus and immediately began evacuating villages and towns that were likely in his path. The population of Athens began moving towards the west as well as to the North East in their efforts to avoid the same fate as the people of Tirana and Naples. As Greeks, they instinctively knew to avoid Mount Olympus. They had time on their side because it was calculated that it would take Cronus just under a day to reach the E951 motorway into Athens.

Early the next morning he reached the north western outskirts and stopped to look out across the city where he saw the Acropolis and its iconic Parthenon. It conjured up images in his mind of the palace in which he once dwelled.

All around the world, without exception, people watched the raging walk of Cronus. Many felt his anger was being fuelled as he wiped out every village and town he encountered. They continued watching as the combined air power of NATO, the Russian Federation, Israel and many other countries from all across the Middle East came to the assistance of Greece. They were horrified while watching their weapons being rendered useless by the same ancient magic that was used in Naples. They resigned themselves to a trail of destruction and a devastation that was total.

By coincidence, the night before Cronus crossed the Adriatic Sea, reports of strange lights high in the stratosphere were broadcasted by TV stations across the Middle East. The lights lasted no more than a few seconds, but there were hundreds of them and they defied all explanation. Little did the people know that, after almost two thousand years, the Temple of Olympus was returning to its place beside were the lagoon used to be. It, as usual, was invisible as it settled near a huge city that had built up along that stretch of coastline.

Within the temple, a light film of dust fell from one statue in particular, the statue of Jacob. As the dust fell away a pale complexion appeared across his face and as the minutes passed a magical glow surrounded him allowing him to begin the process of coming back to life. When he was fully restored he stood for a moment and looked around the Great Hall before stepping down from his plinth. Although the sun struggled to penetrate the blanket of night keeping the gods in their deep sleep, some faint rays did get through allowing Jacob to view some of the gods at sleep. He looked up at Odi, then at his parents before again looking around the hall. For just a few moments he felt unsteady and on gaining his strength be made his way to the armoury where on arrival he was surprised to meet a well prepared steward who re-minded him how it was customary for them to awaken in the days before a god arrives; ensuring that all that may be required is prepared.

"While I slept," said Jacob, "I felt a terrible calamity, Naples and Tirana being destroyed. I heard the thuds of pounding steps and saw the rise of Cronus. I sensed him bringing death and destruction. A vision showed me challenging him but how can this be? I never met him. I only know he's evil and full of vengeance so what is it I'm expected to do?"

"My lord," replied he steward, "I was the one who greeted you the day you and your mother walked into the temple for the first time. Remember how the doors just opened and allowed you in? I knew I was in the presence of those who walk in the Light. When you and your mother parted it was from you the Light glowed the brightest, it showed me that you were a most powerful god, possibly the most powerful. Today, you stand before me no longer a boy, but a man who will leave this temple as a king. You mention Cronus, that's because from Maria you came, from Zeus she came and from

Cronus he came, you are of his bloodline." The steward stepped back and bowed towards the statue of Zeus before continuing. "Only one god has awoken and that's you, it seems your task has been set. The Light is unforgiving; you must answer its call and do its bidding. Go with the blessing of Zeus and be the King of Olympus that you're meant to be."

Jacob washed and prepared; he dressed in the robes of an Olympus king and wore the cape of a god over the golden armour created by Hephaestus. He armed himself with two weapons. A sword, one of the ten created by the nymphs, and a golden dagger that he placed in the scabbard, strapped just below his right knee. He clipped his satchel to his belt and checked that it contained all required for his journey.

Just as Jacob was about to place the golden helmet upon his head, the steward stopped him and requested he kneel. He was taken aback while watching the steward open a royal regalia chásse to extract what looked like the imperial crown of Olympus, the very crown that was first worn by Cronus and then by Zeus. He then remembered the dream he had in Gibraltar, a dream showing him hands placing a crown upon his head.

"Zeus foretold that you will be first to awaken," said the steward while raising the crown above his head. "When this comes to pass, he decreed that you were to be crowned king, one you were born to be." The steward then presented to him a staff. "I've also been instructed to present you with this magical staff; it is encrusted with a crystal that can be used to call on the first Light. Use it well for it will be your friend. My king, when you leave this temple you will, in just one day, change the course of the looming battle but it will not be easy, you will suffer much pain and might even lose your strength and confidence. Remember the compassion, empathy and insight your mother shared with you while you lived among man, it's those memories that will come to your aid when all seems lost."

Jacob absorbed what was said and felt quite numb, he waited a few moments to gather his thoughts before moving towards the doors.

On his way he momentarily stopped. He thought he saw a vision, a ghost. He walked a few more paces and saw the vision again. He recognised it to be his sixteen year old younger self and again remembered his night terrors especially the one where, during all the turmoil, he saw himself wearing a crown. He bowed to his younger self and continued on his way. He turned and again looked around the Great Hall at the stone images of all the gods, especially his beloved brother and then went out into the gardens. The sudden brightness momentarily blinded him but it was the heat of the now rising sun that totally revitalized him. Walking through the gardens he thought of Eala and his children, then thought of his school friends and wondered had the battle of Dublin happened yet. He then struggled to put the memories of what happened that day from his mind. He thought of the Sun Gods and wondered if they were about and watching his every move. He then opened a portal allowing him to enter the large city.

The first thing he noticed was the change in the air quality, the dark dust that was blowing around was beginning to choke him making him very uncomfortable. He couldn't see the lagoon or the ancient trees that once grew along its banks, and this troubled him. They were gone and he wondered how the nymphs allowed this happen. He remarked to himself at the stench that was all around and longed for the sweet aromas that used to prevail in these once enchanted lands. He walked through the empty streets and remembered that this was once the site of the village that gave him the love of his life.

As he continued his walk he reached a large block of apartments where on looking through one of the windows he saw the occupants were watching the destructive walk of a Titan and noted that those watching were terrified.

He watched the news reports repeatedly showing images of Dublin and the awful onslaught the Dark Angels visited on that city. He now knew the battle had happened in real time and saw that the reporters were now connecting the destruction of Naples and Tirana with his prophecies given after the battle of Dublin. He also saw that natural disasters were now being questioned and were being associated with all the strange things happening everywhere. He looked closely at the face of the Titan and remembered the face he saw in the caverns off Hell that time when the Archangels were in his head, it was definitely Cronus.

He continued observing secure in the knowledge he was invisible, allowing him to remain near the window to watch Cronus approach Athens. While watching, his insecurities returned and he became fearful, so much so he had difficulty using his inner strength to hold that same fear at bay. When his strength returned he took a deep breath, blinked and transported himself to Athens.

Chapter 2

He materialised in the southern suburbs of the city and immediately felt the panic spreading everywhere. He noticed people pointing and staring, and heard them whisper as they recognised him to be the same warrior who fought in the battle of Dublin, they were beginning to feel hope. Within minutes a news helicopter hovering close by began broadcasting his arrival. Within minutes police officers arrived. "Can I ask what you're doing here?" asked the officer that approached him, his hand firmly gripping his weapon.

"No, you can't," replied Jacob.

"Crowds are gathering," said the officer still holding his weapon. "This means you're causing a breach of the peace. It's my job to remove the cause of the breach."

"Strange how your city is about to be destroyed and all you worry about is a breach of the peace," said Jacob shaking his head in disbelief.

"You are the boy involved in the murder of all those tourists and students in Dublin. You look older," commented the officer.

"I'm two thousand years older," responded Jacob trying not to get annoyed. "I'm here to remove the threat of Cronus, something your military is incapable of doing," He then pulled the officer so close their noses touched.

"The deaths in Dublin happened because of Hells serpents, not because of me, or my brother. They're coming back and no one will be safe, you will need the power of the gods before this battle is over." He then backed away.

He joined his hands together and as he separated them, he used his magic to part the line of police cars, allowing him to walk through unhindered.

He noted the street and helicopter cameras were trained on him which is what he wanted. As a god he wanted to send out hope to all those watching. He smiled and acknowledged the people as he passed, all while steadfastly walking towards the slopes leading up to the Parthenon. The most striking thing was the hope he brought, and it was spreading. Buses, cars, carts and trucks, all carrying the evacuees from Athens, stopped and people exited their vehicles to watch the amazing sight of the boy king they all saw fight the forces of evil during the battle of Dublin. Like the officer, they were intrigued by his appearance, he was a boy while in Dublin but now, just a few months later, he was presenting to the world as a man who was a powerful looking king. He looked strong and fearless but what the people couldn't see was that he was terrified. They watched him walk up the Acropolis and make his way to stand overlooking the city.

It was while making his way to take up a position at the south facing side of the Parthenon when more images were transmitted around the world. It was an amazing sight, his golden cape flapping and spreading widely in the strong breeze created images usually only seen in the epic films. His imperial crown captured the rays of the now high sun but it was his golden breastplate that attracted the most attention. Its etchings not only showed the laurels of Olympus, it also showed the valknut of Asgard, and both were intertwined. What surprised those watching was that he was only carrying a single sword.

He moved to the patio at the side of the Parthenon and stared out into the distance to watch Cronus move south towards the old city. Even from that distance the heavy steps were audible and getting louder as Cronus made his way to the temple of Zeus. From there he continued towards Hadrian's arch.

Another of the helicopters following Cronus broke off and flew towards the Acropolis to assist in sending more images around the world increasing the growing feelings of hope. Those watching gasped when Jacob produced the gem capped staff from his small satchel and were amazed at how the staff, coming from such a small bag, turned physics on its head. They were riveted when, after raising the staff to the heavens, a blinding light arrived and then shot out across the city. At that point TV images were split; one showing the boy king standing before the Parthenon and the other showing the advance of the Titan. The split images captured Jacob plunging his staff to the ground and then emitting a most powerful beam of light, and the second showed that same light attracting the attention of Cronus.

Cronus was about to commence his destruction of Athens when he was temporarily blinded causing him to shade his eyes and seek out its source. When he focused on the Parthenon he saw a young man, dressed as a warrior king. He noted the warrior's sword and the blinding light that was emitting from his staff; he also recognised the light was one he hadn't seen since the beginning of time, and this intrigued him.

Cronus changed direction to make his way towards the Acropolis and while on his way he continued showing his rage by destroying buildings as he passed. He sent debris in all directions. On arrival at the foot of the Acropolis he was taken aback to see the warrior place the staff back in his satchel, fold his arms defiantly and very clearly show he wasn't afraid.

"Your face!" roared Cronus, "I've seen it before, who are you to defy and challenge the lord of the Titans?"

Jacob didn't respond prompting Cronus to look more closely, he furrowed his brow and noticed that the warrior was wearing the crown of Olympus causing him to get more agitated. He leapt forward attempting to capture the crown but wasn't fast enough. Jacob used his powers, blinked and disappeared to reappear some distance away.

"Where are you, coward?" yelled Cronus.

Jacob decided to antagonise Cronus, wondering how far he could push him. He began by tapping his sword against the walls of different parts of the Acropolis while appearing and disappearing causing great confusion, he even landed on Cronus's shoulder and blew in his ear.

"Who are you? Why defy me? You can't win," yelled Cronus again while trying to locate the warrior. "You can play all the games you like and in the end you will still become my dinner. I am the King of the Titans and I'll find you wherever you may hide." He continued demanding a response until Jacob removed his crown to reveal more of his face.

"I know that face," said Cronus looking unsure. "Six moons ago, while in the bowels of Hell, I watched two young warriors battle a legion of Dark Angels on the streets of Dublin. You were one of those warriors, older, broader and more skilful now. I ask again, who are you?"

"Those two warriors did indeed defeat a legion of Hells finest," replied Jacob while placing the crown back on his head. "I was one and my brother the other. Now it's time for you to meet me as a man." Cronus declined and lifted a large clump of masonry which he hurled at Jacob who yet again blinked his way out of danger.

All over the world people recognised the young king as one of the warriors who fought in Dublin and from news reports at the time, knew his name to be Jacob Baker. They clapped and cheered, and considered him a hero, especially while watching him disappear and then reappear as he outmanoeuvred Cronus. At the same time many were praying he was not alone and would bring many more warriors to help protect them, fearing the horrific prophecy he gave in Dublin was about to come true.

They walked the length of the Acropolis, turned and walked back again never taking their eyes from each other. This went on for almost thirty minutes while each waited for the other to make a mistake. Cronus occasionally threw pieces of rubble at nearby buildings, destroying them in the hope of causing more intimidation, he also used the ancient magic, first seen in Naples, to conjure up balls of fire to hurl at Jacob but his efforts didn't work, Jacob never flinched.

Cronus then broke the silence and asked again as to whom he was and this time Jacob answered, "You ask as to who I am? Yet you look on me and feel you know me? Look again and see in my face someone you know. See in me the face of my grandfather, your son, Zeus." Cronus was taken aback and didn't see this one coming. Jacob continued, "I am Jacob, grandson of Zeus and the Goddess Dione. With the blessing of Zeus I wear the crown of Olympus and I alone will be known as the King of Kings. I have founded a new royal house and will rule Olympus for all time."

"That crown is not for Zeus to give," replied Cronus. "It's mine and mine alone."

"Strange," Jacob sneered, "how it sits on my head and not yours."

This comment infuriated Cronus even more forcing him to react so quickly that he took Jacob by surprise. He struck Jacob, sending him tumbling to the ground, and using his sharp nails he tore into his arm, drawing first blood. Jacob quickly recovered and found the strength to retaliate, he drew his sword and using the power of Ares, he transported himself back and forth at such speed and into different positions that he was able to cause maximum pain by slicing into Cronus' chest, back, shoulders and arms causing him to bleed profusely.

"At first I thought the cowardly Zeus had sent a boy to challenge me," said a suffering Cronus while trying to compose himself. "Now I see he has a plan, you will not succeed."

"How can you call Zeus a coward?" said Jacob, "considering you are the one who eats his own children. I'm ashamed to be of your blood, you make me sick." Jacob paced some more before he continued, "What happens here today is not a plan prepared by Zeus. My brother is a War God of Asgard and has laid his plans before me, they are now my plans. My brothers and I will lead the armies of the gods."

"War God of Asgard?" said Cronus while spitting with contempt. "He can only be Magni, imbecile."

"Beware my brother," responded Jacob. "He's not the god you remember, he's now the greatest of them all, hurt me, beware his vengeance."

"I fear no god," responded Cronus while moving closer. "Before them we ruled; the gods will not survive the return of the Titans."

He continued to hurl rubble, demolishing more buildings, this time further out into the city. Jacob watched him intently while pacing back and forth, so much so that he missed a small indentation in the slabs causing him to trip, allowing Cronus to swing his arm with such force that on contact, it broke Jacob's left leg and arm. The screams of pain coming from Jacob shook the very heavens and the force of the impact sent him hurdling out towards the mountains. He was in so much pain he began to lose consciousness, but was not so unconscious that he didn't hear Cronus smirk, "Not much of a plan is it? I'm ashamed that you are a great grandson of mine." The people watching were horrified, they felt their hope fade and the panic return but they should have had more faith. More was to come.

With whatever strength that remained Jacob managed to blink, transporting himself back to the healing waters of Olympus where he used the power given to him by Poseidon to begin healing himself. When healed he took a moment to take counsel from the steward before returning to the battle with a vengeance. The viewers watched him reappear, and noted how he looked much stronger and more determined. He landed on Cronus' shoulder and, using a new spear, he pierced Cronus' neck causing him to yell out in agony. He continued his attack using all his swordsman skills, speed and tactics. He cut into Cronus's ankles, legs and thighs before Cronus could figure out where Jacob was coming from. He then upended Cronus by piercing his knees; caused him to violently fall forward, and on impacting the ground, send a mild tremor rolling out across Athens.

Cronus lay still for a few moments before finding the strength to rise to his feet and when he did he called on his ancient fire to assist by raised his palm and creating a fireball. He fired it towards Jacob but while Jacob was distracted, he cunningly used his other hand to create a second one and fire it in the direction he anticipated Jacob would jump. It was a good call on his part as Jacob received the full force of the second fireball causing him to impact against a partially rebuilt pillar.

Jacob yelled out in pain as the fires scorched his skin and blisters formed, he was also dazed long enough for Cronus to reach in to capture him. This time there was no escape. Cronus proceeded to slowly squeeze the life from Jacob but thankfully his golden armour, having been forged in the fires of Olympus, was strong enough to protect him. Cronus wasn't happy and immediately moved Jacob towards his mouth so as to swallow him as he did his children all those years ago.

Jacob regained consciousness just as he was about to be placed in Cronus' mouth and although in severe pain had to think quickly, he called out and offered a challenge knowing the Titans always liked a challenge.

"Why should I listen to you?" said Cronus. "You have used the tactics of your grandfather but this time they've failed. You are of no use to me."

Although really hurting and refusing to call out in pain, Jacob managed to ask, "Have you ever wondered why Lucifer brought you back?"

"He needs me to remove the threat of the gods and I will," replied Cronus while lowering Jacob from his mouth. "With them gone he will be free to unleash the serpents of Hell and bring forth The Darkness. My reward will be the return of my kingdom."

"Have you not wondered what happens to Olympus when The Darkness returns?" asked Jacob. "From where will Olympus receive its light when all will be subsumed into total darkness?" Jacob was now gasping and seriously struggling, "I'm a Time Lord and can show you what's to come. My challenge is for you to allow me show you a future where The Darkness rules supreme. Will you allow me?"

"Why should I trust you?" asked Cronus remembering how he had lost all his trust many years ago, but he was intrigued as to what the future held for him.

"They say that blood is thicker than water," continued Jacob. "I'm of your blood but unlike you I would do anything to protect my children. Earlier, while on your shoulder, I felt a deep suppressed pain that showed me how once you were in love, once you were a good king and I want to bring that king back."

"I know nothing of what you speak," said Cronus before proceeding to move Jacob back towards his mouth.

"How come I'm here?" asked Jacob trying to suppress his pain. "How come Zeus is your son? There must have been someone you loved, try to remember!"

Cronus hesitated, thought for a moment, began to remember and wonder. The whole world was watching, they heard everything and prayed he would allow Jacob to show him his future. Their prayers were answered when Cronus relented and agreed to the challenge. Jacob asked him to take his human form which he reluctantly did.

When the human Cronus stood before him Jacob remarked on how alike he and Zeus were. He then placed his hand on Cronus, blinked, and they arrived one year into the future. All viewers gasped while watching them disappear.

When they arrived there was nothing, they could see nothing, hear nothing, touch nothing or smell nothing. "To where have you taken me?" asked Cronus. "Why can't I see? Have you blinded me?"

"This is absolute darkness and is your future," replied Jacob. "Lucifer has won the battle because of your help but the fool has allowed in The Darkness and now there is no light."

"Where's my Kingdom?" asked a panicked Cronus.

"This is your Kingdom," said Jacob. "You are king of nothingness and all your subjects are gone. They've been taken by The Darkness and now you've nobody to rule. Is this what you want? Lucifer is the great deceiver. He deceived Hades for millennia and has done the same to you. Think of how he stopped you leaving the Underworld just so his plans would fall into place."

Cronus turned full circle and could still see nothing, he shuffled his feet and there was no sound, he raised his nose and detected no smell, there was still nothing. He spoke and although Jacob was right beside him he had trouble hearing. Jacob moved forward with his arms outstretched and pulled Cronus closer, "The Darkness even takes your words. Hold on to me, we must leave now before it's too late."

They returned to the Parthenon and it was obvious to all watching that Cronus looked bewildered. He paced back and forth, trying to come to terms with what Jacob had showed him, and then said, "I've always known the future is not set in stone, is there a second path to show me?"

"I can't show you an alternative future," replied Jacob. "This is the path you have chosen, and you haven't indicated your desire to change."

"Once I had a wife," said Cronus while still pacing back and forth. "Rhea was her name. Do you know what became of her?" Jacob was surprised at this question and soon detected a weakening,

"The story goes," said Jacob. "When you were quartered your parts were exiled to many hidden places in the dungeons of Tartarus and were never intended to be found. After your defeat Rhea lived among her children for many years and when happy they ruled as fair and just gods she left. It's written that she missed you more than anything else dear to her. She went to Mount Olympus and lay in the high grasses of the south facing slopes where she fell into a deep sleep. Over time the grasses grew so tall that they absorbed her into their roots. Many tried to rouse her but failed. There she still lies and it's believed she will awaken when the just king whom she always loved comes looking for her."

Cronus now had feelings he had long forgotten and as the moments passed all he wanted was to meet Rhea and rekindle the love he now realised he'd lost. He looked at Jacob and noticed he was still wearing the crown he had for so long desired, but it now meant nothing to him.

"Truly you are the King of Kings," said Cronus while kneeling and bowing. "You have my allegiance. Help me make peace with Zeus." Jacob then reached in to read Cronus's deepest thoughts.

"It seems I've awoken the true lord of the Titans," said Jacob while assisting Cronus back to his feet. "Now that you've come back into the Light I will assist on one condition. Never kneel before me again, you are one of the ancients and deserve our respect."

Jacob's well known compassion showed itself again and he suggested they travel to Mount Olympus. He reached in and blinked both of them to the southern flank of the mountain where on arrival they spread panic among the local villagers who started evacuating towards the coast. After a little persuasion from Jacob the villagers accepted that Cronus was no longer a danger so remained to watch him walk among the tall grasses. They watched him climb higher and listened to him continuously call Rhea's name hoping she'd appear.

The higher he climbed the quieter everything became, no birdsong, no wind, no bellowing, even Cronus's steps were silent. It was absolute quietness. Soon the grasses shuddered and then bowed before him, their roots began to release a pale green mist that thickened and then rose to a great height to form a stunningly beautiful woman. When fully formed she was perfect in every way starting with her welcoming face that was framed by moon shadow-black hair that fell gently to rest just below her shoulders. Her slender eyebrows sat perfectly above her grey green eyes that were highlighted by a soft shadow and liner. Her mint green gown, held in place by gem covered clasps and straps, enhanced her hour glass figure. It was her smile on seeing the one she loved the most was what melted all those watching.

Cronus grew to his Titan form and then stood in awe looking upon the only women he ever loved. He remembered all the good that was between them before the greed, envy, fear and jealousy took him. He hoped it wasn't too late.

Rhea walked towards him and offered her hand. He knew then he had a chance to repair all the damage he'd done. No words were spoken, they just held each other.

They took their human form and made their way down the mountain to where Jacob waited. As they approached he bowed, took Rhea's hand and told her who he was. Her face lit up with a beaming smile when told he was just one from among her many grandchildren and great grandchildren. "The crown of Olympus sits perfectly on your head," she said when reaching in to touch his face. "It has found its perfect host."

"It seems the Ancient One has set in place a plan beginning with me becoming King of Kings," said Jacob reaching in to kiss her cheek. "I believe his plans also led to this day, the day when the Titans come in defence of the Light."

"My children," asked Rhea after looking around. "Where are they? Will I meet them soon?"

"I promise you'll meet them but it cannot be this day," replied Jacob. "The return of the Titans must be kept secret. I will explain at another time, we must return to the Parthenon."

"How long has it been?" asked Cronus." How long since we last walked these lands?"

"It's been many thousands of years," replied Jacob. "In fact, way back in the mists of time wouldn't be an exaggeration"

"I fear Olympus will never accept us back," said a dejected Rhea. "Too much has happened. Is there somewhere we can go to live out our lives in peace?"

"I know of a place," replied Jacob while trying to come up with a plan. "Elysium, it's also known as the Elysian Islands or the Elysian Fields. They are Islands of great beauty and the resting place of the virtuous heroes, fallen warriors, kings and gods of myth and legend. It's the home of the blessed dead." He began to get excited, "You'll be free to come and go as you please but only after we deal with Lucifer. These sacred Islands need a Warrior King and a Mother Queen as their guardians and protectors. I believe Zeus will approve of this plan."

Cronus knew by Rhea's reaction that this was a good offer and said, "We accept your offer and promise to protect those sacred lands."

Chapter 3

Jacob brought them to the islands where they walked among the tombs of the kings and queens of old. They saw the resting places of the warriors and wizards who fell in the great battles as well as many long forgotten heroes who died protecting their realms.

They walked through tree lined avenues and spent much of their time reading the names on the headstones. Cronus and Rhea recognised some as old friends but Jacob never heard of any of them.

After a while they located a seating area, sat and talked about the coming battle.

"If Lucifer wins," said a concerned Cronus. "This special place will also fall. This cannot be allowed to happen. If this is now the realm of the Titans, let it be known that we will defend it with all our might. Once there were twelve, their memory calls out to me. The Titans will assist in defeating Him."

Jacob had already thought of this but couldn't think of the best strategy in which to use the skills of Cronus. He knew he only had one option and that was to call on the brilliant war tactics of his brother. He excused himself and left to climb a nearby hill, leading up to sea cliffs that stood over two hundred meters high. He faced out over the northern seas, raised his arms to the heavens, closed his eyes and called out for Magni to answer.

Magni had gone into his well earned and long overdue sleep knowing his protection of Panya and the boys was now complete. He was satisfied they were safe in the caves of the northern ice lands. Unfortunately for him it was not a peaceful sleep, it was so restless it made it easy for Jacob to reach him. He immediately prepared to answer the call, whistled for his chariot and swiftly travelled to the Elysian Islands.

In the meantime Jacob rejoined Cronus and Rhea to continue their walk along the tree lined avenues. This led them to a large temple where, when they walked up the steps, they were surprised to see the doors magically open; allowing them to enter what was the largest mausoleum they had ever seen.

Cronus used his powers to create a flame to light the first torches that were positioned on both sides of the entrance. As the flames rose, the oil resting in the long gullies that travelled the length of the mausoleum ignited to light torch after torch until all were lit, illuminating the whole tomb. They descended forty steps only to stand in awe. What was before them was a line of arches that travelled down both sides of the tomb for as far as the eye could see. Under each arch lay the final resting place of the most revered ancient kings, renowned heroes, warriors and blessed dead of many realms. On reaching the first arch Jacob was speechless, it held a sarcophagus with the carved-in-stone image of King Solomon and it was placed next to that of the Queen of Sheba. Beside them was King David and beyond him were the tombs of Moses and his wife, Zipporah to name but a few.

Just as they were moving to the next arch Jacob heard pounding footsteps that could only mean Magni had arrived. He ran to greet his very excited brother who lifted him high off his feet. "Brother," said an emotional Magni. It's been too long." He stepped back and looked Jacob up and down, "You wear the crown of Olympus. Truly now you are King of Kings."

"Don't be angry," said Jacob looking very nervous. "I've someone for you to meet."

It was then he noticed Jacob was armed, bloody and a bit worse for wear. He asked as to what the problem was and just as Jacob was about to speak he saw a figure walk from behind one of the arches and recognised him to be Cronus. He reacted by pushing Jacob aside, drew his sword and lunged forward but somehow Jacob managed to contain him, hurriedly trying to explain. Magni, although uneasy, calmed down long enough to listen to the explanation.

Jacob told him of the battle he had with Cronus and how both of them seriously injured each other. He spoke of visiting the nothingness and how that visit brought Cronus back into the Light.

"I need a plan to change history," said a now relaxed Jacob. "It must be one that's good enough to deceive Lucifer. He must think Cronus is dead, killed by me, and I need the plan urgently."

"What was the last thing that happened during your battle?" asked Magni.

"Cronus was about to eat me," cringed Jacob, expecting a violent reaction.

Magni gasped, he was furious and approached Cronus to show his contempt but couldn't find the words. It was then he saw Rhea, "My Lady," he said while bowing. "It's been too long. The great stories still speak of your name. You are still the most revered of the Earth Mothers." They last met when he was a boy, and he remembered how her calmness seeped into his very essence allowing him to relax.

Just then he looked over her shoulder and became distracted; he was enthralled when he saw how vast the halls of the blessed dead were.

"How close is the resting place of the Norse Lords?" he asked while putting his plan together, "I hear a whisper; they're restless and it seems, waiting to come to my aid."

"We have yet to explore many of the arches," replied Cronus while walking under the nearest one. "Ah, this is it! I thought I too heard a whisper. Look upon the tombs of Asgard, the final resting place of the Norse Lords."

Magni was drawn towards a large tomb guarded by four carved in stone Viking warriors and thought he saw them move. He closed his eyes and called on his ancestors to come to his aid. He then walked further through the tombs and recognised many names to be of ancient Asgard myth and legend. "Do you hear it?" he said back to Jacob. "There's a stirring, some are our ancestors and they're preparing to answer my call."

"So quiet," said Jacob. "Not a sound, nothing."

"Listen carefully," said Magni, holding his hand to his ear. "It's a high pitched whistling sound, only audible to a dog. Not saying that I'm a dog. It travels from deep within the tombs and carries almost inaudible voices, they were getting louder. Now do you hear them?" Jacob still couldn't hear them.

Centuries of accumulated dust rose up to form the shapes of Viking warriors, there were many and they were moving rapidly towards Magni, and as they got closer he knew they were coming to impart a plan.

Magni changed; he fell into a trancelike state before turning to say to Cronus, "Go back to the moment just before Jacob fell."

He turned to Jacob, "Take your colossus form and face Cronus as an equal. Fight with such vengeance that its venom will break through the barriers of Hell and attract the attention of Lucifer. He will be watching so make it vicious, he must believe it's to the death."

He turned back to Cronus, "Send Jacob to the ground while at the same time, produce your fire ball. Call on all your might and use the fireball to incinerate him."

He turned back to Jacob, "Anticipate this move, roll out of the way, allow the fireball hit the ground and open a sinkhole."

He then said to both of them, "You must restart your fight, draw blood, hurt each other. Be vicious, be unyielding, and then allow for you both to fall into the sinkhole. Continue your now pretend battle, hidden and out of sight. Let the clanging of swords and the vicious sound of battle, resonate across the cosmos. Then, when it's time, let the whole world see Jacob climb from the sink hole and let them watch the head of Cronus show itself. Let all see Jacob raise his sword and smite the mighty Cronus. All will then know he is dead, let them watch the dark mist rise and find its way back into the pits of Hell."

Cronus smiled and bowed to the knowledge of the Norse Lords, he knew this plan would work but Jacob wasn't so sure. He meekly asked, "How do I become a colossus? I haven't learned to take that form and where do we get the black mist?"

"You are a great grandson of two Titans," said Magni, "trust me, you will learn fast and will become a colossus before Cronus is finished with you."

Jacob nervously nodded and then asked again, "From where do we get the black mist?"

Cronus took a very deep breath and when he exhaled, a steady flow of blackness appeared. Jacob was satisfied, and transported both himself and Cronus back to Athens.

They arrived back to the exact time when Cronus was about to throw his second fireball, the very one that originally floored Jacob. This action also allowed for all that had happened in the previous battle, including the rebirth of Rhea, to be erased from the memory of man. The second fireball as planned hit the ground with such force it opened a sinkhole giving Jacob time to regain his composure. Cronus produced his legendary sword and started an onslaught against Jacob forcing him to use all the training Ares and Athena put him through all those years ago.

It was then when Jacob noticed his breath struggling. At first he felt a tugging sensation, his legs trembled but more especially his arms vibrated. His head pounded and then it happened. He expanded and grew. He reached a height of twenty feet allowing him to face Cronus as his equal.

The battle between the two Titans was relentless and merciless. The clanging of swords could be heard all across Athens and was so loud it surely attracted the attention of Hell. It certainly did. From the corner of his eye Jacob watched a portal open and saw that Lucifer was now watching the fight. He beckoned to Cronus to look up at the Parthenon, which he did, allowing him to confirm that it was in fact Lucifer. Every effort to make the fight look as real as possible ensured Lucifer was deceived. The continuous blows wreaked havoc on both their bodies causing hideous purple-black bruises and blood soaked wounds. They then put the final part of their plan into action by moving the fight even closer to the sinkhole and after a few more painful blows they both fell in.

Dust rose as the yelps of pain, and the clashing of swords, went on for what seemed hours. Eventually it got very quiet and soon a hand was seen rising from the hole to grip the rim. It was Jacob climbing out followed by the bloodied and dust covered head of Cronus. Jacob raised his sword and without hesitation smashed it down on Cronus' head causing him to fall back. Soon after he fell, the cameras recorded his dark mist rising, and followed it as it searched for any crevice in which to hide. Those watching believed it to be the spirit of Cronus trying to find its way to Hell.

Jacob retook his human size and as he was shrinking he pretended not to see the portal. Using his shield he was able to see the reflection of fury crossing Lucifer's face and this pleased him. The portal closed and Jacob took the opportunity to grab the hidden Cronus and return him to Elysium.

They arrived at the steps in the mausoleum and went to find Rhea and Magni who had continued walking through many of the side passageways paying homage to all those who lay in rest. Jacob was hurting and still bleeding when he met them, but put the pain out of his mind when they reached the tombs of the Celts. He immediately thought of Shane and their time in history classes where they shared a love of ancient Celtic myths and legends. He walked by the sarcophagi of Finn Mac Cumhaill, Queen Maeve, King Brian, and Chu Chulainn. At the end of this passageway he saw a large sarcophagus where above it stood a most striking sculpture. It was the image of a proud stallion carrying the most beautiful Niamh and beside her stood the image of Oisin, son of Finn. To their right was the final resting place of King Lir and his first wife, Queen Eva, and they were surrounded by four beautiful swans. Jacob remarked, "My friend, Shane, needs to see this place."

Magni was walking ahead of the others when he reached the aisle that contained the tombs of the Anglo Saxons. He was followed in, and together they all paid homage at the tombs of King Arthur, Queen Genevieve, their knights, St George, Queen Boudicca and many more heroes and blessed dead of the Britannia realms.

While Jacob was admiring the effigy of King Arthur he felt a calling drawing him to the next archway. It was the final resting place of the Dragon Lords. There he saw a beautiful effigy resting on an ornate tomb, it was the effigy of a dragon Queen and he felt drawn to her. He stood before her and was moved when he realised it was Heulwyn, consort of Fafner. What troubled him most was that there was another plinth, partially prepared, and it could only be for Fafner. Jacob placed his hands over his mouth; he was becoming upset especially now that he knew Fafner was not going to make it through the battle. Magni joined him, noticed how upset he was and said, "Did you know her?"

"I didn't," said Jacob, "I never met her. She became the Empress Heulwyn when Fafner became Emperor of the Dragons. They had five children, three boys and two girls. She and Fafner ruled as just monarchs and the dragon realm prospered."

Magni said while looking at the half prepared plinth, "You do know, a half prepared plinth doesn't mean Fafner is soon to die, if it was completed then I'd be worried."

"Look," said Jacob while pointing at the stone mason tools resting against the side of the plinth. "They're working on his plinth, his destiny is set. He will rest with his wife in the not too distant future." He was now very upset and his voice was breaking.

Jacob was considered among the gods to be a very stoic individual; he was a war tactician and outwardly seemed to have no fear. It bothered some of them, especially the War Gods, that he so easily shows his emotions. Magni most of all disliked empathy and compassion, and it took a long time for him to recognise this to be Jacob's most endearing trait. He felt very protective of, and always kept an eye on his young brother.

Magni watched Jacob place his hand on the tomb of Heulwyn then lower his head; he watched him place his other hand on the unfinished tomb of Fafner.

"Brother, Fafner's not here," whispered Magni. "Do not grieve for something that hasn't happened. You always speak of a future and its many paths. Maybe Fafner will change his path and will not lie in rest here"

"I'm not able for this and it hurts," responded Jacob. "I wish to be back with my friends in Dublin. There I was carefree and had lots of fun. Why is life so hard? Why is there so much pain and misery? Magni, help me, I really can't do this." He rested his forehead against a nearby pillar. "Why did Zeus make me king of kings?" he asked. "He arranged for his crown to be placed upon my head. Why? Who am I that I should be crowned so?"

"Get a grip, you've been chosen by the Ancient One and there's nothing you can do about that. Let me tell you why it was so easy for Zeus to place his crown upon your head. We ancient gods have always known, since soon after the beginning of time, about how a young boy would rise up and defend the third age of man. You, my brother, are that boy; you are our King of Kings. You are the defender."

Magni stepped back and bowed causing Jacob to leap forward and say while pulling him up, "Magni, never bow to me, I need you to punch me, kick me, clatter me when I make mistakes, I need you to keep me in line." He pulled Magni towards him, hugged him and said, "Will you hold me. Hold me real tight and let me rest my head on your shoulder, never let me go?" Magni held him tight and after some time passed Jacob continued, "I grew up with just my mother, and now I have a father and three brothers. How can it be that you all must bow before me? I can't accept this." Rhea took Jacob by the arm and said,

"Once before there was a king who was powerful and just, then The Darkness took him. The Light eventually came and saved him, you are that light. It's good for that king to stand here today and watch his great grandson rise up with humility and doubts. We are so proud for you and we are pleased it's you to be anointed as the new King of Kings."

"Enough of these doubts," said Cronus while joining them, "walk up those stairs, feel the fresh air of Elysium and stand proud. Puff out your chest and allow the soft wind surround you. Look across the tombs of the blessed fallen and feel their power my King of Kings, go now."

Jacob walked up the first four steps and stopped. He looked back at the arches and froze. His doubts returned. He turned back and looked up towards the doors and found the remaining steps daunting. He couldn't move; the doubts got stronger. While distracted he didn't hear Magni come from behind, but he certainly felt the unmerciful kick that sent him scurrying. When he reached the door he took a deep breath, he felt the very air Cronus spoke of enter his lungs. He took another deep breath and felt the calmness suppress his fears and doubts. He moved his head from left to right and listened for the voices of the blessed fallen. Soon he felt their strength surround him. He did what Cronus asked, puffed out his chest and stood proud. He turned and looked down at Magni who clenched his fist and placed it across his chest. Magni bowed again and this time Jacob accepted his homage.

Cronus, Rhea and Magni soon reached the top of the steps and together with Jacob looked out across the vastness of the Elysian Fields. They were aware of the many vacant tombs created by the stonemasons, and sensed they would soon start filling up. Their visions showed them the spirits of the dead, victims of the End Times battle and it was getting closer.

"Look up and see how the stars are fading," bemoaned Magni. "The Darkness is relentless, showing no mercy. Out there is Bel Marduk, someone I Lo...." He stopped on realizing what he nearly revealed, then continued, "I worry for him."

"It seems it's my time to comfort you," said Jacob while reaching across to take Magni's hand. "Brother, stop worrying. Bel Murduck is powerful, a renowned Sun God. He'll be fine. You need all your strength for what's coming, so put him from your mind." He reached in and whispered, "Your wait is nearly over, I've seen it."

"Today Jacob showed me what The Darkness brings," said Cronus, tactfully changing the subject. "He showed me how it consumes all senses. The Ancient One will show vengeance when the time is right but expects us to play our part before that time comes." He turned to Magni, "When your father calls, the Titans will answer and I will lead them to assist."

"How can you do this?" asked a confused Jacob. "Are you both not the last of the Titans?"

"Look at us," replied Rhea. "I was consumed by roots and grasses on Mount Olympus. Cronus was quartered and placed in the far reaches of Hell, now we've returned. Worry not about our kin, we will soon find their hiding places."

"Trust us," said Cronus, "the Titans will rise when the time arrives."

Jacob slightly turned his head. He was hearing another calling and announced that he must leave immediately, "Lucifer is moving and his legions are prepared. I smell his vengeance and hear his commands, he's close," He turned to Magni, "Brother, you must return to Asgard and prepare your armies. Watch for my Light, it will be the brightest." He then bowed and disappeared back to Olympus.

It was then when everything changed, Magni was about to mount his chariot when Cronus became alarmed, "Rhea, what is it?" She didn't answer. Magni remained and watched Cronus try to wake her.

"I see deception," she mumbled from deep within her trance. "It's Jacob he's after. I see the last battle, two will fight and then he will be vanquished. All are being deceived, I see him. Even the light struggles. Jacob is in great danger. There is a 'Shadow' and it's near."

"Who will be vanquished?" screamed Magni, grabbing Rhea. "Who will be vanquished? What shadow do you speak of?"

"I don't know?" she said after coming around. "There are two paths. Jacob's on one and he's fighting Lucifer. I can't see which one falls. The other path; is the deception of Lucifer."

Just as he made a second attempt to leave, Rhea said, "Magni, I'm first among all Earth Mothers and there are nine others. Seek them, and send them to me. Lucifer will know Cronus still walks if I reveal myself too soon so do this for me. Call on the Wizards. They'll know what to do."

A very troubled Magni then left. He struggled to remove the image of the last battle between Jacob and Lucifer from his mind hoping it wouldn't come to pass. Occasionally he looked up at the stars, watching in horror as another one fell to The Darkness. He was pleased to see them fight back and wondered was it the Sun Gods on the offensive led by his dearest friend, Bel Marduk. He headed to the western realms and called on the wizards to answer.

Chapter 4

Magni found himself following a dim light leading into an ancient forest close to the never-ending marsh lands. He continued following the light and eventually found an inviting fire burning brightly in the long lost ruins of a temple dedicated to the Goddess Danu. He rested by the fire and waited, all the while holding his sword by his side. He sensed he wasn't alone and only relaxed when he felt a friendly and familiar presence. He was joined by the wizards, Merlin, Apollonius and Mygon and he brought them up to date on the efforts put in place by Jacob in preparation for the battle with Lucifer. He then told them of the request from Rhea.

Rhea's return surprised the wizards, they thought that like all Earth Mothers, she was long gone, hidden and protected until dire times came to threaten earth. They were alarmed and suspicious when Magni told them how Jacob had brought Cronus back from the evil side. They also accepted the secrecy required about the return of the Titans and understood they weren't to ask any more questions.

The wizards knew what they had to do and immediately prepared their search for the Earth Mothers. Magni presented each of them with a gjallarhorn only to be used when alerting Asgard to the location of any Earth Mother they found.

Before leaving, Apollonius said, "We've know of a goddess who walks alone in the forests of the northern ice lands. She's a nature goddess and is considered to be an Earth Mother; you should go there and seek her out. We will travel to the south, the east and the far west. Together we will locate all Earth Mothers."

Magni was pleased to be heading north, he always felt close to home in the twilight of the Ice lands and this pleased him. He soon arrived and immediately sensed a presence but failed to locate it, even the clues were hard to follow. He walked towards a frozen waterfall and searched for a way to get behind it, which he soon found. He made his way into a concealed ice cave that was being heated by a most inviting fire and his senses were telling him that the presence he felt earlier was getting stronger. He didn't have to wait too long when he heard a sweet voice reach out from behind him. It was Medeina, the Lithuanian Goddess of Nature.

"Are you not a little too far north of your realm, my Lady?" he asked.

"My home is safe," she assured him, "I've been walking in the realms of my sister Earth Mothers but they're lost, I can't find any. Tell me, God of War, why is that?"

"No one can find any, my lady," he replied. "It's because everything has changed." It was then when he felt her warm hands rest beneath his tunic; she gently turned him and reached up or a kiss,

"It's been too long since last we held each other," she said while snuggling into him. "Ours was a great love, why did you leave me?"

"I could never love the way you wanted," he said trying to explain, "I'm a War God and preparing for battle has always been my way." She placed her hands around his waist before he continued, "You, you are the only woman ever to steal my heart. Your hair always felt like silk. Your eyes always drew me in, the very same way that the waters of the lagoon in Olympus drew in the gods. Your touch always made me feel lost in love but I don't understand how it was never enough. Even now I feel your power, it, it, it yet again draws me in, and I find you hard to resist."

"My love for you never left," she said holding him tighter. "Seeing you again has awoken something I can't control."

"I feel your love and it creates desires I too can't control," he said after closing his eyes to allow her sweet scent intoxicate him. "I cannot resist and my resolve fails me." He leaned forward and gently moved his arms to surround her bringing her closer if that was at all possible. They kissed and then the passion grew, before long they were lying on his cape in a sensuous embrace that led to them becoming one.

Magni had a reputation for being rough with women, only ever interested in what he could get and never considering the needs of others but with Medeina he was different. Her touch caused every nerve in his body to be electrified. To her, his scent penetrated deep into her consciousness leaving her with no words to describe how she felt. Each kiss, each touch, sent her into a trance-like state that seemed to have no end. Their lovemaking was so intense neither noticed the light that shot out across the universe announcing the conception of another god.

For many hours they lay together before Magni plucked up the courage to say, "You do know that there's another who's never far from my thoughts?"

"I've always known your desires lay elsewhere," she said while closing her eyes before asking, "how is he, how is Bel Marduk?"

"I, I, I haven't seen him in eighteen hundred years," he stuttered wondering how she knew, "and before that it was during the cosmic wars. He was turned by the serpents of Hell and it took all my powers, as well as the powers of a goddess and her two guardians, to bring him back into the Light." He sat up before continuing, "He's a powerful Sun God and was devastated that he fell so easily. When we released him we briefly spoke and then he called on the sun to take him out into the cosmos. He left to fight against The Darkness."

"You will always have a special place in my heart," she said while leaning in to kiss him on the cheek, "and I'll always love you. I'm no fool, I know our time together will always be fleeting but heed me when I say, 'Do you not think it's time for you to follow your heart and be happy?'"

"Since last we met I've been gifted with two more brothers," he said after resting his head on his arched knees. "They're twins, Jacob and Odi are their names. I came close to telling Jacob, but I think he already worked it out. Odi is always in and out of Jacob's head so I suspect he also knows, they've never said anything to me or anybody else for that matter. It would be too much of a distraction for me to follow my heart. It's my plans as well as the plans of Ares and Jacob that the gods are following; those plans need my full attention. The coming battles could be the end of all we cherish and that's why I'm here." He let her go and backed away, "Rhea is back and she has asked me to find the last of the Earth Mothers; will you join her?"

"Of course I'll join her," replied Medeina. "It's my duty to answer a command from the most powerful of all Earth Mothers."

They left the cave and mounted his chariot and as they were leaving he said while looking around, "This is a wondrous place, look at the frozen waterfalls and streams. See how the frost wraps itself around the trees as though to protect them from what's coming. The snows reflect the star light and the moon shows all of nature the way."

She linked and then snuggled closer, "Let's go, Rhea should not be left waiting." They immediately departed.

Chapter 5

The wizards, in the meantime, commenced their search but were having great difficulty. The Earth Mothers had faded out of all memory due to the relentless attacks on their domains by greedy men and incompetent governments. Pristine forests were being logged at an alarming rate with no replenishment. Grasslands were being scorched by the incessant heat of the sun due to climate change. Mountains were being eroded, losing their soils, caused by the melting of the glaciers. What was most troubling was the lack of concern expressed by those in power.

The wizards never gave up, they knew that somewhere the Earth Mothers would be asleep waiting to be reborn and would always come to the aid of their realms when hope showed and as wizards they were bringing hope.

Mygon headed to Africa but while on his way he diverted, his instincts told him he should start in the Middle East. He made his way to the ancient land of Samaria which is now part of the West Bank. There he presented as a vagabond and because of his eccentric appearance was regularly stopped by Israeli security and then by the police from the Palestinian Authority. He always talked his way out of trouble but as he neared his destination he found that he had to use his magic to protect himself.

He reached an ancient orchard, surrounded by columns and walls which were once part of an old palace. He explored the orchard and at times he again used his magic to conceal himself from prying eyes. When the orchard emptied and he was sure he was alone he called out,

"I hear you, my Lady. Your heart still beats in this ancient place. Please show yourself." He received no reply and tried again,

"Why does my Lady Earth not show herself to an old friend? Reveal yourself!" He looked around hoping for a response, "My Lady Ninsar, supreme Samarian Goddess, and Earth Mother to these sad lands. It is I, Mygon, an old friend. Come to me."

Mygon didn't have to wait for much longer. He heard the sound of pebbles falling, and when he turned he saw a sprinkling of the finest dust as one of the columns began to give up its secrets. From the front of the column stepped out a most beautiful Sumerian Goddess. She stood almost six feet tall and was wearing a traditional woven full length skirt and shoulder wrap, held in place by a golden fibula. She was of dark complexion with the most stunning green eyes. Her hair colour was as dark as the feather of a raven, it fell passed her shoulders and was tied in place by a gilded gold band. Her beauty was spellbinding, accentuated by her eyeliner makeup, similar to that of Egyptian royalty, "It's been so long," she said on seeing Mygon. "How is it the peoples of these lands have forsaken me?"

"Yes," replied Mygon, "the people of these lands have indeed forgotten the old ways. Many years ago the old religions were suppressed. The power of the Ancient One has been forgotten." He paused for a moment while waiting on a reaction, "The battle of the End Times is upon us and the shadow of The Darkness approaches. A council of Earth Mothers has been called and your presence is required, Rhea awaits your answer."

"So much has passed since last I met with Rhea," replied Ninsar. "I look around and see no trees. All of Nature is struggling, water is hidden from me, and the fresh air I left behind is heavy with ash and dust, how can this be?"

"Everything has changed," replied Mygon. "There's much too tell, come now and help usher in the next age of man." She reached across and took his hand.

Mygon retrieved his gjallarhorn and alerted Asgard as to where he was. Within moments a chariot carrying a charioteer and two fully armed Asgard warriors arrived to take Ninsar into the presence of Rhea. Mygon then made his way to the ancient lands of Babylon.

He travelled to Iraq and made his way to Baghdad before walking the eighty five kilometres towards what was once Babylon. In what used to be the palace gardens he found a low wall where he sat for many hours just waiting, remembering how in ancient times this was once the most populace city in the world. He felt its history ooze from the surrounding ruins.

He left the palace gardens and soon reached one of the terrace walls that was once a tree trough in the hanging Gardens of Babylon, and there he became emotional. He sat on a stone bench and allowed his mind drift back to the special times he had in this most wondrous place, especially the enchanting time he spent with his once great love, the Goddess Kishar. His thoughts were interrupted when the sound of gunfire and explosions reached his ears. He stood and looked out across the horizon at the destruction caused by fighters from both sides of a horrific conflict that had erupted in these ancient lands. He pounded his staff off the ledge to call on his light and when it came he beamed it out across the desert.

"Why do you defy the Ancient One?" he shouted as his anger grew and his light illuminated all before it. "Don't you see that you are the same, from the same and will always be the same?"

The soldiers ceased fighting and stared back at him, but there was no pity, no empathy or no love in their eyes. All he saw was the mark of the serpent and this alarmed him. When the light departed the fighters showed they didn't care, they just resumed their attacks on each other.

It was then he heard the sound of flapping wings and when he turned he smiled, it was the sound of a winged creature coming into view. The creature landed and said while taking her human form, "For two and half thousand years I've slept, and all I dreamt of was you, my greatest love. I prayed you'd come back for me."

"My beautiful Kishar," he said showing his delight at seeing her again. "You still have it! You've caused my heart to yet again miss a beat but I fear I'm now too old for love. Strange how I again feel warmth long missing from my very being."

She placed her hand to the side of his head then moved it slowly down his face. Within seconds his hair darkened and shortened to land just below his ears. His face lost its age and by the time her magic was finished he was again a twenty five year old wizard. He looked at his hands and watched the wrinkles fade and all signs of a great age disappear. He was thrilled feeling so young again, but then sadness crossed his face, "You've, this day, made me the happiest man in the world," he said while embracing her, "time has again deceived us, today is not our day, you are needed elsewhere. The Darkness and the armies of Lucifer have joined forces and are about to attack this age of man. The Ancient One has brought forth a young god, Jacob is his name, and he leads the armies of the Light. Rhea has returned and summons the last of the Earth Mothers. She asks for your assistance, will you go to her?"

"I'll always answer the call of Rhea, where is she?" she asked. "Why are there always obstacles in the way of our happiness?"

"Trust me," he replied, "before this battle is over, you and I will walk together and this time it'll be forever."

"My love," said Kishar. "That's a time that can't come too soon."

Mygon then produced the gjallarhorn and within seconds a chariot arrived. He assisted her to mount the chariot and with a heavy heart waited until she disappeared over the horizon. He then returned to his elderly form and made his way to Egypt.

On reaching Egypt he knew exactly where he had to go. Again, just like in the West Bank, he was harassed as a vagabond, but this time he aggressively pushed his harassers aside. He was more focused while seeking the most revered of all ancient Egyptians. He was seeking Isis, Goddess mother to the Pharaohs and Earth Mother to all North Africans. He knew she was a wise and cautious deity who would, no doubt, hide herself in plain sight. The Light guided him to the Egyptian Museum of Antiquities, indicating it to be the site of her resting place. He used his magic to walk through a side wall without being detected.

His search took him some time but he eventually found her in a section dedicated to her son, Horus. She was in her human form, seated on a throne that stood no more than 90cm high and she was exactly as he remembered her. She was wearing the frontal uraeus, the image of a sacred serpent, showing to the world how she commanded supreme power, being the wife of the mythical first Pharaoh of Egypt. She was also holding the symbol of life in her hands.

He waited until the museum closed while still using his magic to evade the gaze of the cameras. When sure he was alone he materialised then spread out his arms, "Earth Mother," he called while pounding his staff off the tiles. "Your time has come. Rhea seeks your council. Arise and let the world see the beauty of your being."

Soon the statue moved. Its surrounding black crust fell away revealing a most pristine gold colour. It continued moving then began coming to life. Isis opened her eyes, stood and looked around. She was four feet tall before expanding to six feet.

She stood before Mygon wearing the golden gown of an Egyptian Goddess. Her headdress was also of gold allowing the image of the sacred serpent to become more pronounced. Her heavy black eyeliner accented and highlighted her amazing brown eyes showing how she was considered to be the most beautiful woman in all of ancient Egypt, "Two thousand years have passed since I last walked this Earth," she said. "I attended the council of the gods and on returning I find my people have all but forgotten me, what has changed?"

"All has changed," replied Mygon. "A new religion has taken your people. Grave robbers have brought about the desecration of the tombs of your kin. Only remnants of the great Pharaohs lie in this unholy of places." Isis got angry.

"Leave me, wizard," she demanded, "I will bring forth the wrath of the gods and they will regret their desertion of me."

"No, my queen," insisted Mygon. "A council of Earth Mothers has been called. Rhea has risen and she asks for your assistance, she fears the combined power of Lucifer and his ally, The Darkness, will bring the dominion of man to an end. Will you help her?"

"When Rhea speaks all Earth Mothers must listen," said Isis. "Even my anger succumbs to her power. So yes, I'll go to her."

Mygon again produced the gjallarhorn and called for a chariot and within seconds Isis was whisked away to meet with Rhea.

Mygon then made his way to Nigeria. He was on a quest to find the elusive Asase Yaa, Earth Mother to the tribes of the western forests. On arrival he immediately met up with the elders of the Akan tribe where he presented his case. He noted their mistrust. They feared to deal with a white man; memories of slavery still strong in their minds. He was able to show them how he was a friend of the Orisha and spoke of his many adventures with their gods. When they were convinced he was actually a friend they brought him deep into the forest to meet up with the remnants of the empire of Ashanti where within these remnants Asase Yaa was still revered.

The Ashanti held regular festivals in her honour and invited Mygon to attend the latest one. The festival always concluded with a vibrant primal dance around a huge bonfire built in the centre of the village. It was a dance that went on for many hours, sometimes until morning. It was well after midnight, almost dawn when Mygon, while standing alone, felt a hand rest on his shoulder. It was Asase Yaa.

The dancers froze and the pounding of the drums stopped, all were shocked knowing they were in the presence of their goddess. They fell to their knees and kissed the soil hoping she would walk among them. She did move among them encouraging them to stand. They found her eyes to be calming and her smile to be very soothing. Her colourful robes and gem laden crown glowed under a bright light that completely surrounded her. Her glow also illuminated Mygon showing that he too was blessed by the gods. When she spoke her voice was soft and reassuring.

"Look on me, wizard," she said. "I'm the last of the West African Earth Mothers and wonder what it is you require of me. Do you bring me news of The Darkness? At night I see it smite the stars, it can only be your reason for seeking my assistance."

"I've been asked by Magni, Asgard God of War, to find the Earth Mothers," he replied while bowing. "Rhea has risen and seeks your power, she needs your council. Will you go to her?"

Before answering Asase Yaa looked at her subjects, "So few are left," she said feeling very sad. "So many sold into slavery, and those who are left now hide in the forests. Even after four hundred years they still fear the white man. Will going to meet Rhea help smite their pain?"

"I've no idea," replied Mygon shaking his head. "So much has changed. Everything good about mankind is threatened all because the serpents of Hell have bitten so many. These victims now wait for the call of Lucifer and they will bring much pain. Please meet with Rhea, she has a plan."

Asase Yaa agreed and watched as Mygon produced his gjallarhorn. Soon a chariot appeared above the forest, and slowly descended down to the leaf-covered forest floor. Asase Yaa mounted the chariot and was joined by Mygon, he had concluded his quest and together they left to meet with Rhea.

Chapter 6

While Mygon travelled through Africa and the Middle East, Merlin made his way to the Americas. He went to the stacks near the Grand Canyon to seek out the descendants of the Hopi nation. He was horrified to see so few were left but happy there was enough. He met with the last of the elders and made his request. They listened carefully to what he said and agreed to call a council of the tribes, the first in over two hundred years.

The powwow drummers climbed the highest stacks where they lit enormous bonfires, and as night fell they commenced their rhythmic beating. Initially their gentle heartbeat-like pounding was at first slow and mournful but as night progressed, the beat increased, and got louder. Its percussive sound travelled in all directions, reaching into the heart of all tribes to remind them of the old ways. The continuous pounding brought about a spiritual peace that reminded the elders to lead their tribes in thanking their all-mighty creator; they then called out for the return off the Earth Mothers.

As dawn broke the responses began and all listening knew something special within the American First Nations was about to show itself. All across the grasslands wild mustangs got restless and the strongest stallions left their herds to gallop north. As they travelled they avoided capture and continued their journey until they reached the waiting elders of the many different tribes. The elders wore the eagle feathers and war paint of their ancestors showing their status within their tribe.

They quickly returned south carrying the hopes of each downtrodden nation and were being guided by the continuous drum beat that didn't cease until forty-eight hours had passed. The sound travelled into every village, town and city keeping the residents awake, and it didn't stop until all chiefs and medicine men had reached the gathering. It was said that the White Buffalo walked in their wake, the wolves howled as they passed, and the eagles gathered near the stacks.

The elders sat in a large circle and waited silently for Merlin to join them. When he arrived he acknowledged all those in attendance with a bow of respect, then said, "As the silence takes the pounding of your drums, so too does The Darkness take The Light. Have you not seen the stars die as each night passes? I'm here to warn you of a great calamity that will soon be upon us."

"There's no need for us to look to the sky," said one of the elders speaking on behalf of all nations. "We've seen the dimming stars, and the dark spaces in the night skies."

"What you've seen is the death of the stars," explained Merlin. "They're falling to The Darkness and soon our beloved sun will succumb." He looked around at the alarmed expressions before continuing. "There's another problem, the Archangel Lucifer has taken control of the Underworld and is within days of releasing his serpents of Hell. Their purpose is to destroy mankind, including all in these lands. I seek the Earth Mothers, two of whom should still be concealed among you, will you help me?"

The elders spoke among themselves and after a while they began chanting what was known as the ancient songs of the gods. The drummers joined them and the combination of chanting and drumming soon broke through the veil separating the living and the dead. The young ones only ever heard of elder-magic, never did they expect to experience it for themselves.

After roughly two hours a wintry-white mist developed that eventually formed a thick fog and through that fog appeared two Native American Goddesses. The first to arrive was Maja, the Sioux Earth Mother, the bearer of the tree of life and with her was Atira, the Pawnee Earth Mother, and bringer of the corn.

Merlin recognised them immediately, greeted them and told them of the request from Rhea. They listened carefully to what he said and agreed to meet with her. There was no delay, Merlin produced his gjallarhorn, called on Asgard, and a chariot quickly arrived. He assisted the goddesses to mount the chariot before joining them. His quest was now over.

Chapter 7

Apollonius' quest took him to India where he searched for the last two Earth Mothers. On arrival he immediately sent out his light hoping to attract the attention of the goddesses. He travelled through the central plains, making his way towards the northern mountains aware he was being followed. His light was detected by Bhavani, the Mother Goddess of India. When they finally met she greeted him as a long lost friend and after explaining why he was there she directed him towards the ancient Hindu temples of the far North West; the ones built near Mount Kailash. She assured him it was there where he would find Kali, the black Earth Mother, the Indian Goddess of Creation, Preservation and Destruction.

Bhavani joined him on his quest and together they reached a long sealed cave, reputed to contain the stone image of Kali. He pounded his staff off the entrance, encouraging his light to penetrate its walls. Within minutes the entrance burst open revealing Kali to be already awake. She stood before him as the renowned black-skinned deity of great power. On seeing Apollonius she asked, "My visions showed a wizard and now one stands before me. Why disturb my sleep?"

"My Lady," replied Apollonius. "Forgive this intrusion but my quest is most urgent. The End Times approach and Rhea has called the last of the Earth Mothers into her presence. Will you answer her call?"

She agreed and said she was only too pleased to answer. More than any of the Earth Mothers she was the one who wielded the greatest power because her expertise was in destroying demons. She was there at the creation and helped nurture it along. She prided herself in her preservation of the great rivers, the lushness of forests and the bounty of the deepest oceans. Both she and Bhavani stood back as Apollonius produced his gjallarhorn and called on Asgard, and as was done for the other wizards, a golden chariot arrived and collected all three to bring them to meet with Rhea.

None of the Earth Mothers actually made it to meet with Rhea; instead they were taken to a secret location a short distance from Elysium. Rhea, being the wiliest of them all knew her search could be responsible for revealing the fact that Cronus was still alive so she put in place a plan to conceal their location until they were needed. This change of plan didn't concern the Earth Mothers; they were telepathically connected and understood Rhea's concerns.

Magni had achieved all Rhea asked of him so he travelled back to Elysium to meet with her. She thanked him and then said, "There's one last thing I need you to do. I'm asking you to trust me, and keep this from Jacob."

Magni was taken aback reminding Rhea that Jacob was his King of Kings, and he felt it was his duty to tell him everything. He was uncomfortable but Rhea was able to convince him that what she was about to request was for the best.

"I've seen the battle of the End Times and there'll be many losses," she said. "There'll be much heartbreak but the Light must prevail and for that to happen it'll need the combined power of the Earth Mothers and the Goddesses of the Light. Eala and Panya are particularly powerful and will have to leave Olympus to lead the assault on The Darkness. Jacob will have great difficulty accepting that and must be kept in the dark. I fear that if he knows

Eala and Panya are leaving, he will lose focus. I need him to concentrate on the battle against the armies of Lucifer and if he finds out you must help him understand they have to leave. Swords and warriors are no match against the evil of The Darkness so I need you to support my plan. "

"You have my word," said Magni. "I won't tell him of what you ask but I will tell him there are other plans in play, and that I believe in those plans. I'll tell him not to ask of the plans, he will trust me."

Magni was about to leave when Rhea reached in and whispered in his ear. "My dear Magni, always a War God, always thinking of others and seeking to protect the ones you love. Happiness is coming your way and it won't be long before you'll be with the one you've always truly loved. I see you living out among the stars and only then will I send to you a most unexpected gift, it will be a gift that will make your life complete." He attempted to ask as to what she meant but was stopped when she placed her finger over his lips. He then left for Olympus.

Chapter 8

After Jacob left Elysium he returned to Athens to repair any damage caused to the Parthenon during his battle. He used his magic to fill in the sinkhole hoping nobody questioned the defeat of Cronus. He made sure all who saw him could see he was well and uninjured. When satisfied he returned to the temple and placed the crown back into the care of the stewards. He then excitedly ran to the Great Hall to find many more stewards had arrived giving him hope that Odi and his mother were among them. On his way he met Ares and Athena, who greeted him with a formal bow, but he had difficulty giving them the respect they deserved because he kept looking over their shoulders.

"Your mother still sleeps, as does Odi," said Athena noticing his distraction. She saw his disappointment and stepped aside to allow him enter the Great Hall.

He made his way to greet Zeus and on his way he acknowledged Apollo, Hera, his grandmother and many others as he passed.

"I see the younger ones still sleep," he quipped on seeing Perseus, Odi, Eros and Dionysus still in their stone form. "It must have been a good party? Me thinks' too much drink has been taken?"

Even though he was being jovial he felt the tension among those who had already arrived, especially when looking back at Ares and Athena. Only then did he realize they were dressed in their war robes and armour. When looking around he sensed an awareness that Lucifer was about to unleash his armies.

He reached Zeus and bowed before sitting alongside him. There they discussed the happenings of the last two thousand years. At one point he reached in and whispered, "You must keep what I'm about to tell you secret. Grandfather, I've fought the mighty Cronus and beat him. He now walks in the Light. Rhea has also risen and stands with him. I've used the powers you bestowed on me to make them the guardians of Elysium and I'm hoping you'll accept my decision."

Zeus was shocked and not impressed, but he kept his counsel. "When you gave them Elysium," he asked after gaining his composure. "Were you wearing the crown?"

"Yes," replied Jacob. "At that time I was King of Kings."

Zeus decided it wasn't his place to question the decisions of the King of Kings but did enquire, "I'm curious, did they ask after me?"

"They both asked after you," replied Jacob. "Cronus is full of remorse and has asked to meet up with you. I refused because too much is happening for such a meeting to take place. I did promise a meeting would happen in the near future."

"Why keep this news a secret?" asked Zeus.

"Lucifer thinks Cronus is dead and I want to keep it that way," replied Jacob. "He watched through one of Hells portals just as I pretended to slay him. I felt that if Lucifer became aware that Rhea was back he would work out how he's being deceived and will start searching for the location of both Cronus and Rhea."

"That was a wise decision," said Zeus while nodding in agreement. "I'm impressed; you really are a master tactician. It becomes clearer that

Olympus is safe in your hands." He paused for a moment then continued, "I'm curious about the messengers, do you know of their progress?"

"Yes, I do." replied Jacob felling proud and glad to be asked, "They're still sleeping and are well protected from his gaze. They completed their tasks and all we can do now is hope the message has been successfully passed on. I intervened on several occasions, Raphael also intervened but Magni was the most active; he had no choice especially as he was protecting Odi's babies."

"Odi's babies? Odi's a father?" exclaimed Zeus. "I wondered whose light it was I saw that last night before we slept. When were his babies born?"

"No, no, let me explain," responded Jacob. "They're not born yet, they still sleep. They're Goddesses of the Light, and targets of Lucifer."

"And what about your babies?" enquired Zeus. "Have you seen them?"

"They're no longer babies," beamed Jacob, smiling with pride. "They're toddlers, two year olds, and already have powers. Many years ago I woke and it was arranged for me to visit the realm of the elves and there they were. Soon after, Eala and Faer, escorted by Lord Yaz and his army, arrived. It was my most magical time."

"Aah, how is my old friend, Yaz?" asked Zeus.

"He wasn't really happy," replied Jacob while getting subdued. "He and his people are moving into a new dimension, they've had enough. The glaziers are melting and their homes are threatened, they're being assisted by the elves."

"But for the elves," nodded Zeus knowingly, "all would be lost."

Jacob asked as he stood to leave, "Why are my parents, Odi and the younger gods still sleeping?"

"Worry not young god, they will wake when it's their time," replied Zeus. "Jacob, two days from now all will see me crown you King of Kings. You've been chosen to defend the Light and there'll be no going back. Rest well and prepare yourself. You're going to need your strength."

Jacob bowed and was about to walk away when he felt a tap on his shoulder, it was his mother. He reacted with an exuberance showing how much he missed and loved her. He leapt forward wrapping his arms around her. He closed his eyes taking in the love she had for him. He then felt a powerful arm surround him and knew his father was also with him.

They left for the gardens and located a secluded corner where they talked and enjoyed each other's company. Jacob was surprised they didn't pick up any of the momentous events that had happened to him, Odi or Magni. He got great pleasure telling them about his children and that Odi was also soon to be a father. He then spoke of how he felt about Magni.

"Magni is the greatest. Over the last two thousand years, he never once slept. He and Asgard watched over Panya and intervened when necessary. He even gave me a good kicking when I screwed up. Father, I almost revealed the most secret location of Eala and my children, how could I be so stupid?" he then stood and began pacing. "Lucifer knows my babies are born and has sent his legions to seek them out. One of his generals discovered Panya is pregnant and carrying two goddesses but we don't know if Thanases managed to slay him before he got a message to Lucifer."

"This news is very disconcerting," said Thor becoming very uneasy. "I need to leave for Asgard and meet with Magni and Modi. This news changes everything. Magni might need me."

"When I brought danger to my children," continued Jacob, "they showed no fear. They called for Magni by repeating, Magni, Magni, Magni, and immediately he answered. He took them into his arms and I saw him melt. He's my greatest ally; he called me his King of Kings and then bowed to me. I was horrified."

"That's because you are my King of Kings." Jacob swung around to find Magni standing there smiling from ear to ear. Thor leapt to his feet to greet him. He checked him over trying to satisfy himself that all was well. He then turned to Jacob, "Son," he said. "Enough of these doubts, you are the King of Kings."

"If you think we're going to bow to you in private," said Maria with a stern look on her face, "you've another thing coming."

"I find it difficult when family members bow to me," replied an unhappy Jacob, "even Cronus went to bow, but I stopped him…."

"Cronus," yelled an alarmed Maria, "he's a killer, how did you.....?"

She in turn was interrupted by Jacob, "I brought Cronus back into the Light, but that's a story for another day. I must go; I'm hearing things and need to be alone."

"I too met with Cronus and Rhea." said Magni. "It's true; Cronus does indeed walk in the light. He has no desire for the crown of Olympus. He knelt before Jacob and swore his allegiance. He has also promised to seek out the Titans and lead them into war alongside the gods."

"Magni," asked a curious Jacob, "I thought you were preparing Asgard?"

"Worry not about Asgard," replied Magni. "Modi is there and as we speak, he and our uncles prepare the four armies. I've come to make you aware of other plans and I trust those plans. There's no need for you to concern yourself, trust me, those plans will assist. I'm here to be by your side." Jacob just nodded and left for a short walk in the meadows.

While in the meadows he received fleeting visions showing realms from all across the Astral Plains suggesting he should visit. He rushed back into the temple seeking Magni and when he found him said, "I want to ensure each realm is well prepared for what's coming. Will you to be my guardian?" Magni agreed. He then sought out Chiron and asked for his assistance in dealing with the Centaurs.

To both Magni and Chiron, Jacob suddenly looked stressed and no assurances they gave him seemed to help. They didn't realise he was hearing voices and they were coming at him from all directions. He was having difficulty separating those same voices; he was even picking up the wailing sound of the lost souls. He sensed that the time was approaching for the carriers to rise and prayed there would be millions. A vision showed him his friends, the messengers, especially their resting places. It showed him the dust falling from those taken by the stone. He then saw the slow flowing trickles as the ice-melt fell from those frozen in time. Another vision showed the malevolence of The Darkness as it gathered in the near galaxies and he shuddered. He then saw Lucifer instruct his generals and this emboldened him. He excused himself and went to the one place in the temple that always gave him comfort, the sill of the south facing window.

While alone he reassessed the plans and realised there was no more to be done. He valued the input Magni, Ares and Athena offered him but knew he was now on his own and had to trust that all those plans would work. He decided that when ready he would return to the Parthenon and direct the battle from there. He tapped into the minds of his friends in Dublin and quickly established that panic and anxiety was taking hold, brought on by the continuous broadcasting of supernatural happenings from all across the world.

After a few more moments alone he rejoined Magni and Chiron and when ready they began their journey to meet the Astrals. Their first port of call was the land of the Cypriot Centaurs and there they sought out the herds that once ruled these lands.

Chapter 9

Within moments they arrived on one of the most visited beaches in Cyprus. It was Aphrodite's beach; a place Shane always spoke of, and was somewhere he and Jacob planned to visit when they finished school.

"Aah," said Chiron. "I remember this place, it's said that this is the birthplace of the Goddess of Love." He pointed at the heart shaped rock rising from the sea close to the beach. "She came from among the sea foam near that rock, and now it's known as a place for those who seek eternal youth and everlasting love."

"It surely is a beautiful place," said Jacob, "pity it's now threatened. Everything that is beautiful is so hated by Hell."

"Come," said Magni. "We must move towards the peat grassland in the Troodos mountains, it's there we may find the herds."

While making their way up the mountain they decided to remain invisible until safely away from the few remaining tourists. They were no more than a few moments in the grasslands when a large herd of angry centaurs surrounded them. Chiron was shocked by their aggression forcing him to use his status as the Centaur God of Olympus to calm what were a wild and untamed herd of liminal beings. Jacob dismounted and greeted them but he was taken aback by their appearance. They had ox-style horns and enlarged heads making them a lot uglier than what Chiron had led him to believe. He saw how they had trouble containing their wildness but noted that, in the presence of Chiron, they were trying to behave themselves. He also noted they were keeping their centaurides and younglings out of sight. Chiron then commanded them to listen to what Jacob had to say.

"My friends, I am Jacob of Olympus, King of Kings." He pointed at Magni, "And this is my brother, Magni of Asgard. I'm here to ask for your assistance against the legions of Hell. An enemy of the Ancient One is about to unleash his armies and he will show no mercy. He plans to attack the gods and all astrals, and is in league with a far more dangerous foe, one who is bent on killing the Light." He waited for a response, and when none came he continued, "Look to the night sky and see how the stars are dying, succumbing to that dangerous foe, known as The Darkness. The Sun Gods bravely fight but they're losing the battle and need our help. Will you help us?"

One centaur stepped forward, his name was Keteus, "Why should we assist, you are of the realm that harbours Hera, our nemesis. Look what she did to us. She cursed us with weighty horns making us appear as ugly Liminals and we'll never forgive her. Until she's dead we'll not support Olympus." He then raised his spear and fired it to land at Jacob's feet. Magni drew his sword but Jacob gestured for him to relax and put it away.

"Your anger is misplaced," continued Jacob hoping to negotiate. "I'm still being taught the ways of the gods and have much to learn, so bear with me. I was granted access to all powers held by every god and I'm sure I can access Hera's powers to undo her curse but I'll not do so without her permission. I've chosen to respect the independence of all gods and won't go back on my word even if it means not getting the support of the centaurs. I promise to seek her out and hopefully she'll undo her curse."

Another Centaur called Spargeus stepped forward, "For thousands of years we've carried the heavy weight of these ox-horns. At the birth of our children we got the pleasure of being parents until they reached their third year, and then their horns would grow. Their screams of pain still ring in our ears; we can never forgive her for what she put our younglings through. I will not support your battle, leave us now."

Jacob looked around at the hundreds of centaurs and saw they had their bows raised, ready to release their arrows. He looked up the hill at Chiron and knew by the look on his face that they were wasting their time. Although disappointed he was prepared to keep trying, he said to Keteus and Spargeus, "Allow me show you what's coming to your homeland."

"No!" yelled Spargeus. "Go now, our patience is thin, our anger at Olympus still burns deep."

Jacob, Magni and Chiron left and made their way to Mount Pelion. On the way Jacob said, "My first attempt to confirm the support of the Astral armies and I fail. Did I miss something?"

"They're still hurting and their pain certainly runs deep," said Chiron trying to reassure him. "When looking into the sea and they see their reflection, it breaks their hearts. Once they were the most handsome and the most beautiful. Today they see themselves as ugly and took their anger out on you, give them time, they will respond."

"I once fought alongside the centaurs," said Magni. "It was in the Russian realm, they're the most valiant so it surprises me that they hold such hatred."

Jacob remained quiet for the rest of the journey and only spoke when they reached the foothills of Mount Pelion in Greece.

"I feel the beauty of this most special of sanctums," said Jacob. "Look at the oak trees; they remind me of those that once surrounded the lagoon. I can hear them, they share stories and their rings speak of the valiant history of this magical place. See how the mists lift, it's as though we're expected. A passageway has opened."

Jacob dismounted and placed his hand on the grass. He looked up at Chiron, "We're not alone!"

"They're all around us," smiled Chiron, "and they're curious, it's been a thousand years since a God of Olympus last visited."

"I feel the hooves of a thousand horses," said Jacob looking around and still seeing nothing. "Is there a threat?"

"There's no threat," replied Chiron. "They will reveal themselves as soon as their queen arrives,"

Jacob led his horse along the mist shrouded passageway towards a clearing in the forest. In the centre of the clearing there was a concave shaped dip with a small pond towards which he walked. Magni dismounted and walked alongside him.

Jacob raised his hand for them to stop. He waited and listened as the sound of hooves grew louder. Chiron remained near the tree line and went back into invisibility. Within minutes well over a thousand centaurs materialised and what surprised Jacob was the amount of centaurides who were also present. He was smitten by their beauty and when their queen arrived he was awestruck.

"Welcome, King of Kings," she said. "I am Queen Zephyra. It's been a long time since we've had a visit from Olympus let alone Asgard. Hello Magni. How long has it been?"

"My Queen," said Magni as he bowed. "You look as beautiful as always. I agree; it's been too long."

Jacob clenched his fist, crossed his heart and said as he too bowed, "I'm Jacob of Olympus and seek an audience."

"Our oracles spoke of your visit," said Zephyra acknowledging his status, "They also told us of what's coming. What is it you ask of us?"

"I'm building an army of Astrals," he said while walking away with her. "I've come to ask you to break through the shields. I need the power and speed of Pelion to assist in the defeat of Hell and this can only happen when you ally yourself with the Dragon Lords and the Emperor of the Birds. Together you will be so powerful that Hell will quake in your presence. Can you do this for me?"

Zephyra thought for a moment than asked, "How will we know when to answer?"

"You'll know when my Light shoots across the sky," he replied. "It will be the brightest."

He didn't have to wait too long for her response. "You have our bows and our swords," she said.

He was surprised when she bent forward and whispered in his ear, "Near the tree line, I see Lord Chiron. I alone see him and wonder why he chooses not to show himself to my people?"

"I too wondered, he will have his reasons," surmised Jacob. "He showed himself to the Cypriot Centaurs, they behaved in his presence. Maybe he can see that you have total command of your realm."

A worrying thing then happened, there was a fuss near the outer lines of the centaurs and they began to part creating an opening. Zephyra was taken aback when she saw who was approaching. It was her brother, Keteus, and he looked dejected and beaten, "In the woods yonder are the last of my people," he said. "We were attacked by serpents of Hell and they've decimated our warriors. They've bitten our children and taken their souls leaving us with no choice but to seek the protection of Pelion."

"You and your people will always be welcome in my realm," said Zephyra while leaning in to hug her brother. "Call forth your kin and allow them rest in the shadow of our sacred mountain."

Keteus called his people and they began walking through the meadow. Zephyra was shocked by their condition, "So few left! So many sick and injured; how can this happen?"

It was then when Keteus noticed Jacob and briskly turned his head away. He was ashamed of his actions when they met earlier and didn't know what to do. Jacob noticed his discomfort and offered to help,

"My lord Keteus," he said, "I'm a grandnephew of Poseidon and have many of his skills. Allow me call on the healing powers of the seas, rivers and lakes. Bring your people one by one into the pond and watch a God of Olympus take away their pain."

"Will the waters take away the memories?" mumbled Keteus.

"No," replied Jacob, "but a most powerful Earth Mother will. She'll bring calm and make the bad memories subside. Do you want me to help?"

Keteus looked out across the remnants of his people and saw how the men were broken; and how the women and children were listless. He too was broken and said as he lowered his head, "You would do this for us after the way we rejected you this morning?"

"I'm a God of the Light and will always help my friends," replied Jacob, trying to comfort him. Keteus just nodded, he was still embarrassed.

Jacob blinked himself to Elysium and sought out Rhea. He said as he bowed before her, "Come my lady, your powers are needed." He didn't give her time to reply, just blinked and they arrived back among the centaurs.

Mumblings and murmurings spread through the ranks of the centaurs and they wondered as to who this enchanting goddess was. Zephyra recognised her immediately and went to greet her. Jacob noticed her recognition and placed his finger across his lips as a sign for Rhea's identity not to be revealed.

Rhea watched Jacob make his way to the edge of the pond and go to his knees. She watched him close his eyes and place his hand in the water to call for the assistance of Poseidon. Immediately the waters rippled before wildly bubbling. Within moments Poseidon rose up and moved to place his hand on Jacobs shoulder. When he saw Rhea a smile of recognition crossed both their faces. For Rhea and Poseidon there was no time for a reunion as the mental pain of the injured was now getting unbearable.

Magni gestured for Keteus to lead his people through the pond, which he did, and by the time his people reached the far side their healing was well under way. It was also noticed that the younglings who were going through the change were no longer screaming and crying out in agony; the growth of their horns was now painless, and they no longer resembled ox-horns. They also regained the beauty they were once renowned for. Rhea had undone the curse placed on them by Hera. This was a gift Jacob had organised to be bestowed upon them.

When the last of the injured centaurs had crossed the pond Rhea raised her arms and called on the Light, and when it came it sent out a soothing beam bringing a gentle calmness to all who needed it. When Jacob was satisfied the bad and sad memories had been erased he immediately returned Rhea to Elysium.

On his return to Pelion he was met by both Keteus and Spargeus who had been speaking with Magni and now understood the approaching dangers for all life. "We were wrong," said a chastened Spargeus, "and can clearly see how you are a wise and just king. We speak for the remnants of the Cypriot Centaurs; will you accept our swords and bows?"

"Of course," said a delighted Jacob. "Olympus will accept your swords and bows. Let your warriors return to Cyprus and retake your realm. Leave your elderly and younglings in the care of Pelion, they will be safe here. While in Cyprus, hide and wait for the Light, it will shine brightly. I'll see to it," he looked at Magni for support. "Asgard will send its army to patrol the sky above your homeland. They will be your support." Jacob looked up at the tree line just in time to see a smile cross Chiron's face as he faded to return back to Olympus.

Just then Magni became unsettled and drew his sword. He said while looking around showing alarm, "Beneath my feet I feel the march of a vast army and wonder why Pelion is not alarmed. Who can they be? Are they friend or foe?"

"Magni," said Zephyra, shaking her head. "Always the War God, what you hear is a sound familiar to the centaurs, look towards the northern tree line."

Magni did just that and watched. Within a few moments, thousands of centaurs from the Russian realm had arrived. They were being led by Pol-kan, a formidable warrior. He made his way to greet Zephyra and on reaching her he said, "Today I received word from an esteemed visitor who spoke of an approaching menace. He is a powerful wizard and asked me to join with Pelion. I'm here to offer my armies in the hope you'll accept them?"

"I've already put my armies at the disposal of Olympus," replied Zephyra as she greeted him. "We will answer the call of the gods when needed." She pointed at Jacob, "Here stands before you a grandson of Zeus, his name is Jacob and he has been crowned King of Kings. Today we witness the aftermath of the attack in Cyprus, it showed us the terror that awaits us if Olympus fails. Your armies are definitely required and your offer gratefully accepted."

"I know of you, young king," said Polkan as he bowed to Jacob. "Once I raced a goddess through the nymph lands, and while there she told me of her love for the mighty God of Thunder. You bear their likeness. It will please me to lead my armies in your name, what is it you ask of me?"

"Return to Russia," suggested Jacob. "Protect the hot springs where once my messengers rested. I see Hell rise through those same springs, surround them and wait for the call of the Light."

Polkan turned to Magni and offered his hand, "Magni, Son of Thunder, it's been too long. Does our wager still stand?"

"Oh yes, Lord Polkan," replied Magni with a smirk that went from ear to ear, "drinking you under the table will be my pleasure."

"When this battle's ends," replied Polkan, "I'll hold you to that." He turned, bowed to Zephyra and, along with his army, left and rushed to a portal that took them to the springs near the town of Turinsk.

"My lady," said Jacob while mounting his horse. "Magni and I must leave; we've many more realms to visit and not much time. It's been a great pleasure, until we meet again." He bade his farewells and they made their way towards Elysium.

Jacob had difficulty holding back a smile as they were leaving, so much so, Magni noticed and said, "Proud of yourself, are we? You now have all centaurs on your side."

"No!" responded Jacob. "I'm smirking over something else. Lord Polkan, is he another one of your 'Friends'?"

Magni stretched across and gave Jacob a clatter across the back of his neck causing him to yell, "Ouch, that fucking hurt."

"Another comment like that," threatened Magni, "and the next one will hurt even more."

Jacob flicked his reign and took off at such speed Magni had difficulty catching up. They raced each other, throwing the odd punch and trying to avoid each other's kicks. They soon reached the shores of Elysium.

Chapter 10

On arrival in Elysium they were met by Rhea, who was pleased to see them, "I foresaw your return but didn't think it would be this soon. Come! Let me show you what we've assembled." Jacob and Magni crossed the beach and then the dunes to be greeted by those whom Cronus and Rhea had brought together. It was a gathering of the Titans.

Jacob knew how at the creation there were twelve, six brothers and six sisters. He was surprised to see that Cronus and Rhea were able to find seven, bringing their total to nine. They were all standing just beyond the dunes in their colossus form.

Jacob and Magni bowed as a sign of respect to those who ruled at the beginning of time. Jacob noticed Magni was uneasy and asked, "Brother, everything all right?"

"My path," he whispered, "and some of these Titans crossed in the past, they may not be happy to see me."

"No need to worry, Lord Magni," said Rhea. "All are aware that we are now on the same side, you might get the odd few kicks but no ill will is intended."

Her comment was a cue for the Coeus to quip, "This day gets better; the only god that knocked my pillar stands before us,"

"I'm sure Magni has long forgotten your last encounter," said Rhea trying to calm a developing row.

"I was a toddler, young and innocent," said Magni acting coy. "When there was anything that could be knocked. I was always there to oblige."

"But!" replied Coeus. "You knocked one of the four pillars built to keep the sky and the Earth apart. You then ran and hid,"

"I was only a three year old!" protested Magni.

Jacob had difficulty containing himself. He was trying to prevent a smile, but eventually had to say, "Brother, another 'Friend'?" The look Magni gave him quickly wiped the smile from Jacob's face.

"Enough of this tension; we have a war to win," said Cronus.

It was then when, way out at sea, the sound of sloshing water was heard. It got louder and more violent causing waves to travel in all directions. It attracted the attention of the Titans especially when a head rose from beneath the waves. It was their long lost brother, Oceanus, the Titan of water.

He was the eldest of all the Titans and estranged from his siblings since Cronus usurped their father. He walked towards the beach and Magni was heard to say, "This should be interesting,"

"Why?" asked Jacob.

"Oceanus," whispered Magni, "refused to take part in the attack on their father and was banished when Cronus came to power. He hasn't been seen for thousands of years. It was rumoured he had died of a broken heart but other rumours said that he swore vengeance on Cronus and would one day return and claim his crown."

"I wear that crown." said Jacob.

"Now," nodded Magni. "Now you know why this meeting will be interesting." Oceanus quickly reached the beach and stood there waiting for the droplets to stop falling. He initially stood as a twenty foot high water creature before taking his human form.

"I can see the crown no longer rests on your head," he said as he moved to greet Cronus. "I wonder as to how this can be, after all, you usurped our father so you could reign as King of Kings." He looked around for a moment, "Why are you hiding in this most sacred of places? I get more confused. Strange to see the light shine around you, why is this?"

"Elysium is now our realm," replied Cronus, "we are the guardians of these hallowed tombs,"

"And Olympus?" asked Oceanus.

"My lord Oceanus," interrupted Jacob. "I'm the King of Kings and I alone will wear the crown."

"Ah," said Oceanus, "I stand before the boy King, the one whom Lucifer hates the most. I understand you too are of my blood, what is it about you? How did you fight the mighty Cronus and win?"

"I've no time for this," said Jacob losing his patience. "You stand before us as though you want to challenge the Titans. My crown is not for taking. Can't you see all is threatened? We need to stand together?"

"I'm not here to fight you, or my brothers," assured Oceanus. "I'm here to offer my sword and stand with my brothers and sisters in their hour of need. I've watched from crevices deep beneath the oceans and I too can see the stars as they fall from the Light. I was there at the creation and clearly remember the venom of The Darkness. I will never allow it to rule again," he paused for a moment then continued, "I've watched Poseidon scour the deep while gathering his armies. I've also felt the Mer-People swim in fear as they rush towards the volcanoes. The mythical creatures of the deep, those still unknown to Poseidon, wait for the call of Pegasus. No longer will I hide while my realm goes to war."

"How do you know Pegasus will lead the creatures of myth and legend?" asked a concerned Magni.

"Fear not, God of War," replied Oceanus. "Long ago, before the long sleep, when you and Jacob were talking about your plans. Do you remember the pitcher of water between your beds? You discussed the plans of Asgard and you mentioned Pegasus. I was there. Need I remind you who I am? Lest you have forgotten, I am the first and the eldest; I am the Titan God of Water and was there before Poseidon. I am water and wherever water is, I'm there. I heard everything you shared. Without water, all is lost."

"Oceanus," said Cronus. "Welcome back among the Titans. Your skills and wisdom is much appreciated. We need your guidance, and we accept your sword."

Rhea took her human form and asked Jacob and Magni to walk with her. She said while linking Jacob's arm, "The coming battle begins within days, I see the first blood and in that flowing blood I see a great danger for you. Lucifer will target you, draw you out but I cannot see who will survive. Beware his malice and his deceit." She hesitated before continuing, "I've prepared another strategy, an attack on The Darkness using the power of the Earth Mothers but we will not be strong enough, we'll need more support."

"What can I do?" asked Jacob.

"There's nothing you can do," she replied. "I discussed my plans with Magni and he supports me, I don't want you distracted so I'll withhold them from you."

"Magni already mentioned alternative plans," said Jacob after turning back to face Rhea. "I trust his judgement but he never said you were involved. Although I'm worried about the outcome of my battle with Lucifer I do get solace from my dreams. There I saw a bloodied warrior walk with his sword in hand. I saw him walk through the grasslands, the lakes and the rivers and then reach a cave where I watched a goddess run from a cave to sit with her three children. I saw that I was that warrior and because of that I believe I will survive the battle and go on to be with my family."

"Truly you are of my blood," said Rhea while placing her hand upon his shoulder. "I say again to you, beware the deceit of Lucifer." she momentarily froze, and then said, "There...is...a...Shadow!"

When they returned to the beach all the Titans had taken their human forms and were sitting together, reminiscing and sharing stories that spanned all time. They spoke of their missing sisters and wondered if they were still alive. They listened to Oceanus speak of his domain and how he had nurtured and protected the seas for millennia. He expressed his concerns and then his anger because of the pollution caused by mans careless attitude towards the natural world. He told them how he worried about the creatures of the deep, as well as the fish stocks, but all agreed that none of his concerns compared to what was coming.

Magni and Jacob listened carefully to the Titans as they put in place their plans to defeat Lucifer and they were delighted with the strategy that was now unfolding. They said their farewells and made their way towards one of the portals that gave them access to their next destination, the Realm of the Elves.

Chapter 11

The portal they chose brought them to within sight of Stonehenge where on arrival they met with Merlin and Apollonius who were expecting them. All four walked through another portal taking them into a parallel universe that seemed to be the very same space they had just left. They could still see the Stonehenge monument, but the A303 primary road that should have been close by no longer existed. The air was pristine; and the shrub lands, which for millennia grew across Salisbury Plain, travelled as far as the eye could see. The juniper bushes stood as guardians along a well worn pathway leading towards stone sculptures depicting the majesty that is the Realm of the Elves. The pathway led them to an ancient hexagon shape folly built on the summit of Easton Hill. Apart from the entrance the five other sides were solid walls, each carrying the carved image of stone doors. Merlin tapped on each door and waited. The door, second on the right, opened and allowed them through. Beyond the door they reached a wide stone staircase that led them into a most mystical land.

At the bottom of the stairs they turned right along the banks of a babbling creek that flowed over moss and lichen covered pebbles. They continued walking until they reached sentinel trees whose branches hung low only allowing the faintest of light to reach the woodland floor. On reaching their first sunlit clearing they were not only greeted by rays of fluorescent white light bringing everything it touched to life, they were also greeted by hundreds of colourful butterflies chasing vibrant dragonflies from flower to flower. Further along the pathway they reached a stand of trees hung with vines and covered in the most colourful of flowers, flowers that seldom lost their petals.

All around them seeds wisped amidst floating spores deflecting the light and creating beautiful colours. The flowers oozed fragrances Jacob had never experienced before, and the trees were so enormous they looked as though they were in existence since forever. He had difficulty closing his mouth; he was in awe of the beauty that was all around him. Everywhere he looked was now full of a shining gold light and a spectrum of amazing colours.

They soon reached a column of intricately carved sculptures depicting the Elvin Kings and Queens of old. On passing the sculptors they reached cave dwellings that were chiselled into the cliff-faces, and decorated using the most exquisite carvings. For Jacob and Magni this was surely the most magical realm they had ever visited.

They were greeted by six Elfena who escorted them through to the far side of a gigantic doorway, an entrance that took them into a vast and regal hall. It was a large gothic style room that was open to the skies and it held nine thrones. Behind the thrones was a cathedral style series of pointed windows filled with stained glass depicting battles of old.

"You are about to meet the supreme masters of the nine Elf realms," whispered Apollonius as they continued their walk. "Be aware that it is unheard of for anyone other than the wizards or fellow elves to enter this most magical of places." Apollonius and Merlin walked ahead leaving Jacob and Magni behind.

"I feel unworthy entering these hallowed halls," said Jacob after sniffing his tunic. "We've been riding our horses since early this morning and now we stink."

"It's too late to freshen up," said one of the Elfena after hearing Jacob's comments. "I can give you a fragrance that will make you feel better." Jacob accepted her offer.

He removed his cloak and crown from his satchel while watching the Elfena approach a flowering plant in a nearby urn. He watched her place her palm below a cluster of flowers and whisper reverently, encouraging them to open wider. The flowers released a most fragrant yet masculine scent, strong enough to subdue the smell of horse.

Jacob inhaled the odour and was happy to wear it whereas Magni threw his eyes to the heavens, shook his head and quipped, "You young gods?" Jacob was now happy to present himself as a God King of Olympus and felt better with the fragrance surrounding him. He waited until he was invited into the presence of the supreme elves.

When invited he walked up the centre of the hall with Magni close behind. On looking ahead he found the sight of the wizards and the elves astounding. The wizards stood to the side but the elves all sat stiff and upright, their arms resting motionless on the armrests and they were so still one would think they were handsome wax models.

When he reached the steps he was greeted by Kalen who said, "We meet again, Jacob of Olympus. I can only apologise for my tetchiness when we last met." Jacob bowed again. Kalen continued, "For us it's always a pleasure to be in the presence of a God of Olympus, you are most welcome into our hallowed halls."

He turned to Magni, "Our welcome extends to you too, Lord Magni, Warrior God of Asgard." He then said, "This is a council of Elf kind, on my extreme right is the Lady Lirissa of the Meadow realm, next to her is Lord Aeson of the Forest realm, then we have the Lady Elvina of the Fire realm and lastly, Lord Cassiel of the Storm realm. On my extreme left is the Lady Ariella of the Water realm, next to her is Lord Azrael of the Mountain realm, then the Lady Thalia of the Woodland realm and lastly, Lord Evander of the Ice realm." Jacob and Magni together bowed to the council.

Kalen said while rising from his seat, "You've come before a council of the elves. See how all nine realms are represented. Look upon the Lords and Ladies of Elf kind and be happy we've come together to show you our support. We've discussed the threat posed by the armies of Lucifer but we are more worried about the power of The Darkness that now stalks the universe." He moved to stand before Magni, "We fear for mankind because their armies will be useless against the power of Hell. The elf armies are ready and will go to their aid but only after your call to war."

"The nine armies, where are they?" asked Jacob.

"There are eight doors," said Azrael of the Mountain realm as he pointed to the four doors on each side of the hall. "Behind each door is a tunnel that leads to one of our realms. At this time, in each, there are ten thousand elf warriors, sleeping and waiting for the call of the gods."

"Come," said Kalen moving towards one of the doors. "Let me show you what elf kind has placed at your disposal."

Ariella opened the door into a tunnel lit by burning torches all the way to the far side. She beckoned all to walk through to eventually reach an exit high on a cliff top overlooking a vast expanse with lakes, rivers and streams. In the far distance was a turreted city, surrounded by a white light and to its left was what looked like a gathering of upright sleeping warriors, armed and ready for war.

"Welcome into the realm of the water elves," she said. "This is my domain; it's where my ancestors have been queens since The Darkness was vanquished."

They walked down from the cliff and made their way towards the city where they soon reached a colonnade of stone sculptures depicting queens of the realm that go so far back in time they are now out of memory. As they made their way along the colonnade Magni enquired, "My Lady, don't you trust us? Why are mounted and armed warriors shadowing us? Is there a problem?"

"Magni, always the one to notice," she replied with a smile. "We're being escorted because my generals are uneasy. Sightings of serpents slithering near our borders have reached our ears. Even the best defences can be compromised especially by one as deceitful as Lucifer. It's precautionary."

They soon reached the outskirts of the city and mounted a platform allowing them a view out over the plains. It was then when the sight of ten thousand elf warriors at sleep became clearer. They stood as twenty, five hundred strong columns and they looked formidable.

"What you see before you is one of nine elf armies and they stand ready to answer your call," said Kalen.

"Forgive me, my Lord Kalen," said Jacob, "I'm still learning the ways of the gods. Where is your realm?"

"I am the supreme lord of all elves and my realm is of the sky," replied Kalen. "I am of the Spirit realm and we know everything. We see, hear, smell and feel everything."

Magni turned back to Ariella and asked, "How will you know from where to leave when the call comes?"

"Look into the distance," she replied. "See the dark shadows on the walls, they are doors and there are many. Each one takes us to a different place. In each realm there are many exits, all through waterfalls. Two hundred years ago, Eala and her guardians passed one of our falls, they sensed our presence and we allowed them see the power of our army. With them was the lady, Danu."

Jacob lit up and asked, "How were they? How was my Eala? Did she look well?"

"I was there," said Kalen. "Let me assure you that although looking tired, they were well. Their resting place is in the valley of the two lakes guarded by the spirits of the great elks."

"Lord Kalen," continued Jacob, "my children! Are they here?"

"No," replied Kalen, shaking his head. "They are elsewhere and are very safe. My lord, be patient, it won't be long now." He then asked, "Do you wish to view the armies from our other realms?"

"No, my lord," responded Magni, "we trust your preparations, we need to move on, time is running out and the drumbeat of battle beats louder as each hour passes."

Chapter 12

"I too hear the drumbeat," said Jacob turning to Magni. "It's a call that's getting louder, we need to go."

He then turned to Ariella and asked, "Tell me, my Lady. Which tunnel takes us into the realm of the Yeti?"

"That tunnel takes you to mountains in the east," replied Ariella pointing to a tunnel not too far away. "It will leave you close to a frozen waterfall, behind which is the passageway that allows you reach the Yeti homeland before the sun reaches its Zenith."

Jacob and Magni bade their farewells and made their way through the tunnel, and as said by Ariella, they soon reached the frozen waterfall. The wizards also left and their journey took them to the dragon realm.

"Why the Yeti lands?" asked Magni.

"I've no idea," replied Jacob. "The urge to visit is overwhelming."

On arrival near the Yeti lands Jacob became alarmed, "This is strange," he said. "There's something wrong, stop!" He anxiously looked at Magni who drew his sword.

"I look high into these mountains," continued Jacob. "I recognise them to be those we see from the north facing side of the temple. Six hundred years ago, Yaz and the Yeti nation were to leave for the Alps; it was to be their last journey before moving into another dimension. Those who refused to leave were to express their loneliness by bellowing their pain when the great blizzards blow. All to remind man that once there was a nation native to these high mountains, beings who were the bringers of the snows and the guardians of the glaziers."

"When last I met Yaz," said Magni. "He and his people had already left this place, today it looks as though they never left. I don't understand. Do you feel threatened?"

"No brother," replied Jacob. "Yet, like you I don't understand."

"You are bringing me to some of the most wondrous of places," said Magni looking around at the endless whiteness. "I've never seen such beauty. The snows, they glisten under the high sun, look at the houses, they are everywhere and it seems that the snow protects them."

"It certainly is a wondrous place," agreed Jacob. "And it is as I remember. I sense Yaz is here, but his village is heavily shielded; he must have sought more protection."

Jacob briskly walked ahead of Magni only to impact against an invisible shield, bounce back to be submerged in a tall snow bank, much to the amusement of Magni. Both were surprised because a god should always be able to pass through any shield created by magic. Magni tried and he too failed but it was his attempt that alerted the Yeti.

"Who goes there?" cried one of the guards.

"A War God of Asgard," replied Magni. "And Jacob, King of Kings, God of Olympus,"

Yaz arrived almost immediately and said while opening a portal, "It's always a pleasure to welcome the sons of Thunder." He turned to Magni, "I see you and Jacob have made your peace."

"Ah sure," replied Magni while reaching across to pinch Jacob's cheek. "How could anybody be annoyed with someone with such a cute face? A few clatters and my anger didn't last too long."

Jacob cringed while recalling being kicked and clattered. He then asked, "I thought you left for another dimension, was that not over six hundred years ago?"

"When we reached the high Alps," replied Yaz. "The elves greeted us, you were there. Remember? I led my nation with confidence and just as I was about to enter the portal I looked back and saw fear, a fear I never saw in my people before. I hesitated, and then heard the call of our homeland. I smelt the pine needles resting on the floor of the great forests, and then sensed the loneliness of those we left behind." He took a deep breath before continuing, "I looked into the faces of my people and saw their delight when they realised I was changing my mind. I looked at Kalen and saw him close the portal; he foretold our reluctance and promised the assistance of Elf kind. He sent a message to the mountain elves instructing them to protect us on our way. They created a magic shield to hide us from prying eyes, especially now that man is climbing higher into the mountains."

Jacob saw Yaz was getting upset and encouraged him to continue, "We travelled under cover of darkness, escorted by the elves. After many months we reached our homeland. It wasn't easy; we were attacked and suffered under a constant onslaught by serpents and Dark Angels. They were everywhere and getting more ruthless in their attacks. There were loses but thankfully both Elf kind and the Yeti nation triumphed. Hell paid dearly. I fear 'His' revenge will come when least expected." Yaz then asked them to walk with him.

They walked higher up the mountain and soon reached Yaz's cabin and on their way, more of the Yeti nation materialised. The younglings and the not so young were in awe of Magni, they only ever heard of him from the great stories and to see such a powerful god of Asgard was a great honour for them. Jacob smiled to himself when he noticed how Magni was enjoying all the attention. He saw a different side to his brother while watching him go to his knees and encourage the younglings out of their shyness.

A fire was burning brightly outside Yaz's home inviting them to sit and enjoy its radiant glow and warm heat. Yaz then asked as to the reason for such an unexpected visit.

"I'm visiting all Astrals," said Jacob. "But I couldn't understand the urge to visit the Yeti nation. I thought you were gone. I assumed it was to meet with the few scouts left behind. Never in my wildest dreams did I realise you and I would meet again." He paused then explained why he was there, "The End Times battle is upon us. Lucifer and his armies are ready, and I expect Hell to unleash its power in the next few days. I'm hoping your nation will join the armies of the Astrals under Pegasus and assist in the defeat of Hell. Will you do this for me?"

Yaz sat back and thought carefully about how he wanted to answer. He then stood and beckoned Jacob and Magni to again walk with him. He took them to a platform overlooking his village and let out a loud and throaty growl, a roar that was so loud it would surely waken the dead. It was a sound familiar to the mountain peoples, but never identified. When he stopped roaring he said as the rest of the yeti nation materialised, "Jacob! Look before you, this is the last of the Yeti, there is but five hundred warriors and their families. Is it right to ask them to forsake their homeland yet again, all to fight a force so evil the future of our species will be in doubt. How can I ask my people to fight?"

"May I speak to them?" asked Magni. Yaz agreed and Magni moved to stand before the warriors,

"Warriors of the Ice Mountains, look on to me. My name is Magni, War God of Asgard, and today I call on you to join us in defence of the Light. There's a great sadness coming and many will be lost. Lucifer is about to unleash his armies and the gods need all Astrals to rise up and support us. Look upon your loved ones, look on your younglings and find your spirit. Be the warriors you have always been. Will you stand with us?"

Yaz stepped forward and raised his sword high. Within moments many warriors joined him, and then all warriors raised their swords. Jacob said while thanking them, "I know this is difficult but if we do nothing The Darkness will take power and the Light will be extinguished, if the Light dies all will be lost. You are needed to stand with Pegasus and when he calls you will know it's time."

Well, that didn't take much," replied Yaz. "I thought we were battle weary, look at them. They are true warriors of the Light."

"I bow to the might of the Yeti," said Jacob. "Watch for my Light."

Jacob and Magni thanked Yaz and then continued on their journey.

Chapter 13

While Jacob and Magni were visiting the Yeti, the wizards travelled to Wales. They reached the mountains and climbed close to the summit of Snowdonia where they sought out an entrance to the realm of the dragons. The entrance they sought was concealed by magic and heavily guarded against the most proficient of mountain climbers. This magic was so strong it took some time or them to gain entry, but when they did they were greeted by Andras, who immediately acknowledged them and welcomed them into his realm. They spoke for a few moments before a messenger alerted King Derwyn to their arrival. A short while later the sound of a battle horn was heard, "Ah, a call to arms," announced Andras.

It was just over three hundred years since Merlin and Apollonius last visited but neither of them had used this particular entrance before. They were taken through a lengthy tunnel that was wider than the others. Its walls caked in soot from years of fire-breathing as young dragons learned the ways of their kind. They passed alcoves containing an abundance of treasure causing them to gasp in disbelief.

"I've always heard how dragons were like magpies, now I see why," said Merlin as he looked from side to side. "In each alcove I see hordes of gold, silver, precious stones, works of art, all long missing from the realm of man. Is it true?"

"For millennia," replied Andras, "dragons ruled the skies. Man felt threatened by us and soon began their attempts to wipe us out of all memory. Their stories speak of St. George defeating a dragon. Never happened, he failed, I was there. We always vanquished our adversaries. If they hurt us we retaliated by ceasing their wealth, something we never really wanted or needed, it was them who cherished their wealth and we soon learned that the only way to hurt them was to take it as our reward, hence the gems and precious metals you see in these caves. Even after all this time it still means nothing to us."

They continued their walk and reached a large cavern containing the stone effigies of the nine first dragons. There were four on each side of the aisle, and they were presided over by the original King of the Dragons standing majestically at the rear of the cavern. Each effigy was painted in very vivid colours and each had a one word engraving to tell who they were. Apollonius recalled his mastery of the language only spoken by the ancient dragon lords and read out each name, "Winged, Underground, Horned, Spiritual, Hidden, Yellow, Coiling, Celestial and King."

"I know of the Celestial dragon," said Merlin. "She's the guardian of the gods. I know nothing of the others"

"They are 'The Nine', the founders of the dragon nation," said Andras. "Many years after Fafner became Emperor he decreed that our younglings should begin to understand who they are at a much younger age than in the past, so we bring them to stand before their ancestors and seek inspiration. Our younglings learn that they have nothing to fear, especially the change, we tell them of the great stories and the hero dragons of old and how they rest in Elysium."

"Apollonius and I spent some time in Elysium," said Merlin. "We saw the tombs of the Dragon Lords, there are many."

They continued to walk through the cavern and soon reached an ante-chamber through which they exited and found themselves in the vastness of the dragon realm. The vista before them was breathtaking. Ancient temples and civic buildings dotted the landscape. The atmosphere was one of total calmness, where the sky was so blue and bright that a cloud would be afraid to show itself. In the distance, the turrets and spires of the dragon city stood proud.

As they approached the city, the presence of the great dragon army came into view. They stood in their human form, assembled in honour of the arrival of two esteemed wizards.

"How many warriors are there?" asked Merlin.

"Five thousand," replied Andras.

"When do they appear as dragons?" asked Apollonius.

"When we exit through the three doors of our realm," replied Andras. "We release our flame and transform to take to the sky. It's then we bring terror to any adversary."

Their walk soon took them into the presence of the sons of Fafner; they bowed and were warmly greeted.

"Merlin, Apollonius, this is a great pleasure," said King Derwyn. "You are both most welcome into my realm. I'm curious, what is it that brings you to the domain of the dragons?"

"It's worrying news." said Apollonius. "The End Times battle approaches and The Darkness draws near. Jacob's concern grows and he's reviewing all plans. Is the army of the dragons ready to assist the gods?"

"Look out across the meadows," replied Derwyn. "See my army. They are ready for the call of Pegasus. They'll be led by the sons of Fafner."

Apollonius backed away as though in a trance, he was receiving a vision.

"Send your brothers to the Parthenon," he said while rejoining Merlin and Derwyn, "there's unfinished business unrelated to the battle. I see your mother. I see Jacob and he awaits their arrival. He will impart a gift before he releases his Light calling on the Carriers and the Messengers to awaken."

"A gift?" wondered Derwyn. "What could it be." he turned to Afan and Evan and instructed them to leave for Greece. He also instructed them to confirm to Jacob that the might of the dragon armies will be at his disposal." Merlin and Apollonius expressed their gratitude, bowed before bidding their farewells.

❧❦

While Merlin and Apollonius were in the dragon lands Jacob and Magni arrived in the town of Fira where they had a panoramic view of the Santorini caldera.

"This is another island I always wanted to visit," said Jacob. "Shane and I planned to come here during our third year summer holidays but mother had other ideas, she brought me all over Europe instead."

"I've been here before," replied Magni. "My chariot was in a holding position high above when the Island exploded. That was 3600 years ago. I watched its city and all its towns and villages just disappear. Everything happened so fast even the gods couldn't assist. Tsunamis travelled in all directions devastating all coastlines. It was carnage, well over twenty thousand souls perished. It destroyed the ancient and noble Minoan civilization and took years for the surrounding islands to recover."

"I look around at what can only be described as a rare natural beauty," said Jacob. "Look at the cliffs - so impressive, and the white buildings - so charming. I look at the sea and wonder what remnants of the past lie under its deep azure waters, and then I hear them."

"Look at that island," said Magni pointing towards the centre of the caldera, "Kameni is now its name, see how it grows even in the few moments we've been here."

Jacob stepped back, he received a vision and it unsettled him, "Now I see them, there are thousands. It's from beneath Kameni one of the armies of Hell will attack. Feel the pounding against the walls, soon they will break through. The eruption is imminent and Hells wrath will know no bounds. I can see Lucifer planning a similar eruption to the one you spoke of. This one has Egypt, Libya, Turkey, Israel, Lebanon and Greece in its sights. It will carry thousands of serpents. His plan is to show the world his power by bringing terror using the strength of the waves, and the viciousness of the serpents. Millions will die under this first onslaught. We must warn the Mer-People."

Chapter 14

Jacob and Magni made their way to the port of Athinios where they found an isolated spot near the water's edge. They removed their robes, weapons and headbands, placing them into their satchels before entering the water. They swam into the depths and soon reached the flanks of one of the Mer-People armies, one that was sent as a first line of defence. They made themselves known and requested an urgent meeting with Lord Toyesh, which was arranged.

They were ushered to the northern side of Kameni Island where the main body of the Mer-Army was gathered. Lord Toyesh and several of his generals were in attendance and when Jacob and Magni came into view they were greeted as welcomed allies.

"It's a great honour to be in the presence of two powerful War Gods," said Toyesh. "But it worries me as to why you're here. Is there a problem?"

"Yes, my lord," nodded Jacob, "there is. We fear you have been led into a trap. Lucifer plans to unleash one of his armies through Santorini's volcano, we believe its sole purpose is to overwhelm your army. He will use the power of the eruption to conceal his serpents. They'll be hidden in a tsunami, equally as powerful as the one that destroyed all in its path over three thousand years ago. We suggest you move your armies to the Atlantic, and await the call of Pegasus."

"Lord Magni," said one of Toyesh' generals. "You of all War Gods should know better. You fought with us. How could mere serpents undo the power of the Mer-Army? After all we are aligned with Poseidon and under his protection. It is us alone who know the ridges, crevices and hiding places. Hell has no chance."

Magni swam over to the general. "My friend," he said hoping to address the general's comments. "Only a fool would question the bravery and power of the Mer-Army. We all know it is legendary. But this time you will be fighting alone and it saddens us not to be able to assist. There is one thing that might raise your spirits. Oceanus has returned. He is with nine of the Titans and they're preparing their own plans. He tells us there are hidden creatures deep in the ridges, creatures that will fight when the time is right."

"Oceanus!" exclaimed an excited Toyesh. "He lives? Where is he?"

"Ten of the twelve have gathered in a secret location," said Jacob. "Oceanus was last to join them. They've sworn allegiance to me and have vowed to fight for the Light."

Toyesh turned to his generals, raised his hand to stop any further discussion. "When a god appears before you," he said, "you listen to what is said. When two gods appear, especially one as powerful as a War God of Asgard, you take them seriously and follow their commands. We leave immediately. Send out the signal and we assemble in the waters off the Algarve."

There was no delay; the Mer-Army immediately left for the straits of Gibraltar. Jacob and Magni waited with Toyesh until the last warrior left.

"My King of Kings," said Toyesh while moving away to catch up with his army. "We're a frightened nation and unlike those on land, our hiding places will easily be located. I promised the gods that the Mer-People will defend the seas and fight to the death. We will do everything in our power to stop the serpents of Hell from ruling the deep."

"Poseidon has great faith in you," replied Jacob. "He assured us that the armies of the deep are ready, both Magni and I can see he speaks the truth." Toyesh acknowledged the kind words with a bow as he went out of sight.

On the surface a battle group of twenty vessels from the United States sixth fleet was travelling towards the Eastern Mediterranean. Their sonar was showing unusual activity beneath each vessel and they went on alert. That was until their look-outs informed the commanders that they were surrounded by thousands of dolphins. This spectacle was recorded and broadcast all over the world. It initially showed dolphins diving and swimming in formation towards the west, led by a magnificent male. Then, as the minutes passed, what begun as dolphins diving below the surface, changed to the Mer-Army surfacing, fully armed and showing their power. What the world was witnessing was a gathering of the massed armies of Mer-kind.

"There's one last thing I need to do and you're not going to like it," said Jacob just as they reached Athinios. "I need to go to Dublin."

Magni definitely didn't like it, he felt a visit Shane was unnecessary at this time, "Is that wise?" he asked. "You do realise Zeus won't be happy"

"He's my friend" retorted Jacob, "and sometimes friends come first."

They dried, dressed and then mounted their horses. Jacob stretched across to grip Magni, blinked, thought of Shane and they disappeared.

Chapter 15

They materialised in the school grounds quite close to where Shane, Al, Callum, Stevie, Joey and Davie were having their lunch. Jacob dismounted and looked over to where Shane was sitting waiting for him to look up. Hundreds of pupils began to move towards where Jacob was but they weren't interested in him, it was Magni they were all staring at.

"Is that Thor?" was whispered.

"It looks like him!" was suggested.

Magni dismounted to gasps of disbelief. It was his height that surprised those watching. He stood taller than Jacob, especially with the silver band bearing the golden wings of Asgard resting upon his head.

When Shane finally looked up he at first froze, unable to react, he than leapt up and ran. Tears had already gathered as he reached and then embraced his best friend. The embrace was long and lingering causing Magni to say, "I think everybody knows how close you are, time to separate."

"No! Not yet," responded Jacob. "Just a little longer."

"I watched you fight Cronus," whispered Shane, "We all did, and I was devastated when he beat the crap out of you. It was terrible to watch. I wanted to be with you just to say everything would be OK. Then it was over and you stood for the whole world to see how you were fine. I was so proud but you didn't fool me, I saw in your face that you were up to something."

"It seems I can never fool you," replied Jacob still holding Shane tightly, "You're right, sometimes all is not what it seems. Say nothing." After a few more moments they parted.

"We meet again, Lord Magni," said Shane while reaching in to shake his hand.

"I hope you've all continued your training?" replied Magni.

"Of course we have and the odd thing is - the training you and Ares gave us has come in really useful. The skills we learned allowed us win the Senior Cup and now all opposition is terrified to play against us."

"I was referring to your swordsmanship," responded an unimpressed Magni. Shane looked away.

"Don't mind him," said Jacob. "He wouldn't understand. Anyway, there's a reason I'm here. Are all the boys here today?"

"Yes," replied Shane. "They'll all come running as soon as they realise you're here."

Sure enough, it wasn't long before all eighteen were together. Jacob walked among them and greeted each one individually. He then asked them to listen carefully to what he had to say,

"Tomorrow the world will see me stand alone at the Parthenon. I'll be there for the next six days, that's when everything will begin to change. Lucifer will have unleashed Hell. On the sixth day I will send out my Light. I expect all those who received the message to answer, it will be the largest army ever assembled. My messengers will awaken and be brought to Olympus." He paused for a moment allowing the boys absorb what he said, then continued. "You too will be called upon. Remember, these are the sacred lands of the goddess Danu, you've already met her. When my Light shines she too will rise, but not to assist you, she will leave for Olympus. She trusts you and is depending on your skills to protect her realm. When you see the

Light you must prepare to make your way to the seat of the High Kings, the stone of destiny. And from there you will lead the carriers in defence of these lands. Can you do this for me?"

As each of them placed their hands to their right side their invisible swords began illuminating prompting Shane to speak for them all, "We've been waiting and we're ready to defend the Light."

"Pegasus will send you his fastest steeds," said Magni. "They are magical and no obstacle will stand in their way. They will take you to meet a most powerful and ancient goddess. She is from whom this land got its name and she'll be there to fight by your side." He then said, "It's time for us to go."

They mounted their horses and both clenched their right fist, crossed it over their hearts and bowed to Shane and the boys. All other pupils saw the swords disappear but were more enthralled by the fact that two gods bowed to Shane and the senior rugby team.

❧❧

Jacob and Magni returned to the temple. On meeting Zeus Magni reported that all realms have bowed before Jacob and have sworn their allegiance. "They have faith in him," he said. "And they know he has been blessed by the Ancient One."

"Jacob, why look so anxious?" asked Zeus. "Think of the formidable forces you've gathered. You are a Warrior King, a god with great powers, be strong, allow your confidence grow. Go now and rest."

Even with those words of encouragement Jacob still felt nervous, but when he looked at his brother he got a new strength and inspiration from his stoicism. He stood, bowed to Zeus and then moved towards his favourite resting place where he sat alone and eventually fell asleep.

Chapter 16

It was now very late in the afternoon when, with a jolt, Jacob awoke and reached into his satchel to retrieve his I-phone, his curiosity was getting the better of him and he wondered if Shane had left any messages. There was no coverage so there were no messages. The phone still had power and what jumped out at him was the date, 24th September 2017. He forgot to ask Shane how transition year went and wondered how fifth year was going. All this wondering soon left his mind when he felt the rolling pangs of anxiety again gather, and he wished for all that was ahead of him to disappear.

With a heavy heart he looked out at the desolate city that had built up where the lagoon once sparkled. He wanted to leave but he had to face his coronation before travelling. He left the sill and went to his room where, on arrival, he summoned the stewards and arranged for the finest Olympus robes to be prepared. He called for his weapons to be sharpened and his armour polished.

"Tell me," he asked the attending steward. "Why is it necessary for me to suffer a coronation when so many bad things are coming?"

"My lord," replied the steward while assisting Jacob to remove his clothes. "It's necessary because it ensures continuity. It shows all attending what we are fighting for. It also confirms the chain of command."

Jacob just slowly nodded and stepped into a suds-filled bath where he relaxed and allowed himself to be totally immersed in the soothing hot waters. An hour later he emerged and began preparing himself. When dressed he caught his image in nearby shields and saw he looked every bit a powerful Warrior King.

When it was time, he left his room and made his way through the corridors where temple guards were standing three meters apart all along his route towards the Great Hall. The guards were dressed in their imperial robes and armour, and as he passed, each one stood to attention offering a spear salute at their right shoulder.

Before walking through the doors he stopped and took a deep breath. He allowed a steward check that all straps and clasps were secure, that his cape flowed freely, and his head band was centred properly. "All is ready," said the steward. "Go now and be our King of Kings."

Jacob stepped through the doors and stood for a moment on the highest step looking every bit a powerful warrior king. His white tunic rested just below his knees and was secured by his golden armour, armour that was emblazoned with the laurels of Olympus, surrounding the Valknut symbol of Asgard. His armour captured the sunlight entering the temple through the southern windows enhancing his aura and sending his light all around the temple. His cape draped perfectly from his shoulders, held in place by two circular discs etched with Celtic designs. His golden head band, partially obscured by his thick wavy shoulder length hair, was still perfectly centred allowing the laurels of Olympus to form a light halo on his head.

He looked around at those gathered and was taken aback at the pomp and ceremony that was arranged. The gods and goddesses who were awake were all dressed in the finest robes and wearing the most exquisite crowns and jewellery ever crafted. For Olympus this was truly a grand event.

Jacob looked for Odi and was disappointed to find he was still asleep, he wanted him by his side when Zeus raised the crown. He looked for his mother and when he saw her, his face lit up. It wasn't her amazing robes or her sparkling jewellery that caught his eye; it was her smile that really lifted him. He then looked at his father and found himself in awe at how powerful he stood as a King of Asgard, and God of the Norse realm. He found his strength just by looking at his parents and when he saw Magni, tears gathered. The heralds then raised their trumpets and the choir sang, announcing the arrival of the new King of Kings.

He moved down the steps and through the Great Hall with a confidence so rare in one so young. His cape flowed behind him as though blown by a gentle breeze. While walking, and with a slight bow, he acknowledged all those present holding a special one for his parents. He then turned to Magni and lowered his head while sneaking in a quick wink showing how much he loved his brother. On reaching his grandfather he clenched his fist before placing it over his heart and again he bowed.

Zeus summoned a steward to bring forth the crown and before he raised it above his head he said, "For thousands of years this crown rested upon my head, before that it adorned the head of Cronus, today it's been gifted to the new King of Kings." He gestured Jacob to step forward.

"The ancient writings spoke of a boy entering the realm of the gods; we now know this has come to pass. This boy is filled with integrity and chivalry, and is one who will fight for those who cannot fight for themselves. The stories speak of you, Jacob. You've been chosen by the Ancient One to wear the crown because you are pure of heart and carry the hopes and dreams of all whose lives you've touched. Wear it well for a great burden has now fallen to you." He then placed the crown upon Jacob's head.

Jacob stood and turned to face the gods, watching as they bowed before him. It still bothered him to see his parents bow but this time he accepted their homage. He then said,

"The burden Zeus speaks of is mine and mine alone, given to me by the Ancient One and in the end I will be the one to fight Lucifer. This is one of two battles; the other is against The Darkness. The Darkness fears the gods and has tasked Lucifer with destroying us, a distraction allowing him to advance without being challenged. This is not going to happen because while you slept our messengers have built an army of millions and right now they are all waiting on my call. It pains me when I see how our armies will hurt but I promise you Lucifer will hurt more. He believes it's he who is in control, believe me he's not, he's being deceived. Recently I walked in the nothingness where The Darkness dwells, and I felt its power. Its savagery knows no bounds. Nothing will survive its onslaught, not even Hell. As I speak I sense it's getting closer and its advance is relentless. I read its mind and learned there is no intention of allowing the Light to survive anywhere, including in the Underworld." He took a deep breath before continuing,

"We must use all our resources to defeat Lucifer's armies and this must be done as quickly as possible. We must do this by unleashing our armies in a simultaneous attack that will overwhelm Hell before it has time to entrench itself in our domain. Only then will we be able to focus all our efforts in defence of the Light." He paused again to allow those listening to absorb all he said then continued,

"In a few moments I will walk through the doors of this temple and enter the realm of man, visible to all. I will move towards the great city of Athens, at times using magic to display my power. Mankind will then know war is imminent and they will be terrified but hopefully they will get solace when they see the astral armies take up positions across the sky, near the waterfalls and beside the volcanoes. My friends, I'm appointing Ares and Athena as commanders of the Olympus gods and you must follow them. The senior gods will stand back and only come to our aid when all seems lost. Go now and prepare." He bowed again before moving towards his parents.

He kissed his mother, rested his head on her shoulder while taking in the loving embrace she was giving him. While hugging his father he said, "Who would have thought that the two babies you cradled on that beach in Crete would grow to help lead the armies of Asgard?" he hugged his father again then said, "Go to Asgard and be there to witness your four sons lead Asgard in defence of Earth."

Jacob made his way to the doors and before exiting he glanced back to see tears gather in his mother's eyes, he also saw the anxiety in his father. He was taken aback when he saw Magni rush through the Great Hall to tightly embrace him.

"Magni," he gasped. "If I didn't know you better I'd swear I see a tear."

"You do," replied Magni. "Don't tell anyone."

Chapter 17

Jacob walked through a portal taking him to the centre of the city. He was surprised at the lack of people on the streets, that was until he reached the nearest building and looked through the ground floor window. He saw the residents were watching news reports being broadcast about the attack on Naples and Tirana as well as many towns and villages in Italy, Albania and Greece. They were also watching replays of the attack on Dublin. He continued his journey through the city maintaining a high profile by walking in the centre of the roads. He followed the one road that took him towards the coast.

Word was now spreading and people gathered on the streets. The elderly were first to approach him, especially those ladies wearing the traditional black shawls and headscarves, they'd raise their hands towards the heavens as though greeting someone special. These ladies believed in the old ways and knew their future and the future of their families depended on this young man. Jacob never said a word.

He continued walking and as he neared the coast he was met by permanent barricades built by that countries army. Close by there was a makeshift barricade erected by the opposition, and both groups had their guns trained on him but he didn't care. He increased his pace and refused to obey any instructions to halt. On reaching the barricade he brought his two hands into a praying position and when they parted the barricades magically separated, allowing him through. The opposition fighters cheered and lowered their weapons believing they had a god on their side. The government soldiers were now vulnerable and fired on him but unfortunately for them their bullets disintegrated before reaching him. He never flinched, he just kept walking.

People cheered on realising the warrior from the battles of both Dublin and Athens was back. For the young people watching he was an awesome sight and they saw in him a determination that led them to believe he had a plan. They followed him in their hundreds and then thousands; even government soldiers joined this mass movement. Images of Jacob were now appearing on social media, and news agencies were sending reporters to the area using high speed helicopters. People tried to talk to him but he never responded; he continued at the same pace until he reached the very spot where he first met his beloved Eala. He noted that the ledge she sat on was still there but the water was putrid. He shook his head in disappointment and moved further down the beach before walking to the water's edge. He went to his knees, placed his hand into the polluted ripples, and within seconds the sea began to churn as though a great storm was passing through. He summoned Poseidon for assistance, a summons that was immediately answered.

From beneath the waves a trident appeared followed by a massive colossus. As the moments passed the colossus became more recognisable. He was quickly identified as the God of the Seas. Jacob and Poseidon bowed to each other, instinctively knowing what to do. They placed their hands into the waves causing the sea to get even more violent. Their actions churned up the sea bed, displacing layers of sticky discoloured sands, pebbles and rocks. On the surface centuries of marine debris accumulated. There were sunken vessels, discarded vehicles, derelict fishing gear, all kinds of rotten organic material that had absorbed manmade chemicals, but the worst was the tiny micro plastics. For years the plastics had prevented rays of light from reaching plants and algae that depended on the sun to create the nutrients required to sustain all sea life.

The continuous churning not only displaced the polluted water it also forced the debris on to the beach where Jacob used his power to compress it into smaller manageable pieces before turning it to dust.

Then the calm came, and when it did the sea was pristine again, all pollution was gone. People could smell, the first time for most, the sweet scent of what the sea had to offer.

Jacob then said to Poseidon, "I've sent Toyesh and his army out to safer waters. They were vulnerable around Santorini."

"I agree," responded Poseidon. "Your actions will have saved many of my friends this day." He then returned beneath the waves.

With Poseidon gone Jacob felt very alone even though surrounded by thousands of locals. He tried to cheer himself up by remembering the happy times he had in this very spot all those thousands of years ago. He thought of the boys spying on the girls and their embarrassment at being caught. He thought of the first time he felt Eala's soft skin against his and longed again for this burden to go away so he could be with her one more time. He then dipped his hands into the sea and asked for more assistance.

Those watching saw the sea rise creating a magical stairwell. At the highest step a bridge began forming and it travelled towards the northwest, to reach the coast of Greece where a second water stairwell formed. Jacob quickly made his way up the stairs to begin his journey towards Greece. His walk was not only defying physics it was showing the world the power of the gods.

By the time he reached Greece all major news organisations had helicopters trailing him, including the BBC World Service which was the first to break the news of the return of the Boy King. Speculation was rife but Jacob never stopped to explain why he was back, making things worse. Programme interruptions began and experts in physics, religion, the classics and politics were called upon but none could offer any explanation for the astounding events that were unfolding.

Jacob rested for a few moments on reaching the outskirts of Athens before making his way to the base of the Acropolis. He then made his way up to the south facing side of the Parthenon where he took up a position looking out over the city. He extracted an ornately carved long sword from his satchel and after checking the sharpness of its double edged blade he plunged its tip into the ground, rested his hands on its cruciform hilt and took the 'At Ease' position. As a light wind blew, flapping his cape and tossing his hair, all he did was stare out over the city. Even when approached by dignitaries and police officers he never acknowledged or answered their questions. He just held this position throughout the night.

The Parthenon flood lights where redirected keeping him permanently on view. Efforts by the Greek government to stop news organisations from broadcasting these momentous events were thwarted when emergency court sittings prevented the censorship. Jacob never once moved, continuing to hold the same position for the next two days. Those watching couldn't understand how he just stood there without the need for food, drink or even a toilet break. Speculation mounted, almost to the point of conspiracy, especially as the worlds waterfalls turned from torrents into trickles, volcanoes stopped spewing their lava and animals quietened before seeking hiding places.

On the evening of the third day a loud, thunderous rumbling sound was heard but its location or direction couldn't be identified. Jacob briefly smiled trying not to respond but his heart was bursting with excitement. He knew that sound, he had heard it before. It was the sound of an Asgard chariot and he knew it could only be the one warrior he really wanted to see. The rumbling stopped and a golden chariot materialised in a holding position just off the south facing wall. It was Odi and he was equally as excited.

"About time brother," said Jacob while embracing Odi.

"I woke earlier and knew you'd need me when all Hell breaks loose," was Odi's reply.

"I missed you and I'm so glad you're here," continued Jacob while moving to retake his position looking out over the city. "Do you hear them?" he asked.

"No! I hear nothing," replied Odi while taking up a position roughly six feet away from Jacob. He extracted his sword and, like his brother, plunged it into the ground and then rested his two hands on its handle. They both went quiet and listened.

Twenty four hours passed before Odi lost his patience, "How long more?" he asked.

"It's getting closer and I don't like it. Did you notice the stars last night? How many died while we watched? The Darkness is now so close I can taste its creeping poison."

Little did they know that Sky News had employed a lip reader and she was telling the world what was being said between the two warriors? The diminishing light of the stars was already noticed by observatories around the world, confirming what Jacob and Odi were talking about was really happening.

"Have you thought of Eala?" asked Odi.

"She or my babies are never far from my mind," replied Jacob. "I know they're safe but I'm still worried."

"Same here," said Odi. "I can't believe I'm in love and soon to be a father. Do you think she too is safe?"

"Of course she's safe," replied Jacob, "Magni never took his eyes from her or the boys, he had to intervene on a number of occasions but it was usually the boys who were in trouble."

"Speaking of Magni," said Odi. "I do worry about him. He never seems happy. In Asgard he spent a lot of time with girls but never seemed to meet one he really liked."

"Don't worry about Magni," replied Jacob attempting to change the subject. "We've much bigger things to concern ourselves with and just for the record, there is one he loves and I think they'll end up together. Put it this way, when this is over I'll do all in my power to make it happen."

"Don't leave me hanging," said Odi getting very interested in his oldest brother's love life. "Who is she? Tell me."

"Forget it," said Jacob. "You are the last person I'd tell, so don't be so nosey."

"I'm tempted," said Odi trying to suppress a smile.

"Don't you dare!" threatened Jacob. "If you enter my head, I'll beat the living daylights out of you."

"You and whose army?" said Odi puffing out his chest. "Too late, I'm in."

Odi didn't know what to say but managed, "Oh!"

"Now you know," said Jacob.

Several more hours passed when slight tremors rolled across Athens. "They're getting closer," said Jacob.

"Are you sure?" replied a confused Odi. "I still feel nothing."

"I'm sure," said Jacob. "Look at the sun, see how it dims. Listen for the birds, their silence is deafening, do you not smell the stench of death or feel the fear?"

"Are you afraid?" asked Odi.

"I....am....terrified." replied Jacob.

"With all my training," continued Odi. "And with the guidance of father and the support of Magni and Modi, I thought I knew no fear but this is petrifying me. This is something nobody could possibly be trained for. Please don't tell them I said that."

"I hear them chipping away, tap, tap, tap," said Jacob. "No more than seventy two hours and they will break through."

Odi still felt nothing but knew that if Jacob was preparing so should he, and when Jacob reached for his satchel to retrieve his staff so did he. The nearby news cameras continued filming.

❧❧

In the far distance, what looked like two large birds were seen to be flying towards the Parthenon. They were being tailed by two Greek helicopter gunships, both acting aggressively. As the birds approached the Acropolis, the gunships opened fire much to Jacob's ire. He reacted by creating a fireball similar to the ones Cronus produced and after raising his arm, he fired it in the direction of the gunships.

"They're not birds to be shot down," he yelled. "They're Dragon Lords, friends of the gods. Dragons only show themselves when invited or if there's a great need. Odi, go escort them to safety."

Odi whistled for his chariot and it soon materialised, he quickly moved out to protect the dragons by positioning himself between them and the gunships.

The pilots were under instruction to shoot down anything that flew over Athens and were determined to follow orders. They launched more rockets causing Odi to lose his patience. He decided not to rout the helicopters but to take them down by placing his chariot between the gunships. He raised his sword and severed the rotor blades causing the helicopters to crash to the ground.

"You fools!" yelled Jacob, expressing his fury with military command. "Your weapons are useless against the power of the gods." He demanded NATO send a delegation to meet with him.

Odi and the dragons joined Jacob and for the first time ever the transformation of a dragon into their human form was witnessed all over the world causing gasps of disbelief. People couldn't believe that they were now witnessing two more beings of myth and legend. Everyone watching the broadcasts listened intently to what the lip readers were saying.

The Dragon Lords went on to one knee; clenched their fists across their hearts and bowed to Jacob.

"Let me introduce myself," said the first dragon. "I'm Evan, son of your friend, Fafner. This is my brother Afan. We are princes of the Dragon Realm."

"This is unexpected, but very welcome," said Jacob. "I understood the wizards were to confirm the allegiance of King Derwyn's army."

"Fear not my King of Kings," replied Evan. "Five thousand dragon warriors are trained and ready to fly in defence of the light."

"It's true my lord," said Afan. "Two wizards did visit our realm, after meeting us they suggested we fly to meet with you. We thought it a strange request but found it difficult to resist. King Derwyn insisted we meet with you."

"I agree, it is strange," replied Jacob. "If the wizards suggested it, there's a reason. Will you allow me to enter your head?" Evan agreed. Jacob entered his head and called up his memories.

"Ah, I see their concerns," said Jacob after withdrawing. "They fear a weakness in the command of the dragon army. That weakness is both of you."

"I must protest!" interrupted Afan, showing his contempt. "We are the most trusted and the most trained. How dare they question our abilities?"

"No, no, you misunderstand," replied Jacob trying to reassure them. "I saw what the wizards saw and it's easy to resolve. You are both still grieving for the Empress Heulwyn. Your grief at times effects your judgement and we can't have that when the battle begins. There's a way for you to let her go, and I can help. Do you want my help?" They both agreed.

"I can take you both to see she rests among your ancestors. She is with the blessed dead and is guarded by the Titans."

"Please take us," said Evan. "At that time everything happened so fast, we had no time to grieve. We were too young and didn't understand."

Chapter 18

Jacob placed his hands on Afan and Evan, blinked and transported all three to the beach surrounding Elysium where they met with Cronus and Rhea. "We've been expecting you," said Rhea. "You are most welcome."

Cronus greeted Jacob, before acknowledging Evan and Afan; he noted how they were all dressed for war. He also sensed Evan's anxiousness to visit his mothers resting place. He escorted them to the mausoleum and guided them down into the vaults. They walked through the archway to where the tombs of the Dragon Lords lay.

"I'm about to show you the final resting place of your mother," said Jacob after stopping them from walking any further. "This'll be very emotional especial when you see an identical plinth resting alongside your mothers. Your father's name may already be engraved. Don't worry, he's still alive. Plinths are always prepared in advance for the loved ones of the blessed dead."

Afan and Evan stood in awe at what was before them. The tombs of their ancestors travelled as far as the eye could see. Many with human effigies resting upon them, but the older ones had impressive sculptures of all shapes and sizes depicting the most renowned of dragon kind. These were the ones who ruled near the dawn of time. They walked a short distance and reached a plinth bearing an ornately engrave inscription that read,

Here rests the beloved Empress Heulwyn

Goddess of the Light,

a loving mother and wife.

"I never knew she was a Goddess of the Light," said Evan leaning in to rest his hand on the beautifully carved effigy depicting his mother.

"To me she was just my mother," said Afan as tears gathered. "I miss her so much." He stretched across and began rubbing her stone face while Evan stretched in to hold her hands and together they both descended into a much delayed grief. Rhea gestured to Jacob and Cronus suggesting they back away and allow the boys to grieve in private.

After a while Rhea rejoined the boys and saw how they were still struggling.

"I've allowed you grieve but time is impatient," she said while embracing both of them. "You must now find your strength and continue preparing for the coming battle. I'm the first among the Earth Mothers and was there at the creation. I feel your pain but you must leave this grief behind. I can help." She closed her eyes while still embracing the boys. The Light came, bringing her calmness to surround them.

They quickly recovered and rejoined Jacob and Cronus who waited on the steps outside the mausoleum. "Nice to see the Light shine so brightly around both of you," said Jacob reaching in to hug them. "Now you are true Warriors of the Light."

"I don't know how to thank you," said Evan as he backed away and slightly bowed. "You've no idea what you have done for us this day. I feel the calmness for the first time in so long."

"We were very young dragons watching our mother's body being placed on a boat," said Afan. "The lanterns were carried by the elders, emitting a solemn light. The singing still rings in my ears; it was like what I imagined the songs of elves sounded like. One young boy sung the 'Song of the Dragons' as the incense wafted in the air. My mother's body was sent out across the great lakes. No one told us where she went and that broke our hearts. We are now at peace knowing she's been taken to this sacred place. Our sisters will be so relieved."

"We noticed the plinth beside our mothers is almost completed," said Evan. "The stonemason's tools lie alongside it. The letter F and A have already been carved, does this mean our father's death is imminent?"

"As I said earlier," said Jacob, annoyed at himself for not checking when he was in the vaults. "It's written that the tombs of the blessed dead always include a place for their loved one. If you say his inscription is being carved it would seem his place is prepared and his destiny set. I believe the dragon execution of the witch Morgana has made him a target of Lucifer and his generals. I promise you that if his death comes to pass I will, after his funeral and with the permission of Cronus and Rhea, bring you, your sisters and King Derwyn to this place to mourn alone. Your father, alongside Faer, protected my Eala for two thousand years and I'll be forever grateful. When the time comes I too will share your grief but it is not this day."

"The gates of Elysium will always be open for the Dragon Realm," promised Cronus

"Where does my father sleep?" asked Afan. "Maybe we should be nearby, just in case."

"I believe he sleeps in the far west," replied Jacob. Even I know not where, but it's deep in the land of the Goddess Danu. My visions show me the spirits of the great Elks; they patrol the forests and the mountains, guarding his resting place. He's safe?"

"Will we see him soon?" asked Evan.

"Yes," replied Jacob after closing his eyes and searching. "You will see him soon; your wait is nearly over. My visions show him leading the dragon armies, his sons by his side. I see him leaving the battle and joining the Light. He too is a God of the Light and will share the last line of defence when the battle is almost lost, he will then….." Jacob froze and said no more.

"I fear Jacob's sudden silence means that when he leaves the battle is the time when we must say our goodbyes….." said Afan.

"But at least," replied Evan. "At least we know he will rest among the blessed dead."

Afan was walking up the stairs when he suddenly stopped; he froze and mumbled incoherently.

"Are you Ok," yelled Evan. "Answer me, is it happening again? Tell me brother, what do you see?"

Jacob and Rhea quickly placed their hands on Afan's head and were now sharing his vision. Rhea backed away and said to Cronus, "Jacob's hunch is right. Lucifer still thinks the battle is all about him. He doesn't realise he is just a distraction and will never accept that he is being deceived. He prepares his legions and will bring on a great calamity to all of mankind but all the time it's The Darkness whom we should fear the most. Nothing survives its grip."

Jacob continued watching Afan's vision and it broke his heart. He said hoping to comfort Afan, "Together we've just witnessed the fall of an emperor. He falls only when he sees the Light getting stronger. Did you not see the spirit of you mother? Did you not see her lift your father into her arms and take him away? He didn't fall to battle, he fell to Love. He waited until he was sure his sons were safe and then allowed himself to fall. He is with the one he has loved the most. They were always destined to share eternity together, and when the great stories are written, theirs will the greatest love story of them all."

Evan and Afan were again trying to stay composed but they were having great difficulty. What surprised Rhea and Jacob was when Cronus pulled them towards him and said, "You will have time with your father, he is a powerful god, I feel his spirit reach out to all he loves. You must return to the dragon lands and await his arrival. Greet him in a way that he will know how you have both seen his future, let him know that you will be by his side at all times and will hold his hand as he falls. Let him know that you understand, and let him rest in peace."

"Are we not allowed to grieve?" asked Afan. "Are we not allowed to show our sadness and loss?"

"He's not gone yet" replied an annoyed Cronus. "You all have a battle to fight and he needs his sons to fight as generals of the dragon armies and not be distracted by constantly watching his back. Let him go."

"What you ask is so difficult," said Evan. "But let me assure you we will not be distracted. The blood of Emperor Fafner runs through our veins and it's that blood that will give us the strength to lead the dragons on an onslaught against the serpents and Dark Angels. We will not be defeated."

Jacob then placed his hands on both boys and immediately transported them back to Athens.

Chapter 19

On returning, Jacob immediately assisted Odi who was struggling with a violently vibrating staff. "Thank Odin you're back," he said through gritted teeth. "It started vibrating a few moments ago. I don't think it likes me. Strange how I still feel nothing, why's that?"

"You may feel nothing," said Jacob as the staff calmed. "But it's telling me to send out the light, and it's also showing me images of Lucifer's growing army." He then asked Odi to call on Asgard to send chariots.

Odi produced his gjallarhorn and within minutes ten chariots appeared, each one carrying a commander and two archers.

"Instruct them to provide protection to Evan and Afan until they pass into the western lands." said Jacob as he sent them on their way. All around the world, people watching were in awe of the sight of ten chariots, surrounding two dragons, travelling across the sky on a journey into the west.

Jacob then turned his attention towards a delegation of generals from various armies that had arrived. He berated them, loud enough for the cameras to pick up and it was obvious he was angry, "What is it about you so-called military men?" he yelled. "What allows you to think you can do what you like?" He paused for a moment waiting for a reaction but when none came, he continued, "You can see the strange and magical things happening all over the world, and yet you fire on dragons without knowing whether they're friend or foe. You shoot first, ask questions later and care less about the consequences. After the attack on Dublin, I warned you about what was coming, and still you allowed the evil in some men's hearts to thrive. You allowed tyrants and despots to take over countries bringing fear and death with them. Those murderers are the spawn of Hell and are descendants of those bitten by the serpents in the distant past and now they carry their mark. They have been attacking my carriers and feeding their souls to Lucifer. To them I say 'Beware the vengeance of the gods'. All this time you stood back and did nothing. You allowed diplomacy and expediency instead of righteousness influence your decision. Now look at the consequences."

He was interrupted by one of the generals who said, "Our whole purpose is to protect our own citizens and in some cases, our allies. That is what we have been trained for. How do you expect us to react when we see the strange things that are happening?"

Jacob shot him down, "Do you think we're fools? Do you think the gods haven't noted how the so called powerful countries have used their armies to suppress countries whose governments they don't like, and used their wealth to keep in power tyrants who suit their purposes? All this is now academic because there's nothing you can do against the evil of Hell, and what happened in Naples and Tirana should have convinced you of that. For two thousand years you've been warned about the power of Hell and still you did nothing, now The Darkness threatens Earth and without us there will be no hope. If you want to assist, be our eyes and ears and train your weapons on the volcanoes, they will slow down but not stop the wrath of Hell, but will give the gods time."

When no reaction came he shook his head in contempt then continued, "Very shortly you will see me call on the Light and then you will see the arrival of the immortals. It is they who will control the defence of Earth. When this happens all will know that Hell is on the march. Within twenty four hours you will see the arrival of the Asgard armies, it is then you will see the power of the Astrals. Do not interfere when they take up positions all over the world."

After dismissing the generals, Jacob went quiet. All watching saw him move his head from left to right as though he was in a trance-like state; they then heard him say, "Brother! Stand back."

He raised the staff and with all his strength pounded it off the ground sending a shock wave all across the world; he then called on the ancient primordial light to answer, and when it did, he struggled with its power.

Odi moved to assist and using their combined strength they raised the staff and watched it send out the light in seven different directions. The first four beams each chose a different path; they travelled towards the north, south, east or west. The fifth penetrated the seas and the sixth travelled out into the cosmos. The seventh beam travelled no more than a hundred meters before disappearing into a hidden dimension. All light then faded and everything went quiet.

"What happens now?" asked Odi.

"We wait," replied Jacob.

They didn't have to wait too long before the staff began vibrating again, and soon the first response was felt. A very mild but telling light arrived.

"This is an unexpected response," said Jacob with a wide smile crossing his face. "The light has brought some good news. Congratulations brother, your babies are being born."

"How, how, how can this be?" gasped Odi, "I still feel nothing. Brother, this is getting on my nerves. Where is she? I need to go to her."

"Use your powers and think of Panya," encouraged Jacob. "Blink and you will be there in a second."

"I have only ever blinked once," replied a scared looking Odi. "Remember! You were there. I'm afraid I might mess it up. Help me?"

"OK! Let me in," suggested Jacob. "I'll help, but only for a second."

They blinked and disappeared. Jacob reappeared within a second and again, took his position holding the staff waiting for the true responses.

Odi had arrived on a section of the Kings road in the far north of Scandinavia and immediately made his way up towards the glaciers. He blinked several times allowing him to move closer at a faster pace. He could see the Light Jacob sent and it was hovering above two frozen doorways. He paced and paced while waiting on the doors to thaw but his patience was wearing thin. He used all his strength to pound his fists off the doors but still couldn't get through. He was becoming more agitated and then it happened.

The light descended and penetrated the glacier causing the doorway to burst open from the inside out. Suddenly two powerful warriors emerged and they were no longer the boys who left the temple two thousand years earlier; they now presented as two young men who were clearly Gods of the Light.

Odi acknowledged them while rushing past, all he wanted was to see Panya and on entering the cave he heard what every father loves to hear, the first cries of his babies. He stood in awe while watching the Elfena lifting his daughters from Panya allowing her a clear view of who stood before her.

"Is this a dream?" she said after looking up. Are you real?"

Odi fell to his knees while at the same time raising his hands to cover his mouth, getting very emotional. He said while reaching in to touch her cheek before leaning closer to kiss her lips,

"This might feel like a dream but it's not, I'm real. Apart from visiting the east I slept for two thousand years, and through all that time my thoughts were only of you. Trust me, being apart must never happen again."

This magic moment was interrupted by one of the Elfena, "The Light is impatient and wishes to return to Jacob, you must leave now and allow Panya prepare to release its power."

Panya struggled to her feet and waited for the Elfena to assist. They dressed her in the most exquisite robes and jewellery, and placed on her head a crown of golden laurels as foretold by Jacob. Odi by now had taken his daughters into his arms and was besotted by the two sets of beautiful blue eyes looking up at him. He couldn't take his eyes from Panya until the Elfena again asked him to leave.

He left the cave and watched Baldor and Thanases raise their staffs to prepare for the arrival of the Light. An Elfena joined them and removed their helmets for them to be replaced with crowns of laurels matching Panya's. He then met Irina for the first time but when he saw Viktor he gasped, he suddenly had a vision showing him the brightest of light, it then showed one of his babies and he wondered? At the same time he was struggling with his daughters prompting Irina to come to his rescue; she took one of the babies allowing him to raise the remaining baby up to rest her head upon his shoulder. He was taken aback when the baby moved her lips and nuzzled his neck. He looked at Irina and she immediately knew to place the other baby in his free arm and when he raised her to rest on his shoulder, he just melted. Like Magni, he was a warrior, and never expected to be besotted by the sweet breath of babies softly breathing against his neck.

He watched Panya arrive and was awestruck; he had never seen her look so radiant. He watched her take her place between the boys and then pound their staffs against the ice. She called on the light and when it arrived, it entered the staffs and then exited with such force that it shot out in all directions to begin its long journey over all the northern lands. It travelled through Russia, Ukraine and the Baltic states; it moved south through Poland, Hungary, Romania, into Georgia then Armenia. It arrived in Turkey before making its way throughout the Middle East and then it joined Jacob at the Parthenon.

In all these lands thousands of carriers began to change. They left their places of employment and some left their homes, soldiers even dropped their weapons and left their bases. They all drifted into a kind of trance then raised their arms and waited for the appearance of a magical sword. When the sword arrived it was glowing with a blue-white light. They then began their walk to the nearest volcano.

Panya's work was now done and all she wanted was Odi and her babies. When she joined him she said, "Seeing you has made all what has happened during our journey fade out of memory." She reached in and said while taking one of the babies, "Before we leave I think we should name them? Have you chosen any names?"

"You mean you'd trust me with names?" he said looking concerned.

"Of course I'd trust you," she said with a devious smile. "I'd then make sure your choice matches mine." They laughed.

"Today is the last day of this age of man," said Odi while leaning in to kiss his daughters. "The survivors will need the power of the celestial beings to secure the next age and when they hear of you, my daughters, they must know that you are of Asgard and their friend." He placed his hand on one baby and closed his eyes, "I see you, my beauty, as a bearer of the hammer; it will answer to you and be your guide. You are a granddaughter of the God of Thunder so I name you, Thora, Goddess of War and bringer of the Storms. You will be a protector of survivors, and defender of Asgard."

Panya then placed her hand on the second baby and she too closed her eyes, "Like your sister you are a Goddess of the Light and you too will be of Asgard. The sun will always be your ally; you will be the bearer of gifts and the carrier of all legend. I name you Sunniva, the gift of the sun, and you will bestow your warmth on all of mankind. You, my beloved daughter, are our Sun Goddess."

Odi said while nodding his approval, "That turned out to be a lot easier than I thought."

He then called on two Asgard chariots to take Panya, Baldor and Thanases as well as Viktor, Irina and his daughters back to Olympus. On the way his mind was racing, he was gently cuddling his daughters and couldn't wait to present them to his parents.

On arrival in Olympus they were met by Maria and Thor who immediately doted on their new granddaughters, but the excitement was not to last long. Thor backed away and took Baldor and Thanases aside, "Your part in this story isn't over. You must join Jacob at the Parthenon. The great battle approaches and your swords will be needed to guide the forces of the north." He turned to Thanases, "Irina and Viktor will be safe in Olympus. They'll have the full protection of the gods."

Thanases took his family out into the meadows to spend a few more moments with them, but their time together didn't last long. Irina whispered in his ear, "In the few moments I've spent in this wondrous place I've gained the power of prophecy. I see a daughter in our future so I'm not afraid. Go now and make Asgard proud, be the warrior god you were called to be and lead the carriers of the north to victory. You are a god of the north and the north will follow you."

Odi, Thanases and Baldor then bade their farewells and using Odi's powers they arrived near Jacob who said as he embraced them, "You are most welcome, I can't wait to hear your stories."

Thanases and Baldor backed away; clenched their right fists across their hearts. They knelt and bowed before Jacob. The TV cameras picked up this moving event and broadcast it worldwide. Jacob said to Odi, "It's time to travel south. Think about the land of the thousand hills. Oba is awake, you know what to do."

Chapter 20

Odi blinked and arrived near where Oba and the boys had entered their long sleep. He saw the Light and immediately made his way to a hill where it was shining at its brightest. On his way he absorbed the sights and sounds of the rain forest, allowing him to pick up every movement. He quickly identified the sound of the trees creaking while being bent forward by the mass movements of the herds. When he reached a clearing he witnessed a number of magnificent Tuskers slowing making their way towards the Light. He became distressed when he realised he was watching the last of their kind, once there were thousands and now there were only twenty five left, survivors of a species almost poached into oblivion. These twenty five were being escorted by the remaining great elephant herds.

On reaching the hills he noticed he was being escorted by troops of great apes who had travelled from the misty mountains of Rwanda. The king of the silverbacks, Khalfani, made himself known and walked with him. Odi was slightly concerned and said while walking close to a cluster of volcanic vents, "We see Lucifer unleash his legions through the volcanoes. Have you noticed how they have changed?"

"Yes we have." nodded Khalfani in agreement. "The mists of these high mountains protected us since the beginning of time, but no more, man has broken through our defences and decimated our kin. The volcanoes grow more silent and as they quieten, the mists leave, betraying us to the poachers. I fear our time is coming to an end." He lowered his head in despair.

"Ask the Gods," he continued, "Ask them to look on us with compassion for we have guarded the entrance to the elf lands since the messengers fell into sleep. Under our watch and at a great cost to us, their safety has never been compromised."

Odi placed his hand on Kalfani's head and showed him the future, he showed him more tragedies, but then he showed him five goddesses ushering in the next age of man, and gorillas were everywhere. When finished he said, "The End Times battle is close and when it's over the Astral gods will be your friend. Did you see how Pegasus has amassed the Mer-armies and the centaurs; they will be the guardians of the animal kingdom. The wizards and the elves will also be your allies."

They continued their journey and soon reached a protruding ledge set high on one of the most remote hills which were bereft of trees and covered by lush ferns and grasses. Odi couldn't help looking back to watch the arrival of the Tuskers and their escorting herds. When he saw the troops of gorillas he was shocked, "Khalfani," he asked, "Is this all that's left of your kin? There are so few!" Kalfani just nodded.

He then turned to face the entrance to the elf lands and watched the rocks crack and fall away as it widened. He entered the cave and was greeted by Kalen who said, "Oba is awake but the boys still sleep. We are preparing her but she will not leave until she's sure her baby is safe."

"More babies," laughed Odi, throwing his eyes to the heavens. "I come to bring the messengers home only to find I have many more than were sent away."

"It seems," said kalen, shaking his head. "It seems that even for gods, nature always finds a way. Be warned that there are more surprises, some in the east and others in the west,"

Odi stood back as Oba came into view, she was carrying her son and she looked radiant. She was dressed in the royal blue robes of the Orisha, colours preferred by Yoruba Goddesses, she was also wearing a Gele Head-dress that really enhanced her beauty. He stepped forward and greeted her.

"So handsome," said Odi while admiring her baby. "Looks like Jomo, what's his name?"

"We named him Zane," she said while placing him in Odi's arms,

"Zane - One of noble birth and well born," he said while turning back to Oba, "I see him as an emperor and great things await him."

Just then Oba's face lit up causing Odi to turn around to see Jahiri exiting the cave with a beautiful woman and a child. There was great excitement but also a sense of urgency. Jahiri introduced Jamilah as his partner and the mother of his daughter, Sagal. Odi was delighted for them and announced that he too was a father. It was around this time when Zane began to cry causing Jomo to suddenly wake and run out to comfort his son. While running he tripped and fell forward straight into Odi's arms,

"Jomo, buddy," laughed Odi. "I never thought you felt this way about me,"

"Be careful what you wish for," replied Jomo. "I've been asleep for hundreds of years and have needs. What's that old saying - any port in a storm?" All laughed.

Kalen interrupted, "The Light is impatient. You must get ready." They immediately left to prepare themselves.

When they returned Odi was taken aback. They appeared not of Olympus but as African gods and presented as two most powerful warriors, not unlike the God Shango. They wore calfskin skirts and were gifted with many feathers from the birds of the rift valley. The feathers formed crowns upon their heads and adorned their knees and arms. Their satchels never left their sides and while exiting the cave they extracted their staffs and moved towards the rim of the ledge where they waited for Oba to join them. When she did, she leaned in and kissed Jomo before placing her hands on both staffs. With a firm grip she then pounded them off the ledge and called on the Light, and when it arrived it entered the staffs before shooting out at a speed that was breathtaking. It was then when the tuskers raised their trunks and trumpeted to the whole world that the Light had arrived and was now released to awaken the carriers.

It made its way to the far south where it lit up Table Mountain then travelled back and forth across all of Africa. It penetrated deep into the Great Rift Valley before moving across the Serengeti. It reached Somalia then found its way into the Sahara desert. It turned back to illuminate the Atlas Mountains before travelling up towards Egypt. It rested for a short while and then made its way to Sinai where it stopped in reverence above the most holy of sanctums once guarded by the wizard Mygon, before heading to Israel and crossing the Mediterranean to reach Jacob.

All across Africa, descendants of the carriers began to awaken. They went into a trance and left their offices, homes and farms before moving towards the centre of the roads where, in unison, they raised their right arms and waited. Within moments the blue-white fluorescent light appeared and a magical sword formed in their hands. The armies of the south were now ready and they began to instinctively move towards the volcanoes.

Odi knew what he had to do. He again called on two Asgard chariots and prepared for the journey to Olympus where, on arrival, they were greeted by Maria and Panya. There were now four babies and one toddler in

Olympus and this was unheard of. Panya ran to embrace Oba and couldn't believe she and Jomo had got together. She then ran to Jahiri and hugged him to the point of almost squeezing the life from him. What was strange was the four babies began to change and almost within minutes, they too were toddlers.

Thor had to break up this happy reunion; he sensed it was now urgent for the boys to join Jacob at the Parthenon and insisted they leave immediately. He called Jomo and Jahiri aside and assured them that their families were safe in Olympus."

Odi placed his hands on their shoulders, blinked and then all three materialised alongside Jacob. The whole world was still watching and were mesmerised when the new arrivals clenched their fists, and crossed their hearts before going on one knee and bowing. There were now six immortals on view.

Jacob turned to Odi and said, "The east is calling, Mount Kailash is waiting, go, Lord Shiva calls." Odi immediately left; he was chuffed that he was truly mastering long distant space and time travel. Meanwhile, Jomo and Jahiri were in the midst of a reunion with Thanases and Baldor.

Jacob backed away; he sensed the impending arrival of two chariots and knew it could only be his brothers, Magni and Modi. His heart lifted when he saw them land and he ran to embrace them but before he reached them, they clenched their fists and bowed. There were now seven immortals gathered at the Parthenon and all watching were beginning to feel hope grow.

Chapter 21

In the meantime Odi had arrived on Mount Kailash and was greeted by Lord Shiva who said, "You're just in time. The Light arrived a few moments ago and the glaciers are melting. See how the doors are now on view." Both looked then Shiva continued," I wish to travel to Olympus with the messengers. Can this be arranged?"

Odi didn't seem surprised, "I've been to both the north and the south and in each case I've brought back more than expected, new immortals and their children, there will be no problem bringing you............," he was interrupted by Shiva raising his hand to his ear.

"Listen," said Shiva. "The doors open. My heart bursts with excitement; it's been too long since last I saw Manasa and my grandson."

"Girish and Manasa?" remarked Odi. "I believe they're certainly a match made in Heaven. The gods knew all those years ago, the night their Light lit up the skies and raced across the heavens. It announced the conception of a new god and showed how they were meant to be together. We worried you mightn't be happy about the baby?"

"How could the gods think like that?" responded Shiva. "My grandsons name is Hemish and he was born just before they arrived into my domain. When I took him into my arms I just melted. I'm the happiest god in the universe?" He then sniggered, "I think Girish was terrified, but how could I harm him? He's the father of my grandson and the most important thing is; I know he absolutely loves Manasa."

They walked into the cave and watched the Ice elves begin the preparations for the Light to be answered. Hemish was first to awaken and Shiva immediately took him into his arms. Mulan and Manasa then awoke and were taken aside by the elves. A few moments later Garuda and Girish stirred. Girish leapt from his throne and ran to check on Hemish while Garuda immediately sought out Mulan.

The elves had difficulty preparing the boys because they were so distracted but they managed, and when they were finished the boys appeared not as Olympus warriors but imperial gods of the east. The colours on their Sherwani and the array of gems they were wearing made them look spectacular but nothing prepared those watching for the appearance of Mulan and Manasa. When they arrived, they were emblazoned in the most amazing gem encrusted gowns. Mulan wore the silk gown presented to her by the Emperor of the Fire Islands, she also wore the jewellery fashioned for her by the tribes from the Americas and she wore a crown gifted to her by lord Shiva. Manasa was equally as beautiful.

It was now time to answer the call. Garuda and Girish were first to exit the cave and they made their way to the edge of the ledge where, while waiting, they gazed in awe over the great plateaus of India. The pilgrims who gathered at the foot of this most holy of Hindu mountains watched Mulan join them and place her hands on their staffs before raising them to release the Light. When released it circled the mountain before travelling towards Iran. It then went out to sea to arrive in Australia before moving to South America. It then travelled through central and north America before making its way across the ocean to Japan and then China. It made its way through Vietnam and Cambodia before heading to Burma and then crossing back into India. After India it continued its journey west, to join up with Jacob and like before, as it travelled, the descendants of the carriers stopped what they were doing, went into a trancelike state and waited for their magical sword to appear. When it did they made their way towards the nearest volcanoes. Only when the Light faded and the carriers began their journeys did Odi call for two Asgard chariots.

On arrival in Olympus a great fuss was made of Mulan and the boys and a special welcome was prepared for the arrival of Lord Shiva and Manasa, who was cradling a sleeping Hemish. This time Zeus was present just to ensure all went smooth. As soon as Hemish woke he began to change into a two year old and like all strong toddlers, he wriggled his way out of his mother's arms to run around the temple with all the other toddlers.

Thor again had to be the bearer of bad news. He called Garuda and Girish aside and said, "Your part in this story is not over, there's more to be done. You must leave with Odi and join Jacob at the Parthenon, he's waiting. Don't worry about your families; they'll be safe in Olympus." Odi linked to them, blinked and all three materialised before the Parthenon, and like those who arrived earlier, they bowed to Jacob.

All around the world people were beginning to cheer while watching ten immortals gather at the Parthenon and wondered if more were to come. Jacob nodded to Odi and was greeted with a huge smile, "I know, I know, you want me to go again. This is the one journey I've been wishing for; I can't wait to meet my niece and nephews. Be back soon."

Jacob said, "Hurry he's getting close, I can feel his menace, he's leading the charge, but it's not to this place and this worries me."

Chapter 22

Odi blinked and soon arrived at the glen of the two lakes where he was confronted by a pack of wolfhounds that, alongside the spirits of the Great Elks, were guarding the entrance to the cave.

"The time is close and the signs are everywhere," said a voice that came from behind, it was the spirit of a Golden Stag. "The Light shines brightly above our heads and has attracted our foe, be aware of serpent sightings on the western edges of these lands. The elves are active and the Little People grow nervous. I fear the battle is but hours away and hope all is ready."

"The Light sure does shine brightly above this holy place," replied Odi while bowing. "You've done well, but now it's time for them to awaken. I've been sent to escort the Queen of Queens to Olympus. My chariots will arrive as soon as she awakens, see how the Light is impatient and is calling; see how it glows?" He became unnerved when he noticed a figure standing near the round tower and asked, "The one who stares, who is he? Is this a safe place?"

"You are looking upon the spirit of the hermit monk," said the stag. "Kevin is his name; he is the one who placed Danu's wolfhounds to stand guard over this sanctum and it is they alone who have ensured the safety of the goddesses who rest here."

"There's more than one goddess?" asked a confused Odi.

"Yes, there are two. The Lady Danu, Goddess of the Celtic peoples, she too rests here. Once, she asked a warrior to seek the Fair Land and he did. He saved her from the pain of Hell and, in time, he sought the Fair Land and found her. The story of their love is now written and it will be among the greatest stories ever told, stories of a great love between a Goddess of the Light and the son of a fisherman who became one of the greatest Warrior Gods of Olympus."

Odi was intrigued and wanted to know more but the cave doors opened and the elves arrived carrying three toddlers. Prince Demetrius, on seeing Odi got very excited and began calling, "Pappa, Pappa, Pappa." When he got closer he was confused "You're not pappa!" and began to cry. Odi took him into his arms,

"Hey, little man. Your pappa is my brother and he sent me to bring you home."

It was then when the wall at the back of the cave collapsed to reveal an even deeper cavern where four thrones came into view, and when the dust settled, images of two goddesses guarded by two warriors appeared. Within seconds all four stone images came back to life.

They were assisted by the elves and made ready to answer the call but Eala was having none of it, she had caught a glimpse of her children and ran to reunite with them. Kalen had to intervene, "The Light is getting impatient and you must prepare to answer. Your children are safe with Lord Odi." She reluctantly returned to the cave and was soon ready.

Faer and Fafner were first to exit and when they came into view it was an impressive sight. They were wearing the imperial robes, armour and helmet of the Olympus realm, and when the sunrays bounced off their breastplates beams of light were sent in all directions. When Danu exited, the wolfhounds, the elks and even Kevin, all bowed to their goddess. She effortlessly sauntered over to where Odi, his niece and nephews were standing and together they all waited for Eala to arrive.

When she arrived she was at her most stunning and all present knew she was not only a Goddess of the Light but a most powerful Earth Mother. The light that shone from her was one that was so bright it surely was meant to wrap itself around the soul of the universe. From her shoulders draped an ankle-length, dreamy cream coloured gown made from gold embroidered, silk-like material. Her hair cascaded to rest below her shoulders and was embedded with a scattering of the daintiest of white flowers. "Wow, what an entrance," Odi thought to himself.

She joined the boys and together they pounded the staffs off the ground releasing the light and sending it out all across the west where it spread out over the Fair Lands, into Scotland, England and then Wales. It departed, and travelled to Portugal and Spain, crossed the mountains into France, Belgium, Holland and then Germany. It never stopped until after it crossed the Alps into Italy before making its way to Greece where it joined up with Jacob.

As happened elsewhere, the Light called on the carriers to answer, and they did. They were the descendants of the Celts, Saxons, Franks and the Huns, and like the other carriers they left their homes and workplaces to raise their hands and wait for their magical swords to materialise. Odi then summoned Asgard chariots.

Meanwhile back on the Parthenon, Jacob expressed his concerns about the lack of response from beneath the seas or from the Astrals; that was until Poseidon arrived and he was in his colossus form. "The light has reached the depths of the oceans," he announced. "Those who sleep have awoken. The creatures of the deep are ready and waiting for your call. They will assist the Mer-armies who are now positioned in all seas and oceans. They await your command, my Lord." Poseidon then bowed and left as quickly as he had arrived.

In Olympus, there was great excitement especially for Maria and Thor, they were meeting Jacob's children for the first time and found it very emotional. Zeus, on the other hand, was finding it difficult. There were now nine children in the temple, several of whom had taken a shine to him and never left him alone.

For Eala, being back in Olympus didn't feel right, there was no Jacob and she wasn't happy. She left the temple and went to sit alone in the gardens but was soon disturbed, Zeus arrived with nine children in tow and he seemed to be having the time of his life. He noticed Eala was distracted and joined her, "If I were you I would talk to a Time Lord."

Eala knew exactly what he meant and ran to find Odi, she convinced him to take her to Jacob and he obliged. He gripped her arm, blinked and materialised behind Jacob who was taken aback when he felt two hands wrap around him. When her soft breath drifted across his neck, his eyes involuntarily closed and he gasped, "This can't be real?"

"It's as real as it gets," she whispered.

He spun around so fast he nearly knocked her to the ground and when he pulled her closer all watching saw how much they were in love.

Jacob secured his staff and raised both hands to hold her head then kissed her so passionately some TV stations wondered should they censor the image. He suddenly stopped and asked, "The children, where are they? Please tell me they're safe."

"They're safe in Olympus," said Odi with a snigger. "Poor Zeus is babysitting. Let him look after them. It's the least he can do."

"I don't think so," said Eala shaking her head.

She leaned in and kissed Jacob again, "I'm happy now," she said. "I best go back and rescue Zeus. Hemish and Victor are following him like little lapdogs and I fear they will be the death of him."

Within moments Odi brought Eala back to the temple and collected Fafner and Faer. He brought them to join Jacob, and just like all other guardians, they clenched their fists across their hearts and knelt before him.

The whole world was still watching; there were now twelve immortals standing before the Parthenon and they wondered how many more were coming. T.V. crews continuously panning across the gods, especially the Scandinavian stations, they never took their cameras from Magni or Modi. They recognised them as gods from Norse mythology.

Jacob's anxiety was being picked up and broadcast all around the world and he was heard to say, "Odi, six lights have returned yet the Astrals haven't answered. I don't understand, they should have been the first and this worries me! Hell is marching, I hear the pounding. Why can't you hear them?"

"Brother!" replied Odi. "I hear nothing."

"Odi! Being a dragon, no sound can escape me," said Fafner. "I too can hear the footsteps and there are many. I feel the forces of Hell walking beneath our feet and sense time is up."

People listening to Fafner began to panic. Churches, Mosques and temples, in fact, all places of worship began to fill.

Chapter 23

The words were no sooner out of Fafner's mouth when the brightest of light shot across Athens and it was announcing the arrival of the Astrals. Merlin, Apollonius and Mygon had arrived followed by all nine members of the elf council, led by Kalen. But there was one surprise, especially for Thanases and Baldor. It was the arrival of a Goddess of the Light and it was Mia. Thanases joined her looking very surprised,

"Mia?" He repeated, "Mia, I don't understand?"

Baldor was equally surprised, "We knew you were special and thought you were an oracle. Panya couldn't see your future. She said you were shielded, but this?"

"When you left," said Mia reaching across to hug them. "In the mid-lands you had passed the message to many and I became an oracle to all of them. I never aged and after many hundreds of years the Ancient One came to me with a gift of the Light. I'm to join the goddesses near the End Times and assist in the defence of that Light, there will be six of us and then there will be seven, it will be the last battle."

"You're most welcome," said Jacob after introducing himself. "This is no place for a Goddess of the Light. I'll arrange for you to be brought to Olympus where you'll be safe."

Mia had a special hug for a startled Fafner who had actually never met her, "I saw you fall to the savagery of Morgana and witnessed her venom towards Merlin. It was when I became an oracle and was given an extra power, one that allowed me look back in time. I could do nothing. I watched the Dragon Lords come to your rescue before bringing you to Rome. One of those Lords shone brighter than all the rest and he eventually came upon me. We became one, we are as one,"

Fafner was still confused but eventually worked it out, "Every day I sent out patrols, Derwyn would have continued that policy, our invisibility was always our ally so we were never detected," He paused for a moment, "As they say in these times, the penny has now dropped. There was one dragon who always volunteered, in the morning he was first to leave and always last back in the evening, he's my greatest ally. Andras, am I right?"

Mia lit up just on hearing his name and her face showed her love for him, "Now I can see why he always said you were the wisest dragon of them all."

Jacob interrupted and asked Merlin to use his powers to take the Astrals to Olympus. He was getting alarmed, time was getting short and cracks are beginning to open."

Merlin and the Astrals left to arrive at the temple where Zeus was waiting to welcome them. On seeing Mia, Panya shrieked and ran to hug her. She didn't understand but was happy that they were now six Goddesses of the Light, and together would now be a force to be reckoned with.

It was then when a major tremor shot through the temple, it also rocked the Parthenon. All over the world birds took to the sky in panic and dogs barked in fear. Across the hills, horses, cows and sheep stampeded, then the quietness came and Jacob turned to the immortals and said,

"And so it begins"

Chapter 24

Earlier that day Lucifer travelled through Hell to ensure all was in place by looking out across the vast caverns to be completely satisfied his legions were ready and prepared. He checked the serpent pits and was happy the tormentors were ushering more and more lost and bitter souls into the chambers, to be possessed by the creatures of Hell. Occasionally a lost soul would catch his attention as worthy of being placed among the Dark Angels who occupied the next level; he'd make arrangements for them to be moved. They were the ones who were the mass murderers and bringers of evil during their time on earth. They were to become his most trusted servants; the ones he knew nothing would or could distract them from assisting his mission to claim dominion over all of mankind. He walked among them savouring their absolute loyalty.

He reached the third level and again was satisfied that his most evil spirits, the wraiths of hell, the Ogres, Spectres and Spooks were well prepared for an attack of evil so violent they'd ensure no soul would survive.

As he continued his walk he came upon the level that contained his most prized flying demons, part wraith and part hound. These were an improvement on the ones that attacked Oba, Jomo and Jahiri on Mount Sinai all those years ago. He then walked through the caverns holding the workshops that manufactured the weapons and armour he needed for a full and ruthless onslaught against the gods.

Occasionally an awkward smile crossed his face, showing he was satisfied his legions were ready and then it showed something was bothering him. He couldn't quite put his finger on it so he chose to re-examine everything that had happened since he expelled Hades from the Underworld. He sat on his throne, alone and troubled, while thinking of his expulsion from Heaven and how Michael and the Archangels placed him in the marble cocoon. When the image of his loyal servants, who risked everything to release him, came to him, he stood from his throne and walked to the edge of the platform. He satisfied himself yet again of their loyalty while watching them terrorise and brutalise the latest arrivals into Hell.

He remembered the Ancient One and his disdain for the seven deadly sins, envy, gluttony, greed, lust, pride, sloth, and wrath. He thought of how, over the mists of time, it was arranged for those sins to be forgotten by man. His anger then grew when he thought of them being re-listed by Pope Gregory 1st in the sixth century and then reminded himself of how he was the carrier of those same sins, prompting him to release them as his first line of attack. He returned to his throne and although sensing the impatience of his armies he decided to err on the side of caution, he closed his eyes and called from deep within his self the demons representing each of the deadly sins.

The first to arrive and was Asmodeus who appeared through a black mist that fell from Lucifer's mouth, "Master," he said, "I am lust, set me free and watch as they fill their hearts with carnal desire, I will bring down the armies of the Light." He moved aside and sat on a throne to the left.

Next to arrive was Satan who said, "Master, I am wrath, set me free and I will bring forth my covens as your allies and they will smite all enemies." He too moved aside and took a seat to the right.

After Satan, came Mammon, "Master, I am greed, at last you see my worth, watch as I lead them to acquire everything, let me free and Earth will be yours. The rich and powerful will kneel before you." Mammon then sat to the left.

He was followed by Leviathan who said, "Master, I am envy. Watch as I create discord. See me say one thing to the centaurs and the opposite to the elves, one thing to the dragons and another to the sea creatures. Watch as distrust grows and when they are divided by fear and envy, we will conquer." Leviathan moved aside and sat to the right.

Beelzebub was next to arrive, "Master, I am gluttony, let me free in the arid lands and walk where food is scarce. I will give them food and drink and they will feast for days, my deception will bring forth famine and draught so they will starve. They will then see me bring back the rains and then the harvest for them to again feast. They will then know that it is I who keeps them fed and they will desert the gods." He moved aside and sat to the left.

The last to arrive was Belphegor who announced, "Master, I am sloth. Allow me walk among man, watch me bring laziness and indifference. I am the one who creeps upon them, unknown and unseen. They will sleep when the need is greatest and will not answer the call." He moved aside and sat to the right.

Lucifer then stood, turned and said, "My brothers you are all most welcome, sit and listen to the pain travelling through my caverns. Watch as the lava glows and prepares for its release. I am Pride. Together our greatness will rule the world." He then took his seat and all seven looked out across the lava lakes and revelled in the suffering and howls of pain emanating from all around them but most of all they got solace from the terror that was their constant companion. They sat on the platform with the fires of hell lapping at their feet. They wore black capes with large stiff collars and presented as identical demon beings bearing two horns that rested proudly above their heads. The exception was Lucifer who maintained his chiselled good looks and showed no horns.

It was then when the horsemen were summoned, beings of great power. Each rode a different coloured horse and each bore the signs of the apocalypse. They were greeted as saviours of Hell and the bringers of terror into the minds of mankind. The white horse was the most fearsome and it was riderless, saddled and prepared. He was the mount of Lucifer and would be the one to announce the release of the legions of Hell.

Each horse was the bearer of a great calamity. The black horse bore the rider who was known as Famine, the Red horse carried the rider known as War and the pale horse the rider known as Death. They all moved into the background and waited for their master to release them on mankind.

Lucifer got more confident, but he still had those niggling doubts and hated the fact he couldn't see Olympus or the plans they had in place. He didn't really trust his generals especially the way they assumed mankind was going to so easily fall to the power of Hell. He called for another council and presided over generals who seemed to believe they were invincible and this worried him. His twelve generals presented as eight foot tall dark angels similar to the one who commanded the attack on Jacob and Odi during the battle of Dublin. He and his six brothers sat and listened intently to what they had to say.

The first general to speak was one of the four who risked everything to infiltrate the Underworld, successfully securing the freedom of Lucifer. He was trusted but his arrogance didn't go unnoticed. "My lord," he said. "Our spies tell us that the armies of the west, under the command of a NATO supreme general have been called up but they're in disarray, they are unsure of what they are to fight. We know that a council of countries in the Americas was also called and all agreed to fall under the command of a three star general based in North America, again they have no idea who their enemy is. In China and the Pacific ring there is much confusion and general distrust of each other. The use of atomic weapons is now a strong possibility. The countries of Islam have all united in fear of an unknown force. They have been training together and are ready for any attack."

Lucifer stepped from his throne and with a smirk said, "The fools, do they not know their weapons are useless against the power of the Underworld. Let them make a mistake and fight each other; their deaths will be welcome as many souls will fall into my clutches allowing me to take earth faster. Tell me of the Gods?"

A second general stepped forward, "Master," he said. "Our spies tell us there are twelve immortals standing upon the Acropolis in Athens; they are on full view and give hope to all watching."

"Strange that they have chosen that place," said Lucifer while sitting back on his throne. "I once observed a battle between a Titan and the Boy King, and it was at that very spot. Have I been deceived? Tell me more."

The general continued, "Our spies have observed a boy wearing the crown of Cronus. There's a second boy, almost identical and possibly his twin, he is the Asgard boy King and he wears the markings of Asgard. They stand as two powerful gods and have the ability to move through space and time. Dragon Lords have also been observed but were earlier escorted away by chariots of Asgard. Two of the twelve are Gods of Asgard and it is said that one of them is Magni, a powerful warrior and he was seen to bow to the Boy King."

Lucifer wasn't fazed, "Magni, I fought him once. Although powerful, it'll be my pleasure to send him out of all memory. Tell me more"

A third general stepped forward, "My lord, eight guardians are present at the Parthenon. It's said they have been trained by Ares and Athena, training that took place over two thousand years ago. The one called Thanases is the one who killed our spy. It's rumoured that our spy was about to reveal the existence of two Goddesses of the light who are as yet unborn, they are daughters of the Asgard boy King. We were never able to confirm the rumour but it was noticed that Asgard patrolled the skies above where we suspected the messenger carrying the babies walked."

"How long have your spies been aware of this?" enquired Lucifer.

"Sixteen hundred years," replied the now panicked general.

Lucifer exploded and sent out a shaft of fire that propelled the general into the far reaches of hell, and unluckily for him he landed in the pit housing the hounds. It was from there his screams of terror echoed throughout Hell as he was torn asunder.

"Is there more to tell me?" asked Lucifer as he turned to the remaining generals. "Is there anything else you neglected to report?"

The most senior general cautiously stepped forward, "My lord, the wizards and the elves are against us; they are secretly working with the Boy King,"

"I fear not the Astrals," said Lucifer clenching his fists before responding. "They'll be consumed as soon as I take Earth. I'll force them to kneel before me, especially Kalen and Merlin. I will make them watch the destruction of their realms before smiting them, tell me more,"

"Our spies heard the Boy Kings speak of The Darkness as a bigger threat than the forces of Hell. It's said they fear The Darkness more than they fear you."

Lucifer didn't like what he heard and again exploded. He grabbed the general by the throat forcing him to his knees.

"Only for I need you as my supreme commander," he said while tightening his grip. "I'd send you to the hounds. Let me make myself clear, it's me whom The Darkness is in league with, not the other way around. Do you understand?" The general just nodded.

"Go now," said Lucifer after calming. "You eleven secure more souls, we attack soon." He then returned to sit upon his throne; satisfied with the knowledge he was strong enough to secure Earth as his new domain. He didn't fear the gods believing they were ill prepared for what was coming. He thought for a few more moments and then, with his brother's agreement he chose to open a portal to the Parthenon and show Jacob what he was up against.

When opened it was one of the largest portals ever seen. It opened behind Jacob and it took a few moments for him to realise Lucifer was now present. Magni was first to react, followed by Modi. They both lunged forward with their swords drawn only to be stopped by an invisible shield. Through the portal, viewers not only saw the seven thrones and their occupants, they also saw the orange glow, and they imagined the searing heat of Hells fires. They heard the tormented screams of pain and despair. The four horses were on view and those watching wondered if they were about to announce the Apocalypse. Jacob's warning was coming to pass.

Jacob approached the portal, ignoring the fires and screams of terror. He solely focused on the seven thrones, especially the one where Lucifer was sitting. Just as he was about to speak one of Lucifer's brothers, Asmodeus, leapt from his throne and rushed to the rim of the portal.

"You," he said while staring at Fafner. "You, Dragon Lord, are the one I will take greatest pleasure in skewering. I took the mother of your children, that time in Spain. I made your son suffer in London. Now watch me take your daughters. Think of the pleasure I'll get using them as my playthings. You will always be looking over your shoulder and I will never allow you rest. I will make you pay for the death of my beloved Morgana."

Fafner swiftly drew his sword and raced towards the portal. His sword penetrated the shield and plunged into Asmodeus's heart but he was deceived, what was before him was a sniggering hologram. Fafner looked towards Lucifer and his brothers and felt sick. They knew they had him worried and were enjoying his pain.

"Fafner my friend," said Jacob after entering his head. "Odi will leave for the dragon realm and will bring your family to Olympus. They'll be safe under the protection of Zeus, trust me."

Odi was in Jacobs head and understood what he had to do. He immediately disappeared and arrived near one of the hidden gateways into the dragon realm. On reaching the entrance he was surprised to be greeted by Andras who immediately took him to meet with King Derwyn.

"You're welcome, Odi of Asgard." said Derwyn. "Our oracles told us to expect a son of Thunder."

"I am indeed, Odi, son of Thunder, grandson of Odin and Zeus. I've been sent by my brother to take your sisters, and your family, to Olympus. It's for their safety, and they must leave immediately."

"We are well protected in this realm," said Derwyn. "My father built our defences thousands of years ago and they've never been breached. He was trained by the gods so why now are we threatened?"

"Long before you were born your father heard a calling. He answered and flew into the west, there he met with Merlin. Within minutes they were attacked by a most powerful sorceress, Morgana was her name. Unknown to the gods, she was consort to a brother of Lucifer. Your father fought just as he was trained, but because he wouldn't succumb to her relentless sorcery, she used her magic and almost sent him into sleep. He managed to trap her by using his last line of defence, his golden dagger. Through her foot he pinned her to a tree stump giving time for the dragon guardians to arrive and smite her," he walked over to join Andras then continued. "The dragon guardians were ruthless in their treatment of Morgana and now Hell seeks vengeance. Your father has been in the gaze of Hell since that faithful day. We believe all born of Fafner is in severe danger, we believe Lord Andras is also in danger. The attack on Isabella's home village in Spain was part of their plan, the murder of your mother was arranged in Hell, and Asmodeus, that very brother of Lucifer, was one of the Dark Angels who was present that day. He was also present when you and your brothers were attacked in London."

"Brother," said Afan. "You must accept the offer from Jacob. Isabella is heavily pregnant and you will be distracted. It's the End Times battle that's coming and we need your full and undivided attention as our supreme leader. Olympus is protected by the power of the gods; they will all be safe from the gaze of Hell."

Derwyn was still unsure, his anxiety showed while looking at Isabella and his daughter, he felt it was his duty to protect them but knew deep down they'd be safer in Olympus. Before making his decision he turned to Odi and asked, "How's my father?"

"Your father is fine," replied Odi. "He stands with Jacob at the Parthenon. Alongside Faer, he has been chosen to lead the armies of the west. I can take you to him but be aware, there's a standoff between him and Hell at this very moment." Derwyn accepted Odi's offer and within seconds they materialised alongside Fafner.

Just as Derwyn materialized, a black crystal tipped spear exiting the portal and was travelling towards his father. He reacted so fast he was able to raise his shield, divert the spear and grab its shaft.

"You may have used your evil magic to kill my mother," he yelled while firing the spear back at Asmodeus. "But today you will have to use more than that to get by me. You will not hurt my father."

Lucifer leapt to his feet as the spear reached Asmodeus and impaled him against the fire scorched wall of the throne room. All watching saw Asmodeus turn to a black mist and enter Lucifer's mouth, causing him to all to his knees in pain. That was when the gods realized he had a weak point. Lucifer was furious but before he moved to close the portal he moved closer to Jacob,

"In my dreams," he said. "It's your face I see, it never goes away. What is it about you?"

"It's written," said Jacob as a smile crossed his face, "how once, at the beginning of time, the Ancient One blew a speck of dust out into the universe. Remember my face, Hell lord, for I believe I'm that speck of dust, and I'm now the King of Kings. I'm warning you that when both of us finally fight it will be a battle where only one will still stand. Trust me! I will be the one to stand."

The portal then closed and Jacob went to his knees, he was drained. Lucifer was using Asmodeus as a distraction so he could attempt to enter Jacob's head. He failed; Jacob's defences were too strong.

"Brother," said Magni rushing to assist him back to his feet. "You are our King of Kings. Even a King of Kings must wait for his strength to return."

"He tried to enter my head and steal our plans," said Jacob while gripping Magni's arm. "The more he tried the more my power drained. He got nothing."

"He got nothing because I was there," said Odi. "I broke our agreement. When you weakened, I took over. I know that when I weaken you will come to my aid."

"This time I'm grateful you were there," replied Jacob.

In the meantime, Derwyn remained between his father and where the portal had appeared. He was ready for another attack and wouldn't let his guard down even when Magni, Modi and Odi joined him. He continued to look passed them fearing the portal would reopen.

"Lower your weapon, Dragon Lord," said Magni while reaching in to lower Derwyn's sword. "There's no presence of evil here. Lucifer didn't get what he wanted."

Fafner was still in shock, eyes widened and breathing erratic. He only recovered when he felt the warm embrace of his son. "I don't know what to say," he said. "Your speed was breathtaking. Our realm is certainly safe in your hands."

"I'm not so sure," replied Derwyn. "I did everything you asked of me yet this coming battle frightens me. Afan is a more worthy leader."

"Afan might be a more worthy leader," responded Fafner still trying to reassure his son. "But he hasn't got your wisdom or experience, so stop doubting yourself. You are well trained, just look at how today you saved my life. I'm so proud of you."

He then turned to Jacob, "My instincts tell me I should return to the dragon realm. I might be of more assistance when the three gates open and the full might of the dragon army is unleashed."

"No! My friend," said Jacob. "I need you to take command of the Asgard armies in the west. Derwyn is King of the dragons and should be the one to lead them. Remember, he has the support of his brothers."

Derwyn and Fafner were taken aback but accepted Jacob's decision. Odi then brought Derwyn back to the dragon realm and as soon as they arrived he produced his gjallarhorn and called for two Asgard chariots. When they arrived, he arranged for Derwyn's family and his sisters to be taken to Olympus.

On arrival they were made very welcome, especially Fafner's daughters Aneira and Glain, who had never met their father's friends. There was much surprise that the queen of the dragons had also arrived until they saw how heavily pregnant she was. Maria assisted by taking Isidra to join the other children who were having the time of their lives while being looked after by Zeus out in the gardens. Priceless is a term used many times in Olympus but the look on Zeus's face when another young girl arrived certainly warranted that term. Odi said his goodbyes and then rejoined Jacob at the Parthenon.

"It's time we took up our positions," said Jacob just as Odi returned.

Magni raised his gjallarhorn and summoned the assistance of the Asgard army and within second's twelve chariots, each drawn by two winged Camarque horses, appeared on the horizon and quickly made their way to the Parthenon. Each horse had a foot long horn built into their armoured headdress, not unlike the horn of a unicorn. They were well protected, wearing golden body armour covering most of their bodies.

Magni arranged for Baldor and Thanases to leave and take their positions at the head of the northern armies. He sent Jomo and Jahiri south to take up their positions at the head of the southern armies. He then sent Garuda and Girish East, one to lead the armies of the Near East and the other to lead the armies of the Far East. Faer then left to take control of the America's, while Fafner left to take control of the west.

Jacob watched them leave but never took his eyes from Fafner, when they were out of sight he turned to his brothers, "It's breaking my heart," he said. "Knowing I've just sent my friend Fafner to his death."

"Brother," said Modi while resting his hand on Jacob's shoulder. "Fafner's fate is sealed and no matter where you send him; Death will be lurking, ready and waiting. Let's try to be close by when it happens and assist in sending his spirit on its way. Elysium has his tomb carved and will bestow on him a great honour."

Jacob was about to answer when he backed away and moved his head from side to side. He was receiving messages from the Dragon realm informing him that serpents are active in Scotland and France. The message was also telling him that they are attacking carriers and sending their souls to the Underworld.

Magni said after receiving the same message, "It can only mean Lucifer has not filled the ranks of his armies. He's sending serpents to harvest more souls. We must send assassins."

"No!" disagreed Jacob. "We shouldn't waste our resources. The battle is imminent, he's ready. We should really leave now and hurry back with the full might of the Asgard army, it's becoming more urgent to have them in a holding position above the battle fields."

Chapter 25

The four brothers mounted the remaining chariots and began their slow assent into the sky. Jacob allowed the T.V stations follow their journey, including when they reached space. The passing space station transmitted images of their progress back to both NASA and Roscosmos, that was, until they reached the dark side of the moon. All transmissions then ceased. They soon passed Mars and then moved towards Jupiter, from where they could see in the far distance, the magnificent structures of a now materialised Asgard. They moved towards the outer rings of Saturn and from there they now had a full view of their home world.

Asgard looked magnificent with its numerous turrets, many steeples and magnificent columned civic buildings. The imperial palace stood out the most and was surrounded by a vast amount of flag bearing staffs and flaming lanterns. The nearer they got the clearer they saw that a guard of honour was in place and to their delight, up on the highest platform, just outside the city stood their father and grandfather.

For Jacob, the image of his father, standing with his cape fluttering wildly in the solar winds looked awesome and as he got closer he could see the faint rays of the now distant sun bouncing off his father's imperial crown and this filled him with pride. When he saw the hammer resting upon his shoulder he knew he was indeed one of the most powerful of all the gods, and this was an image forever to be imprinted on his mind.

On approaching the guard of honour, Jacob and Odi pulled back allowing Magni and Modi to be the first to pass, and as they passed they both clenched their right fists and placed their hand across their hearts before bowing to Odin.

Jacob and Odi did the same but were met with the sight of Odin and Thor returning the bow. Thousands upon thousands of Asgardians saw, for the first time, Jacob, King of Kings. They also knew that Odi was soon to be elevated to be their King of Kings and cheered while watching him pass. All four sons of Thunder continued until they were out of sight of Asgard before they took a holding position. There they waited until the stewards blew their trumpets, announcing to the cosmos that the armies of Asgard were now on the move. On hearing the trumpets the boys used firm reign flicks to begin the movement of just over a million Asgard warriors, three to a chariot. The army was split into four, each travelling across different levels of space, all on full view while passing the viewing platform. For Thor, watching his four sons take control of the Asgard armies was one of the proudest moments of his life.

After passing Asgard the four armies quickened their pace, endeavouring to reach earth as quickly as possible. Jacob's anxiety was again building; he was receiving visions showing minor yet violent serpent attacks. His three brothers were also receiving those same visions. Within three hours they reached the moon where their approach was filmed by the international space station. For the astronauts watching the approaching army was awe-inspiring yet terrifying, it was so vast. Images were then transmitted back to earth to be broadcast around the world giving hope to all those watching.

Initially on entering Earth's atmosphere the approaching Asgard army could only be viewed through telescopes or binoculars, but as they descended they soon became visible to the naked eye. On reaching Central

Europe the our armies split into four, Magni in command of those heading to the Far East, Modi led his warriors to Africa, Odi took control of all territories just south of the Arctic Circle up to the North Pole and Jacob led his army towards the west.

Before splitting, Jacob sent a number of chariots in all directions. They were the scouts tasked with awakening the long dead tribes in all territories. Each chariot carried a herald who blew a trumpet gifted by the Archangel Gabriel. They announced their arrival by blowing three loud elongated blasts.

In the north the heralds called out, "Warriors of the north, listen on to me. I call on the Norse Lords, the Huns and the Goths. Arise from your long slumber and leave your tombs. Find you place among the carriers of the Light. Rise now and answer the call of the gods."

In the south they called out, "Warriors of the south listen on to me. From beneath the sands and forests of Africa we call on the Yoruba, the Zulus and the kingdom of Kush. Arise from your long slumber and leave your tombs. Find your place among the carriers of the Light. Rise now and answer the call of the gods."

In the east they called out, "Warriors of the south, listen on to me. From this vast land we call on the Mongols, The Han and the Manchu. Arise from your long slumber and leave your tombs. Find your place among the carriers of the Light. Rise now and answer the call of the gods."

In the west they called out, "Warriors of the west, listen on to me. From these enchanted lands we call on the Celts, the Saxons and the Francs. Arise from your long slumber and leave your tombs. Find your place among the carriers of the Light. Rise now and answer the call of the gods."

In the America's they called out, "Warriors of the America's, listen on to me. From the mountains and forests, deserts and scrublands, prairies and

Ice-lands, we call on the First Nations. Arise from your long slumber and leave your tombs. Find your place among the carriers of the Light. Rise now and answer the call of the gods."

In Australia they called out, "Warriors of Terra Australis, listen on to me. From the beautiful lands of Uluru we call on the First Nations. Arise from your long slumber and leave your tombs. Find your place among the carriers of the Light. Rise now and answer the call of the gods."

The heralds returned to their positions in the ranks of the Asgard army and all around the world the long dead waited for Jacob to send out his Light.

❧❧

In the mean time Lucifer had recovered from the attack on Asmodeus. He called his five remaining brothers to rejoin him and soon they became one leaving him standing alone in the centre of the platform. He was aching to attack but decided on one last inspection of his realm. He walked to the edge of the platform revelling in the sound of terror as more souls were being corralled into the pits. He particularly loved the high-pitched screams that reached his ears knowing those screams were coming from the late arrivals, many who, before being captured, were destined to be part of Jacob's army. When their possession was complete the new invigorated snakes would make their way to the tunnels in preparation for the unleashing of Hell.

Lucifer rejoined the horsemen and mounted the white steed. They rode out through the bowels of Hell as the four Horsemen of the Apocalypse. They soon arrived at the level containing the Dark Angels and were pleased to see eleven generals stand fully armed and facing their armies. He knew these generals could be trusted and would be the ones to unflinchingly carry out his commands, including fighting to the death. He joined them and asked, "Impressive. How many stand before us?"

"There are twelve armies," said the supreme commander. "Each army consists of a million angels. Eleven generals hold our positions and await your command, my lord."

"Is there one who can take control of the twelfth army?" asked Lucifer.

"There is one who has suffered the most," replied the commander. "His screams have echoed around Hell since just after the fall of Paradise. He's strong and unbroken. They call him Cain and he's the first murderer."

"I remember him," nodded Lucifer knowingly. "I destroyed his parents and many of his siblings. It might be time to offer him a reward. Bring him to me,"

It took some time for Cain to be located but Lucifer didn't mind, he had a great respect for the first human soul to enter his domain. Cain finally arrived, naked, bloodied and bruised. He still stood proud and defiant, and Lucifer liked that.

"In your face I see Adam and Eve," remarked Lucifer reaching in to touch the mark of chaos on his left temple. "How easy was it for me to deceive them? An apple, imagine, just one piece of fruit." He stepped away then said, "You too fell to my ways and because you were my first, I considered you special. I never allowed the torturers, or my demons to apply the full force of Hell because I knew that one day I'd need you. You will lead my twelfth army and freedom will be your reward. Will you do this for me?" Cain remained quiet, trying not to show his excitement.

Lucifer produced a sword out of nothing and dipped it into a nearby lava flow. As the sword glowed he said, "Ferro afferam ex inferorum iras." (From this sword bring the wrath of hell)." He placed the sword in Cain's hand and using his magic he gave back to him his dignity by removing all lesions, bruises and encrusted bloodstains, but not the mark. He created clothing so black it allowed Cain blend into the soot covered walls. His armour was equally as black making him more sinister than the other generals.

When prepared, Cain climbed a nearby rocky outcrop to look out across the vastness of the twelfth army. He raised his sword and yelled so all could hear, "For the glory of Hell, the glory of Lucifer, we march towards the domes of fire."

The sight of so many Dark Angels, just one of twelve armies, stretching back as far as the eye could see was awe inspiring for Lucifer. He joined Cain on the outcrop and accepted the homage being paid to him.

"Those of your lineage," whispered Lucifer. "Those who bear your mark, see to it they're spared."

Lucifer remained on the outcrop to watch the twelve armies move towards their exit points. He then moved to the next level where the souls of his most monstrous minions dwelled. He moved among them.

"It pleases me to walk among my murderers, rapists, tyrants, despots and violent criminals," he said while demanding silence from them. "They call you Ghosts, Spectres, Spooks and they fear you the most. They hide from you as you play on their fears of the afterlife. To me, you are the Wraiths of Hell, the lovers of lies, the tormentors and tempters of man. Follow the curses and terrorise their souls. I'm now calling on you to leave this place and do what I ask of you. Be my Wraiths of Hell."

It was then when a dense black mist made its way towards the realm of man. It waited for nightfall before leaving Hell through the graveyards. It used shadows to conceal itself allowing it to reach every home, church, Mosque and Temple without being detected. It remained hidden waiting for the white horse to appear.

What the black mist didn't know was that the wizards and the oracles almost immediately became aware of them and started working on spells strong enough to contain their power. Merlin immediately informed Jacob and he was taken aback by this news. This form of attack was something he didn't anticipate, he expected something more direct. He knew from his time living among man that there was an in-built fear of ghosts, and this fear was capable of destabilising the people causing problems for the gods. He pleaded with Merlin to work as hard as he could to find a way to contain the Wraiths. He then used his magic to telepathically send a message to the soldiers of Asgard and all astral realms.

"Hell has moved the Wraiths among man," he said. "They hide in shadow and wait for the call. Close your minds to the spirit world and don't let them in. Don't be distracted by the black mist, it's very powerful."

In the meantime Lucifer had moved to his next level where he walked among the hound demons of Hell, his newest attack force. They were a favourite of his; he loved their half dog, half demon appearance. These particular ones could fly to great heights and at considerable speed and they knew no fear. They had the ability to tear their prey to pieces while flying across the sky. His only concern was that they were untested. He walked among them, patting as many as time allowed.

"My beauties," he said while encouraging them into frenzy. "Beware the Dragon Lord. He's blessed by the gods and I want him alive. He will suffer my vengeance and my vengeance alone. There is another, he travelled east. He is known as the Emperor of the Birds and commands great power. His piercing call will bring all birds into his presence. He too is blessed by the gods. Beware his screech." He then encouraged them to take their places beneath the dormant volcanoes and prepare for their entry into the realm of man.

Lucifer then made his way to his workshops to satisfy himself that the weapons his smiths were creating were so lethal no adversary could survive an impact. He assisted them by reviving an ancient poison designed to take down the gods.

He left the workshops full of confidence knowing everything was now in place. He returned to his platform and mounted the white stallion. Alongside the other three horsemen he looked out over his vast armies as they made their way towards the exits.

It was then when Jacob, his brothers and the eight guardians drifted into a deep trance. All twelve were watching the march of Hell, they were also aware that the four horsemen were preparing to leave but were being blocked by a dense bank of smoke. They remained to watch the smoke take the shape of a tall pillar bearing the face of terror. It was The Darkness.

"Have you come to witness the fall of mankind?" they heard Lucifer ask.

"You've gone against my wishes for the last time, Hell lord?" replied The Darkness. "Can you not feel how close I am? Why have you broken our agreement knowing it's I who makes the decisions? Remember this is my war, my revenge and you are but a distraction. Jacob's carriers are awake, created to defend the domain of man and with the help of the gods they stand a good chance of prevailing. You've forgotten that it was I who stood alone before the beginning of time, that only I heard the Ancient One say 'Let there be light'. That light vanquished my domain and I learned to hate. My hatred grew when you and the Archangels were created, I won't forget that. When this is over, beware my vengeance."

Lucifer was taken aback at been threatened. He remembered what was said about the gods fearing The Darkness more than they feared him and he was slightly rattled. He then looked out at his armies and said as his confidence again grew,

"The domain of Hell is mine and mine alone," Lucifer yelled back. "Leave and allow me continue with my plan. My forces are about to break through and the demise of earth will be swift. You failed me; you promised to be by my side long before now. We watched the distant suns fall but still you stayed away. My patience ran thin and I've chosen to make my move."

"Tell me, Hell lord, why has Cronus not taken Olympus?" asked a now frustrated Darkness. "You promised to have him deal with the gods, and you failed, I trusted you and you didn't deliver. I believed the decimation of the gods would include the Sun Gods but no, I've been thwarted everywhere I go especially as I near this accursed place you call your domain. Those Sun Gods are more resilient than expected. They are led by the one called Bel Marduk, a Sun God who also commands the thunder and lightning. He gets his power from a young and vibrant sun, making him a most powerful adversary. He is valiant, resourceful, vengeful and cunning. He fights with a strength that tells me he either fights out of hatred of me, or he fights to protect someone he loves more than life. He's delays me, harries me, repels me and defies me. He is the wiliest of them all, and if he succeeds you won't. I'll remind you again, the Darkness will rule supreme."

Jacob now understood the prophecies about the deception of Lucifer. It's now obvious The Darkness has no intention of allowing Hell to survive. It plans to rule supreme which means absolute darkness. He was now convinced as to who the true enemy is.

"You must be getting old and weak," sneered Lucifer on hearing Bel Marduk's name. "We consider him a weakling, easily possessed. We had him until rescued by a God of Asgard. It was in the Temple of Bel, near the city off Palmyra."

A heartbeat was heard; it got louder before beating faster. It became distracting.

"Calm down," said Jacob knowing it was Magni's heart that was loudly beating. "Breathe easy and be happy Bel Marduk fights for you."

"Whom do you speak of?" asked a confused Modi.

"Brother," interrupted Odi trying to deflect the questioning. "Jacob speaks of the heartbeat. Let us concentrate on The Darkness and the unleashing of Hell."

"You're not telling me everything," insisted a now irate Modi. "You're hiding something from me. Who is the heart beat?"

"Modi," said a now exasperated Jacob. "I spoke out of turn. You should know me by now, if something is none of my business, then it remains so."

"Magni," asked Modi who was now very agitated. "Why don't you speak? You're very quiet."

"Modi," said a now very annoyed Odi, "Drop it! The volcanoes are rumbling close to where Magni waits, his hands are full."

"The volcanoes are indeed rumbling and glowing brighter," said Magni. "They speak of war and tell me it's near, let us concentrate on battle and forget gossip."

They continued to listen and watch the happenings in Hell and were certain Lucifer was about to defy The Darkness and unleash his power. They then watched the pillar of smoke disintegrate and make its way out into the cosmos.

It was obvious to the gods that Lucifer was ready to attack. They watched the four horses leave the platform and race through the tunnels towards the highest level of Hell. They saw an exit but couldn't identify where it led to.

Before exiting he dismounted and walked to the edge of the ledge, giving him a view across all levels, one last look at the largest army o evil the universe had ever seen. It was then when he called for silence,

"Today is the day mankind will rue. Today is the last day of this age of man and for them there will be no more. I will hold dominion over Earth and make what is left of them pay for all that's been done to me. Prepare now and do your duty, bring terror throughout the realm of man. Move to the gates and wait for my sign." It was then when Jacob's heart pounded faster.

Lucifer then continued through the tunnels to exit in Jerusalem, the most monitored city on Earth. He and the other three riders burst through the revered Western Wall on to the courtyard at the foot of the Temple Mount where they appeared as four of the most terrifying images of Hells wrath.

Within seconds, the eyes of the world focused on the one who was riding the white horse. They watched him ride out to the centre of the courtyard where the horse reared so high that Lucifer looked as though he stood twelve feet above the ground. When he raised his sword the whole world then knew Hell had been unleashed.

In the meantime, Jacob sensed Lucifer had entered the realm of man but couldn't figure out where. He handed command of the western Asgard forces to Fafner then transported himself back to the Parthenon. On arrival he looked more determined and showed no fear. He was confident his plans were ready and the armies of the Light would prevail. He turned and faced the TV cameras, "Let the writings show the gods once again coming to the aid of man. We will prevail."

The TV stations transmitted everything Jacob said and maintained their coverage of him for as long as he was visible, that was until reports from Israel showed the four horsemen at the Western Wall. TV stations immediately split their screens, one side showing Lucifer and the other side showing Jacob.

People were shocked when they saw Lucifer, they were expecting a horned demon but instead saw a very handsome man. Reporters ran to Jacob seeking comments prompting him to blink and transport himself to Jerusalem where Lucifer had already dismounted and was on one knee with his hand resting on the slabs, he was heard to say, "At last I once again feel the cold stone of earth and it will soon be mine, all mine," he then said on seeing Jacob, "Welcome to my domain, Boy King. Have you come to watch the fall of the third age? The armies of Hell wait for my call and when they answer, your demise will follow." Jacob wasn't fazed.

"Trust me Dark Lord," he sneered. "The gods are aligned against you and we'll not allow you destroy what has been created by the Light."

Lucifer said no more, he was savouring his first touch of earth since the fall of Paradise and was not prepared to allow these magical moments be taken from him. Jacob inched his way closer and raised his sword into an attack position. The three horsemen anticipated his move and leapt forward to create a barrier using their staffs preventing Jacob from reaching his target. Jacob swung his sword wildly, using every move taught to him by the War Gods, but he couldn't get near Lucifer or the horsemen. He changed his strategy and reached into his satchel to retrieve his staff. On raising it, he called on the Light and when it came, its power burst forth and sent Lucifer and his horsemen back through the wall, collapsing the portal and bringing sighs of relief.

"Is he defeated?" yelled a nearby reporter. "Did you destroy him?" asked another. "Are we safe?" said a third.

"I'm afraid not," said Jacob turning back to the reporters. "He's probing and testing and won't give up now he has touched the slab stones of this sacred place. His desire to take earth will only grow so don't be fooled, he'll be back and his vengeance will know no bounds."

"We saw the Light send them back into Hell," said another reporter. "Surely it's stronger?"

"Look to the sun and see how it dims." answered Jacob. "The Darkness is close and looks on Lucifer as a distraction. The Darkness takes no prisoners, it takes everything and that's the real threat but because Lucifer believes it's an ally he just gets stronger. He still plans his attack and, trust me, it's imminent." He looked directly into the camera and tried to reassure those watching, "The Gods are all in place and we are ready to fight for man but we can't move until Lucifer attacks."

He paused again and raised his hand to his ear, "Listen carefully to the quietness, the birds have stopped singing, the wind no longer blows, animals are cowering, even the waves have no energy. All of nature knows Hell is on the march." He went very quiet and began to move his head from left to right, then said with a shudder,

"The wrath of Hell has been unleashed"

Chapter 26

Just then tremors were felt everywhere. All over the world volcanoes began erupting, even long dormant domes exploded. Extinct cones began to move. Panicked reports about legions of Dark Angels filing out from the shadow of pyroclastic flows started reaching Jacob's ears. The hollow sounds of sonic booms caused by explosions in the far distance could also be heard, sending pangs of terror wherever they were felt. The Wraiths of Hell began to show themselves and commenced their possession of those living close to the graveyards.

In the seas, fishing boats, cruise liners and navy ships were reporting thousands upon thousands of dolphins swimming and jumping in formation through the waves. One ship described how the phenomenon started, it described how one dolphin jumped high above the waves, dived and came back up again but this time escorted by two more, then, when they dived, they'd emerge followed by five more and this continued, time and time again, until the ship reported what seemed to be a mass movement of dolphins who, after many more dives resurfaced as a Mer-Army, armed with tridents and swords. Reporters near Jacob asked if he knew anything about the strange behaviour of dolphins and he replied,

"What you are witnessing is the movement of the massed armies of the Mer-People, under the command of their emperor, Toyesh, lord of all sea creatures. They are preparing for an attack on the serpents of Hell."

Santorini's volcano then erupted. It was as powerful as its eruption in 1646BCE. It took out the surrounding islands before sending a tsunami in all directions. The difference between this tsunami and the one in antiquity was that this one camouflaged thousands, possibly millions, of serpents. As the tsunami travelled, helicopters above were picking up dark and sinister images in the waves.

Almost simultaneously a second volcano erupted west of Sicily, it was the small island of Lipari and it was equally as violent. It also sent tsunamis in all directions but it was the one heading towards the east coast of Spain that attracted the most attention. It had the highest concentration of serpents and was the most threatening of them all. Toyesh, at the behest of Asgard had his army off the coast of the Algarve but intuitively, and being a clever tactician, he had earlier decided to send several large columns deeper into the northern seas. He watched the wave flow through the straits of Gibraltar and waited for it to dissipate, as it crossed the Atlantic, before launching his attack.

Splitting his armies transpired to be a wise move because within a few moments of his attack he learned that he was up against a formidable force. They were targeting the throats of his warriors and had a speed that made them almost untouchable, they showed no mercy and were having a horrific success rate. They were eliminating his warriors at such a rate that while sinking; their demise conjured up images of bronzed and wilted leaves falling during a great storm. He soon realised that the forces of the Light were in serious trouble and when he looked at his guards he knew by their faces they were preparing for a disorganised retreat.

He sent messengers to his hidden armies, alerting them to the new skills of the serpents, and then moved the remnants of his now fractured forces out into the deep Atlantic, where they descended down into the Puerto Rico

Trench seeking hiding places near the vents on the ocean floor. It was all to no avail because they were soon located, surrounded and then a continuous and savage attack ensued. The ocean floor became littered with more Mer bodies, and a red bloom spread out across the sands. It was this red bloom that alerted the gods.

In Olympus, Dione got agitated, she contacted Poseidon and together they put in place a plan to rescue the Mer-army. They were both aware of Jacob's promise 'When all seems lost, the senior gods would act' and they decided to act. They immediately made their way towards the ocean and descended the twenty eight thousand feet to the depths of the trench where they located the serpents slithering in a wide circle. They were too late, aid had already arrived and an onslaught of power was in train as serpent after serpent fell to the might of an ancient force that hadn't been seen or experienced since the death of the first Titan.

The aid that had arrived was one of the twelve, it was the Titan Oceanus, and he brought the power of the Kraken, Hydra and the Nirgen, three monsters of the deep who had been asleep since long before the time of the gods. He called on them to be allies of the Light and they agreed. The Kraken was the most feared because of the way it used its many tentacles to suction its adversaries towards its ever hungry mouth. The many heads of Hydra moved so rapidly that nothing could evade her sharp teeth, and the thirty foot long Nirgen used its quivering ghost white and smooth human like skin to sent targeted shock waves that brought terror to those it met. All three worked together and quickly vanquished the serpents bringing a great relief to Toyesh and his warriors.

Poseidon and Dione grew to their colossus form and were soon joined by Oceanus who was beaming from ear to ear on seeing Poseidon. They had not seen each other since Zeus struck down Cronus during the battle between the gods and the Titans and that was thousands of years ago. Poseidon acknowledged the presence of his uncle and introduced him to Dione. All three agreed to work together before thanking the creatures of the deep and asking them to come to the assistance of the Mer-Peoples when required.

What they didn't expect was the reaction of Toyesh, he was furious. He swam to be among the gods but directed his anger at Poseidon, "How could you? How could you watch while my warriors were savaged?" he yelled. "The souls of many have been captured and taken to Hell. Some were princes and princesses of my realm, my sons and daughters. Today my spirit is broken, how can we fight this evil? They're too powerful."

Poseidon reminded him, "You were warned that the gods would be unable to assist, and that you would bear the brunt of Hells underwater attack."

Dione intervened trying to calm things, "Poseidon and I are gods of the seas and we did feel your pain. That's why we're here. We left the safety of Olympus to fight by your side and although we are late, look at your allies. The mighty Oceanus has revealed himself and brought creatures of the deep to assist. What you have suffered is horrendous but what's happening above is much worse. Lucifer has opened volcanoes beneath the seas and through them he's releasing the serpents of Hell. From land based volcanoes he is sending out his Dark Angels. His Wraiths are already terrorising and possessing those living near the graveyards and they will soon spread. We know his flying hounds are near showing themselves. The Astrals are moving into their battle positions but for them to have a chance they need to be sure that your armies will contain the serpents. Your armies need to regain their spirit and move towards the volcanoes,"

Toyesh was confused, he had witnessed the massacre of many of his strongest warriors and wondered how those remaining could possibly take on the armies of Hell. He then felt a presence, it was Jacob. "Lord Toyesh,"

190

he said, "remember how some time ago Odi said to you, 'look to your young, allow them lead, theirs is where you will find your triumph, let them lead.' I say to you, look to your young."

Toyesh thought of Odi's comments and began to feel hope again. He thought of his young warriors and remembered how they were smarter, fiercer and in particular, they were faster. On regaining his confidence he retrieved his Queen Conch shell and sent a message across all oceans hoping the message was loud enough to reach the Mer-Armies hidden in the deepest trenches.

From the Java trench, deep in the Indian Ocean, thousands of Mer-Warriors rose up to form two armies, one made its way towards the volcanoes of Indonesia and Malaysia; it was led by Valda, the eldest daughter of Toyesh. The second army made its way towards the Red Sea.

From the Mariana trench, the vast Pacific Ocean Mer-Army rose up and moved towards the volcanoes that stretched from New Zealand to Japan on the western side and from Chile to Alaska on the eastern side. This western army was under the command of Marcus, the eldest son of Toyesh, and the eastern army was under the command of Briella, twin of Marcus.

Toyesh swam back towards the Mediterranean Sea where on his way he was joined by a number of warriors who were injured during the initial attack. He was also joined by the columns he had sent north before that attack. After passing through the straits of Gibraltar all they saw was widespread chaos with serpents everywhere. Every coastal city, town and village, from Spain across to Israel, was under attack and the onslaught was relentless. This created a dilemma, should he assist or should he continue towards Santorini?

His decision was made easy when he received reports that Lipari had ceased erupting but columns of Serpents were still pouring out from beneath

Santorini. This became his target and after a brief discussion with his generals he modified his plan by splitting his army. He remained near the straits to assist the stricken cities while sending the majority of his younger warriors to cut off the flow from Hell. This movement was led by Alika, his youngest son who approached the remnants of Santorini in a pincer movement allowing his warriors to attack from all sides. Even with their speed and the continuous decapitating of serpents the warriors couldn't stem the flow and this became alarming,

Toyesh sought assistance from Oceanus and requested he use his power to close the portal to Hell. When Oceanus arrived, he was invisible to the serpents because he was of water, he was water and because of that, he alone had the ability to show himself. On reaching the portal, he crouched for a moment before launching himself up through the surface into the sky and as he travelled higher all watching saw him take the shape of a man, all be it a Titan. When he reached a great height he turned and with his arms stretched out before him he headed back into the sea. He gathered speed and using his full might he entered the water and targeted the subterranean cliffs, causing them to collapse and crush the thousands of serpents who were still making their way through.

With the flow stemmed Alika's warriors changed their tactics; they spread out and began attacking the flanks of the serpents swimming towards the cities. They were pleasantly surprised when they were joined by a much larger Mer-Army that was led by Pantos, another son of Toyesh. In fact this was the army that had earlier split from the main eastern force and they had travelled from the Indian Ocean through the Suez Canal.

The two brothers while working together led their warriors in the annihilation of any serpent still swimming. They succeeded in destroying many but unfortunately hundreds of thousands had already reached land and couldn't be followed. These same serpents brought great pain to those they met, showing no mercy. They were more vicious than those previously encountered and seemed to be driven by an insatiable hunger for flesh and souls. They were also driven by a desire to join up with the Dark Angels pouring from the land based volcanoes and the numerous sinkholes that were dotted throughout the world.

The coming together of the serpents and the Dark Angels was the signal for the wizards to raise their staffs and call on Pegasus to summon all those of myth and legend. On receiving the call, Pegasus chose to materialise at the Parthenon where all watching saw him appear as the greatest white stallion of all time. When he took his human form it was clear by his appearance he was a son of Poseidon, same height, same muscular build, and same face. He raised his staff before pounding it off the slab stones sending his light in all directions.

The Centaurs of Cyprus were the first to answer his call. They were led by Keteus and together with the remnants of his warriors they became visible to the Cypriot people. "To the Gods," yelled Keteus. "Assist us; the pain of Cyprus is unbearable. To my warriors I say, let your revenge be felt as this day begins, remember our elderly, remember our younglings, remember our fallen warriors, revenge, revenge, revenge."

On seeing the centaurs the people of Cyprus felt hope, they were aware of the ancient stories and knew that like in those tales, the centaurs had the power to protect them, but it was not to be. The serpents released by the Tsunami had developed the ability to shape shift, they became Dark Angels that stood as seven foot tall demons. These angels used Hells poison tipped lances to slaughter many of the centaurs causing havoc in their ranks.

High in the sky the Asgard army had placed scouts to monitor the happenings below. They saw the difficulty in which Keteus had found himself and contacted Fafner who immediately took action. He ordered a thousand chariots from the western army to descend towards the island and while watching his warriors attack, he chose to join them, not as an Olympus warrior but as Emperor of the Dragons.

The people of Nicosia were traumatised by the images being broadcast into their homes. They cowered behind sofas, under beds and in cupboards while trying to suppress images of serpents attacking their coastal towns and villages, led by vicious Dark Angels.

Their initial hope when they saw the centaurs materialise was replaced by despair when they saw centaur after centaur fall to the power of Hell. Their despair was again replaced by hope when the Asgard army arrived and was being assisted by a fire-breathing dragon. They hoped that, like in Dublin, the dragon's fire would incinerate all it touched. Their hope rose further when they saw the skills of Asgard, especially when the angels that evaded the flame were mangled by the blade-laden undercarriages of the fast moving chariots.

Odi entered Fafner's head so as to watch the battle and was pleased to see so many Dark Angels turn to dust. He worried when he saw how many serpents there were, but relaxed when he saw the warriors release arrow after arrow into the slithering mass, also turning them to dust. The gods had learned how arrows dipped in the first source light were lethal to Hell.

When the battle of Nicosia was over Fafner moved away, there was something bothering him and he wanted to check it out. He wondered why there were no carriers about: he felt there should have been. On reaching high above the Troodos Mountain he noticed wisps of white mist rising and it was continuous, He moved closer and found the source, his worst fears were confirmed. Below him was a slaughter camp being used to kill disarmed carriers that had earlier been possessed by the Wraiths of Hell. He watched the possessed carriers arrive and then struggle as the Dark Angels systematically slaughtered every last one. He watched white mists rise but also saw black mists, and it troubled him to see the black mists drift into cracks and crevices knowing they were going into Hell to join Lucifer's army. He closed his eyes and thought of Jacob who on answering listened to Fafner warn him of the strategy of Hell.

Jacob called for the wizards and when they arrived he said, "Hell is more powerful than at first thought, the Wraiths have possessed many carriers and the Dark Angels are slaughtering them by the thousands. Have you found a way to destroy the Wraiths?"

"We've searched everywhere," replied Mygon. "We've called on all oracles, sorcerers and witches. We've been to the ancient libraries, even those so well hidden that the power of the wizards had trouble finding them. We travelled through time, to the second age of man, all to no avail. The book of life is hidden from us. We've failed."

Jacob raised his hands to his head in despair and shouted, "How can this be? We've put together the greatest army of Astrals ever assembled, how did we not see this?"

"I know you don't want to hear the obvious," answered Mygon, "But it's because we're dealing with the wiliest deceiver of them all."

Chapter 27

It was then when Jacob felt Odi enter his head, "Brother," he said. "Don't despair. I've been summoned to Elysium, wait for my return."

Odi reached Elysium to be greeted by a wondrous sight. Ten of the twelve Titans of legend were standing along the beach in their colossus form, all just over twenty feet tall.

"We're watching the battle," said Rhea as she greeted him. "Unless I act, the destruction of the Astrals will be complete. Asgard too will succumb. It's an ancient magic Lucifer has unleashed but he has no idea that in my woodlands, forests and grasslands, is where the defences against the Wraiths sleep. The Earth Mothers know of these defences, it's time to bring me to Jacob."

Rhea then took her human form and allowed Odi to place his hand on her shoulder, he blinked and they arrived at the Western Wall.

"My lady," said a surprised Jacob. "I thought you were to remain hidden?"

"Relax brother," interrupted Odi. "Rhea might be the saviour of man. Watch her call forth the Earth Mothers."

The wizards bowed on seeing her, they were her guardians in the old times and carried on protecting the natural world when the Earth Mothers fell into silence. Odi said his goodbyes and returned to his position at the head of the northern Asgard army.

Soon after a most powerful Elfena arrived, she was Ellaweise, consort of Kalen and she too bowed to Rhea, "We've been awaiting your return. The woodlands, forests and the meadows are all ready to give up their secrets. Call forth the Earth Mothers."

"My ladies," said a concerned Jacob. "This is a most dangerous place, you must leave. The horsemen have already showed themselves on these most sacred slabs."

"Fear not for us my King," said Rhea trying to reassure him. "Wherever the Earth Mothers walk, evil hides in fear. Lucifer knows better, he fears our power. He or his minions will not show themselves."

"I don't understand?" said a perplexed Jacob. "What can you do?"

"Since the beginning of time," she replied. "When souls left their vessels the mists had to go somewhere. Those who became the black mist made their way to Hell; there was nowhere else for them to go. But the white mist? It had a choice. Some went to Heaven but most chose to stay; they found a home among the souls of the trees. There are millions and they will answer the call of the Earth Mothers. They will defend the light. The Wraiths will fall to their power."

Jacob, Ellaweise and the wizards stood back and watched Rhea walk to the centre of the courtyard. She closed her eyes and raised her arms. She called out in an ancient tongue, "Veni meis sororibus, fructum vestrum, sta mecum." (Come my sisters, bring forth your power, stand with me.)

It was but five seconds when a gentle mist started rising, thickening into a dense fog, from that fog emerged the nine Earth Mothers who had been hidden by Magni. Each one in turn bowed to Rhea, they then faced Jacob and acknowledged his position as King of Kings. He was awestruck looking upon nine goddesses of such beauty and power. They formed a semi-circle facing the ascending sun. Maja, the Sioux Earth Mother, left her position to be replaced by Rhea. She walked among the Olive trees surrounding the Temple Mount. It was noted that the trees all shook as though with excitement as she approached, little did those watching know that they were looking upon a goddess who was in fact the Tree of Life. She raised her hand and commanded one leaf to dislodge itself to rest in her palm. She then moved to place the leaf at the centre of the semicircle and returned to a position among the other goddesses.

Jacob in the meantime was receiving messages informing him that the centaurs of both Pelion and Russia were now in action. He was also aware that the great waterfalls had stopped flowing and portals were opening. He even received a message of allegiance from Japan where a portal had opened and an army of elves, unheard of for over ten thousand years, had began to march in defence of the Light. This was a welcome addition as Japan was under an onslaught of pain because the serpents were seeking revenge for the actions of Garuda and Girish in centuries past.

"I feel and see everything you are experiencing," said Ellaweise entering Jacob's head. "It's one of my greatest powers. The Elf army of the Fire Islands was once known as a most formidable force. They suffered constant attacks from the legions of Hell. We thought they'd succumbed. What this means is you now have ten armies of Elf kind under your command."

Jacob's mind returned to the happenings at the Western Wall, he was trying not to show his anxiety especially as nothing seemed to be happening.

"Calm down," whispered Merlin. "Trust the Earth Mothers, all will be revealed when the time is right, magic only shows itself when it's ready."

It was as the Earth Mothers each raised their right arms when the leaf began to vibrate and expand to become a most magnificent tree. Maja said, "Es e me, non est arbor vitea, opus tuum magicae" (You are of me, you are the Tree of Life, work your magic.) A translucent light shot from the finger tips of each Earth Mother and entered the now fully grown and majestic tree.

The light travelled into the sky and proceeded to form a cocoon around the whole world. It continued its work and then left the cocoon to enter every grove, woodland and forest, seeking out trees that held the white mists of long gone souls. In all lands, souls hidden deep within the rings of the ancient trees began to rise from their long sleep. They instinctively knew they were being called back to battle against the dark mists.

Jacob felt a new presence, it was the Archangel Michael, "Protect the Earth Mothers, move them to Olympus. The seven Archangels will take control of the white souls and together we will deal with the Wraiths of Hell. We know of these ancient spirits and will retake the vanquished villages, towns and cities. This is a battle only we can fight. The wraiths and the black mist will not survive our onslaught."

The Archangels did as they said they would, taking huge pressure off Jacob. They led the white mists to victory against the Wraiths. They used the power of the Light and chased them, harried them, then expelled them from those who were possessed. They drove them back to the graveyards where they were corralled until the guardian angels arrived to consume them by fire. There was no compassion or feeling just a determined use of the Light to ensure they never returned.

Jacob was delighted with the early intervention of the Archangels as this freed up Asgard to assist the Astrals. He remembered Michaels promise that they would only intervene when Lucifer showed himself, and Lucifer had showed himself. He did what was asked of him and moved the Earth Mothers to Olympus. He informed his brothers, and the messengers, that the Wraiths were being dealt with. Rhea rejoined the Titans in Elysium.

Jacob, although relieved, felt his pangs of anxiety again grow. He was thinking of his imminent battle with Lucifer, a battle he feared as he knew everything depended on him defeating Lucifer once and for all. He then felt Odi enter his head and heard him repeat what he said time and time again, "Brother, less of this fear, you are well trained and I'll always be by your side, together we'll be unbeatable, together we will bring down Lucifer."

Chapter 28

Mainland Greece was next for to be attacked. The long dormant Methana volcano erupted for the first time in over three hundred years, releasing thousands of Dark Angels who immediately took to the air. They were in formation and for over five hundred kilometres they flew towards Mount Pelion; their mission - the destruction of Pelion.

The Greek army, assisted by NATO, mounted a major aerial assault before being decimated by the power of the Hell. Their weapons failed miserably in containing the flight of the Dark Angels forcing NATO to consider using nuclear weapons but this was discouraged when an emissary of Queen Zephyra arrived and convinced the commanders to allow the Astrals to unleash their power. The emissary let it be known that the Centaurs of Pelion were about to enter the battle. As the Greek armoured divisions were withdrawing they were taken aback as thousands of warrior centaurs materialised all across the hills of Pelion.

Thousands more appeared on the plain of Thessaly where a gathering of serpents that had left the Aegean Sea earlier that morning was sited. On the hills, the armies of Pelion continued to show themselves, and when ready they slowly cantered before turning to a gallop, racing to confront the armies of Hell. They leapt across all obstacles including the retreating Greek army leaving the soldiers in awe and bewildered. On approaching the serpents they raised their swords and bows but were taken aback that the serpents, in their arrogance, never flinched. They knew they had an advantage because the Dark Angels were hidden on the southern edge of the plains and behind them were the demon hounds ready and waiting for the order to take to the sky.

Queen Zephyra held her position on a nearby hill. "This is too easy," she said while watching her forces advance, she showed her uneasiness when she spoke to one of her guards. "I fear we're being deceived, they think I can't see them but I can. Why is the Dark Angels standing with arrogant smiles crossing their ugly faces?" It was then she received a message from Russia.

On the tree covered foothills near Turinsk the Russian army were engaged in battle against legions of serpents and Dark Angels, who were pouring out from under the hot springs. Just like in Greece, every modern weapon being used had no effect. The Dark Angels were taking control of the area while the serpents sought out as many Russian citizens as they could find. It was a lost cause for the Russian army causing Moscow to order an immediate retreat; this decision prompted Lord Polkan to reveal himself. He materialised on a hill within sight of the battle field in full view of the soldiers who couldn't believe they were looking upon their hero, the one who was known as leader of the Russian Centaurs of myth and legend.

When he knew he had their full attention he made his way down through their ranks, "There's no disgrace in retreating from a battle such as this," he said on meeting with their commander. "From the start you couldn't win, but there is something you can do for me."

"What can we do?" asked the commander.

"Look," said Polkan pointing towards the springs. "See the steam rise and settle in the skies above Turinsk. Use your weapons to collapse the walls and cause the springs to close, this will give my army time to deal with the Dark Angels and serpents already here."

"I've been ordered to retreat," said the commander. "I would need instruction from Moscow."

"Look to the hills," pointed Polkan. "Tell me what you see?"

"Nothing, I see nothing," replied the commander.

"Look again," suggested Polkan.

The commander looked again and this time, and as far as he could see, was a gathering of the largest centaur army ever assembled. The commander gasped and was awestruck. He immediately ordered his soldiers to redirect their weapons and launch a series of precision targeted rockets in the direction of the hot springs. The attack was a sustained onslaught that collapsed the springs and as expected it stopped the exit of thousands more serpents.

Polkan then raised his standard and so began the march of his army. His warriors moved down from the hills and soon reached the retreating, yet very excited Russian army. They appeared as giants alongside the armoured cars and tanks that were protecting the retreating soldiers. Many of the centaurs moved at such speed they had no trouble leaping high above any obstacle they encountered, including the military hardware. The soldiers cheered as the centaurs reached their targets and commenced their attack.

Their excitement soon turned to despair when Hell's second line of attack was launched. It was the flying demon hounds and it soon became obvious why they were the ones much feared by the gods. Their attack was relentless and so savage the centaurs struggled and many fell. Polkan looked on in horror watching his army get decimated and just as he about to call a tactical retreat he felt a presence; it was Chiron,

"My lord Polkan," he said, "great warrior of the Russian realm. I am Chiron, Centaur God of Olympus. Don't retreat, look to the west and watch for the dragon army. Hold your nerve."

Polkan never before felt the presence of Chiron and was unsure if the presence was real or not, and as a result he was having difficulty holding his nerve. He looked around at his panicked generals and saw that their nerves were also frayed, and this rattled him. He looked to the west as requested and when he saw nothing he decided to order a retreat.

It was then when a distinct and shrill dragon roar was heard, it was a scout who landed and announced the approach of the dragon army. This time when Polkan looked west he saw a dark cloud on the horizon and it was so dense it dimmed the sunlight. It was an advance party of the dragon army consisting of one hundred dragons led by Afan. They wasted no time; they fanned out across the battlefield and commenced their attack by releasing their fire using elongated breaths. They targeted the outer ranks of Dark Angels before working their way towards the main body, incinerating them on contact. All across the battlefield, the screams of agony and the stench of seared flesh permeated the air.

The dragons continued their onslaught until from behind they were attacked by Hells demon hounds. These flying hounds were different to those experienced in the past. They were fiercer, more cunning and seemed to have the power to resist dragon fire. Their spears were tipped with a potent poison, lethal to dragons, and as the battle progressed many younger and inexperienced dragons fell.

Afan, concerned by his mounting losses, called his remaining dragons higher into the sky, knowing the demon hounds couldn't follow. There, they momentarily rested, and reassessed their strategy. Their plan of attack changed when, from their great height, they saw an army of carriers arrive.

The older dragons recognised many carriers to be ancient Huns, Goths and Celts who, as foretold, had risen from their graves to assist the gods. Among them were thousands more carriers whose ancestors had received the message and had answered the call of the gods, they wasted no time. They immediately attacked the legions of serpents that were now slithering across the battleground.

Afan now saw his advantage and ordered his dragons to attack the demon hounds by darting from their great height at such speed that nothing could stop them. They travelled in formation as they ploughed into the demon hounds, sending their unconscious bodies onto the swords and spears of the carriers and centaurs waiting below.

The battle was now swinging back in favour of the armies of the Light but it was not to last. Polkan again felt a presence, "Hell has opened a new portal," it was Chiron. "Thousands more serpents and Dark Angels will soon surround you. These are two far bigger armies and they'll soon be upon you. You must trust me, split your army and send help to Pelion. Queen Zephyra is a prisoner and is being taken towards the gates of Hell. There's no time, you must send help now."

"I'm confused," said Polkan in the hope of actually seeing Chiron. "Until the dragons arrived we were in serious trouble. Now you ask me to split my army? With two far bigger armies of darkness approaching how can we possibly survive?"

"Fear not," answered Chiron. "Listen carefully for the rumbling thunder, the sound of chariots. Lord Odi has sent four thousand chariots and they'll close by."

In the meantime the two armies of Hell had arrived and took a holding position on the hills surrounding the battlefield. They were hissing, loud and angry, hoping to spread terror among the armies of the Light. Within minutes they proceeded down the hills and immediately were in action against the carriers and the dragons.

Polkan, although uneasy, decided to follow Chiron's instructions. He split his army and sent two thousand warriors to Pelion, a decision that horrified his generals. He reassured them when he pointed north and showed the approaching Asgard army. "The gods," he said, "this day, are by our side." He then sent his remaining warriors into action.

Odi was at the head of the Asgard army and as he approached the battlefield, he split the chariots to form a classic pincer movement. When in position they waited for his signal, which quickly came, and then they attacked using their light-dipped swords and arrows. All across the battlefield serpents began succumbing to the pain of the Light as the arrows impaled them into the hardened ground. The charioteers used their blade laden undercarriages to decapitate as many Dark Angels as they could. With all this, Hells armies were still too numerous, they seemed to be coming from everywhere.

Afan and Odi took up positions high above the battlefield from where they observed everything unfolding below them. From there they saw another portal had opened allowing more of Hells legions to join the battle. Odi shot down to where the Russian army was observing, he ordered them to target their missiles at the new portal. There was no argument. Within seconds a blizzard of rockets was launched, and on impact, they successfully closed the portal. Odi then joined Polkan on a low hill and called on Afan to join them. As immortals, their acute senses allowed them feel the continuous cracking, snapping and shattering of bones. They could also hear their fallen warriors wail in pain before the silence took them. They could smell the putrefying stench of congealed blood wafting in the air and this sickened them. Although devastated by their losses, they were proud of how those warriors of the Light who were still standing held their stoicism, fighting bravely and showing no fear.

Odi mounted his chariot preparing to join the battle when a silence fell across the battlefield causing great confusion. A number of portals had opened, allowing the serpents, Dark Angels and remaining demon hounds scurry into the protection of Hell.

"How can this be?" asked Odi after rejoining Afan and Polkan. "Are we being deceived? Why would such a formidable force leave?"

"Look out upon that theatre of despair," replied a despondent Polkan. "Look at the brains and innards, they glisten in the setting sun, the blood sodden grasses will forever be imbedded in our memories."

"I fear we underestimated the power of Hell," wondered Afan. "Look at my dragons, there's only thirty still standing. Look at the carriers, so few are left, those remaining are distraught. I cannot count the number of crashed Asgard chariots and as for the centaurs; they are by far the ones who have spilt the most blood."

"Enough of this," yelled an angry Odi. "This is war. My lord Polkan, take what is left of your warriors and help with the rescue of Pelion, Asgard will follow. Afan, inform your King of this day, tell him of what we fight."

Just as they were about to depart, Odi climbed a large boulder where he stood as a Warrior God. With his right hand he raised his imperial staff and summoned the Light. He then called out across the battlefield, "Fallen warriors of the Light; come on to me, rise up and answer the call of Elysium. Allow your bodies find their place among the fallen heroes and the blessed dead. Go now and rest in peace, your battle is over."

The Light shot out over the battlefield and all watching saw the bodies of the fallen warriors begin to rise. The Russian soldiers paid their respects while watching so many bodies, surrounded by a white mist drift towards the west, and they will never forget the sight of carriers, centaurs, dragons and Asgard warriors clenching their right fists, placing them over their hearts, and then bowing to their fallen dead. Only when the last of the white mist had disappeared did the armies of the Light split to go their separate ways.

It was close to nightfall when Polkan and his army arrived in Pelion, and they arrived to a pitiful sight. The torches lighting this enchanted land were still burning brightly, but this day, instead of showing the beauty of a once magical land, they were illuminating the devastation that was everywhere. Bodies of centaurs littered the Thessaly plains but it was the moaning and groaning of the sick and wounded that was the most distressing.

In the fading light a column of captured warriors and younglings were being taken towards portals that had opened in the north. Polkan ordered his warriors in pursuit fearing they were too late. He needn't have worried, some hours earlier the waters that flowed from Mount Olympus were held back allowing the Enipeas Waterfall to dry out. From a deep cave hidden behind the waterfall a five thousand strong army of Water Elves led by Ariella came through and although two hundred kilometres away, being immortals they were able to reach Pelion in less than an hour.

The Elf army came into view just as Polkan and his warriors reached the rear flanks of the column, causing the walk of misery to halt while the Dark Angels assessed their options. They were completely surrounded by two powerful armies who together were far stronger than what Hell had fought earlier so they closed in around their captives and let it be known that if they fall they will take down with them as many prisoners as they could. They brought Queen Zephyra to the head of the column and showed how ruthless they planned to be by publically abusing and beating her until she passed out. They then said that the same fate awaits the rest of the captives if the armies don't withdraw.

At the Western Wall, Jacob had closed his eyes to take in all that was happening around the world. He knew the Asgard armies in the south and in the east were now engaged. He observed the armies in the Americas and noted that as planned Faer had the support of millions of carriers as well as an army of Mountain Elves. He saw that the dragon armies had attacked Hell's defences in Salisbury and near the Stone of Destiny on the Hill of Tara. He also saw a long forgotten War Goddess was assisting the Fair Lands. Even with all that was going on elsewhere he couldn't take his mind from the attack on the peaceful nation of Pelion. He said to the Wizards, "Keep this place sacred, I must go to Olympus." He blinked, disappeared and instantly arrived in Olympus where, to the gods he met; he looked to be seriously stressed. He sought out Chiron and when he found him he could see that he was agitated.

"My sympathies, Lord Chiron," said Jacob as he bowed. "Pelion has fallen and many centaurs are lost. Hell has captured Queen Zephyra and Lord Polkan plans a rescue."

"Each sword that struck a centaur I felt," said Chiron, struggling to reply. "It's like a blade slicing into my hide. There's nothing I can do, I feel helpless."

Jacob was about to seek his guidance when he was interrupted by Ares who said, "There's a way to rescue Pelion." Jacob and Chiron looked at each other and gestured for Ares to set out his plan.

"Athena and I watched the battle," he said. "We saw the weaknesses of Pelion. We saw it fall. Arielle and the Water Elves have arrived and control the north and the east, Polkan has now moved into position and he controls the south and the west, together they have surrounded Hells army. No assault by them at this point can possibly save Zephyra and the last of Pelion but my plan will." He paused for a moment then set out his plan.

"Call forth the nearest Asgard chariots," he said. "Make sure they carry full length body shields. Speak to the wizards and see to it that the shields are protected by their magic. Arrange for Asgard chariots to materialise above the column and drop the shields at such speed that they will form a barrier between the Pelion captives and Hells army. Ensure the chariots carry swords and spears. Let not a moment pass before the full might of a second Asgard battalion materialises and drops as many warriors among the captives as can be arranged. They will be the guardians of Pelion while in the meantime, the Water Elves and Polkan's army attack."

Ares then turned to Chiron, "You alone have the power to enter all their heads at the same time, at my signal do just that and give them hope."

"These plans are so off the wall, they could work," said Jacob in a moment of weakness. He was met by a glare of utter annoyance from Ares, who replied,

"You seem to forget I'm the God of War, my plans will work."

Jacob then called on Odi or Fafner, whoever was the nearest. He was answered almost immediately by Odi,

"I'm close by and was in your head when Ares laid out his plans, trust me brother, Asgard will ensure they'll work. Four hundred chariots are on their way and will be above the Thessaly Plains in a few moments. My warriors know exactly what to do. All we need is the magic of the wizards. Chiron must now speak to the centaurs."

Jacob left immediately to rejoin the wizards at the Western Wall where he briefed them on the plan. Without delay they conjured up a spell, providing a magical protection for the shields that Ares had requested. Chiron at the same time left the temple and went out into the meadows where he closed his eyes and called out for all centaurs to listen,

"Centaurs of Pelion," he said. "Hear me. I am Chiron, God of Olympus. Listen for the sound of the Asgard gjallarhorn then fall to your knees and wait for relief. It will come from the sky above. Hear me, I am with you, do not despair."

Almost immediately Odi raised his gjallarhorn and sent out a sound that hadn't been heard since the time of the cosmic wars. Immediately, the centaurs fell to their knees and as they fell they were in awe of the continuous fall of magic shields, forming a barrier between them and the Dark Angels. This was followed by swords and spears that landed beside them. They were further shocked as Asgard warriors appeared all around them. The glistening golden armour of Asgard made them look so formidable that they passed on their confidence to the despondent centaurs. Ariella and the Water Elves moved forward at such speed the Dark Angels didn't have much time to react. The volleys of arrows falling on the now panicked forces of Hell were relentless and brutal. The elves never stopped and didn't lose one warrior. From the south and the west Polkan's army attacked, seeking their revenge, they were merciless in their routing of Hell. They particularly sought out every commander they could find and summarily executed them.

When the battle ended no presence of Hell was left on the battlefield, all were vanquished. Asgard had lost some warriors, the elves had lost none. Polkan managed with very few losses.

Odi arrived and made his way to meet with Zephyra and Polkan. "It seems the war of the centaurs is over," he said. "You should both go and rebuild your realms. There's no more you can do."

Zephyra was very weak, so much so Odi was alarmed, "My lady, allow me take you to Apollo; he will assist."

"Go my queen," insisted Polkan. "This land will only prosper with you walking on its hallowed grounds. My army will protect your realm awaiting your return." He then turned to Odi and said,

"My army will also be at your disposal, many of our younglings are old enough to carry arms, and they will be trained. My warriors will protect our borders, crossing them if necessary. Call on us when you need us, this battle is but one, there are many more to come." Odi then took Zephyra to Apollo.

Chapter 29

Back at the Western Wall Jacob informed the wizards about the attack on the centaur realms. At the same time he was tuned into what was happening all over the world, most especially what was happening in Ireland. He focused on finding Shane and when he did he found him preparing to leave school after a decision was made to close all schools due to the horrific happenings being reported. He also saw that life in Ireland was continuing as normal except for a strange light that had appeared at the Stone of Destiny on the Hill of Tara and that those witnessing the light couldn't approach it as it seemed to be shielded. He saw that speculation was rife as to what it represented.

The strange happenings all across the world were now being broadcast continuously on all TV stations, but the light on Tara was deemed just to be intriguing. What no one realised was the light, as it strengthened, was signalling for all carriers based in Ireland to make their way to Co. Meath. These were the carriers who were the descendants of the Celtic nation.

As the light intensified its light reached all corners of Ireland and a mass movement of carriers commenced their walk towards Tara. In the school grounds Shane and Jacob's friends came together and descended into a deep trance. A wafting mist gathered around each of them causing their school uniforms to fall away. When the mist departed they had changed. They were taller, stronger and were wearing the light leather armour of ancient Irish warriors. Their swords glowed like beacons and were guiding eighteen stallions from Pegasus's herds towards them. From the motorway a low, almost inaudible sound of horse's hooves was heard, and as they approached the school their clopping got louder and more defined. The sight of eighteen white horses leaping over the high school walls was awesome but the sight of them leaving with their eighteen cloaked and armed riders was spectacular.

They briskly rode from the school to reach the nearby motorway where they continued their swift pace to quickly reach the exit that would take them to the Hill of Tara within ten minutes.

When they reached the hill they made their way to the stone of destiny. It was then when the light took a new form. It was becoming more pronounced and soon took the shape of a most regal woman. To them she looked like a goddess of great power and being young virile boys, they couldn't take their eyes from her, such was her beauty. To the boys she seemed to be framed as though in a portrait, set deep in their minds, the way any beautiful work of art would be. A gold band held her cascading fair hair in place as it rested just below her shoulders ending in a gathering of curls. Her hazel coloured eyes oozed warmth with a sparkle that would warm the hearts of any young man. The boys were smitten, their eyes tracing every contour of her face, but it was her lips that invited their minds to go to places all red-blooded teenagers wished for.

Jacob sniggered while watching, through Shane's eyes, the boy's jaws drop. He then said, "Bud, I don't recognise her, be careful." Merlin stepped forward, placed his hand on Jacob's shoulder and immediately saw who Shane was looking at.

"Relax my friends," he said. "I know her. It's Ériu, War Goddess of the Celts and she's of the tribe of Danu, from her Ireland was given its name.

216

Her beauty has withstood a sleep of five thousand years and for her to awaken means a great calamity is coming to these fair lands. It seems the long gone, ancient gods and goddesses are coming to assist in defending the Light."

Shane heard everything Merlin said, and felt she was vaguely familiar, he didn't understand why. "They say you are the lady Ériu," he said while bowing. "They say you are one of the greatest War Goddesses. My name is Shane and we've been sent by the gods to guard this sacred place; we're at your service."

Ériu acknowledged him then asked, "Why do I sense a great sorrow in my lands? Why is the dragon army on my borders? Tell me, where is my lady Danu?"

"The Lady Danu is in Olympus," replied Shane. "She's with the Goddesses of the Light. The dragon army waits to come to our aid because Lucifer has unleashed his armies and plans to destroy this age of man. The sorrow you speak of could mean anything." He then pointed out over the plains and hills of Meath. "Over the centuries your lands have suffered greatly; no more so than during The Great Hunger, over a million of your people died and many more were sent into exile. Is that the sorrow you speak of?"

"I feel their pain," said Ériu placing her arms across her chest. "The trees still speak of what they saw; the grasses shudder while telling me of those buried beneath. What happened still defines these lands, it's in the very fabric of all around us, even the stones and rivers have a story to tell, but it hasn't broken the spirit of my people."

She lowered her head as though in despair, then turned back to Shane and said, "Once I knew a warrior, Lugh was his name. He was a powerful god and defender of these lands against all enemies. He became my lover and from him came a child that he alone reared. I look on you and see his likeness, you stand in his shadow and your aura tells me you are born of him, his blood is your blood. He ruled as a Sun God, even the storms and the sky answered to him. Through you he will return."

Ériu became more distracted while looking out across the plains. She was seeking something then eventually focused on the almost obscured brow of a distant hill. It was the Hill of Uisneach and it seemed to be calling her. "I see his light, it's very dim and it's coming from under that hill. It's there he has rested for five thousand years." She continued while gripping Shane's arm. "Buried with him is his spear, sword and sling stone. Lucifer must never get his hands on these weapons! They are of a god and must remain hidden."

"Shane!" interrupted Davie. "Look, the dragons, there must be a hundred of them?"

"Never mind the dragons," said Joey. "Look, a massive army approaches from the south."

"Ah, my friend Thalia," smiled Ériu. "Queen of the Woodland Elves."

In the meantime many thousands of carriers arrived. "You've assembled a formidable army and still they gather," said Ériu while turning to face the north. "I see Asgard waits in the northern sky. What is your plan?"

He was just about to speak when a dragon landed and took his human form.

"My name is Evan," he said after offering his hand to Shane. "I've been sent by my brother, King Derwyn. We are to assist in defending the Light. My dragon army is at your service."

Although speaking to Shane he had difficulty keeping his eyes off Ériu, he knew she was special but didn't know why. "My Lady!" he said while bowing. "While approaching the Fair Lands we sensed the presence of an ancient force. It pleases me to bow before such a powerful Goddess of the Light. I'm Evan; my father is Fafner, Emperor of the Dragons."

Shane made another attempt to speak but again he was interrupted, this time by the arrival of Thalia, who was very pleased to see Ériu. After a brief conversation Thalia turned to Shane and was taken aback, "My Lord Lugh," she said furrowing her brow. "It pleases me to see you again!"

"No, no. I'm Shane, a friend of Jacob." Thalia looked confused.

"He is of Lugh," said Ériu. "A vessel for his blood,"

Thalia placed her hand on his cheek and said, "It is written that before the End Times battle a young god will show himself, with another he will lead the armies of the Light and by their side will be a vessel of Lugh. Today I stand before that vessel, one who carries the blood of Lugh."

Shane was overwhelmed, taken aback, and the only thing he could think to say was, "Enough, we've a battle to prepare for."

"Have you a plan?" asked Ériu again.

"Yes, of course I have," nodded Shane. "Sending warriors to Uisneach alone is not an option. Lucifer will surmise Lugh's weapons are there so warriors will be sent to the hills of Slane, Tailte, Donore, Screen and Faughan as a distraction. This will confuse him and give me more time to secure the weapons." He then turned back to Thalia.

"Place a thousand Elves around each of the five hills and what's left around Tara. There are thousands of carriers and they too will be split to assist the elves, they will be under the command of my friends here."

He turned to Evan, "Place the dragon army high in the sky and work with the commanders of Asgard. Only act when the demon hounds show themselves. The fire of the dragons and the arrows of Asgard will be most welcome at that time. I alone will travel to Uisneach."

When all was in place and Shane was satisfied he fetched his horse and galloped at great speed towards Uisneach where on arrival he was drawn to a spot where he felt he should start digging. He used his sword to break the soil and his hands to scoop it away. It wasn't long before he reached a stone doorway bearing old Celtic symbols carved into its lintel. After several attempts he succeeded in breaking through the door allowing sunlight to travel to the back of a wide chamber. The light highlighted a very ornate stone sarcophagus set in the middle of the chamber and inscribed on its lid in an ancient script, yet he could read it, was 'Lord Lugh - Warrior God of the Celts'.

Shane used all his strength to push the lid aside and when he succeeded he was taken aback to see a perfectly preserved body lying within. When he reached in to take the sword he got a shock, he was gripped, and found himself being dragged into the coffin.

"Thief....Who covets my sword?" yelled a loud and thunderous voice.

Shane although terrified found the strength to respond, "I'm no thief. My name is Shane and they say I'm of your blood. I seek to protect the weapons of a god."

"Of my blood, eh?" replied Lugh as he climbed from his coffin still holding a struggling Shane. "You are of my blood? A weakling, how is it you bear my likeness?"

"Trust me, I'm no weakling," said Shane trying to free himself. "I'm as surprised as you considering how it's been thousands of years since you last ruled,"

Lugh released Shane and made his way up the steps to take his first breath of long forgotten clean air, then asked, "Why does the sun dim so?"

"It's The Darkness," replied Shane, "it's feeding on the light."

"The Darkness?" said Lugh. "I remember the Ancient One warning us of its return. It's why so many Sun Gods were created. Do you know of them?"

"Gods are appearing everywhere," replied Shane. "We thought the gods, wizards, centaurs and elves were all stories of myth and legend. Now we're witnessing many strange things. Listen, there's no time to explain. You need to go to Olympus if there are more questions. I have a battle to prepare for and I don't need distractions. The forces of Lucifer are approaching and it will be over my dead body that they will take these lands."

Lugh looked out at the hills of Meath and saw thousands of elves guarding around each of them. He looked up and saw the dragon army as well as the chariots off Asgard patrolling high in the sky. He sensed their determination and saw they were certainly prepared for battle. He turned back to Shane and asked, "On Tara I see a light, a very bright light. Who is she?"

"The light you see is the Goddess Ériu," replied Shane. "She has come to assist in defending her lands. It seems you and she had a 'Thing' back in the day and somehow I might be the result."

"Are you really of my blood?" enquired Lugh. "You look so weak to be a descendant of a god!"

"There's no need to be insulting considering we actually look like twins, same eyes, same hair, same build. There's just five thousand years between us," responded Shane trying to prevent himself from raising his middle finger. "Just so you know. I'm strong, fast and very well trained. My best friend Jacob has given me everything I need to lead the defence of my country. He's a grandson of Zeus and we're inseparable."

"So he's a grandson of Zeus! Now it makes sense as to why you and he became friends. Your godly blood, my godly blood must have brought you together. I fought by Zeus's side during the cosmic wars. He was considered the greatest of all the gods. How is he?"

"No idea, he seems very snarky," replied Shane. "Jacob brought me, and a few friends, to Olympus. He broke the rules and Zeus threatened to use his bolts to zap us. That was a scary moment so I think I'll always be cautious around him."

"Him and his infernal rules," Lugh said while shaking his head. He then patted Shane's horse before clicking his fingers to arrange the appearance of a second horse, "We should make our way to Tara."

They galloped towards Tara and as they approached, Lugh's heart raced as Ériu came into view. He quickened his pace and on reaching the summit he dismounted and just stared in disbelief. After catching his breath he said, "When you left I lost the will to live. I watched you walk away into his arms not knowing you were pregnant. Look at Shane; he's clearly a descendant of ours. I dug my tomb so that I could lie and wait for your return; little did I know it would take five thousand years." He leaned in for a kiss before continuing, "How cruel is life? It separated us all those years ago, and only brings us back together when the battle of the End Times approaches?" Ériu got emotional.

"Life certainly is cruel," she said gently caressing his cheek. "That love we shared is still there. When you slept, I too slept. In the Dream world you were always there, now I ask you to kiss and hold me so I know that this time, it's not a dream." He needed no persuasion, he leaned in and they kissed, this time or real. Their tender moment wasn't to last.

Lugh backed away sensing something disturbing. He took Ériu's hand and they moved towards the north facing side of the hill. Shane followed and asked, "Why look north?"

"Feel the tremors," said Ériu. "They're rumbling and shaking beneath our feet. They flow from the north. Soon we'll see the flames of Hell; torches carried by the Dark Angels, lighting the path for the serpents to slither towards this most sacred of places. Prepare your armies. Hell will soon be upon us."

High in the sky, Fafner, with his hearing of a dragon, heard everything being said and when he looked to the North West he saw the volcanoes of Iceland erupt. He was horrified at the amount of serpents and Dark Angels being released and was dumbfounded at the speed at which they moved towards both Britain and Ireland. The ocean was no obstacle for the serpents, and the winds assisted the Dark Angels. He watched them split, with the smaller of their armies heading towards the coast of Donegal, Derry and Antrim, and the larger one, avoiding Scotland and heading down the Irish Sea before turning towards Salisbury plain. He was also concerned when he saw Evan arrive on to, then leave, the Hill of Tara. He resolved to question Derwyn about his strategy.

Jacob was still at the Western Wall and very aware of what now faced Shane and decided to reach out to him, "Hey Bud," he said after entering his head, "now I know why you always landed on your feet. You're a descendant of two long forgotten gods and now they're back to be by your side. Allow them assist. From what I can see it's you who faces a formidable Hell's army, there are thousands upon thousands on their way so allow the power of Asgard and the strength of the dragons to lead the way."

"Scobie, I'm frightened," said Shane backing away to be alone. "I don't want to let you down."

"Bud, stop worrying, you're not going to let me down and it's OK to be frightened. Remember, lord Lugh might be a powerful Sun God, but he is also a renowned Warrior God. Watch him, learn from him, and follow his lead, but let all around you know it's you who's in command." Jacob then left.

Shane rejoined Lugh who whispered, "I heard everything Jacob said. It's no coincidence that it's you who takes on Hell in these lands, you are of my blood and trust me, spilling my blood is not an option. You will have my guidance," He then said while backing away, "look around and feel the tension. Smell the sulphurous stench; they'll soon be upon us."

Chapter 30

While Evan was high in the sky above Ireland, King Derwyn, alongside Afan, led the main body of his warriors north towards Scotland. Fafner was at the head of the western Asgard armies and aware his three sons had left the safety of the dragon realm. He was still disturbed by Derwyn's decision to send Evan, and one hundred dragons, to Ireland. He felt splitting the army was unwise but knew he had to trust his son's judgement.

Jacob was also aware of what Derwyn was doing and couldn't understand why. Through Derwyn's eyes he saw flames rising throughout England and quickly established that it was UK military bases that were on fire. He also saw a mass movement of carriers heading towards the south and they were easily identified by their magical swords which were now brightly glowing.

What surprised Derwyn was the carriers ignored the plight of the military bases, there seemed to be and urgency to gather on the perimeter of Salisbury Plain. It was then when Fafner decided to lead the western Asgard army south to meet up with the dragons. On meeting Derwyn he asked, "Tell me son, what's your plan?"

Although always nervous in the presence of his father, for fear of letting him down, he knew that this time he had to be assertive.

"I know you're concerned by my decisions but I have to trust my instincts, and I expect you to support me. I decided to send Evan to Ireland because Jacob's friends will soon be up against a formidable force and will need our support. With regards to England, I am aware the army bases are under attack but I'm going to wait, it's the carriers who will need our support. I'll not split my army any further for a very good reason. Look at Stonehenge; see how it shimmers with the presence of so many serpents. Now look among the Juniper bushes and see how many Dark Angels hide within. I fear it's there where one of the epic battles will take place and where the stench of death will prevail for years to come. I will need my full force when that battle starts. Father, can Asgard not assist the bases?"

Fafner said no more, he now agreed with Derwyn's decision. He left and went higher into the sky. He directed four groups of fifty chariots to assist those bases that were in flames.

The first wave of chariots attacked any serpents or Dark Angels they found, the second wave brought warriors who leapt from the chariots to land among the still fighting British defenders. Everywhere they landed they found devastation on a scale that the British forces hadn't suffered since the Second World War. The army got great relief watching the skills and ferocity of the Asgard warriors.

The attempts to secure the bases didn't all go Asgards way as many warriors fell to the constant onslaught of the forces of Hell requiring a third wave, and again many fell.

Fafner didn't want to risk a fourth wave so rushed to rejoin Derwyn.

"We've lost many chariots this day," he reported. "There's a formidable force of Hell in the military bases." He then requested the power of the dragons.

Derwyn was disturbed by the request but knew his father was a brilliant tactician so relented.

"Father," he said, "I fear a trap, as I said before I will not split my army at this time but take fifty warriors and they will raze the bases, use your gjallarhorn and call for Asgard to retreat. I fear what's happening on those bases is a distraction and the real battle is destined to be on Salisbury Plain, note how the bases close to Salisbury have not been attacked. Do they think we're fools? Remove this distraction and let me deal with what's before us."

Fafner followed his son's request. He raised his gjallarhorn and sent out the call for an urgent retreat. It was a slightly modified call as it included an instruction to the warriors to assist in the evacuation of the bases.

The last personnel had just about exited the bases when the dragons arrived to release their flame and they incinerated everything before them. They continued their assault until they were satisfied all serpents and Dark Angels were destroyed, even if it meant burning every building, every munitions dump, every vehicle, plane and helicopter. They totally destroyed everything to ensure none of Hells army survived.

Back in Ireland the first wave of Hell had reached the hills of Meath and caused havoc. The sinister torch lights of the Dark Angels quickly formed a ring of fire around each hill. Shane then issued the order to attack not wanting his forces to be on the defensive.

The swift swishing of swords could be heard now that the carriers were engaged while the Elves immediately released their arrows in a torrent of accuracy that successfully took out the first line of attack by Hell. From the sky, Fafner watched the ring of torches tighten their circular grip and became alarmed while watching the carriers and elves begin to fall. He was pleased to see Evan lead his dragons and attack the rear flanks of the Dark Angels and then use their fire to incinerate so many that hope began to rise, that was until a dark cloud was seen coming from both the west and the north, it was the demon hounds and there were thousands of them.

Fafner was preparing to split the Asgard army when he saw the northern army, under Odi, was engaged in a battle with Dark Angels and serpents that were attacking from both the Ural Mountains, and the north eastern slopes of the Alps. They had attacked Russia, Ukraine and many other eastern European countries and were now massing so as to attack the western countries. He watched the carriers gather along the borders from Germany all the way to northern Italy and was pleased to see the arrival of the ancient spirits of the long gone Franks, Goths and Huns. From his vantage point he saw the arrival of the Elf armies. In England the Meadow Elves under the command of Lirissa arrived from beneath a bank of rocks close to Stonehenge. From the depths of the Black Forest in Germany the Forest Elves under the command of Aeson arrived and in Russia, from behind the waterfalls in the Urals, the Mountain Elves under the command of Azrael arrived. There were ten thousand warriors in each of these armies.

Fafner became suspicious when he saw the demon hounds flying very low and hiding among the Dark Angels, their strategy soon became clear when they swooped into the sky to attack the under-belly of the dragons. It was then when he unleashed Asgard by sending ten thousand chariots to Ireland; thirty thousand to England and the vast bulk that was left he sent to Western Europe. He turned his attention back to what was happening in Ireland and got more concerned because the attack on the dragons was particularly vicious causing many to fall.

He feared for Evan while watching him fly higher into the sky with two demon hounds tailing him. The hounds had evolved and now had the ability to fly higher without suffering the cold. His fears were realised when the hounds reached Evan and bit into his left wing causing him to spiral out of control. He managed to steady his fall and land on the Hill of Slane where he was quickly surrounded by serpents and they were moving in to finish him off. These particular serpents had successfully wiped out the carriers as well as the majority of elves in that area, and were looking forward to adding a dragon to their list of conquests.

Fafner leapt into action and flew at such speed he reached his son before the serpents did. He was delighted to see that another of his sons, Afan, had arrived from Salisbury and was flying by his side. Lugh and Ériu also arrived and between the four of them they formed a perimeter in the hope of protecting Evan. The serpents were ecstatic; they now had two gods and three dragons in their sights and were determined to take their souls to Hell.

They weren't to get their way; Ériu parted her arms and her Light shot out temporarily blinding all before her, she then yelled, "You've defiled my lands for the last time, scum of Hell. This is my domain, now prepare for my wrath." She raised her sword and raced forward taking out as many serpents and Dark Angels as she could, she was quickly joined by Lugh, Fafner and Afan who were equally as successful. Evan, although injured, also managed to assist.

All across the plains the carriers were being slaughtered and the elves were faring no better. It was only after Shane called for Asgard to assist when the tables turned and the forces of the Light began to get the upper hand. Shane and his friends, although seriously battered, continued to fight valiantly and succeeded in leading the discouraged carriers, with the assistance of the remaining elves, towards victory.

Back on the Hill of Slane the battle got more intense. Hidden among a column of approaching Dark Angels was one of Lucifer's brothers. It was Asmodeus and he positioned himself roughly ninety metres back from the hill. From there he raised his crystal encrusted spear and released it with such force that it travelled at a speed making it almost invisible. It hit Fafner, penetrated his armour and pierced his heart. It impaled him against a boulder and all watching knew that for him, there was no coming back.

The silence that fell upon the battlefield was palpable. The remaining serpents and the Dark Angels began retreating back towards the north. On Salisbury plain, King Derwyn fell to his knees in shock, and then grief. At the Western Wall, Jacob raised his hands to cover his face. In Olympus, Zeus and the senior gods leapt from their thrones. Odi was in the midst of a major battle over the plains of central Europe when he suddenly froze, his hands gripped the handle bar of his chariot so tightly blood began to flow, but nothing prepared the world for the reaction of the dragons. When the death of their Emperor sunk in, it was then when the rage came and it took them with a vengeance. They took to the sky in their thousands and made their way to Ireland where they pursued the forces of Hell towards the north. Their revenge was ruthless and swift showing no mercy. Many serpents and Dark Angels were taken high into the sky where they were torn limb from limb before their almost lifeless bodies were released for the dragons flying at a lower level to continue with the carnage before more came to incinerate what was left as they fell. This onslaught continued until every last one of Hells army was destroyed. The dragons, although in grief, got great pleasure from their assault against the demon hounds in particular, and they weren't finished. They flew to join up with the elves near Stonehenge. There they assisted in attacking every serpent, demon hound and Dark Angel that was on the battlefield. None were left. This was a massive defeat for Hell.

In the centre of the battlefield Derwyn was still on his knees, deep in grief and devastated. Andras landed beside him and said while insisting he stand, "My king, show your warriors your power not your grief. We must leave for Ireland. Take to the sky and be our King."

In the meantime Jacob had left Jerusalem and arrived on to the Hill of Slane. He acknowledged Lugh and Ériu with a slight bow; then moved towards Afan and Evan while shaking his head in disbelief, his lips quivering and his face showing his pain. He moved to kneel next to Fafner and gently rubbed his face. He asked all around him to close their eyes while he placed his hands on the spear and jerked it back from the boulder to release Fafner from its grip. He took him into his arms and transported him to the Hill of Tara where he was laid before the stone of destiny.

Within a few moments King Derwyn arrived and together with his brothers they knelt next to their father sharing their grief. Jacob backed away to give them privacy and went to join Shane who was equally distraught, especially when he saw how upset Jacob was.

Andras took control; he was Fafner's greatest general and most loyal friend. He called on the imperial dragon guards to bring the royal carriage. His plan was to take Fafner back to the dragon realm for a state funeral, but this was not to be. A shimmering light appeared in the far west, and as it approached it intensified. It was the spirit of Heulwyn and she had come to take her husband to Elysium.

Her sons watched her lean forward and place her hand on their father's cheek, calling him into her arms. When she removed her hand they watched his spirit rise to excitedly embrace her then together they moved to comfort their sons. They turned to face Jacob, Lugh and Ériu and bowed. Only then did Jacob realise, on seeing the peace in Fafner's face that this was all he ever wanted. He desired to spend eternity with the only woman he ever loved.

After a few moments, Fafner and Heulwyn slowly ascended into the sky and moved towards the west. They were followed by the dragon army escorting Fafner's mortal remains.

On arrival in Elysium they were met by Cronus and seven of the remaining Titans who stood reverently in their colossus form. They stood like pillars guarding the sacred lands of the dead. All Titans then took their human form and went to comfort Derwyn and his brothers before escorting them to the tombs of the dragon lords. The dragons also took their human form and began the slow death march that stretched from the beach, through the tombs of the blessed dead into the Mausoleum. No dragon, other than Fafner's sons, had ever been to Elysium and many of them considered it a place that existed only in the great stories, that was until they marched down the steps towards the arches holding the mortal remains of the dragon lords of myth and legend.

When the ceremony concluded Derwyn secured the lid of the sarcophagus and joined Cronus who said, "My lord Derwyn, you walked into this most holy of places as a King, I'm asking you to look into your soul and see who you are meant to be, walk out through the tombs of Elysium and let the dragon world see you as Emperor of the Dragons." He then presented him with a gift, "This is your father's sword. Over the last two thousand years it rested by his side and assisted him each time he called on the light. Now it's yours. Let the Light in, and become the god you are destined to be; it's your fathers wish."

Derwyn bowed to Cronus and backed away. He moved towards where Evan and Afan were waiting. Together they climbed the steps and when they reached the doors Derwyn stepped forward and took a deep breath. He transformed and appeared taller, his armour changed to the golden colour of the gods. His crown became encrusted with precious gems and his weapons lengthened. He held his sword high calling on the Light, and it came. It sent its power all across Elysium and all dragons went to their knees and swore allegiance to their new emperor. With a new confidence he called out,

"Warriors of the dragon realm; hear me. Today we lost many friends, tomorrow we will lose more; our battle against the forces of evil is not over. Take to the sky and form four armies. Andras, Evan, Afan and I will lead you all to victory. Each army must assist Olympus." He raised the sword again and yelled, "Victory! Victory! Victory!"

In the meantime, Jacob returned to the Western Wall where he felt secure, especially under the protection of the wizards. He had only arrived when he received a message from Odi, "You OK brother?"

"Not really," he replied. "My friend Fafner fell today."

"Brother, you've always known this would come to pass, there will be a time to grieve but it's not today. The west is now under the control of the Light so let's be grateful for the rage of the dragons. Today they came to my aid and soon the north will be secure in the Light, so put your efforts into assisting the east, the south and the Americas."

"Baldor and Thanases!" enquired Jacob. "Do they know what has happened to Fafner?"

"Don't worry about them," replied Odi. "They lead the carriers and the Norse lords. They're bloodied but still fighting, and soon this day will be theirs. I'll make sure they know Fafner died as one of the greatest Warrior Gods of all time."

Chapter 31

Jacob always got inspiration from Odi, his words helped to put the disaster of what happened in Ireland from his mind. He closed his eyes and called out to Faer who was leading the armies of the Light across the Americas. When Faer answered he said, "I felt a terrible pain and a tear trickled down my cheek, has it happened? Is he gone?"

Jacob's voice cracked as he tried to break the news, "It was quick," he said trying to keep himself composed, "he didn't see it coming. Heulwyn arrived and brought his spirit to Elysium." Faer said nothing. Jacob continued, "I feel your pain and I sense your grief, but I need you to find your strength. I need you to be strong and defend the Light as you promised."

Faer remained quiet then after awhile said, "We are ill prepared for what is below me. We battled all morning and lost many warriors, the south has fallen.

Evander and the Ice Elves broke through the glaziers and while making their way from the Great Lakes they were ambushed, the serpents were waiting and their attack was merciless. Evander is missing; I think he's been taken to Hell. Ten thousand Storm Elves, under the command of Cassiel, left the everglades and they too have been decimated. Cassiel survives but his army is seriously depleted. The carriers, there are millions, and they are fighting bravely. All across the tribal lands they're wearing the war paint and feathers of their ancestors. Every Indigenous nation from South and North American has answered the call of the gods and are now at war."

"Hold your position," said Jacob. "Tell the remaining elves to join the carriers and move to the central plains. The dragon army has been split and I've sent Andras and his dragons to assist. Divisions from the western Asgard army are on their way and they too will assist."

Faer was relieved because any attempts he made to protect the cities along the east coast from Boston to Miami were scuppered by a far more resilient Hells army. The savagery they unleashed on New York and Washington DC was horrendous, the death toll was in the millions and what was really upsetting for him was that Hell was replenishing their army in large numbers from the dark souls of people who fell away from the Light many years ago. What gave him hope was the fact that many souls rose as white mists, and this helped him to reaffirm that these lands were worth fighting for.

Jacob had just left Faer's head when a great boom was heard. From high in the sky Fear looked out to the west and saw that Mount St Helens had erupted. A second boom was heard and when he looked to the south west he saw a far more sinister eruption, it was Yellowstone and it was spewing its red hot ash miles into the sky. The ash then spread out all across western and central USA and it brought a darkness unseen on Earth for thousands of years. Temperatures dropped and then the storms came. The ash had a second purpose which was to disrupt the line of sight of Faer preventing him from directing the carriers and the elves. It is also possible that Hell had anticipated the arrival of the army from Asgard.

Hell was right to expect the Asgard army and when it arrived it went into action immediately. The battle was but a skirmish as Faer was only interested in testing Hells resolve but it was at a high price. Hell suffered many losses but Asgard suffered more, many chariots fell and their archers slaughtered.

Hell expected to be engaged with the whole army but Faer only sent a thousand chariots into action, he sent the bulk of Asgard higher into the sky where they split in two, one army went out over the Pacific and the other over the Atlantic. What Hell didn't know was that it was dealing with a well trained commander, a leader whose tactics were taught to him by the Goddess of War.

Mount St Helens and Yellowstone continued to spew, allowing hundreds of thousands more Dark Angels to exit Hell. These latest arrivals made their way towards the central plains and on their way they savaged the people in every town and city they passed. From the east the serpents made their way over the Appalachian Mountains to take up positions on the eastern and north eastern flanks of the prairies.

Faer had difficulty watching their movements as the ash cloud thickened forcing him to move below the cloud cover where he became visible to both the carriers as well as Hells armies. He moved swiftly across the sky and located a place to stay out of harm's way. He watched the carriers and the tribes take up their positions while the remnants of the elf armies formed a shield between the carriers and Hells legions. He was relieved when the spirits of the ancestors came and took up their positions, their greatest warrior chiefs of myth and legend were among them. Then the quietness came. The only sound was that of the gentle breeze whistling through the leaves, shrubs and grasses.

Faer moved again to place his chariot in a holding position just above the carriers. He looked down at his million-strong army and felt there were no more preparations to be put in place. He then looked out over the legions of Hell and saw that his armies were seriously outnumbered, at least three to one. He raised his staff and sent out the Light ensuring his army could see him clearly no matter how far away they were. His army looked upon him as a most powerful Warrior God of Olympus and guardian of the Light, they listened carefully when he said, "Warriors, look upon my staff and see it send out its light. Feel its power and know what you are fighting for. Look upon the legions of Lucifer as they bay for your blood and remember that the gods will not forsake you, they will send their power when our need is at its greatest," He waved his staff about then continued, "Warriors, when you feel all is lost, fall to the ground and await rescue. The gods will show their power. Victory! Victory! Victory."

Faer then moved his chariot to a safer location and waited for Hell to make the first move which wasn't long in coming. The Dark Angels from the south and from the west began marching. They moved in formation and were so numerous they presented as a most terrifying sight. The serpents based in the east and the north began slithering, many of them transformed into demons of great power. They too marched in formation and were ready for battle. The rest of the serpents continued their slimy slithering towards the carriers. As the Dark Angels closed in, it was the elves that attacked first by releasing their arrows in such numbers that the sky darkened creating what looked like starling murmurations. The arrows reached their targets but didn't achieve what was intended, as one Dark Angel fell two more appeared creating a greater difficulty. The carriers then went into action by racing ahead of the elves. Their swords were more effective, each Dark Angel defeated was decapitated before turning to dust. This time they weren't replaced.

In the meantime Jacob became aware of a plan by the Joint Chiefs who had gathered in the Pentagon and he wasn't happy. He was being telepathically informed of what was being discussed by a four star general who was a descendant of a loyal carrier. He also felt that if he had a general in place then Lucifer could also have allies planted, and his suspicions were confirmed when several generals advocated more ruthless action. They insisted that nobody, not even the gods, tells the United States what to do. Jacob's concern grew so he sent Merlin to the Pentagon with an instruction that no action was to be taken.

By the time Merlin arrived it was too late. Hells allies had persuaded the president to launch two nuclear missiles towards were the battles were being fought. The joint chiefs had been persuaded to wipe out both armies whether they were friend or foe. Merlin was furious and sent out his light, immediately highlighting the generals who were part of Lucifer's spy circle. He sent a second blast and this one pierced the generals sending them back to Hell. Merlin then returned to the Western Wall, knowing Faer would deal with the missiles. He also wanted to confirm to Jacob that the US military won't interfere again.

The two missiles had reached the stratosphere when they were intercepted by four Asgard chariots, one being driven by Faer. Two chariots aligned themselves alongside each missile with a view to changing their directions. One was sent towards Yellowstone and the second towards Mount St. Helens. Faer's plan worked, both missiles penetrated deep into both volcanoes before exploding so violently that both volcanoes collapsed in on themselves, preventing radiation escaping. Faer's quick thinking also caused the flow of serpents and Dark Angels to cease. Jacob was pleased when Faer reported that the volcanoes had been neutralised.

Back on the battlefield the serpents from the north and the east were now in action. They slithered towards the first line of defence and were met with a barrage of arrows from the remaining ranks of elves whose launching of arrows was continuous and relentless. They successfully impaled thousands of serpents using arrows that were dipped in the first source light, making them lethal. The carriers then stepped in and joined the elves in a vicious sword battle, the likes of which hadn't been seen since the Punic wars between Rome and Carthage, and that was over two thousand years earlier. Faer then used his gjallarhorn to summon into battle the two Asgard armies stationed over the Atlantic and Pacific Oceans.

On the Great Plains all armies of the Light were now fully engaged. As far as the eye could see those of the Light were now preparing for hand to hand battle. The sound of clashing steel grated and the whooshing of flying spears and arrows was terrifying. Exhaustion was not an option. The death toll among the forces of the Light was so numerous it was almost uncountable but the destruction they brought upon the Dark Angels and the serpents was far worse considering Hell outnumbered them by such a vast number.

Faer was horrified at the nauseating, sickly odour of blood and guts that prevailed in the gathering wind. He cringed listening to bones being fractured, snapped and shattered. The choking and groaning of his warriors as the last vestiges of life departed, broke his heart. He prayed for this battle to end and as the afternoon progressed he could find no hope.

It was around this time when the ash clouds dissipated, allowing the warm glow of the late afternoon sun to bring relief to the tangled mess that was the remnants of the warriors from both sides. For the Light the battle was all but lost and the remaining elves, carriers and tribesmen were now acting as though cornered in a cave. Faer was in despair, he had used the full might of Asgard and it failed to wipe out enough demons. Each fly past took out numerous Dark Angels but there always seemed to be more to replace them, it was as though they had found a new magic that kept replenishing their lines. The Asgard generals got more concerned as each attack resulted in more chariots crashing and the warriors being slaughtered by the thousands. Faer couldn't understand how his formidable defences crumbled so easily and was becoming more dejected until he remembered something Jacob once said, 'When all seems lost the senior gods will act.'

It was then he noticed a glimmer of hope gallop across the skies, it was Pegasus and he halted above the battle field, he reared to his hind legs, neighed loudly, sending out a call to arms. It was a call that travelled in all directions and it soon reached Nevada, North Carolina and Nova Scotia. It awoke the greatest and most powerful symbol of the Wild West, the formidable Mustangs. They answered, and all sixty thousand galloped to join with their god.

They circled the battle field and then the charge of the stallions began, they were so swift and powerful that in one attack they were able to break the ranks of Hell. This was followed by the mares and foals, who, between them finished off the remaining Dark Angels and serpents before all that was evil had a chance to realise what happened.

Faer leapt from his chariot and ran to assist the carriers through what looked like a graveyard of slime and entrails. They made sure every close by serpent and Dark Angel was dispatched. Those who survived tried to use what little strength they still had to inflict as much pain as they could but they didn't last long as Faer and his warriors now had a new purpose and energy.

When he was satisfied his work was done he made his way back to his chariot and went to meet with Pegasus. Although bloodied and bruised, he didn't care, he dismounted, clenched his fist, raised it to cover his heart and bowed to his saviour, then said, "My lord Pegasus, your intervention was most timely and welcome."

"You've done well against all the odds," replied Pegasus. "The battle of the Americas is now over. Leave what remains of Asgard to patrol the skies above, make your way to Olympus. There's a goddess who needs you, her strength wanes in your absence." Faer immediately left for Olympus.

Chapter 32

At the Western Wall Jacob was having difficulty keeping up with the events happening all across the world. He hadn't heard from either Magni or Modi, and this concerned him. In his mind he searched around and again thought of Modi, almost immediately he heard, "Hi Brother, wondered how long it would be before you contacted me. Be aware that this will be some battle Asgard is about to fight." He went quiet for a moment, then said, "Jacob, I felt your pain; I liked Fafner. I hope you're OK?"

"I'm devastated," replied Jacob, "but I'm doing well. Just so you know I can't feel or see Jomo or Jahiri, can you see them?"

Modi moved his chariot higher and soon reported that both were engaged against the forces of Hell. He reported Jomo had moved south and his battle was centred on Table Mountain.

"Jomo," he said, "is in command of thousands of carriers and has just been joined by the Zulu nation. His flaming spear is returning to him leading thousands of long dead warriors from among the mountain and forest tribes. I hope he prevails."

He then spoke of Jahiri, "That Jahiri, he is one handsome devil, wherever he appears, they fall before him. They see him as a powerful god and they just drop everything and follow him; I wish I had that power. The kingdom of Kush and their descendants have risen and, as planned, have joined him. He seems to be having difficulty along the northern coast. The serpents from Santorini are doing a lot of damage. Be aware brother," he continued while moving higher to get a better view. "The Great Rift Valley is volatile today, the long silent volcanoes are belching, those already erupting are releasing thousands more Dark Angels, thankfully the demon hounds of Hell haven't as yet showed themselves. I fear Hells attack will be so dire that the lack of preparations in these lands will leave all but a few dead. I see serpents pouring in from the Atlantic and they're moving towards cities and towns along the western seaboard. There are many more serpents slithering on to the beaches along the eastern seaboard."

"What of the Gods of Africa?" asked Jacob.

"Shango met with me," replied Modi. "He has called the Orisha Gods to come together and they're assisting the Yoruba peoples. The ancestors of the western tribes have risen and are also under their guidance. The minor gods are doing their best but they still argue among themselves, unfortunately they don't seem to understand their only chance of survival is if Jomo and Jahiri succeed."

"Modi," said Jacob getting annoyed. "Need I remind you that you are a Warrior God of Asgard, and you are in command of the south? Get those gods on board now. If what's happening in the north and across the west comes to pass in the south, it suggests they are ill prepared."

"Jacob," it was Jahiri. "I'm under pressure," he said, "the serpents are more resilient than the ones I've met in the past. The carriers fight valiantly and have succeeded in forcing them back towards the sea but they're now regrouping and seem to be getting stronger. They've inflicted carnage on the population and the problem is, the more we smite, the more come out of the sea."

"Your problem is about to get worse," interrupted Modi. "There's an army of Dark Angels flying low across the rain forests, they'll soon be over the Sahara Desert and will be on your flanks, prepare for their attack. I will send Asgard to assist." He looked towards the horizon and said, "A second army is flying south, it's as powerful. Lucifer is throwing everything at this sad land." He looked towards the south east and said, "Oh my."

"Jacob," said Modi. "I see something else. There's thousands upon thousands of serpents crossing the Serengeti, the plains are deserted, it's as though all of animal kind has fled." He moved closer for a better view then continued, "From what I can see four great battles will be fought in the south this day. It seems Lucifer has sent several armies of Dark Angels and two of serpents, a strange decision. Why would he send a serpent army to the centre of the Serengeti? There are but two thousand carriers present. It makes no sense."

"There are strange decisions being made by Lucifer," replied Jacob, "and I fear much of what is happening is a distraction. He's up to something and I can't put my finger on it." He paused for a moment, listened before continuing, "I've heard nothing from Magni as yet, but what we do know for definite is that millions upon millions have died across the world. The harvesting of souls for the army of Hell goes on unabated. Everywhere Lucifer's army has walked is now a hellscape of butchery and despair, yet he has not shown himself since he walked these hallowed stones."

Modi then reported the serpents surrounding the carriers who had gathered in an area of the Serengeti called Seronera. He also spoke of the destruction of towns and villages near the plains, all with thousands of deaths.

Jacob remained in Modi's head and through his eyes he watched the happenings below, he watched the carriers move towards the front line of the serpents, "Modi," he said. "I think it's time to release the arrows of Asgard, assist the carriers."

Modi agreed, raised his hand and with a quick flick ordered the launch of volley after volley. Much to their horror all flights of arrows were deflected showing the gods that Hell had a new power, one that shielded the serpents from the source Light dipped arrow tips. Modi prepared to send his warriors to further assist but was stopped by Jacob who wondered if it was wise to send the Asgard warriors into hand to hand combat. His wondering didn't last long.

Modi looked across the acacia forests and saw the trees heaving just like when once he watched the great beasts of legend move through them, he saw that whatever beasts they were, they were moving towards the plains. Jacob heard him gasp and say, "Oh, wow!" What he was watching was the arrival of the Tuskers.

From the tree line they stepped out and there they stood for a moment. There were twenty five majestic animals, seven bulls and eighteen cows, all with their tusks touching the ground. When they fully exited from beneath the trees they raised their trunks and trumpeted out a call that travelled across the plains. Behind them were the walking skeletons of the fallen emperors who once reigned supreme and had long gone to the elephant necropolis. As the skeletons walked they began transforming. Flesh appeared over their bones, then the grey coloured skin appeared, and before long they were fully formed enormous elephants. Their trumpeted calls left the plains and penetrated back through the Acacia forests before crossing the mountains, and they came from everywhere. Thousands upon thousands were on the move. What Modi was showing Jacob was the Last March of the Tuskers.

The elephants moved at a steady pace and proceeded to completely surround Seronera; they watched the fierce fighting and were horrified by the scale of savagery that came to pass between the carriers and the serpents, a savagery that brought on a glimpse of what the future held under the rule of

Hell. It was carnage for the serpents, their ripped skin, sliced veins and decapitated heads showed how the carriers showed no mercy, but still there were thousands left. It was then when the elephants moved to intervene. Modi remained in situ and watched the herds make their move. It was a silent and determined walk, and before long they reached the outer line of the slithering mass of writhing slime that was the serpent army. For their defence, the elephants used their trunks and tusks to deflect any attempt by the serpents to inject their poison. They just kept marching, nonstop, until they had impaled and trampled into oblivion any serpents in their way. The aftermath was a scene of blood, flesh and bones splattered all over the trampled grasses of these beautiful plains.

When Hell was defeated Modi was aghast at the carnage. He placed his hand against his forehead, closed his eyes and called out, "Father, hear me. Bring the rains; cleanse these lands of the slime of Hell."

He then left his position and met with the carriers, "You've fought valiantly with so few losses," he said. "I'm troubled, why here? Why this place? It bothers me that so few souls should be of such interest to Lucifer! There is something else at play!"

"We too fail to understand why here?" replied the nearest carrier. "We too wondered why a place so devoid of all life? Strange how the message given by the goddess Oba to our families over a thousand years ago should bring so few yet there are millions of us."

"I too don't understand," acknowledged Modi. "It's as though the eyes of the gods are being diverted."

The Emperor of the Tuskers then arrived and bowed. He rested his trunk on Modi's shoulder allowing them to communicate telepathically.

"My lord Modi," said the Tusker. "I think I have the answer. Once in the distant past, a messenger and her guardians walked these lands, they were the ones who passed on the message to the ancestors of these carriers. They bore witness to an attack by Hell on their guardian Tuskers and when the Tuskers fell, the vengeance of the elephant herds was unleashed. They showed no mercy, they impaled and trampled all soldiers of evil in their path. I fear what happened here is a distraction, and it is revenge for that attack. Look around and see how all of elephant-kind is present in one place. Look to the horizon, look in all directions, smell the smoke and see how the fires of Hell surround us. Now watch the flames race towards us giving us no escape. He has deceived us. He has brought all elephant-kind into one place and it would seem he plans to wipe us out of all memory; then his revenge will be complete."

Jacob entered their heads, "It's true, we have been deceived, while you watched the march of the Tuskers, Lucifer released his demon hounds, and they are attacking on three fronts. Jomo and Jahiri are in severe trouble. The Orisha is in disarray. Take to the sky and split Asgard, defend the carriers. Leave the fires of Hell to me."

Modi immediately left to join up with his army and on his way he heard Jacob call out, "Father, aid the Tuskers, release your thunder and bring the rains, give relief to the Serengeti."

In Asgard, Thor heard Jacob's call and immediately summoned his chariot. He crossed the Bifrost Bridge, and after travelling through a nearby portal he arrived in the sky above the Serengeti from where he saw the chaos and panic spreading through the herds. It broke his heart to see the flames lapping at the feet of mothers trying to revive their fallen calves. He quickly assessed the situation and then flew in a large circle around the grasslands, increasing his speed as the seconds passed. At first the clouds formed, and then the lightning came. After that came the loud rumblings. He was announcing to the world that the God of Thunder had arrived and was taking control. The clouds rolled across the sky and hovered over the flames then they released their bounty. The rains fell in torrential pulses, not only filling the rivers causing them to burst their banks, the plains were also drenched bringing great relief, dousing the flames and cleansing the grasses.

When satisfied the herds were now safe Thor moved north to assist the army sent by Modi. He soon arrived and sought out Jahiri but had difficulty finding him as the battle was being fought all across the northern lands from Egypt to Morocco. While searching he came across a powerful fighter, a giant who was alone and valiantly fighting off a column of Dark Angels. He recognised that the giant was seriously outnumbered and raced to his aid but was too late. A volley of poisoned spears was launched bringing the giant down. The Dark Angels didn't wait about, they quickly departed. Thor reached the giant hoping to ease his passing.

"I know not your name," he said, "but I saw your valour. I will see to it that you rest among the heroes of old. Sleep now for your battle is over."

The giant gasped his last few breaths as a single tear flowed down his cheek. He gripping Thor's arm,

"I'm the last of my kind and worry there will be no one to mourn my passing. Will there be a place for me in Elysium, resting among my ancestors?" He whispered while looking around one last time. "This is the beloved lands of the giants, a land I've protected since that time when Heracles slew my kin. Do you know of Oba?" Thor just nodded. "Tell her I answered the call of Pegasus, tell her of my battle. Remind her that my name is Antaeus."

"Fear not great warrior," said Thor. "The Titans guard Elysium and will be proud to mourn your passing." Antaeus passed away.

Thor continued searching for Jahiri and finally located him close to the city of Benghazi. He was out of his chariot and at the head of the carriers who were battling serpents and Dark Angels that had arrived earlier that day.

"The rage of Hell is everywhere and much stronger than we expected," he said on joining Jahiri. "I've a suggestion."

"Anything that helps," replied Jahiri.

"Concentrate on the serpents emerging from the Mediterranean; leave the Dark Angels and hounds to me."

Thor immediately took to the sky and sent the gathered Asgard charioteers in two directions, one to the east and the other the west. The chariots that flew east were chariots that carried the bladed undercarriages and they were preparing to attack the dark Angels. The chariots in the west were much lighter and more manoeuvrable, ideal for attacking the flying hounds. When ready, Thor unleashed both armies, opening two more battle fronts.

The eastern chariots attacked by gathering speed to reach the Dark Angels before they knew what was happening, many were decapitated on contact with the blade underbellies. Those that survived were quickly dispatched by nearby carriers. Eliminating the Dark Angels allowed the western charioteers to attack the demon hounds that were attacking the carriers from behind. The hounds couldn't cope with the swiftness of the lighter chariots and quickly succumbed. They were brought down at such a rate it was felt that this particular battle would soon be won. On the beaches Jahiri and the carriers successfully drove the serpents back into the sea but not before a mass slaughter.

The annihilation of Hells forces across the Northern African coastline was vicious leaving bodies littering the land and seascape. Thousands of Hells army that survived escaped through nearby portals.

"They've done it again," said Thor after rejoining Jahiri. "They attempt to overwhelm us using their superior numbers, and then when they do damage they disappear. Why?"

"It is strange," replied Jahiri. "I fear Hell is trying to drain our forces, I noticed when they slew a carrier, they captured the soul and took it somewhere. Are they taking it to the Underworld? Replenishing their armies?"

"You might be right," said Thor. "That's something I need to think about? I must leave, the south calls."

Thor headed further south planning to assist Jomo but when he arrived, he found the battle was over. Everywhere he looked there were bodies of carriers and fallen chariots of Asgard and this broke his heart. Even seeing the amount of Hells army lying across the battlefield didn't raise his spirits.

He sought Jomo and on finding him said, "Earlier this day I joined Jahiri and saw the grizzly after effects of Hell's savagery. This evening, before me, is that same savagery, yet there's no need of Asgard, you've done well."

"This battle was all but lost," replied Jomo. "My flaming spear did its part, its flame crossed the sky bringing more tribes into the Light and that helped, but it was Modi's action that saved the day. He sent Asgard and while under my command they routed the power of Hell. Here on this ancient land all would have been lost but for Asgard. We are so grateful. Furthermore, the Mer-armies based in the Indian Ocean cut off the advance of the serpents preventing any more from reaching the east coast."

"No matter, young warrior," said Thor. "Your training made you a great commander, you did what was expected, so be proud. I must leave; something isn't right on the west coast. I fear a calamity."

Thor left and raced towards Nigeria all the time receiving visions showing his old friends, the Orisha, really suffering. On arrival he found chariots of the Asgard army strung out across the rain forests and fighting rearguard actions against a far more formidable Hells army. He was horrified at the amount of chariots that had fallen and hoped there were survivors. He also saw the carriers were being decimated making him wonder as to where the warriors of the Yoruba were. He also wondered where Modi was.

He climbed higher into the sky so as to get a better view. From there he saw a clearing and in the clearing he saw eight large wooden posts. Impaled on seven of the posts were renowned Orisha Gods and on the eight was Modi. The Dark Angels were using them for target practice by shooting arrows at non vital parts of their bodies, keeping them alive and in severe pain for as long as possible. Thor was furious, and after racing towards the clearing, then leaping from his chariot he landed between the posts and the tormentors. He took his colossus form and showed his rage while yelling in a clear and thunderous voice, "I am Thor, Asgard God of Storms and Thunder. You will rue the day you hurt my son, prepare for my wrath."

He swung his hammer and as its speed increased, the winds came to form a twister that sucked up the Dark Angels. As they reached the highest clouds the lightning was waiting and it used bolt after bolt to cause maximum pain before incinerating every last one.

Thor retook his human form and ran to free his son. On reaching him he feared it was too late. "Father, forgive me," Modi managed to say, "I've let you and Asgard down. The light calls me, Elysium calls." Just then he began to give up his spirit and begin his long journey to rest among the fallen warriors of Asgard.

"No son," pleaded Thor, his voice trying to break through his grief. "Not now, you're a God of Asgard, an immortal. I see you in my future, you must fight this pain. Please son, help is on the way."

At that very moment Odi arrived, he reached in, gripped Modi and blinked. Within a second he arrived in Olympus where Apollo was waiting.

"Odi, go," said Apollo. "You're needed elsewhere. He's safe in my care. Remember, death cannot enter this sanctum. Go!"

Odi had difficulty backing away, so strong was his love for his brother. He was devastated. Of all his brothers, Modi was his biggest tormentor but was also his most loyal ally. He knew that no matter what, Modi always had his back and could always be relied upon in any crisis. The shock of seeing Modi fall got to him and when he left the room he fell against a pillar and went to his knees in despair. Panya arrived and said while embracing him, "Modi is safe here, and you know that. Stay in my arms until your strength returns then go south and be by your father's side. He needs you more than ever now"

"I don't understand why you are sending me south," wondered Odi. "I'm supposed to be in command of the armies of the north."

"Because of your efforts," Panya replied. "The north is now safe, go and join your father." She went quiet for a moment as a look of concern crossed her face, "Something's wrong and I don't understand, I just glimpsed your father and, it's you who's going to need him."

"I'm a trained general and a God of Asgard," said Odi while looking confused. "Why would I need the protection of the God of Thunder?"

She didn't answer; she leaned in and kissed him. He then left and joined his father in the clearing.

Odi found his father still on his knees, frozen to the spot such was his grief. On hearing Odi return he looked up hoping for good news but nothing came. He only rose to his feet when rustling sounds were heard coming from among the trees causing them both to reach for their swords but there was no need to fear, it was Lord Shango. He arrived all bloodied and battered, looking the worse for wear.

"Throughout these lands," he said, "we fought and many have fallen. Asgard chariots litter the forest floor and the stench of death is everywhere.

Hell just disappeared, into thin air they went! I felt a god fall and can't find as to who it is. Why is there now an eerie silence?"

"The fallen god is my brother Modi," replied a glum Odi. "He's now with Apollo in Olympus."

"My lord Odi," said Shango reassuring him. "Why so glum, he's safe in Apollo's hands. You already know death cannot enter Olympus. I see him back by your side."

"Enough," said Thor. "Let us release the Orisha Gods from their binds and move on." While cutting the binds he turned to Shango, "I too cannot understand this plan of Lucifer. He was winning here and yet he retreats, is there something we're missing? He's after something or is it someone?"

"Go to Asgard," suggested Shango. "Speak to the elders, see what we're missing." Thor agreed and left with Odi by his side.

The two chariots went high enough so as to view all of Africa. When Odi raised his staff and sent out his light, he quickly established no presence of serpents, Dark Angels or demons. He called on Jomo and Jahiri to join him and like him and his father, they too were equally confused. Although confused, all four made their way towards Olympus. While heading north they noticed millions of carriers from all across Africa moving rapidly towards the Middle East. "Strange how briskly they move," remarked Thor. "This is too easy. My fears are growing that there's definitely something else at play. Odi, bring me one of the carriers."

Odi left and a short while later returned with a carrier by his side. "Why such a hurry?" asked Thor.

"Just like the first message we received," replied the carrier. "We've been called upon again. We're to gather on the Aleppo Plateau and what's strange is, our injuries have miraculously healed, we move at great speed, and we feel so much stronger. One thing is clear our battle isn't over."

"Well father," said Odi. "It seems your plans are changed, it's to the Aleppo Plateau we go."

Chapter 33

Jacob, while still standing next to the Western Wall, was telepathically receiving reports from all around the world. He noted that the battles in the north, south and the west as well as the Americas had all concluded with wins for the armies of the Light and this troubled him. Like his father, he felt the wins were too easy. He was satisfied that the Atlantic, Indian and Arctic oceans were secure except for a few skirmishes that were being quickly brought under control. He agreed with Toyesh's decision to send the bulk of his armies into the Pacific Ocean where, all around the ring of fire, volcanoes were still erupting and releasing thousands more serpents and Dark Angels who were making their presence felt. He was pleased to see Toyesh being assisted by the power of Oceanus, the Kraken, Hydra and the Nirgen, but was saddened when he realised how many warriors Toyesh had lost especially Pantos, his son and heir.

Earth was now six hours into the attack from Hell and the death toll had reached at least three billion, no country or continent for that matter was spared. The Mer-armies were dealing as best they could with the serpents who were pouring out from beneath the seas especially near Malaysia and Indonesia, while on land the carriers and the descendants of the Han, the Manchu and the Mongols were in action since earlier that morning. They were up against a most violent and ruthless onslaught. It was in India where the serpents were harvesting the most souls and there was little or no defence. The carriers of India were overwhelmed but were still fighting valiantly and they couldn't understand why nobody was coming to assist. Many millions made their way to the foothills of Mount Kailash in the hope Lord Shiva would come to their aid.

It wasn't Lord Shiva who assisted, it was the Yeti nation who came in their hundreds and commenced an attack on the serpents that was merciless and savage. They began their assault by rolling, just like snowballs, from high in the mountains and then when they neared their targets they evolved into eight foot tall snow people. The serpents couldn't bite through their thick and dense fur ensuring no Yeti warrior fell.

Jacob in the meantime was still trying to reach Magni and was so concerned he contacted Odi and asked him to go find answers. Before Odi left he told Jacob that he and Thor were over the Aleppo Plateau watching the gathering of a vast army of carriers from all across Europe, the Middle East and Africa. He said he couldn't understand what was going on other than one carrier told him that they had all received a second calling instructing them to travel north.

"Odi, never mind Aleppo," said a seemingly disinterested Jacob. "I need you to find out what has happened to Magni, something's wrong, I sense the passing of millions of souls and Asgard is doing nothing, go now."

Odi blinked and arrived into the midst of the Asgard army in the east. He immediately witnessed the slaughter happening all over Asia and was furious Asgard hadn't intervened. He berated the generals and ordered an immediate assault. One very embarrassed general tried to tell him Magni had ordered them to wait for his return before attacking but he never returned. He said Magni had earlier left for Asgard and instructed the generals in charge to only monitor the happenings below but not to interfere.

Odi immediately contacted Jacob telling him he was taking control of the eastern army. "I don't understand?" responded Jacob. "Magni is one of the greatest War Gods, he'd never allow so many to die. This is negligence; there must be something we're missing."

"We'll worry about Magni later," replied Odi while acting on his sense of urgency. "This is some mess; even the Mer-armies are struggling. Yaz and the Yeti nation have attacked and seem to be driving Hell away from the mountains but in the countries of the Far East the slaughter is horrendous. I'll start by sending the bulk of our chariots there."

Odi was known for being a very assertive Warrior God and had no fear of taking decisive action. He immediately called for reinforcements from Africa and Europe and then split his army into four, sending one into action over the central plains of India, his second army entered Chinese airspace and immediately engaged with the flying demons, the third army headed out towards Japan to be rendered unnecessary as the tenth army of the elves had completely annihilated the forces of Hell, albeit with the help of thousands of carriers. The fourth army had the hardest task as they were fighting a rear guard action over Vietnam, Korea and Myanmar.

Back in Wales and deep in the mountains, the dragon oracles were watching the battles in the Far East. They called on Emperor Derwyn and said while showing him what they saw, "My lord, once there was a nation of dragons who ruled the Far Eastern lands. It was written that they were of our blood but then a great wind came and they were no more. The peoples of those lands never forgot and have, for millennia, set aside whole years in honour of their long gone protectors. Their next 'Year of the Dragon' is less than twenty years from now. You must send your armies to assist, let them see how much we care but what is most important is we must show them that their homage was not in vain."

"Our warriors have been so depleted," said a concerned Derwyn. "If we use our resources we will be defenceless in our own lands."

"Trust us," replied the oracle. "You have enough to defend both realms."

After considering his options Derwyn called on Andras and said, "Our battle, it seems, isn't over. Take a thousand dragons, cross the high Arctic and rescue the peoples of the Far East. Let them see you fight by their side. Always remember that in those lands they celebrate in memory of our kin, our long gone ancestors. They now look forward to the 'Year of the Dragon' so let us acknowledge their homage."

"We're exhausted, my lord," said a troubled Andras, "and many are still not healed. Does Olympus not realise we've done our part."

"The war is not over until it's over," said Derwyn. "Many of our allies are still falling to the armies of Hell. While we can still breathe fire, we should breathe fire. My friend and protector, lead my armies one more time."

Andras bowed and called together a thousand warriors and when ready they made their way to the nearest exists. While exiting they were met by Derwyn who was standing high on a very tall stone stele saluting as they passed. Within two hours they reached the Far East and joined up with Asgard,

"My lord Odi," said Andras as he bowed. "The fire of a thousand dragons is all yours, what is your command?"

"Split in three," replied a delighted Odi. "Send an army to attack over India, the second to attack over China and the third to attack over the South East. Send your largest army towards the South East."

Through the ash and smoke filled skies they arrived. For the people, they were an awesome sight, especially when they released their flame. The people cheered while watching them incinerate the serpents and Dark

Angels. Their ruthless pursuit of the demon hounds lifted the spirits of the carriers and emboldened them into fighting even more fiercely. Then everything changed, a quietness came, the armies of the Light were looking all around them, there were no serpents, Dark Angels or demon hounds, they had all disappeared as though into thin air. Odi looked confused and called on Andras to join him, he was equally confused. "How can this be?" he asked.

They looked down on a landscape of devastation that spread from the north east of China to the south west of India and saw cities, towns and villages, all in flames. Stunned survivors exited their hiding places with tears flowing as they comprehended all they had lost. The dragons took holding positions high in the sky before fading into invisibility. Asgard was in deep shock especially when they realised how many chariots had fallen.

"Are we being deceived?" asked Andras. "Where did they go? What is he playing at?"

Odi contacted Jacob, "The war in the east is over and much has been destroyed. There's now no presence of Hell and the carriers have begun moving towards the west. Something's not right. This happened in the south."

"I sense a new presence," said Jacob, "and it's something I haven't felt before, it's calling me to Aleppo." Odi sensed nothing and insisted he stay under the protection of the wizards but this wasn't an option because the wizards were leaving to make their way to Olympus.

Odi was very alert to everything happening around Jacob and wasn't happy that he was now alone, he blinked and immediately appeared alongside him, "There's no way I'm leaving you alone in a place where Lucifer has shown himself, we'll travel together and join father above Aleppo."

Jacob was really pleased Odi had arrived, he felt safer. "Is there still no sign of Magni?" he asked,

"I tried," replied Odi. "I used my powers to search and it was to no avail, it's as though he's shielded from my gaze."

"Maybe together?" wondered Jacob. "Maybe our combined powers will find him?"

They placed their hands on each other's shoulders then moved their foreheads together and closing their eyes, they began searching. Together they thought of Magni and travelled through space and time to search all places to which their minds took them. The images brought them to the east where they saw Magni preparing to send the eastern armies into battle. They also saw he was distracted and then saw him speak with his generals, they watched him race towards the northern lands and then cross the Bifrost bridge into the realm of Asgard. They followed him to where he met with Odin and then watched him move towards the Mountain of the Oracles. They listened to the oracles say,

"Lucifer isn't interested in Earth as his dominion, he cares less that Hells fires will burn all before it, he cares even less for man; it's their souls he wants just so he can spite the Ancient One. All this is but a distraction for he has a far greater desire. He wants one god only, the Boy King. He sees in Jacob something he's hated since the beginning of time."

Jacob and Odi continued following Magni as he left Asgard then watched him enter Earth's atmosphere. They were horrified to see two powerful entities, beings they couldn't identify, materialise on his chariot. There was no shape to identity them, just a dense fog from which arms extended. They watched the fog disable and subdue him, before taking him through a portal to a place they didn't recognise. They managed to penetrate the portal before it fully closed and followed the entities while they placed Magni into a blackened cell. They were prevented from entering, it was shielded by a potent evil magic, yet they were able to see all that transpired within it. They watched the entities strip and humiliate their brother, and their anguish increased when they saw him being impaled against a stone wall before being whipped into unconsciousness. They then watched Lucifer arrive and the two entities disappear into his mouth.

"The great War God of Asgard," Lucifer was heard to say. "Magni, how easy was it for you to fall into my grasp?"

Magni managed to spit into his face before receiving a full force punch that sent blood spatter in all directions, "My tentacles spread out everywhere," said Lucifer while plunging his jagged fingers deep into Magni's chest. "The pathetic Asgardian oracles will never speak again. Their blood decorates the walls of their grotto. Do you think I'd allow them send warnings to the Boy King? I plan to make him suffer a pain that'll be felt all across the universe. I'll relish his screams of terror as he watches his beloved, and his children, torn to pieces by my demons of Hell."

"Why do you hate him so?" gasped Magni as more blows rained down on him.

"Wouldn't you like to know?" said Lucifer while extending one of his finger nails to tear into Magni's chest. He then went to disembowel him but stopped as though frozen. He slowly turned and stared at the entrance then walked over and sniffed the stale air, "Ah, I smell your fear, boy, and you are not alone, you brought your side kick, the one who is nothing without you, a useless excuse for a warrior," he stepped out into the passage way and looked around, then growled, "Cowards, show yourselves."

He didn't get what he wanted, he walked away, and the boys followed him into a vast cavern. When the boys looked out across the vastness, they saw the size and strength of the armies who were preparing to enter the realm of man, and they were shocked. They then knew that the real battle was about to start and it had the makings of what Jacob remembered from his religious classes to be forever known as the last battle, the last war, the last of everything...It was ARMAGEDDON

Chapter 34

The boys slowly parted and were clearly shocked by what they saw. "I don't look on you as my side kick," said Jacob after a few moments of silence. "I wouldn't know what to do if I lost you. You are the bravest warrior I've ever known."

"I don't care what he said," replied Odi shrugging his shoulders. "He's the great deceiver and if he says one thing I will look at the opposite. He called me useless therefore I know I'm useful. He said I was nothing without you, well, I know I'm everything to you, so don't worry, he can't insult me.....I can't believe you're worried about my feelings considering you've just witnessed the strength of the real army of Hell."

"What are we going to say to father about Magni?" asked Jacob.

"We're not going to say anything," replied Odi. "You, my amazing brother, will offer your head and allow him place his hand upon it, he will then see everything. I'm going to hide, because his explosion will send shockwaves throughout the cosmos and I don't want to be in the way when that happens."

"Coward," sneered Jacob.

"This time, brother," replied Odi. "I'm definitely going to be a coward."

Odi produced his gjallarhorn and called for two chariots to take them to the Aleppo Plateau, where, on arrival they separated, with Odi heading to position himself close to Damascus while Jacob joined his father. Odi watched his father place his hand upon Jacob's head. He saw the shock cross his father's face and was surprised there was no explosion. He entered Jacob's head, "That's not what I expected!"

"I think his heart is broken," replied Jacob. "He just looked at me and started talking about the gathering of the carriers."

"Well then," said Odi. "No more should be said, I'm moving back towards Jerusalem, I think I see the hounds but I'm not sure."

Jacob remained quiet for a short while then turned to his father and asked, "Why didn't you react when you saw what's happening to Magni?"

"I didn't react because there's a war to fight," replied Thor. "It's a war that could be the last and if victory eludes us, all will be lost. I intend to win. Be warned, watch me deal a merciless blow against Hell and let me assure you that my revenge will be best served cold."

"My heart's broken," said Jacob while backing away, "I can't get him from my mind. I'm leaving for Olympus. I believe Hades might be able to help."

Before Thor could say anything Jacob blinked to immediately arrive in Olympus. He was so upset and distracted that he passed his children without recognising them. He sought out Hades and allowed him place his hand upon his head and when Hades finished going through his memories Jacob asked, "Do you recognise the place where Lucifer is holding Magni?"

"I do!" nodded Hades. "It's not easy to get to, and it's the most shielded place in the Underworld. It's not part of Hell."

"Can you take me there?" asked Jacob causing Hades to recoil in horror,

"No! Are you mad? That part of the Underworld is beyond law and full of a dark anger."

"You must help," insisted Jacob. "I can't concentrate; the image of Magni suffering is clouding my judgement."

Zeus arrived and when he looked at Jacob he saw his distress and said while raising two of his fingers to stop the gathering tears from flowing, "Since the day we met I saw what was most endearing about you, it's your compassion. You oozed love for those closest to you. Today is not the day for that compassion; you are King of Kings and the whole world needs you to be decisive. Leave Magni to me. I'll see if there's something I can do." He continued while backing away, "Go now, be the leader we all know you to be."

Jacob bowed to both Zeus and Hades and made his way back into the temple only for his heart to leap with joy when he saw Eala was waiting. She saw the smudges around his eyes and said, "I'll say nothing, just come into my arms and let me comfort you." She held him and he involuntarily closed his eyes to take in the love she had for him but nothing matched the feelings that gathered when he felt a number of little arms wrap themselves around his legs, he smiled, looked down and then lit up. He went to his knees and hugged his three children. He looked into their tiny faces and again remembered what he was fighting for. He looked up at Eala, continued to smile, got up and kissed her before moving towards the doors. Within moments he arrived back above the Aleppo Plateau and stood beside his father, "Father, I don't understand why I'm so insecure? Why do I always doubt myself? Yet, why is it I feel so strong in your presence?"

"Jacob, son," said Thor. "I've raised three of my sons as War Gods, powerful and ruthless leaders, any one of them could rule Asgard but you are different. Those sixteen years under the protection of your mother you learned the ways of mankind, developed their emotions. When your mother and I parted little did I know how powerful she was and how she used her powers to take you through time, to hide and protect you, yet teach you to be the greatest Warrior God of them all. What makes you different is that you are so full of compassion, understanding and empathy but most importantly you are full of love. See how Asgard, the Astrals, even man, have laid down their lives just to follow you, you will rule the cosmos when all this chaos is over."

"I don't understand," said Jacob still showing his insecurities. "I played tricks on my friends, played rugby for my school. I broke the rules, drank alcohol behind the school gym. I did all the things teenage boys got up to just to defy my mother and my teachers. How can all this be?"

"Enough," replied an exasperated Thor. "We'll talk of this another time. Now watch as Hells armies make their way across the lands below."

Jacob looked down and saw an army of serpents attack the coastal plains of Israel and Lebanon. They attacked in a line from Gaza in the south to the Lebanese port of Sidon.

"They're splitting," said Jacob. "Some are making their way towards the hill of Megiddo; others are chasing the columns of refugees from Gaza and the cities of Jaffa and Haifa."

"Fear not," replied Thor. "Odi has sent a column of charioteers and they'll provide protection until the refugees reach the mountains. I'm more alarmed at what I see over Megiddo."

"I see it too," said Jacob. "Is this when I get alarmed? Hell's portal is a least two hundred meters wide, they are pouring out in their thousands. This must be the largest army of Dark Angels ever assembled and it seems to be never ending."

"Look at the general who leads the Dark Angels. Do you recognise him?" asked Thor.

Jacob focused for a moment and then saw the Mark of Chaos and gasped. "I don't believe it," he said. "I thought his existence was a myth. Father, its Cain, the first murderer, son of Adam and Eve. How is he leading Hells armies?" There was no reply.

Cain's army just kept coming and Jacob couldn't believe what he was watching; it was an army so large it covered the plains for miles around. He estimated it consisted of over a million Dark Angels and they were still coming. He then saw a second army emerge south of the Dead Sea, moving towards the Judean wilderness. Thor pointed towards the west of Homs and identified a third army emerging from the Anti-Lebanon Mountains. They then saw a forth army appear about one hundred miles east of lake Al-Assad. With the serpent army still emerging from the Mediterranean Sea and the four armies of Dark Angels, Jacob estimated Hell had sent over five million combatants. He concluded that the real battle between the Gods and Hell was about to begin.

Jacob's anxiety grew until he saw several hundred thousand carriers arrive from the north and the west, battle-hardened survivors of yesterday's attacks. He watched them settle west of the Aleppo Plateau, preparing to march on Lebanon. He recognised them to be descendants of the Celts, Saxons, Franks, the Norse lords, the Huns and the Goths. He then watched Faer, Thanases and Baldor move into position as their commanders.

He smiled when from the east a similar amount of carriers arrived and were gathering north east of the Euphrates River; he recognised them to be descendants of the Han, the Manchu and the Mongols. They were under the command of both Girish and Garuda.

His spirit rose when, from the south, he saw the carrier descendants of the Kingdom of Kush, the Zulus and the Yoruba peoples arrive and station themselves in Jordan, ready to move towards the Syrian Desert. He was pleased to see Jomo and Jahiri take control of this army.

It was then when he saw that Hell had released its most formidable Demon Hounds and it was them that sent fear through the ranks of the Light. Three armies took to the sky, one above the mountains of Moav, another between the southern and northern Palmyrene Mountains and the third near the city of Sidon. Hell now had eight armies ready to attack.

In the meantime Odi went into invisibility, feeling something monumental was about to happen. He travelled south to station himself above the Golan Heights where he watched the Israeli army base on Mount Hermon being attacked, leading to the annihilation of the unprepared soldiers. His feelings that something huge was about to happen, and needed to be checked out paid off. While there he witnessed the four horsemen appear, led by Lucifer. He then watched Lucifer dismount, open his mouth and release the black mist that formed into his six brothers. The seven princes of Hell were together again.

Odi reached out for Jacob and reported what he witnessed. He then moved back north to take up his position as leader of the northern Asgard army.

Jacob's anxiety grew again. His breathing was laboured and he gripped his stomach indicating his nerves were getting the better of him. "Relax son," said Thor. "Hell has very little left to show, the Light as yet is not in place. Look north, tell me what you see."

"Wow! Father!" said Jacob looking excited. "It's the dragon army. I see King Derwyn and General Andras, there must be four thousand of them, they span across the northern mountains. They're splitting in two, one army is flying towards the Mediterranean and the other remains stationary over Turkey." Thor then said, "Look south and now tell me what you see."

"I see two armies," said Jacob, getting even more excited. "One must be ten thousand strong. It's Kalen and the Spirit Elves. The second is Cassiel and the remnants of the Storm Elves, and they seem well prepared for war."

"Trust me son," said Thor feeling very pleased. "They are well prepared but there is more to see. Look east and tell me what you see."

Jacob looked east and saw as far as the volcanoes of eastern Turkey into Armenia. He saw the advance of Elvina and the Fire Elves and was pleased that another ten thousand fighters were on their way. Thor then said, "Look across the heavens. Now son; tell me what you see."

Jacob looked up and was soon in awe. The vast Asgard army had materialised and it was spread across the sky as far as he could see. He saw Odi was at the head of the northern army and was delighted to see Modi had recovered to take charge of the southern army. He noted that the eastern and western armies were still leaderless and announced he was leaving to take control of the western army. He clenched his fist, crossed it over his heart and bowed to his father and then turned to do the same to his brothers. Before he left he said, "Father, I thought I was to lead the battle of the End Times but it seems it's you who's in control."

"Son," replied Thor. "I might be known as the God of Thunder but take a good look at me, I'm also an Asgard God of War. Do you think I'd let you carry this burden alone especially since the oracles insist it's you he really wants. You're my son, and I love you more than life itself. It'll be over my dead body that he lays his hands on you."

Jacob felt his spirit soar and was about to speak again when Thor said, "I've one more army to call upon, an army no more than six strong. They're the most powerful of them all and have been sleeping for many millennia. When I called, they answered, look to the west and tell me what you see."

Jacob looked to the west; out over the Mediterranean and his jaw dropped watching them emerge from beneath the seas. "How can this be?" he said. "They said they'd only act when all seems lost. All is not lost, what power do you have over them?" He got more excited then continued, "Father, I know them, they're the Titans, Cronus and his brothers, they will bring terror to Hell."

"They certainly will," replied Thor. "I witnessed the war between the Olympians and the Titans. The universe trembled in fear until Zeus and his brothers used their clever ways and brought about the defeat of Cronus. As brothers they fought each other but working together they can be very loyal. Look at them stand still, they will wait in the sea and then, when called, they'll attack. They are the alpha and the omega, they were there at the creation and with their sisters they are the origin of everything. They see the danger of The Darkness and want Lucifer out of the way so those of the Light can defend it without distraction."

Meanwhile, Zeus and Hades had left Olympus to make their way to the Underworld. They quickly located a long forgotten entrance that took them through a dark and foreboding terrain known as 'The ungodly place'. A place so sinister even the mighty Zeus felt the hairs on his neck rise. There was no colour, everything grey and dank. Lifeless trees looked forlorn, surrounded by discarded twigs and broken branches. Every step they took echoed into the distance, sounding overly loud, but in this place there was no life. At times menacing mists would rise, bringing images of souls hidden in shadow, but there were no souls. Throughout this part of their journey they remained invisible.

Hades knew the way and quickly reached the entrance to the hidden dungeons knowing that's where Magni was likely to be, and seeing one particular dungeon heavily guarded, they knew they were in the right place. He couldn't believe his luck when he saw that the guarded cell was at the end of a tunnel with no exits, but it did have an alcove to the right. Guards were positioned every ten paces along the length of the tunnel with a further six at the door.

Zeus believed Lucifer would have ordered Magni killed if any rescue was attempted so they carefully put in place their plan beginning with an invisible Hades making his way to the alcove and concealing himself from what Zeus was about to do. Zeus then materialized revealing the power of the Olympus God of Gods. He produced his lightening rod and released a continuous flow of bolts that not only eliminated the guards; it also burst through the doors of the cell allowing Hades to rush through and destroy the six guards who, after hearing the commotion outside, were moving to finish Magni off.

Zeus quickly reached the cell, joined Hades and together they released Magni from his binds. They were horrified at the condition in which they found him and worried as to how they could carry him without causing more pain. They had no choice but to put their fears aside. They gagged his mouth, suppressing his screams, and then lifted him into their arms as gently as they could. They carried him back along the tunnel to the secret entrance then made their way to Olympus where Apollo immediately went to work.

The magic of Olympus quickly brought about a miraculous recovery for Magni. His return to health was assisted by Eala and Panya who used the power of the Light to hasten the rebuilding of his strength and as soon as he could talk he made it very clear that he was leaving to join the battle.

Back above the Aleppo Plateau, Thor was still monitoring the advance of Hell while keeping an eye on his sons. He watched them patrol their positions and encourage their warriors, he was satisfied all was ready. His greatest thrill came when he heard a chariot race towards him from the south; it didn't take long to work out who the charioteer was. He felt emotional when he saw Magni dressed in the imperial robes of a War God of Asgard and showing he meant business.

"Father," said Magni. "If I didn't know it was you, I'd swear I saw a tear."

"Well it is me," responded Thor. "And you did see a tear."

Magni felt moved, nodded to his father and immediately left to take control of the eastern army. He couldn't help himself. He headed towards his army using a detour that brought him close to the Golan Heights. He got great pleasure in giving a single finger gesture to Lucifer, sneering at him in a way that became the catalyst for Hells army to launch the first waves of its attack against the forces of the Light.

Thor was prepared for some form of reckless action by Magni, knowing him so well. He knew Magni would use any chance he got to seek revenge and infuriate Lucifer ensuring that what he did would be the first move of the conflict.

When Magni reached the eastern army, Thor raised his staff and commanded Kalen and his ten thousand spirit elves to march on the Israeli coastal plains. He had tasked them with distracting the serpents emerging from the Mediterranean, giving the carrier's time to stop the relentless and savage attack on the cities, villages and towns along the coast.

Kalen's elves had a major advantage being invisible to all but the gods. Being a very well trained army they acted with a precision that sent shockwaves through the ranks of Hell. Their tight formation was also protected by their body length shields that acted like a battering ram to those who couldn't see them. Unfortunately this strategy wasn't to last; Lucifer anticipated this move and held back an army of wraiths who were more powerful than those he had unleashed earlier that week. These wraiths had unnatural speed, cunning and skills that allowed them to out-manoeuvre the elves. They could also see the aura of the elves giving them the means to undo the magic surrounding the shields and this they ruthlessly used to their advantage. They infiltrated the elf ranks and systematically reduced the elves to piles of flesh and bone, their slaughter was merciless.

Jacob immediately mounted a rescue by sending a large force from the western Asgard army. He sent a thousand chariots with the instruction to rescue all survivors especially Kalen, their supreme leader. He then received an order from his father to destroy the serpent army by putting the main body of the western army in a line from Gaza in the south to Latakia in Northern Syria.

When in place Jacob raised his staff and led his warriors on an all out assault that was so swift it took the serpents by surprise. The initial success of Asgard was down to the blade laden under-carriages of the chariots as they rolled across the sands. They churned and minced the serpents leaving a slithery slimy sludge of shredded flesh and innards that soon sent the stench of death across the plains.

While dealing with the serpents he was very aware of the columns of refugees making their way into the mountains, especially a vast column of over half a million residents of Jerusalem. He was so concerned he dispatched several thousand chariots as escorts not knowing that there were no safe zones; he quickly established that the demon hounds and battalions of Dark Angels had taken control of the mountains and had cut off all escape routes.

He soon discovered the Dark Angels had evolved and they too had a new speed allowing them to evade all attempts at being vanquished. Soon all armies of the Light were under pressure bringing about a change of tactics. He decided that the warriors should take on Hell in hand to hand combat and felt the only way his army had a chance was to lead the warriors by example. He jumped from his chariot to land among a large force of Dark Angels where, using his swordsman skills, he proceeded to work his way through their ranks and this action began to have an effect. The Dark Angels may have had a new speed but Jacob was faster. His warriors were in awe watching him leap from one tree trunk to another before bouncing back across his adversaries and taking their heads as he passed. The warriors followed his example and soon a fight back had begun.

In the east, Magni watched the carriers below split, with one half under Garuda moving towards Lake Al-Assad and the other commanded by Girish heading towards the southern Palmyrene Mountains. He looked ahead and saw that Garuda was moving towards a battle against a force of at least two hundred thousand Dark Angels and decided to assist by sending part of his eastern Asgard army. He changed his mind when he saw that the dragons, under the command of Andras, were moving into position and preparing to assist the carriers.

He then became alarmed when he saw several thousand demon hounds take off from the northern Palmyrene Mountains and they were very clearly on an intercept coarse with Garuda's carriers. He sent a messenger, who quickly met up with Garuda,

"My lord Magni sends you a warning of a new threat. Demon hounds have taken to the sky and they're flying low, out of sight, so beware their treachery. Lord Magni feels you are moving into a trap and the Dark Angels waiting for you are a distraction. He alerts you to the dragon army; it's flying to your aid but won't reach you for several hours."

Garuda appreciated the warning but had already anticipated some kind of trap, "Tell my lord Magni" he said. "Tell him to watch me take to the sky and call on my allies. In the past I used my powers to call on all of bird kind, and with those same allies I defeated the serpents and Dark Angels, I intend to use those same powers again this day." He climbed onto the rim of the chariot and held his arms aloft so all could see his power. He then leapt and all watched him transform into a most magnificent bird. He looked every bit an Emperor of the Skies, the mythical bird foretold by Jacob two thousand years earlier. Most importantly, he now presented as one of the most powerful gods of the east. When he sent out his piercing call, it travelled throughout the deserts and across the mountains, and they answered in their thousands.

First to arrive were the Saker Falcons followed by the African Houbara Bustards, next came the Imperial Eagles and then the most majestic Greater Spotted Eagles. Last to arrive were the Egyptian Vultures whose sole purpose was to clean up the mess left after the battle ended. They bided their time and waited in the highest tree branches dotted all across the mountains.

In the far south Modi began to move the southern Asgard army towards the north. He stationed his chariots above where another army of demon hounds were exiting Hell from under the mountains of Moav, they were moving towards the Judean wilderness. He left his position to meet up with Jomo and Jahiri and was pleased to see they were well prepared and eager to enter battle. He also saw they had total control of the southern carriers and commanded their absolute loyalty. After meeting them he had no doubt as to their abilities in defending the Light and routing the demons.

Thor, in the meantime, moved higher into the sky and now had a panoramic view of the six hundred miles long by three hundred miles wide battlefield. He saw that the armies of the Light were well prepared but was bothered because the serpents and Dark Angels on the Israeli coastal plain seemed to be rallying and getting the upper hand. He chose not to send aid, trusting Jacob and the western army would soon prevail. He wanted no distractions while trying to figure out why Cain and Hells army was just stalled in the area between Megiddo and an area just north of the Sea of Galilee. He couldn't understand the strategy until he focused on those standing on the Golan Heights and then noticed that Lucifer was staring back at him.

They stared at each other for what seemed like an age, neither blinked. As one spoke it was as though they were face to face. Thor was first to speak and his face would appear before Lucifer and when Lucifer spoke his face would appear high in the sky, on Thor's chariot, bringing them almost nose to nose.

"Look out across this vast battlefield," said Lucifer. "And see Armageddon! You're outnumbered, Thunder God, and know not what you face. My serpents are close to securing the coastal plains. The Boy King is no match for me.

"It's early yet," smirked Thor with contempt. "My son will prevail. He and Asgard fight valiantly and trust me; your serpents and Dark Angels will soon cower and hide in fear. I've not unleashed my full power."

"Do you think I'm a fool," yelled Lucifer. "I see your strategy, mine is still hidden."

"We know you're still harvesting souls," Thor yelled back. "And have secured many, so yes we know that much of your power is still hidden. We also know your confidence is your weakness. Look to the sun and see how it pales, don't you see that we should be allies in defence of the Light. Your so called ally is no friend, The Darkness takes everything and will take the Underworld; it will get pleasure in taking the orange glow of the fires of Hell."

"The Darkness is my ally," said Lucifer while laughing loudly. "Our alliance will never be betrayed, I have no fear."

"There is an old Asgard saying," said Thor shaking his head in disbelief. "Wisdom rests deep in your head, make sure your head is not just for wearing your helmet."

Lucifer smirked and then turned to the horsemen, and beginning with the Black horse and rider he said,

"Go to the fields and burn their food, bring on the famine, let them starve. Poison the lakes, rivers and streams, let them thirst." He looked at the Pale horse and rider then said,

"See the lines of refugees, pursue them, do your duty and bring death upon them." He placed his hand on the Red horse and whispered to the rider,

"You're my favourite, ride out and bring forth Hell, let them see your power, lead the demon hounds to feed on their flesh. Go and unleash war."

The red horseman moved to the edge of the plateau at the summit of Mount Hermon then pounded his staff off the ridge to send out his signal for the remaining soldiers of Hells armies to attack. All three horsemen then left to do their worst before retreating and returning to the bowels of Hell.

The next of Hells armies to rise up was another army of demon hounds who launched from the city of Sidon in Lebanon. At first an orange glow appeared and it was glowing over Sidon sea castle. Between the two towers a portal opened and an army of ten thousand demon hounds began crossing the eighty metre long causeway leading to the Castle. Jacob was already fighting serpents further south but when the portal opened he was directed to take to the sky and investigate. He brought an escort of five thousand chariots and when he arrived he didn't hesitate, he launched an attack, especially on those demons crossing the causeway.

It was during the attack when Jacob saw the demon hounds drag what looked like a bound, yet very strong and regal man behind them. They were mercilessly beating, trashing and flaying him. He saw that the man was an immortal but didn't recognise him. Jacob used the power of his mind to reach the victim and quickly established the man was Melqart, the Phoenician god protector of all cities and traders based around the Mediterranean.

"Trust me my lord," said Jacob hoping to offer comfort. "Your pain will soon end and when free I can get you to Olympus."

"How is it I now feel the long lost Light?" asked Melqart. "Who is bringing this forgotten warmth into my heart?"

"Jacob, I am Jacob, son of Thor."

"Is it too much to hope that this is a rescue?" asked Melqart. "Thousands of years have passed since I was captured by the forces of Hell. They held me prisoner in dungeons buried deep in the Underworld. I was hidden from the gaze of Hades and then brutalised by Lucifer after he completed his takeover."

"Son, I know him," said Thor after entering Jacob's head. "He's an old friend, long forgotten in these lands. He fought by my side in the cosmic wars. Rescue him."

Jacob quickly put a plan together. He flew out over the Mediterranean while his forces continued their attack. This allowed for the demons to be distracted long enough for him to go into invisibility. While invisible he turned his chariot back towards Sidon and when he reached the causeway he leapt from his chariot, landing just before the six demons holding the binds of Melqart. He materialised and using his outstretched spear he skewered three of the demons; he then extracted his sword and using its swift slicing motion he decapitated the three remaining demons.

He released Melqart, gripped his shoulder, disappeared and brought him to the safety of Olympus where he was treated for his years of torturous abuse. The demon hounds behind Melqart didn't have time to react and their screeches of fury were heard all the way to the Golan Heights causing

Lucifer to explode in a fit of rage. He created, then released hundreds of fire balls, firing them in all directions and didn't care who or what they hit, friend or foe.

Jacob remained in Olympus long enough for Melqart to recover hoping to convince him to fight by his side,

"My father said you carry the strength of Heracles," said Jacob. "Fight by my side, reclaim your lands, the people will follow."

"I'm an angry god, of no use to anyone," replied Melqart. "I'm forgotten in my lands. While crossing the causeway to what was once my temple I recognised nothing, and there was nobody there to honour me."

"I lived among man for sixteen years," said Jacob trying to reassure him. "I can tell you that man remembers nothing of the gods, but over the last six months they've again learned of our existence. They now realise how much they depend on us, especially for their protection. We must protect them as best we can. I need you to join me in that protection." Melqart thought for a moment and agreed to assist.

By the time they returned all armies of the Light were now engaged. The battlefields were theatres of pure savagery, turning red with the blood of thousands of carriers. Jacob was buoyed by the remaining fighters and their determination to prevail but he also saw they were seriously outnumbered. While watching the western carriers he was pleased by how valiant they were, especially as they were fighting the powerful third army of demon hounds, a battle being fought all along the coast of Lebanon. He listened to Faer call out as he dispatched each hound, "That's one for Fafner. That's two, three, and four......." Faer's rage continued as he avenged the slaughter of his closest friend.

Further north, Odi prepared his attack while waiting until Baldor and Thanases had led the northern carriers south across the Aleppo plateau. They were on their way to attack the third army of Dark Angels who had moved north from the city of Homs. On facing each other, both armies wasted no time in engaging. It was a particularly vicious battle where no mercy was shown. Every action was brutal to the extreme leaving casualties mounting up. Odi joined them and used Jacob's strategy by leaping from his chariot into the midst of the Dark Angels. His courage, skill and swiftness brought great confusion to the Dark Angels and when his Asgard warriors followed his lead, a mass rout of evil began. King Derwyn then launched his dragons and this time their breath of fire did its worst sending the Dark Angels to a flaming death.

To the east and the south both Magni and Modi were in their element, they were fighting horrendous battles aiming to deal a merciless blow on Hell. Their two Asgard armies joined up to form a line from south of Jordan through eastern Syria and into southern Turkey. Their archers released continuous barrages of arrows, arrows that were dipped in a beam of the first source light making them so lethal they quickly penetrated the ranks of the vast second army of Dark Angels who had emerged south of the dead sea. They also trained their arrows on the 4th army of Dark Angels who had arrived east of Lake Al-Assad. The Storm elves under Cassiel were also engaged south of the mountains of Moav. They were in action against the very troublesome first army of demon hounds. As Storm elves they had the power to call on the assistance of the winds, which came and brought forth a wall of sand that blinded the hounds allowing the elves to decimate their ranks. They were more successful than Kalen and his Spirit elves. They managed to finish the battle with very few casualties.

The dragons under the command of general Andras had reached Lake Al Assad and were attacking the flanks of the fourth Dark Angel army, they couldn't use their breath of fire as Hell, in this case, was stronger but they did use their claws by grabbing as many Dark Angels as they could, bringing them into the sky and tearing them asunder. Girish and the carriers were now fully engaged and slowly getting the upper hand. They were soon joined by the Fire elves, the most swift and relentless of all Elven armies. Their arrows were successful because they were dipped in the fires of the old volcanoes of Armenia and on impact incinerated all before them.

The tide of war was now turning in favour of the Light and Magni decreed that it was time to finish Hell off. He sent his vast army of charioteers and with the power of the dragons and the remaining carriers they successfully destroyed the massed ranks of Dark Angels. They then turned their attention to the second army of demon hounds that had arrived from the Palmyrene Mountains. Andras saw the danger and again stepped in. His dragons used their claws to great effect and were able to quickly neutralise the hounds. His quick action was instrumental in bringing the battles in the east and the south to a swift end.

Garuda was now high in the sky above the Syrian Desert and saw that Jacob had rejoined the battle against the serpents across the coastal plains. He was in awe of the power of the god assisting him and wondered as to who he was. He watched him protect Jacob and also use his strength to raise boulder after boulder before rolling them out among the ranks of serpents and crushing them into oblivion.

He then sent out a call and the birds came to follow him towards the mountains of Lebanon before moving south to where Jacob was fighting. He could also see that the serpents were still slithering in from the Mediterranean Sea leaving behind them a crimson red slick from the amount of blood they had spilt during their battle with the Mer-armies.

Garuda then sent out another shrill and piercing call that brought thousands more battle birds from all across the Mediterranean and they came in such numbers that the skies darkened. The falcons were first to attack, their speed on impact stunned the serpents, and then the bustards, followed by the eagles, would attack causing alarm to spread through the ranks of serpents as they were hoisted high into the sky. The cold air caused the serpents to fall into a catatonic state before they were released into the path of the fire-breathing dragons of King Derwyn's army.

In the meantime Odi, Baldor and Thanases were concluding their efforts to contain the onslaught of Hell in the north and with the help of Andras and his dragons they began to get the upper hand.

Odi was perturbed because when he went high into the sky he saw his father still staring out Lucifer, he felt his father was being deceived but couldn't quite put his finger on what was bothering him. He was satisfied the battle in the north was now about to be concluded and felt Jacob would soon have the west under his control so he raced to place his chariot alongside his father, "Father," he said. "What is it, why are you still staring at Lucifer? Why is he holding your gaze?"

"He's the great deceiver," replied Thor. "It's as though the turmoil and bloodshed below means nothing to him, something else is holding his gaze. I can't figure it. He knows I'm his greatest threat, yet he shows no fear. We met before and he suffered."

"Father, look down on Cain," said Odi looking out across the battlefield. "He still smirks. He's now leading an army so vast it spreads from Damascus all the way to Jerusalem. There are our different columns with what must be over two million Dark Angels in each, and they still pour from the portal. The demon hounds also gather, are these the elite of Hell? Has he worn our armies down so much that we now stand no chance?"

Magni arrived and heard what Odi said, he responded by saying, "Fear not little brother, Asgard has fought more dangerous battles and we still stand. Look at our allies, they're formidable. The carriers have proven man is worth fighting for."

Modi then arrived looking a bit bloodied and worse for wear, "Father," he said, "night falls, we should wait for dawn and then release the full power of our armies, finish off Hell and let the next age of man commence." All four stayed quiet while watching Jacob and Melqart continue to fight the remnants of the serpent army.

"Look at him fight," remarked Thor with a tear gathering. "He has more skills, tactics and determination than the four of us put together, yet I still worry."

Jacob and Melqart didn't leave the battle until they were sure all were defeated and it was only when the last serpent succumbed when Jacob invited Melqart to join him on this journey to meet with Thor. On the way Melqart said, "When I look up I realise I've forgotten the stars and when I look out across the cosmos I see how so many are gone, have I been away that long?"

"Look closely and watch as star after star is extinguished," said Jacob. "It's the relentlessness of The Darkness. See how our own sun dims, The Darkness has arrived. Out in the cosmos the Sun Gods are still fighting but they're being defeated, The Darkness is too powerful."

"I am one of the ancients," said Melqart. "And I was there at the creation. I saw the Ancient One stand alone and raise his hand before blowing something into the cosmos. He knew I was there and somehow I knew he wanted me to bear witness to what he had done. He blew a miniscule speck of dust and I've forever wondered what it was."

"What was it." asked Jacob.

"The spark that will continue the fight back," said Melqart while staring at Jacob.

Jacob stationed his chariot next to Thor's allowing Melqart to leap across into an embrace of real friendship. They held each other as long lost friends and had difficulty finding the words to fill the gap of millennia that kept them apart.

"I never knew," said Thor. "I often wondered where you went. Never did I think that you were in the dungeons of Hell."

"It was the thoughts of the times we spent fighting together," replied Melgart. "The births of Magni and Modi, and all the things we did together. It was those thoughts that gave me the will to live. Why am I not surprised to find you at the head of such a vast army, fighting the greatest battle since the fall of the angels?"

"You know me too well!" said Thor.

"On my way here I told Jacob about how I alone witnessed the Ancient One blow a speck of dust out into the cosmos," said Melqart whispering in Thor's ear. "It was just before The Fall. I think I now know what that speck was! I remember a presence. I felt that same presence today. As I stand with you now that presence feels even stronger. I see you have twin boys."

Thor backed away. He looked at Jacob and Odi, and was beginning to understand, "I think I've always known, you've just confirmed to me why Lucifer is so focused."

"Come on father," interrupted Odi. "Don't keep us in the dark, what's he talking about, tell us."

"I think it's about me," said Jacob.

"You're correct," replied Melqart. "But this conversation I feel is for another day."

"Again," said an exasperated Modi, raising his hands towards the heavens. "I'm going to be last to find out, so unfair."

"I think my sons all know me by now," smiled Thor. "When I want you to know something I'll tell you, when I don't, you know something! Tough."

That night Thor and his four sons stood in their chariots watching the Golan Heights. A strong wind had developed and the sound of their capes flapping was audible to the armies below. All across the hills and deserts, camp fires burned brightly, and as the night progressed and the wind died down, an eerie silence developed. Occasionally a pathetic scream, one of terror, was heard and all listening knew that another poor soul had been found, was being tortured and then devoured by the forces of evil. Many warriors found it difficult to sleep because of the constant sound of weapons being sharpened. It was a sound that became their bedfellow and many felt that these next few hours were surely going to be their last. What surprised the gods, as they looked around, was the sense of fear. A fear not only affecting the warriors of the Light but also the legions of Hell, it was as though all knew what was coming was a battle to the death with no coming back.

"The sun is touching the horizon," said Modi, looking towards the east. "It's rising rays will soon light up these sad lands."

"Son," said Thor. "You are King of Kings. It's your place to rally the troops, go and prepare them for action."

Jacob looked bewildered and as he pointed his thumb at his chest said, "Me? Are you mad?"

"Get down there and do your duty," insisted Magni

Odi smirked to himself but chose to say nothing. Jacob then flicked his reigns and his chariot slowly descended towards a place where he knew the light winds would carry his words to all soldiers of the Light. He cleared his throat,

"Warriors of the Light! Listen on to me and hear my pleas. Remember your loved ones and remember your beloved lands. The hopes and prayers of what is left of mankind rests with you. Some of those who still walk are your families, your kin, and your loved ones. Hear me, ignore the terror sounds of the baying demons and be assured that what we face is the last vestiges of Hells tyranny. Remember the conflagration they caused in your homelands, remember the soul destroying rage they unleashed on your loved ones. It is said that history is written by the victors so let us, this day, be the victors. I know you are afraid but always remember that without fear there is no valour, let your valour bring forth victory, victory, victory."

All across the battlefield the warriors of the Light rallied, they were inspired, they shouted at the top of their voices, "Victory, victory, victory." The momentous sound of several million voices calling out 'Victory' in unison sent shock waves through the ranks of Hell but it didn't faze either Lucifer or Cain. Magni looked across at Modi and said, "He speaks of valour, look at him; he oozes valour, after this day he will be known as the greatest warrior of them all. He is my brother."

It was then when Cain climbed a protruding outcrop of rocks and raised his staff. He said nothing, just gestured for the forward sections of his army to move in four directions. As they crossed the various ridges they were met by the true extent of the forces of the Light which was rallied against them. What frightened them the most was the fact that the Titans had quietly moved into six positions and between each Titan was a different army under commanders who had sworn to defend the Light. The Titans were in their colossus form looking like they were not prepared to take prisoners.

Cronus stood with his back to the north. He was in the twelve o'clock position and was surrounded by the northern carrier army under the command of Baldor and Thanases. When Lucifer saw him he was furious, especially since he never detected that Cronus was still alive. In the one o'clock position was the remnant of the elf armies followed in the two o'clock position by the Titan Hyperion. In the three o'clock position was the eastern carrier army under the command of Girish and Garuda who were followed in the four o'clock position by the Titan Coeus. Next was half the dragon army, commanded by King Derwyn and they were in the five o'clock position and next to them, in the six o'clock position stood the Titan Crius who was surrounded by the southern carrier army under the command of Jomo and Jahiri. They were followed by the vast Asgard army under the command of the four sons of Thor. It was so numerous they were positioned in four different layers. They held the seven o'clock position. In the eight o'clock position was Oceanus, followed by the western carrier army under Faer and they were in the nine o'clock position. The Titan Ladetos was in the ten o'clock position and was followed by the second half of the dragon army under general Andras and they held the eleven o'clock position.

Together the combined armies of the light had the forces of Hell completely surrounded. There was a determination to totally annihilate them once and for all. Although Jacob's armies were vastly outnumbered there was a new confidence especially now the Titans had shown themselves. The dragon armies were in their human form and had decided hand to hand combat was going to be the most effective way to fight. They were the first to move into action followed by the elves. The carriers were next and then Asgard was unleashed. The Titans stood back, watching as the greatest battle since the fall of the angels commenced.

First blood was drawn by the demons of Hell. Their attack on the carriers mirrored their savaging of them over the previous few days. The carriers showed no fear but their relief was palpable when the Asgard warriors landed beside them. As the hours passed it became apparent that the warriors of the Light were sustaining staggering losses. Asgard was now totally in the firing line forcing Thor to ascend and take a position of command on the front line. The dragons were the most successful and used their skills to tear and rip the Dark Angels to pieces but Hell just kept coming, there seemed to be no end to the evil forces that were travelling through the portal.

Magni and Modi joined their father insisting he return higher into the sky and direct the forces of the Light from there. When he reached his holding position and looked out over the battle field he saw the now almost impossible task that lay before him. He observed the light flashes of the clashing blades as they reflected the gleam of the midday sun. He was disturbed when he saw the extent of the Asgard warriors that had fallen. It troubled him while looking towards were they lay in heaps, with their glazed-over eyes that had earlier released their last tears to mix with their congealed crimson red blood and this shocked him. He was upset while watching the carrier's succumbing and worried that man was beginning to lose the repository of all of Earths knowledge and achievements.

The battlefield was now a mire of blood and guts where the stench grew under the relentless heat of the now high sun. It was to become a place where so many warriors and soldiers of the Light would end their days. Thor was saddened that there were so few left to weep and pray over the graves of the fallen, no one to sing as the white mist left and made its way towards Elysium. He hated it when he saw the swarms of plague ridden flies gather, before feasting on the pale skinned corpses that lay unloved and lost.

Thor yelled at Lucifer, ensuring all on the battlefield heard him. He used his thunder to ensure his voice travelled from one end of the battlefield to the other.

"Lucifer," he yelled. "How could you? Once you were a most favourite of the Ancient One, why do you bring such wanton destruction and violence on his creation? Where did you get this blood lust? You have brought on a holocaust of the innocents and yet you still can't see how it is The Darkness that will bring you down, stop this madness and leave earth in peace."

Lucifer sneered and shouted back, "We've mastered the art of the kill and will ramp up the pain and the terror. Decay and absolute humiliation awaits you, there will be no beating hearts as the sun sets, these lands will soon be mine."

Thor then called out to further rally the forces of the light, he raced from north to south and east to west, and he showed them that he was very confident of victory. He reminded the warriors and carriers of how well trained they were and of how they were considered to be master swordsmen. He sought from them one last charge to be launched with a renewed vigour. He asked them to slash their swords back and forth and bring on the death throes of defeat against Hell. He told them of his awareness that they were winded, battered, bruised, and in agony. He then reminded them why they were schooled in battle and encouraged them to wield their swords without mercy.

He inspired the army and caused Odi to enter Jacob's head, "If we are going to win this battle we need to cut the head off the snake, together we should target Cain."

"Agreed," replied Jacob. "Follow my lead."

Odi and Jacob took their chariots high into the sky causing Thor to ask, "What's that pair up to?" He didn't have to wonder for long. Jacob and Odi parted and headed at speed in opposite directions, one to the north and the other to the south. When out of sight they turned and headed back towards the battlefield.

Cain watched a chariot approach and smirked when he saw it was Odi. He watched him leap from the chariot and charge at him but he failed to notice that a second chariot was approaching from the south. He was ready for Odi but hadn't anticipated the cunning of the twins because when Jacob arrived he sent Cain tumbling to the ground. Odi was upon him in a second but unfortunately he totally misjudged Cain's strength. Cain rose up, produced two swords and then a duel of shear savagery began. Fear never entered any of their heads, they were all so focused. This was an epic battle between the first murderer and two powerful gods.

What the boys found unnerving was that Cain's facial expression was unreadable, he showed no pity. He'd whisk around in fluid movements, fighting with no honour. It was when he produced his crystal encrusted staff when the boys knew they were in trouble. He began to swing it wildly preventing Jacob and Odi from getting close. Each time they did they'd either have to leap high or summersault out of the way. Cain's energy seemed to have no bounds. He acted as though he was just teasing them.

On the Golan Heights Lucifer intently watched the fight, he was intrigued by the skills of the twins, recognised them as the skills that could have only been taught by the War Gods. The boys increased their speed by somersaulting and leaping in all different directions. They never rested and they used every trick they knew causing maximum confusion. It was as though they became one.

Lucifer got uneasy and decided to intervene. He waited for his opportunity and then sent a fast moving fireball that hit Jacob causing him to lose balance. This was the opportunity Cain was waiting for, he plunged his staff towards Jacob as he stumbled. The staff penetrated his armour and impaled him. Cain used all his strength to toss Jacob about and when he was released he was sent tumbling towards a stone wall where he impacted with such force he cracked his skull.

Odi went into shock, he was watching his brother's life force fade and it caused him to lose his judgement. Cain used this distraction to send Odi flying towards the same wall but he managed to save himself. Thor in the meantime was travelling through the sky only to see his son fall. He looked towards the Golan Heights and saw Lucifer change; the fires of Hell came to surround him. He grew the horns of the devil and took on the face of a demon. He was now the image of evil that man so often used to describe him.

Thor looked back at his son and saw the white mist gathering, about to leave. He was broken-hearted. He then noticed Lucifer race towards Jacob's body forcing him to intervene.

Cronus was also watching and when he witnessed Jacob's demise, he went into a rage. His brothers sensed his anger and together they raised their arms, facing their palms towards the sky. They closed their eyes and fireballs materialised. They tightened their grip around the battlefield by sending out shafts of fire that joined them all together. The circle of fire intensified and formed a vice like ring preventing anybody from leaving. They then released their fury on the Dark Angels, serpents and demon hounds.

They sent fireball after fireball into the ranks of Hell and soon increased the intensity of the barrage so that within an hour the armies of Hell began to fall, there was no escape; they were suffering the ancient power of the Titans and they hadn't a chance. Lucifer didn't care, he was after his greatest prize and raced at such speed that those watching couldn't keep up. Thor had by now built up an equally fast speed and was determined to reach Jacob's body before Lucifer.

In the meantime Odi's strength was waning as he continued to fend off Cain. From the corner of his eye he watched Lucifer reach Jacob and grip him by his tunic, he saw him being lifted to rest at the side of the horse; he thought he saw Lucifer pushing his fist into Jacob's mouth before racing off.

Odi, in the throes of all his pain, received a vision of a warrior, all bloodied and torn, his sword in his hand and resting by his side. The warrior crossed the seas, walked through rivers and lakes, then moved across the grasses and through a forest before making his way towards a cave. He saw the warrior walk over to greet three toddlers and then he saw their mother rush out and hug the warrior. He watched the warrior go to his knees playing with the children. He then realised that he was in Jacob's head, witnessing his last memories. He knew of Jacobs dream from two thousand years ago, when Eala first went on her long walk. He remembered how Jacob felt that the image was his future showing him surviving the battle. Odi then knew Jacob's vision was just wishful thinking and nothing more, this broke his heart.

In the meantime Thor was in hot pursuit, swinging his hammer readying it for release. At the same time Odi fell in and out of consciousness and had resigned himself to being killed by Cain. His will to live was now gone. He held his sword before him but soon realised he could no longer fend off the constant probing and pummelling being rained down on him. He needn't have worried because his saviour was close by.

As Thor raced after Lucifer he had to pass where Odi was awaiting his demise. Odi saw his father coming but Cain didn't, he was too intent on finishing Odi off. Thor passed Cain and with the skilful use of his sword managed to decapitate him.

Thor continued his pursuit of Lucifer and again prepared to release his hammer only this time it was too late. A cliff face portal opened allowing

Lucifer through, it closed so fast the hammer could only smash against the now solid rock.

On the battle field the forces of the Light quickly recovered from the shock of the Jacob's death, they regrouped then unleashed a barrage of arrows that continued what the Titans had started. The dilemma for the Dark Angels was that they were now leaderless and began making mistakes. Their attempt at brutality was quickly matched by a new vigour throughout the ranks of the Light. Hell was now in retreat, except they had nowhere to go, all escape portals were closed. This wasn't their lucky day because by nightfall, they were subjected to a constant onslaught of arrows, spears and swords that reduced their ranks to all but a few hundred. Worse was to come for them when one of the ancient gods arrived. It was Hermes and he had come to fulfil a prophecy given by Jacob when he first arrived in the temple. He released a flesh eating plague and directed it to attack those forces of Hell still fighting.

When the battle was over and the slaughter and mayhem had ceased, everything became hushed. A silence of despair descended and settled among the warriors now that Jacob was gone. He was dead and the worse thing for the warriors and for the gods was the fact that he was deprived of his place in Elysium resting among the Heroes, kings and gods of old, it was this that broke their hearts.

Chapter 35

Earlier, while the battles raged on earth, The Darkness made its presence felt. Its insidious attack on the sun brought on what felt like the beginnings of a solar eclipse. For those fighting, the dimming light went unnoticed. Even the dropping temperature went unheeded. For Magni, his anxiety grew while praying Rhea's plan was already in play. He closed his eyes, thought of Olympus, and was able to see that more and more immortals were arriving, seeking its protection. His mind took him out into the gardens where he saw Zeus being hounded by a gaggle of excitable two year olds. He smiled to himself watching the God of Gods become a child minder, but he did notice how Zeus was particularly watching the Princess Helena who was showing signs of having, and using the power of the Light.

He moved back into the temple and saw Eala, Panya, Mulan and Oba sitting together staring at the sun. He saw their distress and became alarmed until Mia and Danu arrived. He then saw the real power of the Light surround all six of them. He continued watching knowing that for Rhea's plan to work, something else needed to happen, and that something else did happen. A lightning bolt hid the ground close to where the goddesses were sitting. It was the arrival of Rhea announcing to the cosmos that she was back, and about to take control.

She greeted the goddesses then enquired as to the whereabouts of Zeus only to be told he was 'Baby-Sitting'. She made her way out into the gardens and was amused to see him sitting on the ground playing with so many youngsters.

"I sense your presence mother," said Zeus turning to greet her. "I wept when I saw the roots of the grasses absorb you into their very essence. Has it really been ten thousand years? You are most welcome into the domain of the gods."

"It has," replied Rhea. "I rested peacefully knowing you were the God of Gods. At times the thought of the hatred between you and your father disturbed me, but now I'm happy he seeks your forgiveness. Can you find it in your heart to meet with him?"

"We'll see." said Zeus while lifting Thora and Helena into his arms. "Meet two of your great granddaughters, Helena and Thora. Their fathers are my grandsons."

"Two goddesses," said Rhea reaching in to touch their cheeks. "One of the Light; the other will be a goddess queen of Asgard. How wonderful to see so many children. I see an Archangel, a Sun God and Goddess, Earth Gods, so much power. That one," she said while pointing at one of the boys. "He's trouble."

"His name's Obelius," laughed Zeus. "He's a son of Jacob, another great grandchild of yours. He will break Jacob's heart but will be his father's greatest ally. He's destined to be a god guardian of Olympus."

Just then a mild tremor rumbled beneath their feet.

"It seems mother we have more visitors, very important visitors. You'd better go into the temple and greet them."

Rhea made her way into the temple and was delighted to be greeted by the arrival of the Earth Mothers, all of whom were old friends of the senior gods and were made very welcome. For Rhea, meeting the rest of her sons and daughters was very emotional, especially after such a long time. Some hours later a dense mist gathered on the inner steps of the temple, followed by a continuous rumble of thunder, then three intense beams of light. From the mist stepped out the three wizards, Apollonius, Merlin and Mygon. All was now in place for the fight back to begin. Rhea's plan was about to be activated.

Rhea led the Earth Mothers back out into the meadows where they found a slightly elevated knoll and formed a perfect circle. The wizards remained on the steps ready to intervene if things went wrong. The goddesses were close by but seemed to be in a trance. They were in a trance, and were being shown a pathway to the edge of the universe. When they revived Danu said,

"It seems we've been tasked with defending, and protecting the Light. What we are about to do has never been tried before."

The ten Earth Mothers stood silently for several minutes before raising their right hands with their palms facing the sky.

It was now mid afternoon and there was no doubt The Darkness had arrived. The light of the sun faded bringing on an eerie atmosphere that felt more oppressive as the minutes passed. It appeared like a giant shadow, slow moving and relentless, with a gaping mouth big enough to swallow all before it. It brought absolute terror.

The wizards showed signs of anxiety wondering why the Earth Mothers were so relaxed but they should have known better, Rhea had a plan, and she was waiting for more sunlight to fade before releasing the power of her kind. When the time came she was the first to speak,

"I call on the sands of this sacred land," she said after closing her eyes. "Come on to me, rest in my palm." A gentle breeze blew lifting grains of sand to rest on her palm. Next to speak was Ninsar,

"From the lagoon," she said. "Send to me your droplets. Let their power moisten, then rest in my palm." Maja then spoke and she said,

"Lord of the trees, send me a leaf, let it represent all of nature, rest it in my palm." Medeina then called out,

"God of the Blooms, send me a flower, let it show the beauty of summer, rest it in my palm." Asase Yaa was next and she said,

"Goddess of the Snows, send me your flake, let its crystals be the bearer of winter, rest it in my palm," Isis spoke next and she said,

"Emperor of the suns, send me your Light, let my palm be its guardian." Then Kali called out,

"God of the Seasons, send seeds and fruit, bearer of spring and autumn. Let them rest in my palm." Atira came next and she said,

"Lord of the winds, wrap around me and let your power rest in my palm," Then Kishar spoke,"

"God of all crafts, rest a nugget in my palm, let it represent all metals." and lastly, Bhavani spoke,

"I call on the torches of Olympus to send me your fire, let it too rest in my palm."

The Earth Mothers each had a different element representing all of life and when they blew the elements into the centre of their circle everything changed. The winds came and churned them together and as the elements spun, they expanded to form a massive sphere. Its ambient light intensified before becoming translucent, and then it split into six smaller pulsating spheres.

The six Goddesses knew what they had to do, they walked into the centre of the circle, each standing before a sphere. Eala, Panya and Oba looked back at their children giving them reassuring smiles. There was no need; their children were gathered around the feet of Zeus and under his protection. They then raised their arms to rest against the outer wall of the spheres only for their hands to slowly meld into the wall allowing them to step in. As the spheres became even brighter, almost blinding, they slowly levitated and took to the sky to form a single line before spreading out to directly face The Darkness.

The Darkness just kept coming even though its attempts to completely destroy the sun were being thwarted by the power of the suns solar eruptions. While its battle with the sun continued it sent its mist to attack the moon and begin its takeover. The goddesses, although distressed watching the moon being absorbed, continued their journey to assist the sun. Their assistance began when Mia, Danu, Oba and Mulan formed a line across its earth facing side. Eala and Panya took up positions on the extreme left and right facing out into the universe. When all was in place they, in unison raised their hands with their palms facing The Darkness and released a most powerful light, four beams directed towards the sun and two directed out into the universe. The four beams joined together before opening up like an umbrella creating what looked like a battering ram. Eala's and Panya's beans were so powerful they formed a barrier, preventing The Darkness from travelling any further. The beams intensified and the push back began. At times The Darkness retaliated but this just motivated the goddesses to increase their power, they never tired, it was as thought the Ancient One was resting his hand on their shoulders.

This battle between the Light and The Darkness went on for many hours but in the end it was the Light that prevailed. The power of the released sun returned, and it sent its beams to burn the stifling mist from the moon. The goddesses were pleased with what they achieved but knew their work wasn't finished. They chased and harried The Darkness out across the Milky Way and never once did their power diminish. Soon they were travelling faster than the speed of light and as they travelled, their light kept getting brighter.

There were times when they came across debris of long lost battles, battles fought by the powerful Sun Gods. They even rescued a few who were in a deep catatonic state as a result of the advance of The Darkness. On their way they used their powers to reignite suns that were extinguished thousands of years earlier but they paid special attention to the suns that had only recently succumbed. They watched those suns assist many dead planets, scattered all across the universe, and were pleased to see them nurture the beginnings of new life. The six goddesses continued their pursuit and were relentless in their efforts to bring back the light to countless solar systems.

They eventually arrived at the furthest reaches of the universe to where only nothingness exists, and to their surprise they were joined by a new energy. They were now seven and together they unleashed a light so bright no evil could possibly survive its power. This light appeared for a second and travelled to the other side of the universe instantaneously, defying science as it should have taken thousands of years to achieve such a feat. In Olympus, the seniors gods were together when the Light passed, Odin declared, "The Ancient One has awoken and is telling us the Light reign's supreme."

The Darkness was defeated. The six Goddesses were now in shock and were drained but it didn't take long for them to start preparing to return to Olympus. Eala was first to speak,

"Although I hear the call of Olympus my very being screams out that The Darkness is not really defeated, I can still feel its power. This war isn't over."

"You're right," said the Ancient One. "It isn't over. All must understand that where there's light, there's always darkness; where there's goodness there will always be badness, where there's love there will always be hate. The challenge for the next age of man is to follow the laws already set by the gods. There is pain ahead because Lucifer has got what he wants and will soon move into shadow. The gods still have much more to do and I will be there to assist. Peace will reign for just a few years then there will be SHADOW. You have defeated The Darkness this time but it will again seek allies." He looked out across the vast expanse of space then continued, "Go now, go back to your families. At the blink of an eye I can send you on your way. Your coronation awaits your return."

The goddesses were in awe, most especially Eala, who was always known for her devotion to the Ancient One. They felt they should remain and serve but feared outstaying their welcome. Their minds drifted back to their loved ones prompting the Ancient One to say, "I understand your desire to serve; you can serve wherever you are. Go now with my blessing." There was no further discussion, they bowed, blinked and in an instant arrived at the portal of Olympus.

Chapter 36

Everything was sombre in Olympus as the Gods came to terms with the death of Jacob, even so they knew that their priority was to assist the injured gods and goddesses who were arriving and seeking the assistance of Apollo. When Magni, Modi and Odi arrived, they were blood-stained and dishevelled showing that they had been very much in the thick of the battle. Odi was totally distraught and had great difficulty dealing with the reception they received. He began to tremble and then ran through the temple, out into the ornamental gardens, where he went to his knees and yelled out for his fallen brother.

Maria was broken hearted and in tears, she was nearby when she heard the cry of despair. She looked back and saw that it was Odi and called him over to join her. On his way she thought, for a fleeting second, that it was Jacob until she focused and saw by his fair locks that it wasn't. She raised her arms and said, "Odi, my boy, is it true? Is he gone?"

"Mother, I was there," he answered as his tears flowed. "I saw the staff penetrate his armour and then Cain send him crashing against the cliff face. I could do nothing, I was stunned and at Cain's feet. I got hope when I looked towards the sky and saw father travel at great speed, it was then I heard the sound of the horseman, it was Lucifer. I saw him grab Jacob and I heard him say 'Elysium will not be your resting place, Boy King. There will be no honour or peace for you.' He took him through a waiting portal." Odi held his mother, both of them sharing their grief.

While resting his head on her shoulder he felt a heat sensation forcing him to open his eyes and when he did, he focused on a vision, and soon realised it was his two year old niece, the Princess Helena, and she was glowing. She looked up at him and in a very childish way managed to say, "Pappa not dead!"

"I can't deal with this," he said, parting from Maria and running away,

"I don't think your pappa is coming home, darling," said Maria while lifting Helena and embracing her tightly.

"My pappa not dead," replied Helena getting more assertive.

Maria said no more, she was trying to suppress her grief. She placed her hand on Helena's head and received a visionary shock causing her to quickly withdraw her hand. She picked up a vision showing her Jacob in a dungeon, fighting for his life. The vision also showed Lucifer forcing the white mist back into him.

Maria placed Helena on the ground and ushered her back into the temple. She then ran out into the meadows seeking Odi and when she found him, he was lying in a heap near the pergola. "Jacob isn't dead," she yelled. "Helena has seen it. She has powers."

"I saw him fall," replied Odi fighting back his tears. "Accept it, he's gone."

"Tell me what you saw!" demanded Maria.

"I saw the staff penetrate his armour," he said. "I saw his head impact the wall and heard his skull crack on the second impact. I saw his blood pool and heard his last gasps. He looked at me and I saw his eyes glaze over as he passed away."

"Did you see the white mist leave?" said Maria while grabbing his collar.

Odi went quiet, he was searching. Maria shook him vigorously and asked again. "Did you see the white mist leave?"

"I did see the white mist," he mumbled while trying to remember. "It came to his mouth, then he was grabbed by Lucifer, the mist was forced back in. Mother, what does this mean?"

They ran into the temple to find Helena challenging Zeus and Magni who were both trying to calm her, trying as gently as they could to help her understand her father wasn't coming back. Those gathered found the stubbornness of Helena heart wrenching but they also noticed, the more agitated she got, the stronger the light surrounding her glowed. To them it was amazing to watch a two year old toddler hold her ground and not back down. Maria and Odi reached Zeus insisting Helena was speaking the truth.

It was then when a new portal opened just outside the temple; it was the return of the six goddesses. On arrival they were cheerful and excited until Eala fell to the ground, holding her chest as she screamed and her tears flowed. At the same time she kept calling out Jacob's name. "I can't feel him," she wailed. "He's dead; I feel the grief in the temple."

Panya couldn't detect him either but said nothing, she assisted Eala to her feet and together they made their way into the temple.

On seeing Odi her temper rose, she charged at him and although she could see he'd been crying, she didn't care. She pounded her fists off his chest.

"You said you'd always protect him," she shouted while trying to catch her breath. "You said you'd always be by his side, so how could you let this happen?" Odi felt humiliated and ran from the temple. Eala then saw Magni.

"You....War God my foot." she yelled on seeing Magni. "Why weren't you protecting him?"

It was then when she felt little arms wrap around her leg, and when she looked down she saw it was Helena who said, "My pappa not dead."

"Helena has powers" said Maria on approaching Eala. "She's insisting Jacob's alive, I saw her vision, he is alive, but none of us know what to do. We can't sense him anywhere. It's as though he's being shielded."

Helena was getting more agitated. She walked towards the doors, gripping Modi's finger as she passed. She turned back and said in her childish way, "Magni, come, come." Magni joined her deciding it was best to humour her.

When she gripped his finger everything changed, her light spread to surround her uncles and all three of them found themselves inside a crystal sphere, not unlike the ones that brought the goddesses out into the cosmos. All three were facing into the temple when the sphere levitated before backing out through the doors with the gods following. "Don't worry," said Magni looked over at Eala. "We'll look after her."

"Like you did my Jacob," she responded sarcastically.

The sphere rose higher into the sky and as it continued its journey its speed increased until it shot out into the cosmos and out of sight. It travelled through the solar system and out deep into the galaxy. It continued its journey, racing past amazing solar displays and strange worlds. It eventually landed on a rock formation that was drifting alone through space. It was a sinister place, bathed in strange coloured beams of light that originated from the surrounding suns. The beams illuminated the rock, causing eerie light formations and mystical illusions all over the rock-scape. There were dark and murky mists rising from the many fissures making it feel like a most foreboding place. Magni went to his hunkers and said to Helena, "Where have you brought us, darling?"

She said nothing, just raised her arm and pointed towards an entrance leading into a blackened stone cavern lit by a cold orange glow. Every now and again a high pitched scream was heard. It was so shrill it sent shivers down their spines.

Magni moved towards the cave, he slowly entered to the sound of muffled voices. He turned back to Modi seeking silence and insisted Helena remains outside.

They slowly and silently made their way through the tunnels and the deeper they travelled the more sinister the caves became. At times they though they saw Dark Angels but there were none, their minds were being deceived. They had their swords drawn and were ready for action.

Every now and again the screams got louder and their hearts would miss another beat. As they got nearer they clearly heard voices coming from deep in the cavern and they worked out that it was Lucifer. They sensed his malice and enjoyment as he tortured his victim. They couldn't sense Jacob but they knew that some poor unfortunate was being punished for something or other. As they got closer they heard, "Why? Why me? What is it I did to you? I've never met you yet you targeted and threatened me. Why?"

There was a guttural laugh and then they heard, "At last, Boy King, you ask the question I've been waiting for." They then knew the victim was Jacob. "At the beginning of time, I was the favourite of the Ancient One. I pandered to his every need and assisted with the creation even though I resented him making man in his own image. I lost his trust and watched as that imbecile Phoenician, Melqart, became his confidant. Once, I followed and then hid as Melqart and the Ancient One stood at the edge of the universe, right next to the nothingness. I watched the Ancient One raise his palm and then blow out into the cosmos a single speck of dust. I saw it drift then fade knowing it was the spark of life. I knew he had created another favourite, one who would push me further away. Even while cocooned I watched you being born; I knew I was right when I saw the light wrap itself around you. I know that speck is you and I'll make you suffer. I plan to keep you alive and ensure your torture will continue until the end of time."

"I'm no speck of dust," Jacob managed to say." I'm a God of Olympus and son of the God of Thunder. Beware his vengeance and that of my brothers, they'll find you and make you pay." It was then when Lucifer extended his finger nails and slowly dragged them down Jacob's chest towards his groin causing the most horrendous screams of pain to echo throughout the caverns.

Both Magni and Modi fell back against the wall in shock, but they quickly recovered. Magni was first to move and he made his way higher up the ridge where he had a better view, he assessed that the platform was reachable and decided to act immediately. He leapt to land close to the stake holding a naked, bloodied and bruised Jacob bound to it. He hoped Modi would remain hidden for the moment, but it wasn't to be, Modi was already in mid-air and on his way to assist in the rescue.

Lucifer was taken aback that his secret hideout was discovered, he was furious and reacted with such speed he knocked Modi roughly against boulders near the edge of the platform. Modi was stunned leaving Magni to fight alone.

The distraction of Lucifer was catastrophic for Jacob as it allowed the white mist to finally leave. Modi while still stunned was alert enough to watch the mist rise and move towards the exit. He looked across at Jacob and saw a sickly grey colour take him; he knew then that he had just died. He was broken hearted and his will to recover was broken, that was until he saw the skills and prowess of Magni. "Father," he said as he closed his eyes and pleaded, "Send me the hammer. Magni needs me, send me the hammer."

Thor, at this point, was with Melqart near the Aleppo plateau, they were ensuring the last of Hells armies were sent back to where they came from. He planned to leave for Olympus and just as he was about to leave his head moved from left to right and back again, as though he was listening to some low whispers. He turned to Melqart, "Modi's in my head, he calls for the hammer even though he knows it doesn't answer to him."

"Send it to him," said Melqart. "It will return if he's unworthy, send it now." Thor released the hammer and it immediately disappeared to reappear in Modi's hand.

Magni and Lucifer were now in mortal combat and were both drawing blood. The constant clashing of steel was grating. They were equally matched in swordsmanship skills, one unable to get the better of the other. It took some time before Magni's tactics started to work but all Lucifer needed was for Magni to make one mistake and the battle was his. That mistake came when Magni looked across at Jacob and saw he had passed away. Magni, staring at Jacob's battered and bruised body allowed Lucifer that one second, a second that was enough for him to toss his sword at such speed it impaled Magni against the wall. Lucifer then extracted his dagger planning to finish Magni off. He moved to decapitate him but he hadn't allowed for the recovery of Modi, who had received the hammer and released it at such speed it sent Lucifer crashing against the wall. His head impacted so forcefully it cracked his skull, the impact also crushed his ribs totally incapacitating him. Modi quickly freed Magni and then turned to finish Lucifer off. He pierced his heart, and then used his axe to dismember his body. He built a Pire and cremated each part individually preventing any future followers from using magic to restore him. In the meantime Jacob's white mist had gathered near the cave entrance, waiting.

Helena had disobeyed Magni and made her way into the cave. She showed no fear making her way towards the platform, even when she looked into a nearby grotto and saw a shadowy figure. The figure got more defined and then entered her head, "Do not be afraid," it said. "Close your eyes and allow your mind to view the cosmos, tell me what you see."

"I see something," she said. "It's tiny, very small. It's a speck of dust." She opened her eyes and moved closer to the platform. She saw Magni and Modi cradling her father's body and felt their grief but she wasn't alarmed.

Modi looked up towards the ridge and asked, "Who's she talking to?"

"I see or hear nobody," said Magni.

"I hear something," said Modi straining his ears, "She's definitely talking to the old man. How come you can't see him?"

"She's alone," said Magni. "That knock to your head must have done more damage than you thought."

Helena raised her palm, waited a few moments and then the tiniest speck of dust arrived. She blew the speck towards her father. It entered his slightly opened mouth and then everything changed. The white mist returned and it too entered Jacob's mouth, within seconds a dim light appeared and his body began to glow.

"That was the spark of Life," said Magni while backing away. "The very one sent at the beginning of time. The Ancient One has saved him. The Ancient One must be the old man you see on the ridge."

Magni was excited and very relieved, he looked across to Modi and was taken aback to see, for the first time ever, tears rolling down his brother's cheeks.

"Brother," he said, "this is a first. I've never known you to cry!"

Modi wasn't embarrassed, he didn't care. He was so happy Jacob was recovering. He stretched across to hug Magni not realising one of his still flowing tears dropped into Jacob's open mouth.

"Yak," said a horrified Jacob. "That's disgusting!" They looked down to be met with a feeble yet broad smile. Jacob then caught a glimpse of the shining light up on the ridge.

"That bright light?" asked Jacob while pointing up towards the ridge. "What is it?"

"That's your Helena," replied Magni.

"Who's that beside her, he's holding her hand?" said a panicking Jacob. "Is my baby in danger?"

"Trust me brother," said Modi. "She's safe."

"I see nobody," said Magni trying to reassure him, "But I sense his presence and know who it is. Helena is in no danger."

"No," insisted Jacob struggling to get up. "I don't know who's holding her hand, she's in danger."

"Brother," said Magni holding him closer. "Trust us, she's safe. It's the Ancient One." Jacob closed his eyes for a moment and relaxed while resting in Magni's arms. After awhile Modi said,

"Come on little brother, let's get you cleaned, dressed and sorted, we can't have you arriving in Olympus showing everything you have."

"Hey," replied Jacob trying to be funny, "I've nothing to be ashamed of."

"I can definitely see that," laughed Magni.

Modi fetched some water and began cleaning the congealed blood away but was stopped when Jacob said, "Listen, as much as I appreciate your help, I prefer to clean myself. Please take Helena outside and give me some alone time. I need to come to terms with what he did to me."

Magni and Modi didn't argue; they assisted Jacob to stand. They fetched Helena and carried her outside.

Jacob found it difficult to stand without the aid of his staff. It took some time for his strength to show signs of returning but when it did he retrieved his satchel to fetch another cask of water. He poured the water over his head and as it flowed down his body it magically washed away the congealed blood and grime that had gathered since his torture began. He used the power of the Light to heal his scars and close his open wounds. He looked across at the Pire and decided he wouldn't leave until he was sure no muscle, skin or even bone remained, he was determined nothing of Lucifer would survive. He sat on a nearby rock, resting his chin on his knees while staring into the flames and thought of the chaos that pile of ashes caused. He then thought of all those he lost. Using the flickering flames he looked down at his naked body and realized he was still in pain, and heavily bruised. He closed his eyes, clenched his fists and called on the Light. When he opened his eyes the cave was illuminated, the Light had come and as his body glowed, and his pain and bruises disappeared.

From his satchel he fetched his spare robes and armour and when dressed he placed is sword and dagger into their scabbards leaving only one more thing to do. He extracted the crown of Olympus and found it had changed; it was now encrusted with the most exquisite gems. When he put the crown upon his head it tightened, then his whole body strengthened. When he felt ready, he took a deep breath and prepared to leave but before moving away he looked up towards the ridge to see that The Ancient One was still there. He smiled and then bowed to be met with a bow in return.

Outside, Magni held Helena in his arms while Modi paced and at times, fired stones out into space. They were impatient, wanting to take Jacob home and share the good news. After a few more moments passed they heard slow and faint footsteps approach while a radiant light developed near the mouth of the cave. The steps got stronger, louder and more determined while the light kept getting brighter until the entrance was totally illuminated. Magni placed Helena behind him, shielding her eyes from the increasing light. He and Modi then shielded their eyes as the light became almost blinding as it exploded out into the universe. While the brothers stood with their mouths open and tears welling in their eyes, Helena was already running up the hill calling, "Pappa, Pappa, Pappa."

For those few moments while waiting for Helena to reach him, he stood as a most powerful Warrior God. His pristine white robes and his golden armour glistened, not only in his own aura, but also because of the rays of the surrounding suns. His crown sparkled while reflecting the light reaching him from deepest space. The brilliant white light oozing from him not only confirmed him to be King of Kings, it was announcing him to be the God of Gods. Magni and Modi bowed and received in return an equally reverent acknowledgement.

Jacob watched Helena run up to him knowing his place was not just to be a King or a God, it was also to be a father, so he went to his knees and stretched out his arms to receive an embrace of love that only a daughter could have for a father. For the first time he could be the father he always wanted to be without any threats or dangers to distract him. What surprised him was when he was embraced by his brothers the feelings were just the same. He was happy and couldn't wait to return home to be with Eala and his sons. They all held hands and this time it was Jacob's power that brought them home.

Chapter 37

They arrived in the ornamental gardens just as the sun was setting. Jacob asked Magni to take Helena into the temple as he wanted some time alone. When he felt ready he made his way up the steps and as in the past, the doors magically opened. The setting sun was behind him and as he entered the temple it created an amazing image of a God of the Light in all his glory. He stood on the highest step and acknowledged the homage being paid by all those in attendance, including his grandfathers. He looked around for his mother and father and couldn't wait to meet them, but it was Eala and his children he wanted more than anything. Eala threw all conventions aside and ran through the temple to leap into his arms and this was followed by the patter of three sets of tiny feet. When they reached him he felt complete.

He soon noticed Odi was missing and decided to break their agreement. He sought him out and entered his head, "Hi, where are you?" Odi wouldn't answer so he tried again, "I miss you, where are you?"

"I'm walking through the forests," replied a reluctant Odi. "I'm in the land of the snow people and want to be alone."

"This is no time to be alone," said Jacob. "I need you with me, get back here or I'll break your neck."

"You and whose army?" challenged Odi. "I'll take someone better than you to break my neck." They both laughed yet Jacob sensed he was hurting.

"What's wrong brother?" he asked.

Odi went quiet for a moment then mumbled, "Eala hates me, she thinks I let you down and that you fell because of me. Everyone saw her attack me. I can't face you or those in the temple right now."

"Are you for real?" said Jacob losing his patience. "Eala loves me more than anything and hit out at you because she knows that after her and our babies, you are the closest to me. Surely you understand how terrible the shock my death was for her. She needed to hit out at somebody and it just happened to be you. Eala loves you so get back now or I really will break your neck."

"Please Jacob, leave me alone. I'm still hurting," responded Odi. "She really did embarrass me. Give me a few hours, I'll see you then."

Jacob was about to speak again when he was interrupted by Eala entering Odi's head, "Idiot, get your ass back here now and welcome your brother home." Jacob tried to stifle a laugh.

"I told you she hates me," said Odi. "Listen to how she's speaking to me."

"It's all right for you," replied Jacob "You'll be living it up with Panya in the palaces of Asgard while I'll have to live with someone else whom I didn't know could enter my head. My secrets are no longer safe." He then yelped while receiving a clatter of affection across the back of his neck,

"The cheek of you," said Eala. "For the record I only recently discovered I can enter your head when I need to."

"Is his head as messed up as mine?" asked Odi with a snigger. Eala didn't get a chance to reply because a fourth presence arrived and this time it was Panya prompting a panicking Odi to say, "When did you learn to do that?"

"I'm not telling you," responded Panya. "It's nice to have a little power over you. I'm shocked at some of the things that are on your mind; suffice it to say you'll need to sort yourself out." All he could think to say was,

"I'll have you know, I'm very young, up for trying anything, and have lots of needs."

"Well as Eala said," replied Panya. "You better get your ass back here and we'll see if I can sort out those needs."

At the blink of an eye Odi returned to the temple and immediately went to hug Jacob.

"You're unbelievable!" said Jacob. "Eala called you an idiot and you know what? She's right! Panya gives you an offer even I wouldn't refuse and you come and hug me, if I were you I'd be getting a room."

"No one is getting any room," interrupted Panya. "You two need to spend some time together, there's probably a lot you need to talk about. Those needs have been around for the last two thousand years, one more day won't hurt."

Jacob and Odi left for the ornamental gardens where they sat on the bench next to the statue of David. They were soon joined by Magni and Modi who reverted to kind, teasing their little brothers.

"Magni," said Modi. "I don't know about you but from memory, that statue doesn't look like Odi, too big. I think it's Jacob! What do you think?" Jacob cringed.

"Yeah," replied Magni. "Come to think of it, you might be right. Maybe we should check again?" Jacob began backing away.

"What are they talking about?" asked Odi.

"When they found me," replied Jacob. "I was naked with my bits on full view, covered in slime and blood. When the fight was over and I was restored, they started to wash me. Their hands were everywhere. I have to face eternity knowing that pair rubbed me down with their wet and bare hands, and the worst thing is they're never going to let me live it down."

He continued to walk away and made his way to his room where he was again joined by Odi. They talked for some time before falling asleep, the turmoil and horror of the last while had finally taken its toll.

❧❧

While they slept, gods and goddesses from all across the universe were making their way to Olympus to celebrate this special day. They arrived knowing the battle was won and The Darkness was back in the nothingness.

For many the gathering was a chance to renew old friendships but for Mia it was her chance to reunite with the man she loved. She knew he'd survived the war and was hoping he made it to Olympus. She searched the temple and the immediate grounds and when finally she looked up at the folly, there he was. She saw him standing alone and looking a bit despondent then noticed that he was dressed in the finest robes of an imperial Dragon lord. She wanted to look her best especially now that she had something to tell him.

She called on the Light and when it came, it worked its way down her body to transform her into a most beautiful goddess. Even the flower sprites went to work as she made her way towards the folly; they commanded the flowers to open, releasing the most fragrant of aromas. The scent was so powerful Andras knew she was close by, and when she joined him he said,

"I arrived some hours earlier to discover you were one of the goddesses who had left to fight The Darkness. I was terribly worried."

"We were never in any danger," she assured him. "The Ancient One was always by our side."

She moved closer and was in awe; she'd seen him many times as a dragon lord, and a few times as a war torn human, but never as one of the most powerful, handsome and muscular of men. He stared back and said while shaking his head in disbelief,

"Since the war ended I'd fly high just to watch the stars do battle against The Darkness and I wondered which Goddess of the Light was assisting. Occasionally I saw The Darkness fight back and my heart would sink, bringing on a terrible pain." He raised his arms to gently touch her cheeks, "I need to know this is real."

She assured him while gently kissing his neck, "Trust me, this is real and our kisses will wipe away all the pain." She then moved his hand to rest on her small bump and without saying anything more he knew.

From the temple those watching saw the light surround them as though providing a protective blanket, but more importantly they knew the bright light was also announcing there was a baby.

❦❧

In the meantime Eala and Panya got anxious, their coronation was rapidly approaching. They made their way to the boy's room and were surprised to find them still asleep.

"The stewards are waiting," said Eala while shaking Jacob awake. "We need to get ready."

Odi awoke and was delighted to see Panya standing over him,

"Have you come to sort out those needs of mine?" he said with a smile.

"You should be so lucky?" she responded.

"I had a most peaceful sleep and my dreams were very powerful," he said. "All I dreamt of was you and our daughters. I've never been this happy."

"Don't be so soppy," she said while hugging him. "I'm not sure which Odi I like the most, the warrior or the soppy one. It's going to take a millennium to find out."

"A whole millennium," said Jacob. "He doesn't have the patience, this should be fun." Odi then threw a pillow at him.

The stewards assisted and after an hour of washing, grooming and dressing they had prepared two Kings and two Queens for the most important day of their lives. When ready they made their way through the corridors leading to the Great Hall. They were nervous, except for Jacob, who had already faced his own coronation some days earlier so for him it was less daunting. He was wearing the crown and looked every part a true God of Olympus. He felt Eala's fear and tried to reassure her with a gentle smile as they reached the Great Hall. He looked at Odi and saw he was petrified, smirked and said,

"I thought you said that you were one of the fiercest warriors known to man? Why are you shaking?"

"He might think he is one of the fiercest warriors known to man but in my hands he is putty," said Panya. "Watch how I take him through the Great Hall to face his destiny. Trust me, he'll not flinch."

The doors opened to a fanfare of trumpets announcing the arrival of two powerful royal houses that were about to take power. While walking through, Jacob said,

"Odi, Panya, walk in alongside us and let all see us as inseparable."

The trumpeting continued while they stood at the top of the steps and to those watching it was an amazing sight. Jacob and Eala were wearing the white and gold robes of Olympus Gods except that Jacob was wearing the imperial crown of the King of Kings. Odi was wearing the robes of a warrior King of Asgard and Panya was dressed in the robes of a high ranking Goddess of the Light.

Their walk through the hall was slow as it was filled to capacity and they intended acknowledging everyone. Visitors had come from all over the world, from the Astral Plains and from out across the cosmos. There was also a delegation from Elysium as well as the Underworld. They didn't ignore the stewards, guards or servants; they planned to be all inclusive. On reaching their friends it was then when it hit Jacob hard that Fafner was gone and this was when he got emotional. They moved on and reached the area where King Derwyn and the dragon nation delegation were seated. When Jacob saw them, he and Odi clenched their fists across their hearts and lowered their heads in homage to the memory of Fafner. Derwyn, along with his brothers and his sisters stood and acknowledged the homage being paid to their father.

They moved on and while passing the ancient Goddesses of Olympus it was noted by Zeus that Jacob was paying special attention to five of them who were grouped together. He saw them slightly bow to Jacob and then leave the temple. He wondered, but chose to say nothing.

On the opposite side the Gods of Asgard were placed. Odi caught Modi's eye and saw he was trying to get his attention, indicating there was something wrong with his breeches. Jacob entered his head, "Odi, he's playing you; the stewards wouldn't allow you to walk through the Great Hall to be ridiculed, ignore him."

"What if he's right?" asked an unconvinced Odi. "Surely he wouldn't pull a stunt on such a solemn occasion?"

"Brother, don't!" Jacob insisted. "Let your revenge be best served cold."

It was too late. Odi placed his hand over his crotch area and started feeling around giving rise to an instant chorus of sniggering and giggling. Magni was seen patting Modi on the back, and Odi was mortified. He found out the hard way that there was no problem with his breeches and that he was again a victim of his older brother's pranks.

"I don't think we should allow them away with that," said an unimpressed Eala. "If it was my man I'd seek revenge."

"What have you got in mind?" asked Panya.

"Remember how briskly we travelled across the universe and the times we travelled so fast, The Darkness couldn't see us." replied Eala. "I think we could embarrass Magni and Modi and teach them a lesson they will never forget. They won't be able to blame us as we will be, as far as everybody is concerned, walking through the Great Hall."

"Don't even think about it!" said Odi. But before he finished his sentence Eala and Panya had dropped the breeches of both Magni and Modi, revealing everything they had, causing a rumble of great mirth to flow through the temple. Jacob said while trying to keep a straight place,

"I can't believe you did that?"

"We didn't do anything," said a sniggering Panya. "After all we haven't left your sides."

"I love this girl," said Odi.

Jacob and Odi had great difficulty keeping a straight face; they'd tried everything to embarrass their brothers and never expected that it would be their girlfriends who would succeed. They composed themselves then continued their walk and acknowledged the Pantheons from the Americas,

Australasia, Africa and the Far East. They finally reached the Indus Gods who were with Lord Buddha, and there was a special greeting imparted to them.

Their walk through the Great Hall was now completed when they reached the four thrones set out for them. Jacob sat to the extreme right and was joined by Eala, Odi took the throne to the extreme left and he was then joined by Panya. Apollonius, as the most senior of the wizards, was recognised throughout the realms as the one gifted by the Ancient One with the powers to grant kingship and he was master of ceremony,

First to be elevated was Eala and she knelt before Apollonius, "Let all here bear witness to the coronation of Ealasaid," he said as he raised the crown above her head. "She is a Goddess of the Light, and now Queen of Queens in the Olympus realm. Let her and Jacob rule as just and wise monarchs." He then placed the crown upon her head as all called out, "Long live the Queen." Those close by could see her crown was identical to the one worn by Jacob.

Jacob and Eala then stepped aside to allow Odi and Panya move to the centre thrones. Odin and Thor stepped forward and raised the Crowns of Asgard high above their heads while Apollonius recited the coronation prayer. All watched the gem encrusted crowns being lowered on to their heads and as the crowns were being lowered Apollonius said, "Let all here bear witness to the coronation of Odi, King of Kings and Warrior God of Asgard, and Panya, Goddess of the Light, and now Queen of Queens of the Asgard Realm." All called out, "Long live the King, long live the Queen."

Jacob and Eala rejoined Odi and Panya and all four accepted the homage offered. Jacob knew it was customary to say a few words so he stepped forward and cleared his throat,

"I'm not one to stand and give long speeches so all I'll say at this time is that I will continue the policies of my grandfather. When I think back to the battles I realise we've interfered in the affairs off Man too many times in the past, making it easy for Lucifer to take control of earth and the Underworld, giving him a base from which to build his armies. This must never happen again. I've lost close friends, as have many of you and I never want to go through that again. As gods we should step back and rebuild our pantheons, we should also remember that although we won this battle the war is one that never ends. The Darkness will keep trying so we must always be on our guard. Having said all that I have a small bit of unfinished business with man and will be concluding that business over the next few days but this evening while you party I will be leaving for Dublin to assist my closest friend who is beginning his journey into the Underworld."

Chapter 38

Jacob linked Eala and together they made their way back through the Great Hall. Although greeting everybody individually it was obvious Jacob was distracted and this distraction was getting unbearable. He reached his parents and had difficulty trying to talk with them, even when his sons and daughter ran to hug him he couldn't give them his full attention. He looked at his mother and felt her grief was also growing; she too was sensing the passing of Shane and mouthed to him, "Go; go now."

Eala also sensed his growing distress and gripped him tightly while whispering in his ear, "Take me with you, you're going to need me!"

He just nodded while holding back his gathering tears, "I'm dreading this," he said. "I've always known this day would come and yet it still hurts. He was my rock when I lived in Dublin; we were so close we finished each other's sentences? We always had each other's back."

Before he left he asked King Derwyn and Odi to join him and when they arrived he reminded them of what Shane did as leader of the Celts and of how his actions had saved many lives. He made several requests which were immediately agreed to. He then took Eala's hand and together they blinked and left for Dublin.

On arrival they maintained their invisibility for just long enough to change from their Olympus robes and crowns into more modern clothing. As they materialised they were picked up by the attending TV cameras and their arrival was immediately broadcasted all around the world. Reporters tried to interview them but Jacob was having none of it, he was too focused on reaching Shane's house. On his way he ignored his many old friends who were all now very aged but Eala didn't, she acknowledged them while at the same time rushing to catch up with Jacob.

When she reached him he was waiting at the gate and she could see his heart was about to burst, she sensed he was praying they weren't too late. He ran up the stairs and stood outside the door of Shane's bedroom listening to the soft weeping of Shane's family. He then heard, "Is he here yet?"

"I'm here," he answered while opening the door. "I promised you I'd travel across the universe just to be with you when the time came. I've come to fulfil that promise."

He went to his knees at the side of the bed and reached across to grip Shane's hand. He noted the difficulty Shane was having trying to open his eyes, and how his breathing was laboured.

"Hi Scobie," said Shane causing Jacob to get very emotional.

"Hi Bud." he replied with difficulty.

"I think I can see the Light," said Shane after briefly rallying. "And it's getting brighter,"

"Hi Shane, it's me, Eala."

"Hi gorgeous," replied Shane with a big smile crossing his face. "Is it your Light I see?"

"When you're ready," she said whispering into his ear. "My Light will take away the pain and welcome you with open arms. It'll escort you to a much better place."

Jacob was now totally distraught with his tears flowing freely. He continuously and gently rubbed Shanes face, pleading for him to wait, "Bud, not yet, I can take you back in time. We can have more fun, just like we did in Ibiza, remember,"

"How can I ever forget," said Shane looking very happy. "Can't believe we spent the whole time partying in our boxers, I had no other clothes with me, that was fun," He paused for a moment then began gasping, "Scobie, Scob, I'm tired, the time is coming, I hear a calling."

Jacob kept calling him back, "Not yet. Bud, not yet, give me a few more moments."

Just then Odi and Panya arrived and Odi, on recognising that the time was now, moved in to take Jacob away. Panya sent out a gentle light and this helped to relax and calm Shane's family. She then joined Eala at the end of the bed and together they raised their hands, calling Shane into the Light.

The Gods were the only ones to see his spirit rise and it was at this time when Jacob became inconsolable. Odi tried to shield him because it was unheard of for gods to show their feelings in this way but if the truth be really known, he was jealous that he never had a friend that would cause the same effect that Shane's death was having on Jacob.

"I wish I had a friend like Shane when I was a child," whispered Odi into Jacob's ear. "Witnessing your reaction shows me all the things I've missed."

"When I arrived in 1st year he made me so welcome," said Jacob while resting his head on Odi's shoulder. "I was being bullied because of my accent, it made me different. One look from Shane and all bullying stopped. He included me in everything and never forgot me; we were inseparable. He and I took on the world and always won, we shared our most secret thoughts. Before Eala and my babies he was everything to me."

Jacob pulled himself together and went to sympathise with Shane's devastated family. He gathered them together and said,

"Your father was the greatest friend anyone could have. He inspired me and when my powers began showing he was never afraid. He kept me grounded and was always compassionate, loving, strong and loyal. It is fitting for him to rest among the blessed dead, the heroes, the kings and the gods of old. Will you allow me to take him to the tombs of Elysium?"

Shane Jr answered, "My dad never stopped talking about you, we saw the old school photo's but never saw any photo's or video's of you or him together during the war, we were beginning not to believe him but now we can see how close you two were. I know my sisters and I would be happy for him to go with you."

Jacob was delighted with their decision and immediately reached into his satchel to retrieve his robes and crown. "I ran into this house to be with Shane as a friend," he said. "I will leave as a King and will allow the world see that your father was escorted to his final resting place by four of the most powerful kings and queens of the Olympus and Asgard realms.

Odi went to the window and blew his gjallarhorn and within seconds two royal Asgard chariots arrived. The first one was extended at the rear. He reached in, lifted and carried Shane's body down to the carriage. It was then when Eala and Panya used their powers to prepare Shanes body. They called on the flower sprites to fly from garden to garden picking the most fragrant flowers then return to lay them around Shane. When prepared, his family, neighbours and friends came closer and were taken aback at how regal he looked especially when they saw the old dusty sword that was hidden in the attic emit a most magical and radiant light. It was also telling the world that he was a hero and a friend of the gods.

The magic of the occasion was to continue with the arrival of a majestic dragon that landed alongside the funeral chariot, the dragon transformed to become King Derwyn who bowed to both Jacob and Odi then went to sympathise with Shane's family.

The magic continued with the arrival of a bright and luminous flash of white light and it was accompanied by a continuous peel of thunder. It was the arrival of Lord Lugh, God of the Celts and after he bowed to Jacob, he went and offered his sympathies to Shane's family, who were shocked at his likeness to their dad. He then joined Jacob, Odi and Derwyn to form a guard of honour around the body of Shane. From the TV drones hovering above, was broadcast the amazing sight of an Asgard funeral chariot surrounded by four Warrior Gods, all in honour of a most respected hero.

The magic was to continue with the arrival of one hundred dragons and they were flying past in formation. Next was heard a loud rolling sound that was announcing the arrival of one hundred golden Asgard chariots and they took up a holding position above the cortege. Jacob then called on Shane Jr and said, "It's time, your dad's place is prepared and he will rest among the Celtic Kings. Shane Jr nodded but looked troubled, he asked, "Will we be able to visit our dad's resting place?"

Jacob was tempted. He looked at Odi, Lugh and Derwyn and he saw them all slowly shaking their heads. He sought inspiration from Eala and Panya and they too were shaking their heads. "There's a way!" he suggested as he entered Odi's head. "I can show them the future that just happens to be Shane's tomb in Elysium, do you agree? Will you assist?"

Odi agreed and walked over to join Jacob. They placed their right hand on each other's foreheads and soon conjured up a portal showing the final stages of Shane's funeral. Shane's family and close friends could also see what was happening. They watched Shane's body being raised as though by magic and then float towards the doors of a grand mausoleum. They continued to watch while pallbearers carried him down towards one of the wide arches and were pleased to see him being escorted by many warriors. They were impressed when they saw the sculptured tombs of the ancient gods, kings, queens and heroes of Ireland. They also saw Cronus open a sarcophagus to make it ready to receive the body of Shane. This was the most emotional part for them as they waved their last farewells to their father. Jacob ended the image and said to the family, "That's the best I can do, Elysium is a sanctum that can never be visited by mortals. Did you note that your mother rests alongside your father? Be happy for them."

It was now time to leave. Jacob and Odi mounted the first chariot while Eala, Panya, Lugh and Derwyn mounted the second. Both chariots rose into the air and a solemn procession of Asgard chariots escorted by the dragons began their slow movement across the sky and out over Dublin bay before turning back over the city and moving into the west. On arrival in Elysium they were met by Cronus and Rhea as well as six pallbearers who carried Shane to his tomb. It was a very moving ceremony and for Jacob it was the toughest part of the day. Only for the solace he received from Eala it was felt he would have suffered another breakdown.

Soon after the ceremony ended and everyone let the tombs, King Derwyn managed to slip away. He returned to the mausoleum and made his way to the arches of the dragons where he was taken aback when the torches magically lit up. Their light spread across the tombs highlighting sculptures of all the great dragons of old, even those who had faded out of memory. He was mesmerised by how many there were but it was the two newest tombs that attracted his attention.

His concentration was broken by the arrival of Rhea, who said, "It pleases me to see you revisit these tombs, you never grieved properly and now it's time. The Titans know of an ancient prophecy that speaks of a young dragon who will lead his armies and assists in the defeat of The

Darkness. That dragon is you and from you will come the greatest dragon dynasty of them all, but this can't happen until you accept your father has already forgiven you."

Derwyn said, "I broke their hearts, I was rebellious, arrogant and rude to them, do you really think they forgave me?" Rhea moved to reassure him.

"Each time I walk under these hallowed archways," she said. "I sense the great love that existed between them. They rest in peace and that peace can only exist because they know the dragon realm is safe in your hands."

After acknowledging her kind words, he said, "My brothers speak of this place and of how their grief was taken away; they speak of our mother and feel it was she who brought the calmness. Will it be the same for me?"

"Place your hands on both tombs," she suggested. "Feel their love. Look out across the effigies of your ancestors and see in their faces the pride they feel while in your presence and then let their calmness take away the pain. When this happens you must reaffirm in yourself as to whom you are. Derwyn, Emperor of the Dragons." She then backed away towards the steps to allow him grieve alone. On reaching the steps she was joined by Jacob, Eala, Odi, Panya and Cronus.

After some time passed Eala and Panya sensed Derwyn's grief was getting more intense and they went to be with him. He was on his knees and seemed to be in shock. Panya reached in and whispered in his ear, "Let your tears flow and feel them take away the pain, you will be stronger after this day. Close your eyes and feel your parents reach out to you. They are talking to you; listen carefully to what they have to say."

Eala and Panya were joined by Jacob and Odi just in time to witness an amazing sight. It was the arrival of Fafner and Heulwyn's spirits and they appeared alongside Derwyn. They placed their arms around him bringing the calmness and to everyone's surprise Fafner's spirit turned and looking directly at Jacob mouthed, "Thank You."

Derwyn's strength returned while watching his parents return to invisibility, he then exited the tomb and said to all present, "I'm now ready to return to the dragon realm and this time I really believe my parents know me as Derwyn, Emperor of the Dragons."

Jacob joined him and said, "It's about time, but not until tomorrow, tonight you join the celebrations in the temple."

He then turned to Cronus, "It's also time for you to join us in Olympus, meet and finally enjoy your family. Oh, by the way, this is Odi, my twin and he's father to two goddesses. This is Panya, his Queen." He took Eala's hand and continued, "And this is Eala, the love of my life and mother of my children."

Chapter 39

Within seconds they all arrived in the gardens of the temple to be met by the sight of many more gods and goddesses arriving for the celebrations. Cronus was very nervous and it showed. He kept looking around as though in fear of what was to come. Rhea was first to light up when she saw Zeus approach. He too was nervous especially when he saw his father. Jacob's children ran from the temple to greet their mother and father and this broke the ice as Helena immediately took a shine to Cronus, "My pappa said you are lord of the Titans and that you were once one of the greatest kings that ever ruled." It was then when Odi's two daughters arrived and they too found Cronus fascinating. He was taken aback by the welcome he was receiving from the children and said when he went to his knees, "Such beauty, such power I feel in you, three Goddesses of the Light and somehow I feel that your real power will not show itself for a very long time. The Ancient One has touched your souls and one day you will be called upon to bring the light to the darkest of places."

Jacob's sons then approached and he said, "Ah, two princes of the Olympus realm. Like your sister your souls have been touched by the Ancient One but I see a parting, one will be a Warrior King and will always be on guard in defence of the realm; the other will become the greatest mystic of all and a guardian of the Astral Plains."

It was then when Cronus felt a real shiver travel through his body. He stood and turned to be met by the icy glare of a still unsettled Zeus who said, "Father, I'm not sure how I feel. When I look on you I still see the Titan whom I hated for thousands of years. I see the one who brought great pain into my life and the lives of countless others, both in the astral world and in the mortal world. I will accept the judgement of Jacob but will not forget. I will do everything in my power to forgive and because of Jacob I welcome you back into Olympus."

He then backed away and said while embracing his mother, "Your cunning and wily ways that saved my life all those years ago has led to this day, look around at your grandchildren and all those who have come after them. See how happy Olympus is now, this is all down to you, we will be forever grateful."

"Enough of this reminiscing," said Odi. "It's time to party. Jacob, let's get the Great Hall cleared and have some fun."

"I know it's been two thousand years since the last party I organised," said Jacob. "Mother, I remember it went down well with the younger gods, maybe we should do the same; what do you think?"

"What's a party?" asked Cronus

"I have no idea," replied Rhea.

"I attended Jacob's last party and let's just say; it's in the gardens you'll find me." said Zeus.

Jacob and Odi ran into the temple and were pleased to see the stewards had already begun clearing the hall and were placing many trestle tables between the columns. In the meantime Eala and Panya were using their powers to create colourful lighting to shine from the numerous torches adorning the walls while Maria, Oba and Mulan worked with the kitchen staff to prepare the widest variety of foods to suit all tastes

When all this was done Jacob blinked and arrived in the private quarters of one of the biggest and most renowned DJ's based in Ibiza. The DJ immediately recognised him from the battle and sat in awe of him. When Jacob asked if he would come to Olympus and perform for the gods, the DJ asked, "Would the gods like my music?"

"The gods will soon be dispersing to their own realms," replied Jacob. "None of them will have ever experienced your kind of music but I did, I remember when my friend Shane and I attended a wild club in Ibiza we had the time of our lives and we were given many happy memories. I want to share those memories."

"What about my equipment and sounds," wondered the DJ? "How do I get them there? What about power?"

"Power will be no problem," Jacob assured him. "We are the gods after all. Asgard will carry your equipment. Will you come?"

"I've played to thousands upon thousands and graced the great stadiums," replied the DJ "I played before royalty and now I've been asked to play for the gods, of course I'll go with you." Jacob summoned Odi and a number of his Asgard warriors, within seconds they transported the DJ and his equipment to the Great Hall.

The DJ wasted no time, he walked to several spots and much to the amusement of the stewards and those gods present; he clapped loudly, listening for echoes. He eventually settled on the steps at the back of the temple as the most ideal site for his turntables and speakers. Jacob arranged for power to be provided using some contraptions created by Apollo and Athena and then the DJ took a deep breath before beginning a practice round of sounds only once before heard in Olympus.

Jacob was in his element but every now and again memories of Shane entered his head and reminded him of the great times they had all those years ago. Eala joined him and soon he was able to push the memories aside. They embraced and soon they began gyrating to the high octane sounds. Jacob wasn't a bad dancer in his day and was determined to show Eala some of his moves; she followed his lead to end up jiving and swinging across an empty dance floor. Odi was horrified, "If you think I am going to dance," he said as Panya was already pulling him on to the floor. "I refuse to make a fool of myself. Keep trying and I'll be out that door so fast it will take your breath away."

Panya held him so tightly he couldn't escape. "Look at Jacob!" she said. "You're his twin, identical in every way. Don't let him out do you on the dance floor." She then pushed him to where Jacob was and gestured for Eala to back away. He entered Jacob's head and soon felt his whole body dance to the rhythm the DJ was producing. It became infectious and within seconds he was dancing in unison with Jacob to that same rhythm. The stewards had difficulty containing themselves; they'd never seen gods dancing and found it amusing.

After a while Jacob and Odi were joined by their daughters, Helena, Thora and Sunniva and together they had the time of their lives. Jacob's two sons, Obelius and Demetrius were mortified and hid behind a column until they were caught by Panya who dragged them on to the floor. They made every effort to escape and were relieved when the DJ stopped the music and confirmed, "The sound is right, the venue is brilliant and the music choice will rock the night away. What time do we start?"

"Two Hours." replied Odi.

After ensuring everything was in place, Jacob and Eala went to their room where they spent the next two hours doing what they normally do when they get some time alone. On returning to the Great Hall they were delighted at how party-like everything looked in the fading evening light.

Every table was well positioned to take up the twelve gods each. The torches were emitting multicoloured beams of light that danced to the music. The ambiance created by the numerous incense sticks and scented candles was mesmeric. While the DJ begun by keeping the music reasonably low, the silhouettes of young couples kissing and cuddling could be seen bringing a sense of love and joy to the hearts of those watching. At the main entrance Jacob and Eala greeted the still arriving gods and goddesses.

In the gardens the senior gods of all pantheons secured tables and opted to enjoy the party from a safe distance. Zeus was heard to say to Dione as they held hands, "Tonight I look at the moon, she's at her brightest and I wonder, as she looks down upon us, how many stories are there for her to tell?"

"I've often watched her move across the sky," replied Dione while snuggling closer, "I fear the stories she has to tell are of heartbreak, war and pestilence. So tonight I pray she witnesses the true happiness and great joy that Jacob's party will bring to the cosmos. Here's hoping this party will erase all the horror of the last few years and give us something special to remember."

Back in the Great Hall the party was in full swing and the gods and goddesses buzzed with excitement. The DJ catered for the sounds and rhythms from all corners of the world making it a raucous and noisy event but nobody cared, they had never experienced such fun and it was the party to beat all parties, destined to become the talk of the cosmos.

The Goddess of Chaos did her best not to cause ructions but she couldn't help it. While dancing through the hall she sent those nearby scurrying in all directions but she didn't care. It was when she sent Modi stumbling towards the wall that everything for her was to change.

Odi was known as the vain one but nothing compared to the effort Modi made especially when dressed in the imperial robes of an Asgard Warrior God. He had plans for this night and wanted to look his best at all times, but he didn't allow for a push that sent his beer cascading all down his tunic as he impacted the wall. While trying to compose himself he turned and was dumbstruck to find he was facing Eris whom he had noticed two thousand years earlier and never really forgot her. He even had her image engraved on to his chariot. "Sorry," she said while lowering her head and acting coyly.

"You did that deliberately," he replied in a flirting kind of way. "I don't think I should let you away with it. Your punishment will be a gentle slapping."

"A gentle slapping, you say? Greater gods than you have tried," she mocked. "You won't be able for my chaos, strife and discord."

"Are you challenging me?" said Modi puffing out his chest.

"As I said, you wouldn't be able for me," was her reply.

Modi furrowed his brow and from the corner of his eye caught Odi and Jacob sniggering.

"I recognise that face, he wouldn't dare?" said Odi.

"What's he going to do?" asked Jacob.

"One thing I can tell," replied Odi. "He knows we're watching and he's going to show off. He will have a satisfied smile on his face before this night is over."

"What do you mean?" said Jacob.

"Watch! One, two, thr....." laughed Odi.

At that moment Modi bent forward and manhandled Eris over his shoulder. He carried her kicking and screaming across the floor, out towards the lagoon bringing great relief to all other guests. The gods now felt safe from the discord she brings and went on to have an amazing party.

At the lagoon Modi held Eris down using his powerful leg as an anchor.

"I won't release you until you stop struggling," he said while holding her hands behind her back. "I know you have the power to kill me with one swoop of your arm so I'm being cautious. I like you and haven't stopped thinking of you since I first saw you all those years ago. I spoke with the oracles and they've told me there's a way to tame you. Will you let me?"

"No man can take me," she screamed. "I am the Goddess of Chaos and Strife."

"I am no man," he yelled back. "I'm a God of Asgard and I don't want to take you. I want you to come to me freely. I saw the way you looked at me and know you have the same feelings, let's try."

He moved in for a kiss and she bit his lip, he tried again and she bit him again. He was persistent and kept trying until he felt her resolve weaken.

"I could kill you at any time," she said as he loosened his grip.

"I know you can, but you won't," he replied. "I felt your resolve leave."

He moved in again and this time they passionately kissed until he released her arms. He thought to himself while her hands caressed his back, 'I'm either going to die or I'm going to Heaven.' He went to Heaven.

Their lovemaking was so passionate it resonated across the cosmos. The moon showed her embarrassment by hiding behind the nearest cloud. Those on the patio pleaded with the DJ to increase the volume so as to drown out the gasping and grunting sounds that travelled across the water. Sometimes when the moon did reveal herself, her beams illuminated two naked bodies rolling around on the grass verge next to the lagoon. This caused much mirth especially among those who knew the two gods involved. Their lovemaking continued for several more hours and only when a bright light shot into the sky did they stop.

Zeus saw the light and turned to Dione, "At last! Someone has tamed her. Is it possible I can now relax when visitors arrive? I wonder who she's with."

"We'll find out soon enough." replied Dione.

Just then Jacob and Odi ran through the garden towards the lagoon. They ran passed Zeus and Dione but were sent tumbling when Zeus tripped both of them."

"What was that for?" yelled Jacob.

"You two were just being nosey," replied Zeus.

"Of course we're being nosey," said Odi while dusting himself down. "That's Modi out there, and he's with Eris. It's time for revenge."

"Thanks be to the Ancient One!" cried Zeus while leaping to his feet, and raising his hands to the heavens. "Few gods in the cosmos have the power to tame Eris; Modi is certainly one of them."

Zeus stopped Jacob and Odi from getting any further, insisting they return to the temple. He planned to patrol the beach and prevent any further interruptions.

It was several more hours before Modi and Eris arrived back into the temple and as foretold by Odi he had a smile that went from one side of his face to the other. That smile remained and lasted well past the arrival of the first rays of the morning sun.

Odi noticed Magni was missing and after a brief search found him sitting alone on the grass verge at the far side of the lagoon. He noticed how sad he looked, sat beside him and said nothing.

"Go away, prick," snarled Magni. "Go back to the temple. I'm Ok."

"No," said Odi. "You're not Ok and I'm worried. You protected my family while I slept, and I will be forever grateful." He moved in to gently nudge him, "I'm not moving until you tell me what's wrong." Just then Jacob arrived.

"Oh, for Odin's sake." said Magni. "Now I've got two nosey pricks pestering me."

"Wrong," said a voice coming from a short distance away, it was Modi. "You're going to be pestered by three nosey pricks!"

On seeing Modi, Odi couldn't help himself, "Was it good for you?" he asked.

Modi leapt to grab him and bury his head in the sand. It was then when Jacob got emotional, he turned to Magni, "This is the last time we're going to see you for a very long time, isn't it?"

"I've no intentions of leaving either you or Odi," said a confused Magni. "I'll always have your backs."

"Jacob's right," said Odi while dusting himself down. "It is the last time we'll see you. You're not in our future, where are you going?"

"I'm going nowhere," insisted Magni. "I'll be patrolling Asgard with Modi by my side and will be visiting Olympus to see my niece and nephews who mean everything to me."

"Odi, shut up," said Modi after landing a punch to Odi's side. "He's going nowhere."

"He is Modi." said Jacob pointing towards the sun. "Look to the left of the sun, what can you see?"

Modi or Magni saw nothing but Odi did and was getting visibly upset but said nothing.

"Look again," said Jacob.

This time they all saw a very bright light, yet still the size of a pinprick and it was travelling at a great speed from behind the sun. They continued watching, and soon they were able to make out its shape. It was the chariot of a Sun God, driven by Bel Marduk.

When he landed he approached Magni and said, "I promised to seek you out so here I am. While with the Sun Gods fighting The Darkness I realised I had no one to mourn me if I succumbed, and after speaking with Helios, and listening to the way he spoke of you I knew it was time for us to be together. There's a sun way out in the galaxy where we can spent eternity together. Will you leave with me?" Magni was visibly shaking and his mind was racing.

"Brother, go," said Odi leaning in to hug him.

"You deserve happiness brother, go." said Jacob stretching across to kiss his forehead.

Modi got upset, "I did wonder," he said shaking his head and embracing him. "I suppose I always knew. You need to go and be happy. We love you and will seriously miss you but your happiness is more important."

On the patio Thor and Maria were watching their boys and were curious as to who the visitor was. Thor's instincts told him to go down and investigate. A sense of loss was developing and he felt he should get there as quickly as possible. When he reached his sons he demanded to know what was going on. Magni stepped forward,

"Father, this is Marduk and he's very special to me. We fought together during the cosmic wars and over time became very close. He has come for me and I've decided it's the right thing to do, we plan to spend the rest of our lives together."

"I don't understand?" said a confused Thor.

Magni placed his arm across Marduk's shoulder and then Thor began to understand.

"Why am I the last to find out?" he asked.

"Don't worry about it, I only found out a few moments ago, that pair knew all along," said Modi pointing at Jacob and Odi.

Thor was now visibly upset and when he composed himself he asked, "Are you happy?" he paused waiting on a response. "If you are, then you must go, but please find a way to keep in touch."

There was no standing on ceremony or long goodbyes, Magni and Bel Marduk just left and were soon gone out of sight. The boys tried to comfort their father but he was devastated and wanted to be alone. Several hours later while making his way back to the temple he met Odin who said, "Odi told me, it's a big loss but he'll always be out there and when you need him he'll be first to answer your call. Always remember you have three other sons and lots of grandchildren with more on the way, they'll need your guidance so you must be there for them. This is now your task." While moving away he continued, "Zeus and I are leaving for the Underworld; Hades still seeks out the last remnants of Lucifer's legions and might need our assistance. We'll return before nightfall."

Meanwhile while sitting alone in the temple, Jacob's expression changed, he looked around as though sensing something troubling. At the very same time out near the folly Odi felt the same menace. Although apart, together they said, "**Shadow**? Who is **Shadow**?"

Chapter 40

Through the gates of
Heaven they walked

Deep in his domain, Hades sought out his imprisoned allies and freed them. His generals and remaining guards immediately moved to secure the underworld but only after they located Minos, Aeacus and Rhadamanthus, the three Judges of the Dead, who on being freed set about clearing the backlog of souls waiting at the gates.

In the meantime Zeus and Odin arrived and made their way up a ramp leading to a platform giving them a panoramic view all across Hades' domain. From there they watched Hades and the three Judges at work; they also saw the great difficulty Hades had controlling the remnants of Lucifer's evil armies. They remained and observed him eventually push the last of the Dark Angels through the gates of Hell.

When this task was completed Hades rushed to join them and together they watched the Judges pass their judgement on the latest souls to arrive. It pleased them that those souls were all of the Light and were being ushered through the gates into Heaven where they were greeted by the seven Archangels.

It was soon after when footsteps were heard and they were coming from behind. On turning they found it was 'The Man' and he was not alone. She was beside him. She was the one who wept at the foot of the cross and was with him outside the tomb. She always said she knew everything but few believed her and by the way she held his arm all saw that she was right. The brightest of light shone from both of them and it illuminated the Underworld. While watching the happy souls making their way through the gates, the Man said,

"They will never hunger or thirst again: neither the sun nor scorching winds will ever plague them, because the Ancient One, who is at the throne will be their shepherd and will lead them to the springs of living water, and he will wipe away all tears from their eyes."

The End

Jacob
Journey of A God
Eamon Blake

'Jacob - Journey of a God' is the first in a gripping series of five books. It chronicles the journey of a troubled youth who, since his twelfth birthday, has been haunted by disturbing visions showing horrific events set in the past. As the visions escalate he learns of a future filled with turbulent and violent times.

Its 2016, and although living the normal life of a Dublin teenager - school, studies, rugby, and girls, he soon discovers his true identity. His mother tells him the story of his birth and her efforts to protect him from forces beyond his comprehension. He begins to understand his extraordinary abilities especially when he realises those abilities are actually the powers of a God.

Amidst the unfolding drama of his life, Jacob's visions show him to be leading a battle against two malevolent forces - one is 'The Darkness' and the other, the nefarious 'Prince of Hell'. Both have made him a target of their venom, they know he has been chosen to be the defender of the Light and they fear his power.

Why does The Darkness loathe the Light?

What fuels the Prince of Hell's hatred of Jacob?

In the face of these existential questions, will Jacob embrace his divine destiny and become the God he was born to be?

Jacob
Walk of The Messengers
Eamon Blake

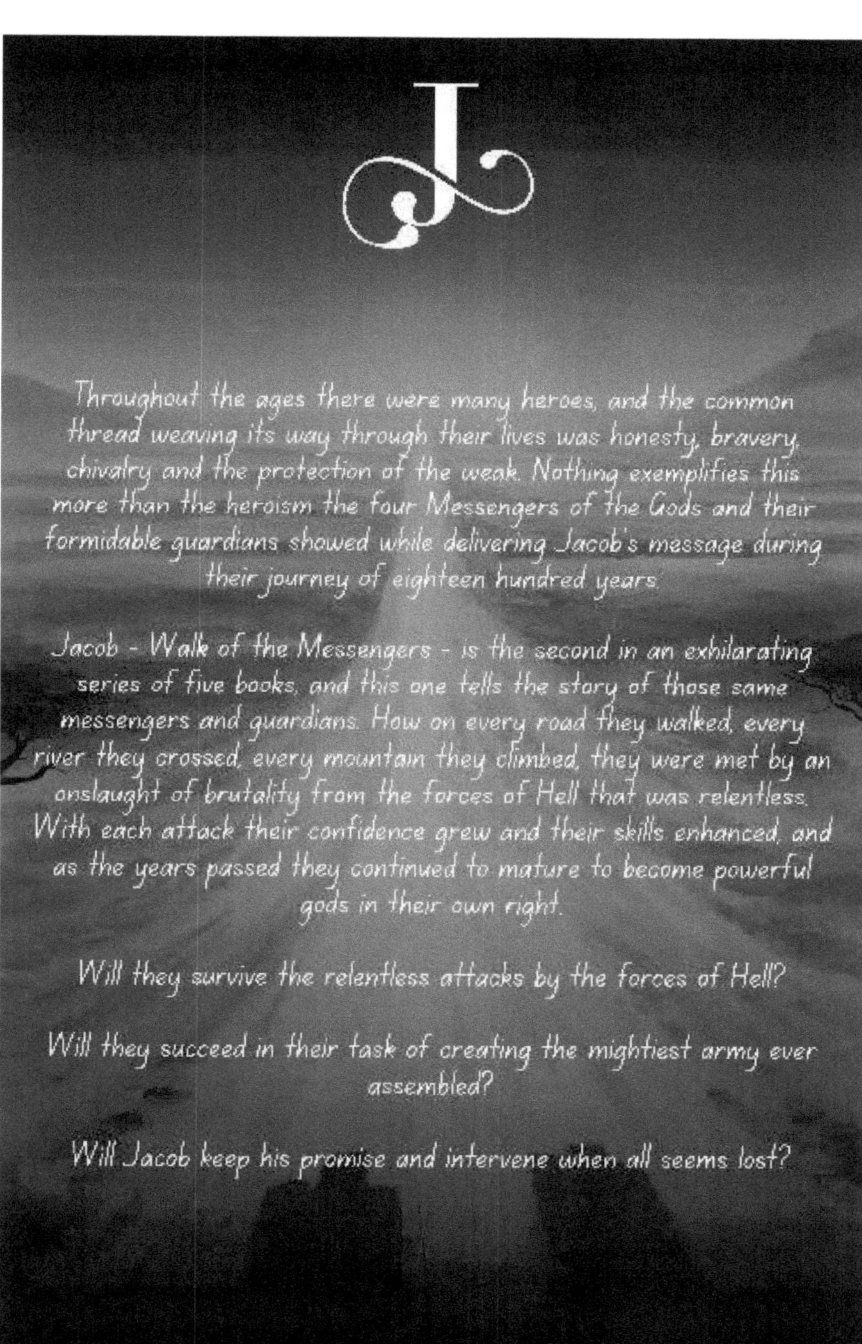

Throughout the ages there were many heroes, and the common thread weaving its way through their lives was honesty, bravery, chivalry and the protection of the weak. Nothing exemplifies this more than the heroism the four Messengers of the Gods and their formidable guardians showed while delivering Jacob's message during their journey of eighteen hundred years.

Jacob - Walk of the Messengers - is the second in an exhilarating series of five books, and this one tells the story of those same messengers and guardians. How on every road they walked, every river they crossed, every mountain they climbed, they were met by an onslaught of brutality from the forces of Hell that was relentless. With each attack their confidence grew and their skills enhanced, and as the years passed they continued to mature to become powerful gods in their own right.

Will they survive the relentless attacks by the forces of Hell?

Will they succeed in their task of creating the mightiest army ever assembled?

Will Jacob keep his promise and intervene when all seems lost?

Jacob
Children of The Gods
Eamon Blake

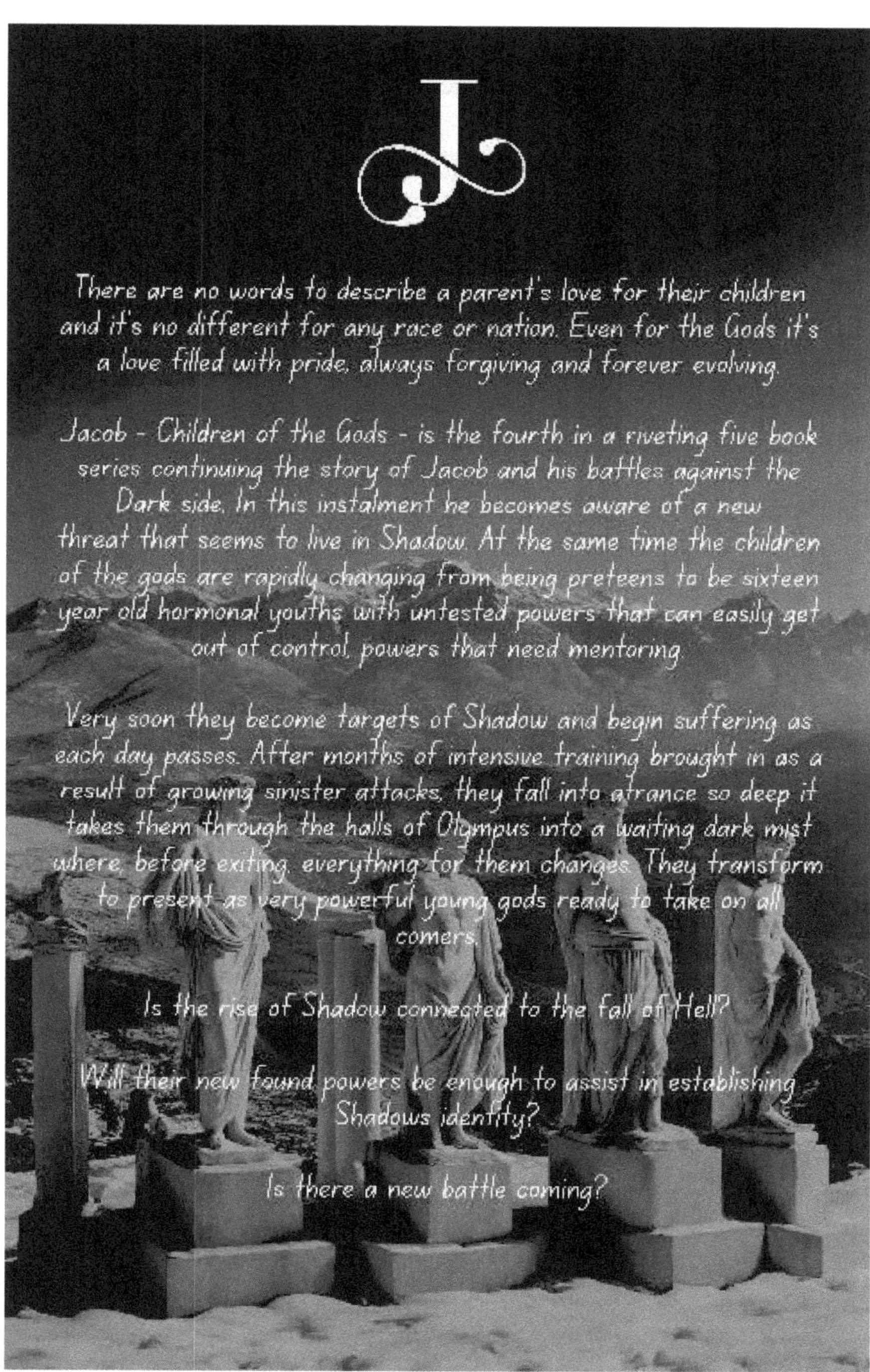

There are no words to describe a parent's love for their children and it's no different for any race or nation. Even for the Gods it's a love filled with pride, always forgiving and forever evolving.

Jacob - Children of the Gods - is the fourth in a riveting five book series continuing the story of Jacob and his battles against the Dark side. In this instalment he becomes aware of a new threat that seems to live in Shadow. At the same time the children of the gods are rapidly changing from being preteens to be sixteen year old hormonal youths with untested powers that can easily get out of control, powers that need mentoring.

Very soon they become targets of Shadow and begin suffering as each day passes. After months of intensive training brought in as a result of growing sinister attacks, they fall into a trance so deep it takes them through the halls of Olympus into a waiting dark mist where, before exiting, everything for them changes. They transform to present as very powerful young gods ready to take on all comers.

Is the rise of Shadow connected to the fall of Hell?

Will their new found powers be enough to assist in establishing Shadows identity?

Is there a new battle coming?

Jacob
Battle for Olympus
Eamon Blake

A mysterious and frightening shadow has been skulking its way through all the realms of myth and legend. Its sinister presence is always followed by an attack of such evil violence that few survive.

Jacob - Battle for Olympus - is the last in a riveting five book series. It concludes the story of his battles against the Dark side. In this instalment he finally establishes who Shadow is and quickly learns it can only be defeated with the assistance of the Ancient One.

Jacob's heart breaks on learning of attacks by Shadow on the Dragon, Elf and Yeti nations and is devastated when he discovers many of his friends and allies have been killed.

When Asgard is destroyed he concludes that Shadow's plan, just like that of The Darkness, is to destroy all that has been created by the Ancient One. This emboldens him to awaken the defenders of Olympus who have, since long before the time of Zeus, been sleeping deep in the caverns below the temple.

Can Jacob rescue the remnants of those of myth and legend?

Will the Ancient One come to Jacob's assistance?

Is the Battle for Olympus to be the battle to end all wars?